W9-DBN-878

THE POCKET BOOK

of

ADVENTURE

STORIES

Edited by

PHILIP VAN DOREN STERN

POCKET BOOKS OF CANADA, LTD.
Montreal, Canada

THE PRINTING HISTORY OF

The Pocket BOOK of Adventure Stories

Pocket BOOK edition published March, 1945

1ST PRINTING ..... FEBRUARY, 1945
2ND PRINTING .... MARCH, 1945

BOOKS ARE WEAPONS IN THE WAR OF IDEAS

THIS IS A WARTIME BOOK

THIS ORIGINAL EDITION, PREPARED ES-
PECIALLY FOR POCKET BOOKS, IS PRINTED
FROM BRAND-NEW PLATES MADE FROM
LARGE, CLEAR, EASY-TO-READ TYPE, AND
COMPLIES WITH THE GOVERNMENT'S
REGULATIONS FOR CONSERVING PAPER
AND OTHER ESSENTIAL MATERIALS.   F-2

Printed in Canada

oncerns the mind as well as the muscles. It would therefore seem that good adventure stories should be written
by good writers, by men who can write with their heads
and their hearts and not merely with their fingers.

It should hardly be necessary to demonstrate this, for
many of our most distinguished novels are long adventure
stories—*Don Quixote, A Tale of Two Cities, Moby Dick,
Treasure Island, Green Mansions, The Red Badge of
Courage, Lord Jim,* and *For Whom the Bell Tolls* among
them. War and revolution, the sea and the ships that sail
upon it, far places and the odd people who dwell there,
escape and pursuit, love, violence, and death are themes
that have fascinated writers ever since they first began to
put words down on paper for the delectation of their
fellow men. It seemed reasonable then to believe that
there were enough really first-rate short adventure tales
written by first-rate authors to fill a book. The editor
soon found that there were—and enough to fill a dozen
books like this one.

But here are an even dozen of them, carefully chosen
from scores of good ones. In these twelve stories, sport,
the man hunt, piracy, shipwreck, tropical romance, and
the other familiar themes customarily dealt with in the
adventure story have been transmuted into bright pieces
of shining gold by that alchemy of which only the great
story-tellers know the secret.

—PHILIP VAN DOREN STERN

Contents

Acknowledgments

Selection from *Twelve against the Gods*, by William Bolitho. By permission of Simon & Schuster; copyright, 1929.

"Fifty Grand," by Ernest Hemingway. By arrangement with Charles Scribner's Sons.

"Flight," by John Steinbeck. From *The Long Valley*, copyright, 1938, by John Steinbeck. By permission of The Viking Press, Inc.

"Red," by W. Somerset Maugham. From *The Trembling of a Leaf*, copyright, 1921, by Doubleday, Doran and Company, Inc.

"Gun Crazy," by MacKinlay Kantor, by arrangement with Sydney A. Sanders.

"Escape from the Mine," by Walter D. Edmonds. From *Drums along the Mohawk*, by arrangement with Little, Brown & Company.

"The Most Dangerous Game," by Richard Connell. By arrangement with Brandt & Brandt; copyright, 1924, by Richard Connell.

"The Fourth Man," by John Russell. By arrangement with Brandt & Brandt; copyright, 1916, by John Russell.

"The Man Who Saw through Heaven," by Wilbur Daniel Steele, by arrangement with Harold Matson.

"The Open Boat," by Stephen Crane, by permission of and special arrangement with Alfred A. Knopf, Inc.; copyright, 1898, 1899, 1926, by Alfred A. Knopf, Inc.

"The Man Who Would Be King," by Rudyard Kipling. From *Under the Deodars*, by arrangement with Doubleday, Doran and Company, Inc., A. P. Watt & Son, London, The Macmillan Company of Canada, Ltd., and Mrs. George Bambridge for the Kipling estate.

"The King's Messenger," by Rafael Sabatini. By arrangement with Brandt & Brandt; copyright, 1930, by Rafael Sabatini.

Introduction

The adventurer is within us, and he contests for o
favor with the social man we are obliged to be. These tw
sorts of life are incompatibles; one we hanker after, the
other we are obliged to. There is no other conflict so
deep and bitter as this, whatever the pious say, for it de-
rives from the very constitutions of human life, which so
painfully separate us from all other beings. We, like the
eagles, were born to be free. Yet we are obliged, in order
to live at all, to make a cage of laws for ourselves and to
stand on the perch. We are born as wasteful and unre-
morseful as tigers; we are obliged to be thrifty, or starve,
or freeze. We are born to wander, and cursed to stay and
dig.

—From *Twelve against the Gods* by William Bolitho

There are three kinds of people in this world—those who actively seek adventure; those who at least seek it vicariously; and those who are so smugly satisfied with their own existence that want none of it in any form. This book is intended for those who like adventure, who enjoy hearing about brave deeds and strange places, and who wish to enlarge their experience of life to include aspects which may thus far have eluded them.

For adventure is the spice of life, the essence of its highest moments, the stuff of which long-enduring memories is made. Good writing about it, however, has been too cheaply imitated, too often put out under false brand names in a commercial effort to make shoddy goods pass as the real thing. True adventure is not merely a matter of pistol shooting, hard riding, and a pretty girl as a reward. It is, as any great adventurer—from Adam, who first dared eat the forbidden fruit, to the latest warrior just returned from overseas—can testify, something that

Fifty Grand

By ERNEST HEMINGWAY

"How ARE you going yourself, Jack?" I asked him.

"You seen this Walcott?" he says.

"Just in the gym."

"Well," Jack says, "I'm going to need a lot of luck with that boy."

"He can't hit you, Jack," Soldier said.

"I wish to hell he couldn't."

"He couldn't hit you with a handful of bird-shot."

"Bird-shot'd be all right," Jack says. "I wouldn't mind bird-shot any."

"He looks easy to hit," I said.

"Sure," Jack says, "he ain't going to last long. He ain't going to last like you and me, Jerry. But right now he's got everything."

"You'll left-hand him to death."

"Maybe," Jack says. "Sure. I got a chance to."

"Handle him like you handled Kid Lewis."

"Kid Lewis," Jack said. "That kike!"

The three of us, Jack Brennan, Soldier Bartlett, and I were in Hanley's. There were a couple of broads sitting at the next table to us. They had been drinking.

"What do you mean, kike?" one of the broads says. "What do you mean, kike, you big Irish bum?"

"Sure," Jack says. "That's it."

"Kikes," this broad goes on. "They're always talking about kikes, these big Irishmen. What do you mean, kikes?"

"Come on. Let's get out of here."

"Kikes," this broad goes on. "Whoever saw you ever buy a drink? Your wife sews your pockets up every morning. These Irishmen and their kikes! Ted Lewis could lick you too."

"Sure," Jack says. "And you give away a lot of things free too, don't you?"

We went out. That was Jack. He could say what he wanted to when he wanted to say it.

Jack started training out at Danny Hogan's health farm over in Jersey. It was nice out there but Jack didn't like it much. He didn't like being away from his wife and the kids, and he was sore and grouchy most of the time. He liked me and we got along fine together; and he liked Hogan, but after a while Soldier Bartlett commenced to get on his nerves. A kidder gets to be an awful thing around a camp if his stuff goes sort of sour. Soldier was always kidding Jack, just sort of kidding him all the time. It wasn't very funny and it wasn't very good, and it began to get to Jack. It was sort of stuff like this. Jack would finish up with the weights and the bag and pull on the gloves.

"You want to work?" he'd say to Soldier.

"Sure. How you want me to work?" Soldier would ask. "Want me to treat you rough like Walcott? Want me to knock you down a few times?"

"That's it," Jack would say. He didn't like it any, though.

One morning we were all out on the road. We'd been out quite a way and now we were coming back. We'd go along fast for three minutes and then walk a minute, and then go fast for three minutes again. Jack wasn't ever what you would call a sprinter. He'd move around fast enough in the ring if he had to, but he wasn't any too fast on the road. All the time we were walking Soldier was kidding him. We came up the hill to the farmhouse.

"Well," says Jack, "you better go back to town, Soldier."

"What do you mean?"

"You better go back to town and stay there."

"What's the matter?"

"I'm sick of hearing you talk."

"Yes?" says Soldier.

"Yes," says Jack.

"You'll be a damn sight sicker when Walcott gets through with you."

"Sure," says Jack, "maybe I will. But I know I'm sick of you."

So Soldier went off on the train to town that same morning. I went down with him to the train. He was good and sore.

"I was just kidding him," he said. We were waiting on the platform. "He can't pull that stuff with me, Jerry."

"He's nervous and crabby," I said. "He's a good fellow, Soldier."

"The hell he is. The hell he's ever been a good fellow."

"Well," I said, "so long, Soldier."

The train had come in. He climbed up with his bag.

"So long, Jerry," he says. "You be in town before the fight?"

"I don't think so."

"See you then."

He went in and the conductor swung up and the train went out. I rode back to the farm in the cart. Jack was on the porch writing a letter to his wife. The mail had come and I got the papers and went over on the other side of the porch and sat down to read. Hogan came out the door and walked over to me.

"Did he have a jam with Soldier?"

"Not a jam," I said. "He just told him to go back to town."

"I could see it coming," Hogan said. "He never liked Soldier much."

"No. He don't like many people."

"He's a pretty cold one," Hogan said.

"Well, he's always been fine to me."

"Me too," Hogan said. "I got no kick on him. He's a cold one, though."

Hogan went in through the screen door and I sat there on the porch and read the papers. It was just starting to get fall weather and it's nice country there in Jersey, up in the hills, and after I read the paper through I sat there and looked out at the country and the road down below against the woods with cars going along it, lifting the dust up. It was fine weather and pretty nice-looking country. Hogan came to the door and I said, "Say, Hogan, haven't you got anything to shoot out here?"

"No," Hogan said. "Only sparrows."

"Seen the paper?" I said to Hogan.

"What's in it?"

"Sande booted three of them in yesterday."

"I got that on the telephone last night."

"You follow them pretty close, Hogan?" I asked.

"Oh, I keep in touch with them," Hogan said.

"How about Jack?" I says. "Does he still play them?"

"Him?" said Hogan. "Can you see him doing it?"

Just then Jack came around the corner with the letter in his hand. He's wearing a sweater and an old pair of pants and boxing shoes.

"Got a stamp, Hogan?" he asks.

"Give me the letter," Hogan said. "I'll mail it for you."

"Say, Jack," I said, "didn't you used to play the ponies?"

"Sure."

"I knew you did. I knew I used to see you out at Sheepshead."

"What did you lay off them for?" Hogan asked.

"Lost money."

Jack sat down on the porch by me. He leaned back against a post. He shut his eyes in the sun.

"Want a chair?" Hogan asked.

"No," said Jack. "This is fine."

"It's a nice day," I said. "It's pretty nice out in the country."

"I'd a damn sight rather be in town with the wife."

"Well, you only got another week."

"Yes," Jack says. "That's so."

We sat there on the porch. Hogan was inside at the office.

"What do you think about the shape I'm in?" Jack asked me.

"Well, you can't tell," I said. "You got a week to get around into form."

"Don't stall me."

"Well," I said, "you're not right."

"I'm not sleeping," Jack said.

"You'll be all right in a couple of days."

"No," says Jack, "I got the insomnia."

"What's on your mind?"

"I miss the wife."

"Have her come out."

"No. I'm too old for that."

"We'll take a long walk before you turn in and get you good and tired."

"Tired!" Jack says. "I'm tired all the time."

He was that way all week. He wouldn't sleep at night and he'd get up in the morning feeling that way, you know, when you can't shut your hands.

"He's stale as poorhouse cake," Hogan said. "He's nothing."

"I never seen Walcott," I said.

"He'll kill him," said Hogan. "He'll tear him in two."

"Well," I said, "everybody's got to get it sometime."

"Not like this, though," Hogan said. "They'll think he never trained. It gives the farm a black eye."

"You hear what the reporters said about him?"

"Didn't I! They said he was awful. They said they oughtn't to let him fight."

"Well," I said, "they're always wrong, ain't they?"

"Yes," said Hogan. "But this time they're right."

"What the hell do they know about whether a man's right or not?"

"Well," said Hogan, "they're not such fools."

"All they did was pick Willard at Toledo. This Lardner, he's so wise now, ask him about when he picked Willard at Toledo."

"Aw, he wasn't out," Hogan said. "He only writes the big fights."

"I don't care who they are," I said. "What the hell do they know? They can write maybe, but what the hell do they know?"

"You don't think Jack's in any shape, do you?" Hogan asked.

"No. He's through. All he needs is to have Corbett pick him to win for it to be all over."

"Well, Corbett'll pick him," Hogan says.

"Sure. He'll pick him."

That night Jack didn't sleep any either. The next morning was the last day before the fight. After breakfast we were out on the porch again.

"What do you think about, Jack, when you can't sleep?" I said.

"Oh, I worry," Jack says. "I worry about property I got up in the Bronx, I worry about property I got in Florida. I worry about the kids. I worry about the wife. Sometimes I think about fights. I think about that kike Ted Lewis and I get sore. I got some stocks and I worry about them. What the hell don't I think about?"

"Well," I said, "tomorrow night it'll all be over."

"Sure," said Jack. "That always helps a lot, don't it? That just fixes everything all up, I suppose. Sure."

He was sore all day. We didn't do any work. Jack just moved around a little to loosen up. He shadow-boxed a few rounds. He didn't even look good doing that. He skipped the rope a little while. He couldn't sweat.

"He'd be better not to do any work at all," Hogan

said. We were standing watching him skip rope. "Don't
he ever sweat at all any more?"

"He can't sweat."

"Do you suppose he's got the con? He never had any
trouble making weight, did he?"

"No, he hasn't got any con. He just hasn't got anything inside any more."

"He ought to sweat," said Hogan.

Jack came over, skipping the rope. He was skipping
up and down in front of us, forward and back, crossing
his arms every third time.

"Well," he says. "What are you buzzards talking
about?"

"I don't think you ought to work any more," Hogan
says. "You'll be stale."

"Wouldn't that be awful?" Jack says and skips away
down the floor, slapping the rope hard.

That afternoon John Collins showed up out at the
farm. Jack was up in his room. John came out in a car
from town. He had a couple of friends with him. The car
stopped and they all got out.

"Where's Jack?" John asked me.

"Up in his room, lying down."

"Lying down?"

"Yes," I said.

"How is he?"

I looked at the two fellows that were with John.

"They're friends of his," John said.

"He's pretty bad," I said.

"What's the matter with him?"

"He don't sleep."

"Hell," said John. "That Irishman could never sleep."

"He isn't right," I said.

"Hell," John said. "He's never right. I've had him for
ten years and he's never been right yet."

The fellows who were with him laughed.

"I want you to shake hands with Mr. Morgan and Mr.

Steinfelt," John said. "This is Mr. Doyle. He's been training Jack."

"Glad to meet you," I said.

"Let's go up and see the boy," the fellow called Morgan said.

"Let's have a look at him," Steinfelt said.

We all went upstairs.

"Where's Hogan?" John asked.

"He's out in the barn with a couple of his customers," I said.

"He got many people out here now?" John asked.

"Just two."

"Pretty quiet, ain't it?" Morgan said.

"Yes," I said. "It's pretty quiet."

We were outside Jack's room. John knocked on the door. There wasn't any answer.

"Maybe he's asleep," I said.

"What the hell's he sleeping in the daytime for?"

John turned the handle and we all went in. Jack was lying asleep on the bed. He was face down and his face was in the pillow. Both his arms were around the pillow.

"Hey, Jack!" John said to him.

Jack's head moved a little on the pillow. "Jack!" John says, leaning over him. Jack just dug a little deeper in the pillow. John touched him on the shoulder. Jack sat up and looked at us. He hadn't shaved and he was wearing an old sweater.

"Christ! Why can't you let me sleep?" he says to John.

"Don't be sore," John says. "I didn't mean to wake you up."

"Oh no," Jack says. "Of course not."

"You know Morgan and Steinfelt," John said.

"Glad to see you," Jack says.

"How do you feel, Jack?" Morgan asks him.

"Fine," Jack says. "How the hell would I feel?"

"You look fine," Steinfelt says.

"Yes, don't I," says Jack. "Say," he says to John.

"You're my manager. You get a big enough cut. Why the hell don't you come out here when the reporters was out! You want Jerry and me to talk to them?"

"I had Lew fighting in Philadelphia," John said.

"What the hell's that to me?" Jack says. "You're my manager. You get a big enough cut, don't you? You aren't making me any money in Philadelphia, are you? Why the hell aren't you out here when I ought to have you?"

"Hogan was here."

"Hogan," Jack says. "Hogan's as dumb as I am."

"Soldier Bahtlett was out here wukking with you for a while, wasn't he?" Steinfelt said to change the subject.

"Yes, he was out here," Jack says. "He was out here all right."

"Say, Jerry," John said to me. "Would you go and find Hogan and tell him we want to see him in about half an hour?"

"Sure," I said.

"Why the hell can't he stick around?" Jack says. "Stick around, Jerry."

Morgan and Steinfelt looked at each other.

"Quiet down, Jack," John said to him.

"I better go find Hogan," I said.

"All right, if you want to go," Jack says. "None of these guys are going to send you away, though."

"I'll go find Hogan," I said.

Hogan was out in the gym in the barn. He had a couple of his health-farm patients with the gloves on. They neither one wanted to hit the other, for fear the other would come back and hit him.

"That'll do," Hogan said when he saw me come in. "You can stop the slaughter. You gentlemen take a shower and Bruce will rub you down."

They climbed out through the ropes and Hogan came over to me.

"John Collins is out with a couple of friends to see Jack," I said.

"I saw them come up in the car."

"Who are the two fellows with John?"

"They're what you call wise boys," Hogan said. "Don't you know them two?"

"No," I said.

"That's Happy Steinfelt and Lew Morgan. They got a poolroom."

"I been away a long time," I said.

"Sure," said Hogan. "That Happy Steinfelt's a big operator."

"I've heard his name," I said.

"He's a pretty smooth boy," Hogan said. "They're a couple of sharpshooters."

"Well," I said. "They want to see us in half an hour."

"You mean they don't want to see us until a half an hour?"

"That's it."

"Come on in the office," Hogan said. "To hell with those sharpshooters."

After about thirty minutes or so Hogan and I went upstairs. We knocked on Jack's door. They were talking inside the room.

"Wait a minute," somebody said.

"To hell with that stuff," Hogan said. "When you want to see me I'm down in the office."

We heard the door unlock. Steinfelt opened it.

"Come on in, Hogan," he says. "We're all going to have a drink."

"Well," says Hogan. "That's something."

We went in. Jack was sitting on the bed. John and Morgan were sitting on a couple of chairs. Steinfelt was standing up.

"You're a pretty mysterious lot of boys," Hogan said.

"Hello, Danny," John says.

"Hello, Danny," Morgan says and shakes hands.

Jack doesn't say anything. He just sits there on the bed. He ain't with the others. He's all by himself. He was wearing an old blue jersey and pants and had on boxing shoes. He needed a shave. Steinfelt and Morgan were dressers. John was quite a dresser too. Jack sat there looking Irish and tough.

Steinfelt brought out a bottle and Hogan brought in some glasses and everybody had a drink. Jack and I took one and the rest of them went on and had two or three each.

"Better save some for your ride back," Hogan said.

"Don't you worry. We got plenty," Morgan said.

Jack hadn't drunk anything since the one drink. He was standing up and looking at them. Morgan was sitting on the bed where Jack had sat.

"Have a drink, Jack," John said and handed him the glass and the bottle.

"No," Jack said, "I never liked to go to these wakes."

They all laughed. Jack didn't laugh.

They were all feeling pretty good when they left. Jack stood on the porch when they got into the car. They waved to him.

"So long," Jack said.

We had supper. Jack didn't say anything all during the meal except, "Will you pass me this?" or "Will you pass me that?" The two health-farm patients ate at the same table with us. They were pretty nice fellows. After we finished eating we went out on the porch. It was dark early.

"Like to take a walk, Jerry?" Jack asked.

"Sure," I said.

We put on our coats and started out. It was quite a way down to the main road and then we walked along the main road about a mile and a half. Cars kept going by and we would pull out to the side until they were past. Jack didn't say anything. After we had stepped out into the bushes to let a big car go by Jack said, "To hell with this walking. Come on back to Hogan's."

We went along a side road that cut up over the hill and

cut across the fields back to Hogan's. We could see the lights of the house up on the hill. We came around to the front of the house and there standing in the doorway was Hogan.

"Have a good walk?" Hogan asked.

"Oh, fine," Jack said. "Listen, Hogan. Have you got any liquor?"

"Sure," says Hogan. "What's the idea?"

"Send it up to the room," Jack says. "I'm going to sleep tonight."

"You're the doctor," Hogan says.

"Come on up to the room, Jerry," Jack says.

Upstairs Jack sat on the bed with his head in his hands.

"Ain't it a life?" Jack says.

Hogan brought in a quart of liquor and two glasses.

"Want some ginger ale?"

"What do you think I want to do, get sick?"

"I just asked you," said Hogan.

"Have a drink?" said Jack.

"No, thanks," said Hogan. He went out.

"How about you, Jerry?"

"I'll have one with you," I said.

Jack poured out a couple of drinks. "Now," he said, "I want to take it slow and easy."

"Put some water in it," I said.

"Yes," Jack said. "I guess that's better."

We had a couple of drinks without saying anything. Jack started to pour me another.

"No," I said, "that's all I want."

"All right," Jack said. He poured himself out another big shot and put water in it. He was lighting up a little.

"That was a fine bunch out here this afternoon," he said. "They don't take any chances, those two."

Then a little later, "Well," he says, "they're right. What the hell's the good in taking chances?"

"Don't you want another, Jerry?" he said. "Come on, drink along with me."

"I don't need it, Jack," I said. "I feel all right."

"Just have one more," Jack said. It was softening him up.

"All right," I said.

Jack poured one for me and another big one for himself.

"You know," he said, "I like liquor pretty well. If I hadn't been boxing I would have drunk quite a lot."

"Sure," I said.

"You know," he said, "I missed a lot, boxing."

"You made plenty of money."

"Sure, that's what I'm after. You know I miss a lot, Jerry."

"How do you mean?"

"Well," he says, "like about the wife. And being away from home so much. It don't do my girls any good. 'Who's your old man?' some of those society kids'll say to them. 'My old man's Jack Brennan.' That don't do them any good."

"Hell," I said, "all that makes a difference is if they got dough."

"Well," says Jack, "I got the dough for them all right."

He poured out another drink. The bottle was about empty.

"Put some water in it," I said. Jack poured in some water.

"You know," he says, "you ain't got any idea how I miss the wife."

"Sure."

"You ain't got any idea. You can't have an idea what it's like."

"It ought to be better out in the country than in town."

"With me now," Jack said, "it don't make any difference where I am. You can't have an idea what it's like."

"Have another drink."

"Am I getting soused? Do I talk funny?"

"You're coming on all right."

"You can't have an idea what it's like. They ain't anybody can have an idea what it's like."

"Except the wife," I said.

"She knows," Jack said. "She knows all right. She knows. You bet she knows."

"Put some water in that," I said.

"Jerry," says Jack, "you can't have an idea what it gets to be like."

He was good and drunk. He was looking at me steady. His eyes were sort of too steady.

"You'll sleep all right," I said.

"Listen, Jerry," Jack says. "You want to make some money? Get some money down on Walcott."

"Yes?"

"Listen, Jerry," Jack put down the glass. "I'm not drunk now, see? You know what I'm betting on him? Fifty grand."

"That's a lot of dough."

"Fifty grand," Jack says, "at two to one. I'll get twenty-five thousand bucks. Get some money on him, Jerry."

"It sounds good," I said.

"How can I beat him?" Jack says. "It ain't crooked. How can I beat him? Why not make money on it?"

"Put some water in that," I said.

"I'm through after this fight," Jack says. "I'm through with it. I got to take a beating. Why shouldn't I make money on it?"

"Sure."

"I ain't slept for a week," Jack says. "All night I lay awake and worry my can off. I can't sleep, Jerry. You ain't got an idea what it's like when you can't sleep."

"Sure."

"I can't sleep. That's all. I just can't sleep. What's the use of taking care of yourself all these years when you can't sleep?"

"It's bad."

"You ain't got an idea what it's like, Jerry, when you can't sleep."

"Put some water in that," I said.

Well, about eleven o'clock Jack passes out and I put

him to bed. Finally he's so he can't keep from sleeping. I helped him get his clothes off and got him into bed.

"You'll sleep all right, Jack," I said.

"Sure," Jack says, "I'll sleep now."

"Good night, Jack," I said.

"Good night, Jerry," Jack says. "You're the only friend I got."

"Oh, hell," I said.

"You're the only friend I got," Jack says, "the only friend I got."

"Go to sleep," I said.

"I'll sleep," Jack says.

Downstairs Hogan was sitting at the desk in the office reading the papers. He looked up. "Well, you get your boy friend to sleep?" he asks.

"He's off."

"It's better for him than not sleeping," Hogan said.

"Sure."

"You'd have a hell of a time explaining that to these sport writers though," Hogan said.

"Well, I'm going to bed myself," I said.

"Good night," said Hogan.

In the morning I came downstairs about eight o'clock and got some breakfast. Hogan had his two customers out in the barn doing exercises. I went out and watched them.

"One! Two! Three! Four!" Hogan was counting for them. "Hello, Jerry," he said. "Is Jack up yet?"

"No. He's still sleeping."

I went back to my room and packed up to go in to town. About nine-thirty I heard Jack getting up in the next room. When I heard him go downstairs I went down after him. Jack was sitting at the breakfast table. Hogan had come in and was standing beside the table.

"How do you feel, Jack?" I asked him.

"Not so bad."

"Sleep well?" Hogan asked.

"I slept all right," Jack said. "I got a thick tongue but I ain't got a head."

"Good," said Hogan. "That was good liquor."

"Put it on the bill," Jack says.

"What time you want to go into town?" Hogan asked.

"Before lunch," Jack says. "The eleven o'clock train."

"Sit down, Jerry," Jack said. Hogan went out.

I sat down at the table. Jack was eating a grapefruit. When he'd find a seed he'd spit it out in the spoon and dump it on the plate.

"I guess I was pretty stewed last night," he started.

"You drank some liquor."

"I guess I said a lot of fool things."

"You weren't bad."

"Where's Hogan?" he asked. He was through with the grapefruit.

"He's out in front in the office."

"What did I say about betting on the fight?" Jack asked. He was holding the spoon and sort of poking at the grapefruit with it.

The girl came in with some ham and eggs and took away the grapefruit.

"Bring me another glass of milk," Jack said to her. She went out.

"You said you had fifty grand on Walcott," I said.

"That's right," Jack said.

"That's a lot of money."

"I don't feel too good about it," Jack said.

"Something might happen."

"No," Jack said. "He wants the title bad. They'll be shooting with him all right."

"You can't ever tell."

"No. He wants the title. It's worth a lot of money to him."

"Fifty grand is a lot of money," I said.

"It's business," said Jack. "I can't win. You know I can't win anyway."

"As long as you're in there you got a chance."

"No," Jack says. "I'm all through. It's just business."

"How do you feel?"

"Pretty good," Jack said. "The sleep was what I needed."

"You might go good."

"I'll give them a good show," Jack said.

After breakfast Jack called up his wife on the long-distance. He was inside the booth telephoning.

"That's the first time he's called her up since he's out here," Hogan said.

"He writes her every day."

"Sure," Hogan says, "a letter only costs two cents."

Hogan said good-by to us and Bruce, the nigger rubber, drove us down to the train in the cart.

"Good-by, Mr. Brennan," Bruce said at the train, "I sure hope you knock his can off."

"So long," Jack said. He gave Bruce two dollars. Bruce had worked on him a lot. He looked kind of disappointed. Jack saw me looking at Bruce holding the two dollars.

"It's all in the bill," he said. "Hogan charged me for the rubbing."

On the train going into town Jack didn't talk. He sat in the corner of the seat with his ticket in his hat-band and looked out of the window. Once he turned and spoke to me.

"I told the wife I'd take a room at the Shelby tonight," he said. "It's just around the corner from the Garden. I can go up to the house tomorrow morning."

"That's a good idea," I said. "Your wife ever see you fight, Jack?"

"No," Jack says. "She never seen me fight."

I thought he must be figuring on taking an awful beating if he doesn't want to go home afterward. In town we took a taxi up to the Shelby. A boy came out and took our bags and we went in to the desk.

"How much are the rooms?" Jack asked.

"We only have double rooms," the clerk says. "I can give you a nice double room for ten dollars."

"That's too steep."

"I can give you a double room for seven dollars."

"With a bath?"

"Certainly."

"You might as well bunk with me, Jerry," Jack says.

"Oh," I said, "I'll sleep down at my brother-in-law's."

"I don't mean for you to pay it," Jack says. "I just want to get my money's worth."

"Will you register, please?" the clerk says. He looked at the names. "Number 238, Mister Brennan."

We went up in the elevator. It was a nice big room with two beds and a door opening into a bath-room.

"This is pretty good," Jack says.

The boy who brought us up pulled up the curtains and brought in our bags. Jack didn't make any move, so I gave the boy a quarter. We washed up and Jack said we better go out and get something to eat.

We ate a lunch at Jimmy Hanley's place. Quite a lot of the boys were there. When we were about half through eating, John came in and sat down with us. Jack didn't talk much.

"How are you on the weight, Jack?" John asked him. Jack was putting away a pretty good lunch.

"I could make it with my clothes on," Jack said. He never had to worry about taking off weight. He was a natural welterweight and he'd never gotten fat. He'd lost weight out at Hogan's.

"Well, that's one thing you never had to worry about," John said.

"That's one thing," Jack says.

We went around to the Garden to weigh in after lunch. The match was made at a hundred forty-seven pounds at three o'clock. Jack stepped on the scales with a towel around him. The bar didn't move. Walcott had just weighed and was standing with a lot of people around him.

"Let's see what you weigh, Jack," Freedman, Walcott's manager said.

"All right, weigh *him* then," Jack jerked his head toward Walcott.

"Drop the towel," Freedman said.

"What do you make it?" Jack asked the fellows who were weighing.

"One hundred and forty-three pounds," the fat man who was weighing said.

"You're down fine, Jack," Freedman says.

"Weigh *him*," Jack says.

Walcott came over. He was a blond with wide shoulders and arms like a heavyweight. He didn't have much legs. Jack stood about half a head taller than he did.

"Hello, Jack," he said. His face was plenty marked up.

"Hello," said Jack. "How you feel?"

"Good," Walcott says. He dropped the towel from around his waist and stood on the scales. He had the widest shoulders and back you ever saw.

"One hundred and forty-six pounds and twelve ounces."

Walcott stepped off and grinned at Jack.

"Well," John says to him, "Jack's spotting you about four pounds."

"More than that when I come in, kid," Walcott says. "I'm going to go and eat now."

We went back and Jack got dressed. "He's a pretty tough-looking boy," Jack says to me.

"He looks as though he'd been hit plenty of times."

"Oh, yes," Jack says. "He ain't hard to hit."

"Where are you going?" John asked when Jack was dressed.

"Back to the hotel," Jack says. "You looked after everything?"

"Yes," John says. "It's all looked after."

"I'm going to lie down a while," Jack says.

"I'll come around for you about a quarter to seven and we'll go and eat."

"All right."

Up at the hotel Jack took off his shoes and his coat and

lay down for a while. I wrote a letter. I looked over a couple of times and Jack wasn't sleeping. He was lying perfectly still but every once in a while his eyes would open. Finally he sits up.

"Want to play some cribbage, Jerry?" he says.

"Sure," I said.

He went over to his suitcase and got out the cards and the cribbage board. We played cribbage and he won three dollars off me. John knocked at the door and came in.

"Want to play some cribbage, John?" Jack asked him.

John put his hat down on the table. It was all wet. His coat was wet too.

"Is it raining?" Jack asks.

"It's pouring," John says. "The taxi I had got tied up in the traffic and I got out and walked."

"Come on, play some cribbage," Jack says.

"You ought to go and eat."

"No," says Jack. "I don't want to eat yet."

So they played cribbage for about half an hour and Jack won a dollar and a half off him.

"Well, I suppose we got to go eat," Jack says. He went to the window and looked out.

"Is it still raining?"

"Yes."

"Let's eat in the hotel," John says.

"All right," Jack says, "I'll play you once more to see who pays for the meal."

After a little while Jack gets up and says, "You buy the meal, John," and we went downstairs and ate in the big dining-room.

After we ate we went upstairs and Jack played cribbage with John again and won two dollars and a half off him. Jack was feeling pretty good. John had a bag with him with all his stuff in it. Jack took off his shirt and collar and put on a jersey and a sweater, so he wouldn't catch cold when he came out, and put his ring clothes and his bathrobe in a bag.

"You all ready?" John asks him. "I'll call up and have them get a taxi."

Pretty soon the telephone rang and they said the taxi was waiting.

We rode down in the elevator, and went out through the lobby, and got in a taxi and rode around to the Garden. It was raining hard but there was a lot of people outside on the streets. The Garden was sold out. As we came in on our way to the dressing-room I saw how full it was. It looked like half a mile down to the ring. It was all dark. Just the lights over the ring.

"It's a good thing, with this rain, they didn't try and pull this fight in the ball park," John said.

"They got a good crowd," Jack says.

"This is a fight that would draw a lot more than the Garden could hold."

"You can't tell about the weather," Jack says.

John came to the door of the dressing-room and poked his head in. Jack was sitting there with his bathrobe on, he had his arms folded and was looking at the floor. John had a couple of handlers with him. They looked over his shoulder. Jack looked up.

"Is he in?" he asked.

"He's just gone down," John said.

We started down. Walcott was just getting into the ring. The crowd gave him a big hand. He climbed through between the ropes and put his two fists together and smiled, and shook them at the crowd, first at one side of the ring, then at the other, and then sat down. Jack got a good hand coming down through the crowd. Jack is Irish and the Irish always get a pretty good hand. An Irishman don't draw in New York like a Jew or an Italian but they always get a good hand. Jack climbed up and bent down to go through the ropes and Walcott came over from his corner and pushed the rope down for Jack to go through. The crowd thought that was wonderful. Walcott put his hand on Jack's shoulder and they stood there just for a second.

"So you're going to be one of these popular champions," Jack says to him. "Take your goddam hand off my shoulder."

"Be yourself," Walcott says.

This is all great for the crowd. How gentlemanly the boys are before the fight. How they wish each other luck.

Solly Freedman came over to our corner while Jack is bandaging his hands and John is over in Walcott's corner. Jack puts his thumb through the slit in the bandage and then wrapped his hand nice and smooth. I taped it around the wrist and twice across the knuckles.

"Hey," Freedman says. "Where do you get all that tape?"

"Feel of it," Jack says. "It's soft, ain't it? Don't be a hick."

Freedman stands there all the time while Jack bandages the other hand, and one of the boys that's going to handle him brings the gloves and I pull them on and work them around.

"Say, Freedman," Jack asks, "what nationality is this Walcott?"

"I don't know," Solly says. "He's some sort of a Dane."

"He's a Bohemian," the lad who brought the gloves said.

The referee called them out to the center of the ring and Jack walks out. Walcott comes out smiling. They met and the referee put his arm on each of their shoulders.

"Hello, popularity," Jack says to Walcott.

"Be yourself."

"What do you call yourself 'Walcott' for?" Jack says. "Didn't you know he was a nigger?"

"Listen—" says the referee, and he gives them the same old line. Once Walcott interrupts him. He grabs Jack's arm and says, "Can I hit when he's got me like this?"

"Keep your hands off me," Jack says. "There ain't no moving-pictures of this."

They went back to their corners. I lifted the bathrobe off Jack and he leaned on the ropes and flexed his knees

a couple of times and scuffed his shoes in the rosin. The
gong rang and Jack turned quick and went out. Walcott
came toward him and they touched gloves and as soon as
Walcott dropped his hands Jack jumped his left into his
face twice. There wasn't anybody ever boxed better than
Jack. Walcott was after him, going forward all the time
with his chin on his chest. He's a hooker and he carries
his hands pretty low. All he knows is to get in there and
sock. But every time he gets in there close, Jack has the
left hand in his face. It's just as though it's automatic. Jack
just raises the left hand up and it's in Walcott's face.
Three or four times Jack brings the right over but Walcott gets it on the shoulder or high up on the head. He's
just like all these hookers. The only thing he's afraid of
is another one of the same kind. He's covered everywhere
you can hurt him. He don't care about a left-hand in his
face.

After about four rounds Jack has him bleeding bad and
his face all cut up, but every time Walcott's got in close
he's socked so hard he's got two big red patches on both
sides just below Jack's ribs. Every time he gets in close,
Jack ties him up, then gets one hand loose and uppercuts
him, but when Walcott gets his hands loose he socks Jack
in the body so they can hear it outside in the street. He's
a socker.

It goes along like that for three rounds more. They
don't talk any. They're working all the time. We worked
over Jack plenty too, in between the rounds. He don't
look good at all but he never does much work in the ring.
He don't move around much and that left-hand is just
automatic. It's just like it was connected with Walcott's
face and Jack just had to wish it in every time. Jack is
always calm in close and he doesn't waste any juice. He
knows everything about working in close too and he's
getting away with a lot of stuff. While they were in our
corner I watched him tie Walcott up, get his right hand
loose, turn it and come up with an uppercut that got Walcott's nose with the heel of the glove. Walcott was bleed-

ing bad and leaned his nose on Jack's shoulder so as to give Jack some of it too, and Jack sort of lifted his shoulder sharp and caught him against the nose, and then brought down the right hand and did the same thing again.

Walcott was sore as hell. By the time they'd gone five rounds he hated Jack's guts. Jack wasn't sore; that is, he wasn't any sorer than he always was. He certainly did used to make the fellows he fought hate boxing. That was why he hated Kid Lewis so. He never got the Kid's goat. Kid Lewis always had about three new dirty things Jack couldn't do. Jack was as safe as a church all the time he was in there, as long as he was strong. He certainly was treating Walcott rough. The funny thing was it looked as though Jack was an open classic boxer. That was because he had all that stuff too.

After the seventh round Jack says, "My left's getting heavy."

From then he started to take a beating. It didn't show at first. But instead of him running the fight it was Walcott was running it, instead of being safe all the time now he was in trouble. He couldn't keep him out with the left hand now. It looked as though it was the same as ever, only now instead of Walcott's punches just missing him they were just hitting him. He took an awful beating in the body.

"What's the round?" Jack asked.

"The eleventh."

"I can't stay," Jack says. "My legs are going bad."

Walcott had been just hitting him for a long time. It was like a baseball catcher pulls the ball and takes some of the shock off. From now on Walcott commenced to land solid. He certainly was a socking-machine. Jack was just trying to block everything now. It didn't show what an awful beating he was taking. In between the rounds I worked on his legs. The muscles would flutter under my hands all the time I was rubbing them. He was sick as hell.

"How's it go?" he asked John, turning around, his face all swollen.

"It's his fight."

"I think I can last," Jack says. "I don't want this bohunk to stop me."

It was going just the way he thought it would. He knew he couldn't beat Walcott. He wasn't strong any more. He was all right though. His money was all right and now he wanted to finish it off right to please himself. He didn't want to be knocked out.

The gong rang and we pushed him out. He went out slow. Walcott came right out after him. Jack put the left in his face and Walcott took it, came in under it and started working on Jack's body. Jack tried to tie him up and it was just like trying to hold on to a buzz-saw. Jack broke away from it and missed with the right. Walcott clipped him with a left-hook and Jack went down. He went down on his hands and knees and looked at us. The referee started counting. Jack was watching us and shaking his head. At eight John motioned to him. You couldn't hear on account of the crowd. Jack got up. The referee had been holding Walcott back with one arm while he counted.

When Jack was on his feet Walcott started toward him.

"Watch yourself, Jimmy," I heard Solly Freedman yell to him.

Walcott came up to Jack looking at him. Jack stuck the left hand at him. Walcott just shook his head. He backed Jack up against the ropes, measured him and then hooked the left very light to the side of Jack's head and socked the right into the body as hard as he could sock, just as low as he could get it. He must have hit him five inches below the belt. I thought the eyes would come out of Jack's head. They stuck way out. His mouth come open.

The referee grabbed Walcott. Jack stepped forward. If he went down there went fifty thousand bucks. He walked as though all his insides were going to fall out.

"It wasn't low," he said. "It was a accident."

The crowd were yelling so you couldn't hear anything.

"I'm all right," Jack says. They were right in front of us. The referee looks at John and then he shakes his head.

"Come on, you polak son-of-a-bitch," Jack says to Walcott.

John was hanging onto the ropes. He had the towel ready to chuck in. Jack was standing just a little way out from the ropes. He took a step forward. I saw the sweat come out on his face like somebody had squeezed it and a big drop went down his nose.

"Come on and fight," Jack says to Walcott.

The referee looked at John and waved Walcott on.

"Go in there, you slob," he says.

Walcott went in. He didn't know what to do either. He never thought Jack could have stood it. Jack put the left in his face. There was such a hell of a lot of yelling going on. They were right in front of us. Walcott hit him twice. Jack's face was the worst thing I ever saw—the look on it! He was holding himself and all his body together and it all showed on his face. All the time he was thinking and holding his body in where it was busted.

Then he started to sock. His face looked awful all the time. He started to sock with his hands low down by his side, swinging at Walcott. Walcott covered up and Jack was swinging wild at Walcott's head. Then he swung the left and it hit Walcott in the groin and the right hit Walcott right bang where he'd hit Jack. Way low below the belt. Walcott went down and grabbed himself there and rolled and twisted around.

The referee grabbed Jack and pushed him toward his corner. John jumps into the ring. There was all this yelling going on. The referee was talking with the judges and then the announcer got into the ring with the megaphone and says, "Walcott on a foul."

The referee is talking to John and he says, "What could

I do? Jack wouldn't take the foul. Then when he's groggy he fouls him."

"He'd lost it anyway," John says.

Jack's sitting on the chair. I've got his gloves off and he's holding himself in down there with both hands. When he's got something supporting it his face doesn't look so bad.

"Go over and say you're sorry," John says into his ear. "It'll look good."

Jack stands up and the sweat comes out all over his face. I put the bathrobe around him and he holds himself in with one hand under the bathrobe and goes across the ring. They've picked Walcott up and they're working on him. There're a lot of people in Walcott's corner. Nobody speaks to Jack. He leans over Walcott.

"I'm sorry," Jack says. "I didn't mean to foul you."

Walcott doesn't say anything. He looks too damned sick.

"Well, you're the champion now," Jack says to him. "I hope you get a hell of a lot of fun out of it."

"Leave the kid alone," Solly Freedman says.

"Hello, Solly," Jack says. "I'm sorry I fouled your boy."

Freedman just looks at him.

Jack went to his corner walking that funny jerky way and we got him down through the ropes and through the reporters' tables and out down the aisle. A lot of people want to slap Jack on the back. He goes out through all that mob in his bathrobe to the dressing-room. It's a popular win for Walcott. That's the way the money was bet in the Garden.

Once we got inside the dressing-room Jack lay down and shut his eyes.

"We want to get to the hotel and get a doctor," John says.

"I'm all busted inside," Jack says.

"I'm sorry as hell, Jack," John says.

"It's all right," Jack says.

He lies there with his eyes shut.

"They certainly tried a nice double-cross," John said.

"Your friends Morgan and Steinfelt," Jack said. "You got nice friends."

He lies there, his eyes are open now. His face has still got that awful drawn look.

"It's funny how fast you can think when it means that much money," Jack says.

"You're some boy, Jack," John says.

"No," Jack says. "It was nothing."

Flight

By JOHN STEINBECK

About fifteen miles below Monterey, on the wild coast, the Torres family had their farm, a few sloping acres above a cliff that dropped to the brown reefs and to the hissing white waters of the ocean. Behind the farm the stone mountains stood up against the sky. The farm buildings huddled like little clinging aphids on the mountain skirts, crouched low to the ground as though the wind might blow them into the sea. The little shack, the rattling, rotting barn were grey-bitten with sea salt, beaten by the damp wind until they had taken on the color of the granite hills. Two horses, a red cow and a red calf, half a dozen pigs and a flock of lean, multicolored chickens stocked the place. A little corn was raised on the sterile slope, and it grew short and thick under the wind, and all the cobs formed on the landward sides of the stalks.

Mama Torres, a lean, dry woman with ancient eyes, had ruled the farm for ten years, ever since her husband tripped over a stone in the field one day and fell full length on a rattlesnake. When one is bitten on the chest there is not much that can be done.

Mama Torres had three children, two undersized black ones of twelve and fourteen, Emilio and Rosy, whom Mama kept fishing on the rocks below the farm when the sea was kind and when the truant officer was in some distant part of Monterey County. And there was Pepé, the tall smiling son of nineteen, a gentle, affectionate boy, but very lazy. Pepé had a tall head, pointed at the top, and from its peak, coarse black hair grew down like a thatch all around. Over his smiling little eyes Mama cut a straight bang so he could see. Pepé had sharp Indian cheek bones and an eagle nose, but his mouth was as sweet and shapely as a girl's mouth, and his chin was fragile and chiseled. He was loose and gangling, all legs and feet and wrists, and he was very lazy. Mama thought him fine and brave, but she never told him so. She said, "Some lazy cow must have got into thy father's family, else how could I have a son like thee." And she said, "When I carried thee, a sneaking lazy coyote came out of the brush and looked at me one day. That must have made thee so."

Pepé smiled sheepishly and stabbed at the ground with his knife to keep the blade sharp and free from rust. It was his inheritance, that knife, his father's knife. The long heavy blade folded back into the black handle. There was a button on the handle. When Pepé pressed the button, the blade leaped out ready for use. The knife was with Pepé always, for it had been his father's knife.

One sunny morning when the sea below the cliff was glinting and blue and the white surf creamed on the reef, when even the stone mountains looked kindly, Mama Torres called out the door of the shack, "Pepé, I have a labor for thee."

There was no answer. Mama listened. From behind the barn she heard a burst of laughter. She lifted her full long skirt and walked in the direction of the noise.

Pepé was sitting on the ground with his back against

a box. His white teeth glistened. On either side of him stood the two black ones, tense and expectant. Fifteen feet away a redwood post was set in the ground. Pepé's right hand lay limply in his lap, and in the palm the big black knife rested. The blade was closed back into the handle. Pepé looked smiling at the sky.

Suddenly Emilio cried, "Ya!"

Pepé's wrist flicked like the head of a snake. The blade seemed to fly open in mid-air, and with a thump the point dug into the redwood post, and the black handle quivered. The three burst into excited laughter. Rosy ran to the post and pulled out the knife and brought it back to Pepé. He closed the blade and settled the knife carefully in his listless palm again. He grinned self-consciously at the sky. "Ya!"

The heavy knife lanced out and sunk into the post again. Mama moved forward like a ship and scattered the play.

"All day you do foolish things with the knife, like a toy-baby," she stormed. "Get up on thy huge feet that eat up shoes. Get up!" She took him by one loose shoulder and hoisted at him. Pepé grinned sheepishly and came half-heartedly to his feet. "Look!" Mama cried. "Big lazy, you must catch the horse and put on him thy father's saddle. You must ride to Monterey. The medicine bottle is empty. There is no salt. Go thou now, Peanut! Catch the horse."

A revolution took place in the relaxed figure of Pepé. "To Monterey, me? Alone? *Sí*, Mama."

She scowled at him. "Do not think, big sheep, that you will buy candy. No, I will give you only enough for the medicine and the salt."

Pepé smiled. "Mama, you will put the hatband on the hat?"

She relented then. "Yes, Pepé. You may wear the hatband."

His voice grew insinuating, "And the green handkerchief, Mama?"

"Yes, if you go quickly and return with no trouble, the silk green handkerchief will go. If you make sure to take off the handkerchief when you eat so no spot may fall on it. . . ."

"*Si*, Mama. I will be careful. I am a man."

"Thou? A man? Thou art a peanut."

He went into the rickety barn and brought out a rope, and he walked agilely enough up the hill to catch the horse.

When he was ready and mounted before the door, mounted on his father's saddle that was so old that the oaken frame showed through torn leather in many places, then Mama brought out the round black hat with the tooled leather band, and she reached up and knotted the green silk handkerchief about his neck. Pepé's blue denin coat was much darker than his jeans, for it had been washed much less often.

Mama handed up the big medicine bottle and the silver coins. "That for the medicine," she said, "and that for the salt. That for a candle to burn for the papa. That for *dulces* for the little ones. Our friend Mrs. Rodriguez will give you dinner and maybe a bed for the night. When you go to the church say only ten Paternosters and only twenty-five Ave Marias. Oh! I know, big coyote. You would sit there flapping your mouth over Aves all day while you looked at the candles and the holy pictures. That is not good devotion to stare at the pretty things."

The black hat, covering the high pointed head and black thatched hair of Pepé, gave him dignity and age. He sat the rangy horse well. Mama thought how handsome he was, dark and lean and tall. "I would not send thee now alone, thou little one, except for the medicine," she said softly. "It is not good to have no medicine, for who knows when the toothache will come, or the sadness of the stomach. These things are."

"Adios, Mama," Pepé cried. "I will come back soon. You may send me often alone. I am a man."

"Thou art a foolish chicken."

He straightened his shoulders, flipped the reins against the horse's shoulder and rode away. He turned once and saw that they still watched him, Emilio and Rosy and Mama. Pepé grinned with pride and gladness and lifted the tough buckskin horse to a trot.

When he had dropped out of sight over a little dip in the road, Mama turned to the black ones, but she spoke to herself. "He is nearly a man now," she said. "It will be a nice thing to have a man in the house again." Her eyes sharpened on the children. "Go to the rocks now. The tide is going out. There will be abalones to be found." She put the iron hooks into their hands and saw them down the steep trail to the reefs. She brought the smooth stone *metate* to the doorway and sat grinding her corn to flour and looking occasionally at the road over which Pepé had gone. The noonday came and then the afternoon, when the little ones beat the abalones on a rock to make them tender and Mama patted the tortillas to make them thin. They ate their dinner as the red sun was plunging down toward the ocean. They sat on the doorsteps and watched the big white moon come over the mountain tops.

Mama said, "He is now at the house of our friend Mrs. Rodriguez. She will give him nice things to eat and maybe a present."

Emilio said, "Some day I too will ride to Monterey for medicine. Did Pepé come to be a man today?"

Mama said wisely, "A boy gets to be a man when a man is needed. Remember this thing. I have known boys forty years old because there was no need for a man."

Soon afterwards they retired, Mama in her big oak bed on one side of the room, Emilio and Rosy in their boxes full of straw and sheepskins on the other side of the room.

The moon went over the sky and the surf roared on the rocks. The roosters crowed the first call. The surf subsided to a whispering surge against the reef. The moon dropped toward the sea. The roosters crowed again.

The moon was near down to the water when Pepé rode on a winded horse to his home flat. His dog bounced out and circled the horse yelping with pleasure. Pepé slid off the saddle to the ground. The weathered little shack was silver in the moonlight and the square shadow of it was black to the north and east. Against the east the piling mountains were misty with light; their tops melted into the sky.

Pepé walked wearily up the three steps and into the house. It was dark inside. There was a rustle in the corner.

Mama cried out from her bed. "Who comes? Pepé, is it thou?"

"*Sí*, Mama."

"Did you get the medicine?"

"*Sí*, Mama."

"Well, go to sleep, then. I thought you would be sleeping at the house of Mrs. Rodriguez." Pepé stood silently in the dark room. "Why do you stand there, Pepé? Did you drink wine?"

"*Sí*, Mama."

"Well, go to bed then and sleep out the wine."

His voice was tired and patient, but very firm. "Light the candle, Mama. I must go away into the mountains."

"What is this, Pepé? You are crazy." Mama struck a sulphur match and held the little blue burr until the flame spread up the stick. She set light to the candle on the floor beside her bed. "Now, Pepé, what is this you say?" She looked anxiously into his face.

He was changed. The fragile quality seemed to have gone from his chin. His mouth was less full than it had been, the lines of the lips were straighter, but in his eyes the greatest change had taken place. There was no laughter in them any more, nor any bashfulness. They were sharp and bright and purposeful.

He told her in a tired monotone, told her everything just as it had happened. A few people came into the kitchen of Mrs. Rodriguez. There was wine to drink. Pepé drank wine. The little quarrel—the man started toward

Pepé and then the knife—it went almost by itself. It flew, it darted before Pepé knew it. As he talked, Mama's face grew stern, and it seemed to grow more lean. Pepé finished. "I am a man now, Mama. The man said names to me I could not allow."

Mama nodded. "Yes, thou art a man, my poor little Pepé. Thou art a man. I have seen it coming on thee. I have watched you throwing the knife into the post, and I have been afraid." For a moment her face had softened, but now it grew stern again. "Come! We must get you ready. Go. Awaken Emilio and Rosy. Go quickly."

Pepé stepped over to the corner where his brother and sister slept among the sheepskins. He leaned down and shook them gently. "Come, Rosy! Come, Emilio! The Mama says you must arise."

The little black ones sat up and rubbed their eyes in the candlelight. Mama was out of bed now, her long black skirt over her nightgown. "Emilio," she cried. "Go up and catch the other horse for Pepé. Quickly, now! Quickly." Emilio put his legs in his overalls and stumbled sleepily out the door.

"You heard no one behind you on the road?" Mama demanded.

"No, Mama. I listened carefully. No one was on the road."

Mama darted like a bird about the room. From a nail on the wall she took a canvas water bag and threw it on the floor. She stripped a blanket from her bed and rolled it into a tight tube and tied the ends with string. From a box beside the stove she lifted a flour sack half full of black stringy jerky. "Your father's black coat, Pepé. Here, put it on."

Pepé stood in the middle of the floor watching her activity. She reached behind the door and brought out the rifle, a long 38-56, worn shiny the whole length of the barrel. Pepé took it from her and held it in the crook of his elbow. Mama brought a little leather bag and counted the cartridges into his hand. "Only ten left," she warned. "You must not waste them."

Emilio put his head in the door. "'Qui 'st 'l caballo, Mama."

"Put on the saddle from the other horse. Tie on the blanket. Here, tie the jerky to the saddle horn."

Still Pepé stood silently watching his mother's frantic activity. His chin looked hard, and his sweet mouth was drawn and thin. His little eyes followed Mama about the room almost suspiciously.

Rosy asked softly, "Where goes Pepé?"

Mama's eyes were fierce. "Pepé goes on a journey. Pepé is a man now. He has a man's thing to do."

Pepé straightened his shoulders. His mouth changed until he looked very much like Mama.

At last the preparation was finished. The loaded horse stood outside the door. The water bag dripped a line of moisture down the bay shoulder.

The moonlight was being thinned by the dawn and the big white moon was near down to the sea. The family stood by the shack. Mama confronted Pepé. "Look, my son! Do not stop until it is dark again. Do not sleep even though you are tired. Take care of the horse in order that he may not stop of weariness. Remember to be careful with the bullets—there are only ten. Do not fill thy stomach with jerky or it will make thee sick. Eat a little jerky and fill thy stomach with grass. When thou comest to the high mountains, if thou seest any of the dark watching men, go not near to them nor try to speak to them. And forget not thy prayers." She put her lean hands on Pepé's shoulders, stood on her toes and kissed him formally on both cheeks, and Pepé kissed her on both cheeks. Then he went to Emilio and Rosy and kissed both of their cheeks.

Pepé turned back to Mama. He seemed to look for a little softness, a little weakness in her. His eyes were searching, but Mama's face remained fierce. "Go now," she said. "Do not wait to be caught like a chicken."

Pepé pulled himself into the saddle. "I am a man," he said.

It was the first dawn when he rode up the hill toward the little canyon which let a trail into the mountains. Moonlight and daylight fought with each other, and the two warring qualities made it difficult to see. Before Pepé had gone a hundred yards, the outlines of his figure were misty; and long before he entered the canyon, he had become a grey, indefinite shadow.

Mama stood stiffly in front of her doorstep, and on either side of her stood Emilio and Rosy. They cast furtive glances at Mama now and then.

When the grey shape of Pepé melted into the hillside and disappeared, Mama relaxed. She began the high, whining keen of the death wail. "Our beautiful—our brave," she cried. "Our protector, our son is gone." Emilio and Rosy moaned beside her. "Our beautiful—our brave, he is gone." It was the formal wail. It rose to a high piercing whine and subsided to a moan. Mama raised it three times and then she turned and went into the house and shut the door.

Emilio and Rosy stood wondering in the dawn. They heard Mama whimpering in the house. They went out to sit on the cliff above the ocean. They touched shoulders. "When did Pepé come to be a man?" Emilio asked.

"Last night," said Rosy. "Last night in Monterey." The ocean clouds turned red with the sun that was behind the mountains.

"We will have no breakfast," said Emilio. "Mama will not want to cook." Rosy did not answer him. "Where is Pepé gone?" he asked.

Rosy looked around at him. She drew her knowledge from the quiet air. "He has gone on a journey. He will never come back."

"Is he dead? Do you think he is dead?"

Rosy looked back at the ocean again. A little steamer,

drawing a line of smoke sat on the edge of the horizon. "He is not dead," Rosy explained. "Not yet."

Pepé rested the big rifle across the saddle in front of him. He let the horse walk up the hill and he didn't look back. The stony slope took on a coat of short brush so that Pepé found the entrance to a trail and entered it.

When he came to the canyon opening, he swung once in his saddle and looked back, but the houses were swallowed in the misty light. Pepé jerked forward again. The high shoulder of the canyon closed in on him. His horse stretched out its neck and sighed and settled to the trail.

It was a well-worn path, dark soft leaf-mould earth strewn with broken pieces of sandstone. The trail rounded the shoulder of the canyon and dropped steeply into the bed of the stream. In the shallows the water ran smoothly, glinting in the first morning sun. Small round stones on the bottom were as brown as rust with sun moss. In the sand along the edges of the stream the tall, rich wild mint grew, while in the water itself the cress, old and tough, had gone to heavy seed.

The path went into the stream and emerged on the other side. The horse sloshed into the water and stopped. Pepé dropped his bridle and let the beast drink of the running water.

Soon the canyon sides became steep and the first giant sentinel redwoods guarded the trail, great round red trunks bearing foliage as green and lacy as ferns. Once Pepé was among the trees, the sun was lost. A perfumed and purple light lay in the pale green of the underbrush. Gooseberry bushes and blackberries and tall ferns lined the stream, and overhead the branches of the redwoods met and cut off the sky.

Pepé drank from the water bag, and he reached into the flour sack and brought out a black string of jerky. His white teeth gnawed at the string until the tough meat parted. He chewed slowly and drank occasionally from the water bag. His little eyes were slumberous and tired, but the muscles of his face were hard set. The earth of the trail was black now. It gave up a hollow sound under the walking hoofbeats.

The stream fell more sharply. Little waterfalls splashed on the stones. Five-fingered ferns hung over the water and dripped spray from their fingertips. Pepé rode half over in his saddle, dangling one leg loosely. He picked a bay leaf from a tree beside the way and put it into his mouth for a moment to flavor the dry jerky. He held the gun loosely across the pommel.

Suddenly he squared in his saddle, swung the horse from the trail and kicked it hurriedly up behind a big redwood tree. He pulled up the reins tight against the bit to keep the horse from whinnying. His face was intent and his nostrils quivered a little.

A hollow pounding came down the trail, and a horseman rode by, a fat man with red cheeks and a white stubble beard. His horse put down its head and blubbered at the trail when it came to the place where Pepé had turned off. "Hold up!" said the man and he pulled up his horse's head.

When the last sound of the hoofs died away, Pepé came back into the trail again. He did not relax in the saddle any more. He lifted the big rifle and swung the lever to throw a shell into the chamber, and then he let down the hammer to half cock.

The trail grew very steep. Now the redwood trees were smaller and their tops were dead, bitten dead where the wind reached them. The horse plodded on; the sun went slowly overhead and started down toward the afternoon.

Where the stream came out of a side canyon, the trail left it. Pepé dismounted and watered his horse and filled up his water bag. As soon as the trail had parted from the stream, the trees were gone and only the thick brittle sage and manzanita and chaparral edged the trail. And the soft black earth was gone, too, leaving only the light tan broken rock for the trail bed. Lizards scampered away into the brush as the horse rattled over the little stones.

Pepé turned in his saddle and looked back. He was in the open now: he could be seen from a distance. As he ascended the trail the country grew more rough and terrible and dry. The way wound about the bases of great square rocks. Little grey rabbits skittered in the brush. A bird made a monotonous high creaking. Eastward the bare rock mountaintops were pale and powder-dry under the dropping sun. The horse plodded up and up the trail toward a little V in the ridge which was the pass.

Pepé looked suspiciously back every minute or so, and his eyes sought the tops of the ridges ahead. Once, on a white barren spur, he saw a black figure for a moment, but he looked quickly away, for it was one of the dark watchers. No one knew who the watchers were, nor where they lived, but it was better to ignore them and never to show interest in them. They did not bother one who stayed on the trail and minded his own business.

The air was parched and full of light dust blown by the breeze from the eroding mountains. Pepé drank sparingly from his bag and corked it tightly and hung it on the horn again. The trail moved up the dry shale hillside, avoiding rocks, dropping under clefts, climbing in and out of old water scars. When he arrived at the little pass he stopped and looked back for a long time. No dark watchers were to be seen now. The trail behind was empty. Only the high tops of the redwoods indicated where the stream flowed.

Pepé rode on through the pass. His little eyes were nearly closed with weariness, but his face was stern, relentless and manly. The high mountain wind coasted sighing through the pass and whistled on the edges of the big blocks of broken granite. In the air, a red-tailed hawk sailed over close to the ridge and screamed angrily. Pepé went slowly through the broken jagged pass and looked down on the other side.

The trail dropped quickly, staggering among broken

rock. At the bottom of the slope there was a dark crease, thick with brush, and on the other side of the crease a little flat, in which a grove of oak trees grew. A scar of green grass cut across the flat. And behind the flat another mountain rose, desolate with dead rocks and starving little black bushes. Pepé drank from the bag again for the air was so dry that it encrusted his nostrils and burned his lips. He put the horse down the trail. The hooves slipped and struggled on the steep way, starting little stones that rolled off into the brush. The sun was gone behind the westward mountain now, but still it glowed brilliantly on the oaks and on the grassy flat. The rocks and the hillsides still sent up waves of the heat ~~ had gathered from the day's sun.

~~epé looked up to the top of the next dry withered ridge. He saw a dark form against the sky, a man's figure standing on top of a rock, and he glanced away quickly not to appear curious. When a moment later he looked up again, the figure was gone.

Downward the trail was quickly covered. Sometimes the horse floundered for footing, sometimes set his feet and slid a little way. They came at last to the bottom where the dark chaparral was higher than Pepé's head. He held up his rifle on one side and his arm on the other to shield his face from the sharp brittle fingers of the brush.

Up and out of the crease he rode, and up a little cliff. The grassy flat was before him, and the round comfortable oaks. For a moment he studied the trail down which he had come, but there was no movement and no sound from it. Finally he rode out over the flat, to the green streak, and at the upper end of the damp he found a little spring welling out of the earth and dropping into a dug basin before it seeped out over the flat.

Pepé filled his bag first, and then he let the thirsty horse drink out of the pool. He led the horse to the clump of oaks, and in the middle of the grove, fairly protected from sight on all sides, he took off the saddle and the bridle and laid them on the ground. The horse stretched his jaws sideways and yawned. Pepé knotted the lead rope about the horse's neck and tied him to a sapling among the oaks, where he could graze in a fairly large circle.

When the horse was gnawing hungrily at the dry grass, Pepé went to the saddle and took a black string of jerky from the sack and strolled to an oak tree on the edge of the grove, from under which he could watch the trail. He sat down in the crisp dry oak leaves and automatically felt for his big black knife to cut the jerky, but he had no knife. He leaned back on his elbow and gnawed at the tough strong meat. His face was blank, but it was a man's face.

The bright evening light washed the eastern ridge, but the valley was darkening. Doves flew down from the hills to the spring, and the quail came running out of the brush and joined them, calling clearly to one another.

Out of the corner of his eye Pepé saw a shadow grow out of the bushy crease. He turned his head slowly. A big spotted wildcat was creeping toward the spring, belly to the ground, moving like thought.

Pepé cocked his rifle and edged the muzzle slowly around. Then he looked apprehensively up the trail and dropped the hammer again. From the ground beside him he picked an oak twig and threw it toward the spring. The quail flew up with a roar and the doves whistled away. The big cat stood up: for a long moment he looked at Pepé with cold yellow eyes, and then fearlessly walked back into the gulch.

The dusk gathered quickly in the deep valley. Pepé muttered his prayers, put his head down on his arm and went instantly to sleep.

The moon came up and filled the valley with cold blue light, and the wind swept rustling down from the peaks. The owls worked up and down the slopes looking for rabbits. Down in the brush of the gulch a coyote gabbled. The oak trees whispered softly in the night breeze.

Pepé started up, listening. His horse had whinnied. The moon was just slipping behind the western ridge, leaving the valley in darkness behind it. Pepé sat tensely gripping his rifle. From far up the trail he heard an answering whinny and the crash of shod hooves on the broken rock. He jumped to his feet, ran to his horse and led it under the trees. He threw on the saddle and cinched it tight for the steep trail, caught the unwilling head and forced the bit into the mouth. He felt the saddle to make sure the water bag and the sack of jerky were there. Then he mounted and turned up the hill.

It was velvet dark. The horse found the entrance to the trail where it left the flat, and started up, stumbling and slipping on the rocks. Pepé's hand rose up to his head. His hat was gone. He had left it under the oak tree.

The horse had struggled far up the trail when the first change of dawn came into the air, a steel greyness as light mixed thoroughly with dark. Gradually the sharp snaggled edge of the ridge stood out above them, rotten granite tortured and eaten by the winds of time. Pepé had dropped his reins on the horn, leaving direction to the horse. The brush grabbed at his legs in the dark until one knee of his jeans was ripped.

Gradually the light flowed down over the ridge. The starved brush and rocks stood out in the half light, strange and lonely in high perspective. Then there came warmth into the light. Pepé drew up and looked back, but he could see nothing in the darker valley below. The sky turned blue over the coming sun. In the waste of the mountainside, the poor dry brush grew only three feet high. Here and there, big outcroppings of unrotted granite stood up like mouldering houses. Pepé relaxed a little. He drank from his water bag and bit off a piece of jerky. A single eagle flew over, high in the light.

Without warning Pepé's horse screamed and fell on its side. He was almost down before the rifle crash echoed up from the valley. From a hole behind the struggling shoulder, a stream of bright crimson blood pumped and stopped and pumped and stopped. The hooves threshed on the ground. Pepé lay half stunned beside the horse. He looked slowly down the hill. A piece of sage clipped off beside his head and another crash echoed up from side to side of the canyon. Pepé flung himself frantically behind a bush.

He crawled up the hill on his knees and one hand. His right hand held the rifle up off the ground and pushed it ahead of him. He moved with the instinctive care of an animal. Rapidly he wormed his way toward one of the big outcroppings of granite on the hill above him. Where the brush was high he doubled up and ran, but where the cover was slight he wriggled forward on his stomach, pushing the rifle ahead of him. In the last little distance there was no cover at all. Pepé poised and then he darted across the space and flashed around the corner of the rock.

He leaned panting against the stone. When his breath came easier he moved along behind the big rock until he came to a narrow split that offered a thin section of vision down the hill. Pepé lay on his stomach and pushed the rifle barrel through the slit and waited.

The sun reddened the western ridges now. Already the buzzards were settling down toward the place where the horse lay. A small brown bird scratched in the dead sage leaves directly in front of the rifle muzzle. The coasting eagle flew back toward the rising sun.

Pepé saw a little movement in the brush far below. His grip tightened on the gun. A little brown doe stepped daintily out on the trail and crossed it and disappeared into the brush again. For a long time Pepé waited. Far below he could see the little flat and the oak trees and the slash of green. Suddenly his eyes flashed back at the trail again. A quarter of a mile down there had been a quick movement in the chaparral. The rifle swung over. The front sight nestled in the v of the rear sight. Pepé studied for a moment and then raised the rear sight a notch. The little movement in the brush came again. The sight settled on it. Pepé squeezed the trigger. The explosion crashed down the mountain and up the other side, and came rattling back. The whole side of the slope grew still. No more movement. And then a white streak cut into the granite of the slit and a bullet whined away and a crash sounded up from below. Pepé felt a sharp pain in his right hand. A sliver of granite was sticking out from between his first and second knuckles and the point protruded from his palm. Carefully he pulled out the sliver of stone. The wound bled evenly and gently. No vein nor artery was cut.

Pepé looked into a little dusty cave in the rock and gathered a handful of spider web, and he pressed the mass into the cut, plastering the soft web into the blood. The flow stopped almost at once.

The rifle was on the ground. Pepé picked it up, levered a new shell into the chamber. And then he slid into the brush on his stomach. Far to the right he crawled, and then up the hill, moving slowly and carefully, crawling to cover and resting and then crawling again.

In the mountains the sun is high in its arc before it penetrates the gorges. The hot face looked over the hill and brought instant heat with it. The white light beat on the rocks and reflected from them and rose up quivering from the earth again, and the rocks and bushes seemed to quiver behind the air.

Pepé crawled in the general direction of the ridge peak, zig-zagging for cover. The deep cut between his knuckles began to throb. He crawled close to a rattlesnake before he saw it, and when it raised its dry head and made a soft beginning whirr, he backed up and took another way. The quick grey lizards flashed in front of him, raising a tiny line of dust. He found another mass of spider web and pressed it against his throbbing hand.

Pepé was pushing the rifle with his left hand now. Little drops of sweat ran to the ends of his coarse black hair and rolled down his cheeks. His lips and tongue were growing thick and heavy. His lips writhed to draw saliva into his mouth. His little dark eyes were uneasy and suspicious. Once when a grey lizard paused in front of him on the parched ground and turned its head sideways he crushed it flat with a stone.

When the sun slid past noon he had not gone a mile. He crawled exhaustedly a last hundred yards to a patch of high sharp manzanita, crawled desperately, and when the patch was reached he wriggled in among the tough gnarly trunks and dropped his head on his left arm. There was little shade in the meager brush, but there was cover and safety. Pepé went to sleep as he lay and the sun beat on his back. A few little birds hopped close to him and peered and hopped away. Pepé squirmed in his sleep and he raised and dropped his wounded hand again and again.

The sun went down behind the peaks and the cool evening came, and then the dark. A coyote yelled from the hillside, Pepé started awake and looked about with misty eyes. His hand was swollen and heavy; a little thread of pain ran up the inside of his arm and settled in a pocket in his armpit. He peered about and then stood up, for the mountains were black and the moon had not yet risen. Pepé stood up in the dark. The coat of his father pressed on his arm. His tongue was swollen until it nearly filled his mouth. He wriggled out of the coat and dropped it in the brush, and then he struggled up the hill, falling over rocks and tearing his way through the brush. The rifle knocked against stones as he went. Little dry avalanches of gravel and shattered stone went whispering down the hill behind him.

After a while the old moon came up and showed the jagged ridge top ahead of him. By moonlight Pepé traveled more easily. He bent forward so that his throbbing arm hung away from his body. The journey uphill was made in dashes and rests, a frantic rush up a few yards and then a rest. The wind coasted down the slope rattling the dry stems of the bushes.

The moon was at meridian when Pepé came at last to the sharp backbone of the ridge top. On the last hundred yards of the rise no soil had clung under the wearing winds. The way was on solid rock. He clambered to the top and looked down on the other side. There was a draw like the last below him, misty with moonlight, brushed with dry struggling sage and chaparral. On the other side the hill rose up sharply and at the top the jagged rotten teeth of the mountain showed against the sky. At the bottom of the cut the brush was thick and dark.

Pepé stumbled down the hill. His throat was almost closed with thirst. At first he tried to run, but immediately he fell and rolled. After that he went more carefully. The moon was just disappearing behind the mountains when he came to the bottom. He crawled into the heavy brush feeling with his fingers for water. There was no water in the bed of the stream, only damp earth. Pepé laid his gun down and scooped up a handful of mud and put it in his mouth, and then he spluttered and scraped the earth from his tongue with his finger, for the mud drew at his mouth like a poultice. He dug a hole in the stream bed with his fingers, dug a little basin to catch water; but before it was very deep his head fell forward on the damp ground and he slept.

The dawn came and the heat of the day fell on the earth, and still Pepé slept. Late in the afternoon his head jerked up. He looked slowly around. His eyes were slits of wariness. Twenty feet away in the heavy brush a big tawny mountain lion stood looking at him. Its long thick tail waved gracefully, its ears were erect with interest, not laid back dangerously. The lion squatted down on its stomach and watched him.

Pepé looked at the hole he had dug in the earth. A half inch of muddy water had collected in the bottom. He tore the sleeve from his hurt arm, with his teeth ripped out a little square, soaked it in the water and put it in his mouth. Over and over he filled the cloth and sucked it.

Still the lion sat and watched him. The evening came down but there was no movement on the hills. No birds visited the dry bottom of the cut. Pepé looked occasionally at the lion. The eyes of the yellow beast drooped as though he were about to sleep. He yawned and his long thin red tongue curled out. Suddenly his head jerked around and his nostrils quivered. His big tail lashed. He stood up and slunk like a tawny shadow into the thick brush.

A moment later Pepé heard the sound, the faint far crash of horses' hooves on gravel. And he heard something else, a high whining yelp of a dog.

Pepé took his rifle in his left hand and he glided into the brush almost as quietly as the lion had. In the darkening evening he crouched up the hill toward the next ridge. Only when the dark came did he stand up. His energy was short. Once it was dark he fell over the rocks and slipped to his knees on the steep slope, but he moved on and on up the hill, climbing and scrabbling over the broken hillside.

When he was far up toward the top, he lay down and slept for a little while. The withered moon, shining on his face, awakened him. He stood up and moved up the hill. Fifty yards away he stopped and turned back, for he had forgotten his rifle. He walked heavily down and poked about in the brush, but he could not find his gun. At last he lay down to rest. The pocket of pain in his armpit had grown more sharp. His arm seemed to swell out and fall with every heartbeat. There was no position lying down where the heavy arm did not press against his armpit.

With the effort of a hurt beast, Pepé got up and moved again toward the top of the ridge. He held his swollen arm away from his body with his left hand. Up the steep hill he dragged himself, a few steps and a rest, and a few more steps. At last he was nearing the top. The moon showed the uneven sharp back of it against the sky.

Pepé's brain spun in a big spiral up and away from him. He slumped to the ground and lay still. The rock ridge top was only a hundred feet above him.

The moon moved over the sky. Pepé half turned on his back. His tongue tried to make words, but only a thick hissing came from between his lips.

When the dawn came, Pepé pulled himself up. His eyes were sane again. He drew his great puffed arm in front of him and looked at the angry wound. The black line ran up from his wrist to his armpit. Automatically he reached in his pocket for the big black knife, but it was not there. His eyes searched the ground. He picked up a sharp blade of stone and scraped at the wound, sawed at the proud flesh and then squeezed the green juice out in big drops. Instantly he threw back his head and whined like a dog. His whole right side shuddered at the pain, but the pain cleared his head.

In the grey light he struggled up the last slope to the ridge and crawled over and lay down behind a line of rocks. Below him lay a deep canyon exactly like the last, waterless and desolate. There was no flat, no oak trees, not even heavy brush in the bottom of it. And on the other side a sharp ridge stood up, thinly brushed with starving sage, littered with broken granite. Strewn over the hill there were giant outcroppings, and on the top the granite teeth stood out against the sky.

The new day was light now. The flame of the sun came over the ridge and fell on Pepé where he lay on the ground. His coarse black hair was littered with twigs and bits of spider web. His eyes had retreated back into his head. Between his lips the tip of his black tongue showed.

He sat up and dragged his great arm into his lap and nursed it, rocking his body and moaning in his throat. He threw back his head and looked up into the pale sky. A big black bird circled nearly out of sight, and far to the left another was sailing near.

He lifted his head to listen, for a familiar sound had come to him from the valley he had climbed out of; it was the crying yelp of hounds, excited and feverish, on a trail.

Pepé bowed his head quickly. He tried to speak rapid words but only a thick hiss came from his lips. He drew a shaky cross on his breast with his left hand. It was a long struggle to get to his feet. He crawled slowly and mechanically to the top of a big rock on the ridge peak. Once there, he arose slowly, swaying to his feet, and stood erect. Far below he could see the dark brush where he had slept. He braced his feet and stood there, black against the morning sky.

There came a ripping sound at his feet. A piece of stone flew up and a bullet droned off into the next gorge. The hollow crash echoed up from below. Pepé looked down for a moment and then pulled himself straight again.

His body jarred back. His left hand fluttered help-lessly toward his breast. The second crash sounded from below. Pepé swung forward and toppled from the rock. His body struck and rolled over and over, starting a little avalanche. And when at last he stopped against a bush, the avalanche slid slowly down and covered up his head.

Red

By W. SOMERSET MAUGHAM

THE SKIPPER thrust his hand into one of his trouser pockets and with difficulty, for they were not at the sides but in front and he was a portly man, pulled out a large silver watch. He looked at it and then looked again at the declining sun. The Kanaka at the wheel gave him a glance, but did not speak. The skipper's eyes rested on the island they were approaching. A white line of foam marked the reef. He knew there was an opening large enough to get his ship through, and when they came a little nearer he counted on seeing it. They had nearly an hour of daylight still before them. In the lagoon the water was deep and they could anchor comfortably. The chief of the village which he could already see among the coconut trees was a friend of the mate's, and it would be pleasant to go ashore for the night. The mate came forward at that minute and the skipper turned to him.

"We'll take a bottle of booze along with us and get some girls in to dance," he said.

"I don't see the opening," said the mate.

He was a Kanaka, a handsome, swarthy fellow, with somewhat the look of a later Roman emperor, inclined to stoutness; but his face was fine and clean-cut.

"I'm dead sure there's one right here," said the captain, looking through his glasses. "I can't understand why I can't pick it up. Send one of the boys up the mast to have a look."

The mate called one of the crew and gave him the order. The captain watched the Kanaka climb and waited for him to speak. But the Kanaka shouted down that he could see nothing but the unbroken line of foam. The captain spoke Samoan like a native, and he cursed him freely.

"Shall he stay up there?" asked the mate.

"What the hell good does that do?" answered the captain. "The blame fool can't see worth a cent. You bet your sweet life I'd find the opening if I was up there."

He looked at the slender mast with anger. It was all very well for a native who had been used to climbing up coconut trees all his life. He was fat and heavy.

"Come down," he shouted. "You're no more use than a dead dog. We'll just have to go along the reef till we find the opening."

It was a seventy-ton schooner with paraffin auxiliary, and it ran, when there was no head wind, between four and five knots an hour. It was a bedraggled object; it had been painted white a very long time ago, but it was now dirty, dingy, and mottled. It smelt strongly of paraffin and of the copra which was its usual cargo. They were within a hundred feet of the reef now and the captain told the steersman to run along it till they came to the opening. But when they had gone a couple of miles he realised that they had missed it. He went about and slowly worked back again. The white foam of the reef continued without interruption and now the sun was setting. With a curse at the stupidity of the crew the skipper resigned himself to waiting till next morning.

"Put her about," he said. "I can't anchor here."

They went out to sea a little and presently it was quite dark. They anchored. When the sail was furled the ship began to roll a good deal. They said in Apia that one day she would roll right over; and the owner, a German-American who managed one of the largest stores, said that no money was big enough to induce him to go out in her. The cook, a Chinese in white trousers, very dirty and ragged, and a thin white tunic, came to say that supper was ready, and when the skipper went into the cabin he found the engineer already seated at table. The engineer was a long, lean man with a scraggy neck. He was dressed in blue overalls and a sleeveless jersey which showed his thin arms tattooed from elbow to wrist.

"Hell, having to spend the night outside," said the skipper.

The engineer did not answer, and they ate their supper in silence. The cabin was lit by a dim oil lamp. When they had eaten the canned apricots with which the meal finished the Chink brought them a cup of tea. The skipper lit a cigar and went on the upper deck. The island now was only a darker mass against the night. The stars were very bright. The only sound was the ceaseless breaking of the surf. The skipper sank into a deck-chair and smoked idly. Presently three or four members of the crew came up and sat down. One of them had a banjo and another a concertina. They began to play, and one of them sang. The native song sounded strange on these instruments. Then to the singing a couple began to dance. It was a barbaric dance, savage and primeval, rapid, with quick movements of the hands and feet and contortions of the body; it was sensual, sexual even, but sexual without passion. It was very animal, direct, weird without mystery, natural in short, and one might almost say childlike. At last they grew tired. They stretched themselves on the deck and slept, and all was silent. The skipper lifted himself heavily out of his chair and clambered down the companion. He went into his cabin and got out of his clothes. He climbed into his bunk and lay there. He panted a little in the heat of the night.

But next morning, when the dawn crept over the tranquil sea, the opening in the reef which had eluded them the night before was seen a little to the east of where they lay. The schooner entered the lagoon. There was not a ripple on the surface of the water. Deep down among the coral rocks you saw little coloured fish swim. When he had anchored his ship the skipper ate his breakfast and went on deck. The sun shone from an unclouded sky, but in the early morning the air was grateful and cool. It was Sunday, and there was a feeling of quietness, a silence as though nature were at rest, which gave him a peculiar sense of comfort. He sat, looking at the wooded coast, and felt lazy and well at ease. Presently a slow smile moved his lips and he threw the stump of his cigar into the water.

"I guess I'll go ashore," he said. "Get the boat out."

He climbed stiffly down the ladder and was rowed to a little cove. The coconut trees came down to the water's edge, not in rows, but spaced out with an ordered formality. They were like a ballet of spinsters, elderly but flippant, standing in affected attitudes with the simpering graces of a bygone age. He sauntered idly through them, along a path that could be just seen winding its tortuous way, and it led him presently to a broad creek. There was a bridge across it, but a bridge constructed of single trunks of coconut trees, a dozen of them, placed end to end and supported where they met by a forked branch driven into the bed of the creek. You walked on a smooth, round surface, narrow and slippery, and there was no support for the hand. To cross such a bridge required sure feet and a stout heart. The skipper hesitated. But he saw on the other side, nestling among the trees, a white man's house; he made up his mind and, rather gingerly, began to walk. He watched his feet carefully, and where one trunk joined on to the next and there was a difference of level, he tottered a little. It was with a gasp of relief that he reached the last tree and finally set his feet on the firm ground of the other side. He had been so intent on the difficult crossing that he never noticed anyone was watching him, and it was with surprise that he heard himself spoken to.

"It takes a bit of nerve to cross these bridges when you're not used to them."

He looked up and saw a man standing in front of him. He had evidently come out of the house which he had seen.

"I saw you hesitate," the man continued, with a smile on his lips, "and I was watching to see you fall in."

"Not on your life," said the captain, who had now recovered his confidence.

"I've fallen in myself before now. I remember, one evening I came back from shooting, and I fell in, gun and all. Now I get a boy to carry my gun for me."

He was a man no longer young, with a small beard, now somewhat grey, and a thin face. He was dressed in a singlet, without arms, and a pair of duck trousers. He wore neither shoes nor socks. He spoke English with a slight accent.

"Are you Neilson?" asked the skipper.

"I am."

"I've heard about you. I thought you lived some-wheres round here."

The skipper followed his host into the little bungalow and sat down heavily in the chair which the other motioned him to take. While Neilson went out to fetch whisky and glasses he took a look round the room. It filled him with amazement. He had never seen so many books. The shelves reached from floor to ceiling on all four walls, and they were closely packed. There was a grand piano littered with music, and a large table on which books and magazines lay in disorder. The room made him feel embarrassed. He remembered that Neilson was a queer fellow. No one knew very much about him, although he had been in the islands for so many years, but those who knew him agreed that he was queer. He was a Swede.

"You've got one big heap of books here," he said, when Neilson returned.

"They do no harm," answered Neilson with a smile.

"Have you read them all?" asked the skipper.

"Most of them."

"I'm a bit of a reader myself. I have the *Saturday Evening Post* sent me regler."

Neilson poured his visitor a good stiff glass of whisky and gave him a cigar. The skipper volunteered a little information.

"I got in last night, but I couldn't find the opening, so I had to anchor outside. I never been this run before, but my people had some stuff they wanted to bring over here. Gray, d'you know him?"

"Yes, he's got a store a little way along."

"Well, there was a lot of canned stuff that he wanted over, an' he's got some copra. They thought I might just as well come over as lie idle at Apia. I run between Apia and Pago-Pago mostly, but they've got smallpox there just now, and there's nothing stirring."

He took a drink of his whisky and lit a cigar. He was

a taciturn man, but there was something in Neilson that made him nervous, and his nervousness made him talk. The Swede was looking at him with large dark eyes in which there was an expression of faint amusement.

"This is a tidy little place you've got here."

"I've done my best with it."

"You must do pretty well with your trees. They look fine. With copra at the price it is now. I had a bit of a plantation myself once, in Upolu it was, but I had to sell it."

He looked round the room again, where all those books gave him a feeling of something incomprehensible and hostile.

"I guess you must find it a bit lonesome here though," he said.

"I've got used to it. I've been here for twenty-five years."

Now the captain could think of nothing more to say, and he smoked in silence. Neilson had apparently no wish to break it. He looked at his guest with a meditative eye. He was a tall man, more than six feet high, and very stout. His face was red and blotchy, with a network of little purple veins on the cheeks, and his features were sunk into its fatness. His eyes were bloodshot. His neck was buried in rolls of fat. But for a fringe of long curly hair, nearly white, at the back of his head, he was quite bald; and that immense, shiny surface of forehead, which might have given him a false look of intelligence, on the contrary gave him one of peculiar imbecility. He wore a blue flannel shirt, open at the neck and showing his fat chest covered with a mat of reddish hair, and a very old pair of blue serge trousers. He sat in his chair in a heavy ungainly attitude, his great belly thrust forward and his fat legs uncrossed. All elasticity had gone from his limbs. Neilson wondered idly what sort of man he had been in his youth. It was almost impossible to imagine that this creature of vast bulk had ever been a boy who ran about. The skipper finished his whisky, and Neilson pushed the bottle towards him.

"Help yourself."

The skipper leaned forward and with his great hand seized it.

"And how come you in these parts anyways?" he said.

"Oh, I came out to the islands for my health. My lungs were bad and they said I hadn't a year to live. You see they were wrong."

"I meant, how come you to settle down right here?"

"I am a sentimentalist."

"Oh!"

Neilson knew that the skipper had not an idea what he meant, and he looked at him with an ironical twinkle in his dark eyes. Perhaps just because the skipper was so gross and dull a man the whim seized him to talk further.

"You were too busy keeping your balance to notice, when you crossed the bridge, but this spot is generally considered rather pretty."

"It's a cute little house you've got here."

"Ah, that wasn't here when I first came. There was a native hut, with its beehive roof and its pillars, over-shadowed by a great tree with red flowers; and the croton bushes, their leaves yellow and red and golden, made a pied fence around it. And then all about were the coco-nut trees, as fanciful as women, and as vain. They stood at the water's edge and spent all day looking at their re-flections. I was a young man then—Good Heavens, it's a quarter of a century ago—and I wanted to enjoy all the loveliness of the world in the short time allotted to me before I passed into the darkness. I thought it was the most beautiful spot I had ever seen. The first time I saw it I had a catch at my heart, and I was afraid I was go-ing to cry. I wasn't more than twenty-five, and though I put the best face I could on it, I didn't want to die. And somehow it seemed to me that the very beauty of this place made it easier for me to accept my fate. I felt when I came here that all my past life had fallen away, Stockholm and its University, and then Bonn: it all seemed the life of somebody else, as though now at last I had achieved the reality which our doctors of philosophy —I am one myself, you know—had discussed so much. 'A year,' I cried to myself. 'I have a year. I will spend it here and then I am content to die.'

"We are foolish and sentimental and melodramatic at twenty-five, but if we weren't perhaps we should be less wise at fifty.

"Now drink, my friend. Don't let the nonsense I talk interfere with you."

He waved his thin hand towards the bottle, and the skipper finished what remained in his glass.

"You ain't drinking nothin'," he said, reaching for the whisky.

"I am of a sober habit," smiled the Swede. "I intoxicate myself in ways which I fancy are more subtle. But perhaps that is only vanity. Anyhow, the effects are more lasting and the results less deleterious."

"They say there's a deal of cocaine taken in the States now," said the captain.

Neilson chuckled.

"But I do not see a white man often," he continued, "and for once I don't think a drop of whisky can do me any harm."

He poured himself out a little, added some soda, and took a sip.

"And presently I found out why the spot had such an unearthly loveliness. Here love had tarried for a moment like a migrant bird that happens on a ship in mid-ocean and for a little while folds its tired wings. The fragrance of a beautiful passion hovered over it like the fragrance of hawthorn in May in the meadows of my home. It seems to me that the places where men have loved or suffered keep about them always some faint aroma of something that has not wholly died. It is as though they had acquired a spiritual significance which mysteriously affects those who pass. I wish I could make myself clear." He smiled a little. "Though I cannot imagine that if I did you would understand."

He paused.

"I think this place was beautiful because here I had been loved beautifully." And now he shrugged his shoulders. "But perhaps it is only that my æsthetic sense is gratified by the happy conjunction of young love and a suitable setting."

Even a man less thick-witted than the skipper might have been forgiven if he were bewildered by Neilson's words. For he seemed faintly to laugh at what he said. It was as though he spoke from emotion which his intellect found ridiculous. He had said himself that he was a sentimentalist, and when sentimentality is joined with scepticism there is often the devil to pay.

He was silent for an instant and looked at the captain with eyes in which there was a sudden perplexity.

"You know, I can't help thinking that I've seen you before somewhere or other," he said.

"I couldn't say as I remember you," returned the skipper.

"I have a curious feeling as though your face were familiar to me. It's been puzzling me for some time. But I can't situate my recollection in any place or at any time."

The skipper massively shrugged his heavy shoulders.

"It's thirty years since I first come to the islands. A man can't figure on remembering all the folk he meets in a while like that."

The Swede shook his head.

"You know how one sometimes has the feeling that a place one has never been to before is strangely familiar. That's how I seem to see you." He gave a whimsical smile. "Perhaps I knew you in some past existence. Perhaps, perhaps you were the master of a galley in ancient

Rome and I was a slave at the oar. Thirty years have
you been here?"

"Every bit of thirty years."

"I wonder if you knew a man called Red?"

"Red?"

"That is the only name I've ever known him by. I
never knew him personally. I never even set eyes on him.
And yet I seem to see him more clearly than many men,
my brothers, for instance, with whom I passed my daily
life for many years. He lives in my imagination with the
distinctness of a Paolo Malatesta or a Romeo. But I
daresay you have never read Dante or Shakespeare?"

"I can't say as I have," said the captain.

Neilson, smoking a cigar, leaned back in his chair and
looked vacantly at the ring of smoke which floated in the
still air. A smile played on his lips, but his eyes were
grave. Then he looked at the captain. There was in his
gross obesity something extraordinarily repellent. He had
the plethoric self-satisfaction of the very fat. It was an
outrage. It set Neilson's nerves on edge. But the contrast
between the man before him and the man he had in
mind was pleasant.

"It appears that Red was the most comely thing you
ever saw. I've talked to quite a number of people who
knew him in those days, white men, and they all agree
that the first time you saw him his beauty just took your
breath away. They called him Red on account of his
flaming hair. It had a natural wave and he wore it long.
It must have been of that wonderful colour that the pre-
Raphaelites raved over. I don't think he was vain of it,
he was much too ingenuous for that, but no one could
have blamed him if he had been. He was tall, six feet and
an inch or two—in the native house that used to stand
here was the mark of his height cut with a knife on the
central trunk that supported the roof—and he was made
like a Greek god, broad in the shoulders and thin in the
flanks; he was like Apollo, with just that soft roundness
which Praxiteles gave him, and that suave, feminine

grace which has in it something troubling and mysterious. His skin was dazzling white, milky, like satin; his skin was like a woman's."

"I had kind of a white skin myself when I was a kiddie," said the skipper, with a twinkle in his bloodshot eyes.

But Neilson paid no attention to him. He was telling his story now and interruption made him impatient.

"And his face was just as beautiful as his body. He had large blue eyes, very dark, so that some say they were black, and unlike most red-haired people he had dark eyebrows and long dark lashes. His features were perfectly regular and his mouth was like a scarlet wound. He was twenty."

On these words the Swede stopped with a certain sense of the dramatic. He took a sip of whisky.

"He was unique. There never was anyone more beautiful. There was no more reason for him than for a wonderful blossom to flower on a wild plant. He was a happy accident of nature.

"One day he landed at that cove into which you must have put this morning. He was an American sailor, and he had deserted from a man-of-war in Apia. He had induced some good-humoured native to give him a passage on a cutter that happened to be sailing from Apia to Safoto, and he had been put ashore here in a dugout. I do not know why he deserted. Perhaps life on a man-of-war with its restrictions irked him, perhaps he was in trouble, and perhaps it was the South Seas and these romantic islands that got into his bones. Every now and then they take a man strangely, and he finds himself like a fly in a spider's web. It may be that there was a softness of fibre in him, and these green hills with their soft airs, this blue sea, took the northern strength from him as Delilah took the Nazarite's. Anyhow, he wanted to hide himself, and he thought he would be safe in this secluded nook till his ship had sailed from Samoa.

"There was a native hut at the cove and as he stood

there, wondering where exactly he should turn his steps, a young girl came out and invited him to enter. He knew scarcely two words of the native tongue and she as little English. But he understood well enough what her smiles meant, and her pretty gestures, and he followed her. He sat down on a mat and she gave him slices of pineapple to eat. I can speak of Red only from hearsay, but I saw the girl three years after he first met her, and she was scarcely nineteen then. You cannot imagine how exquisite she was. She had the passionate grace of the hibiscus and the rich colour. She was rather tall, slim, with the delicate features of her race, and large eyes like pools of still water under the palm trees; her hair, black and curling, fell down her back, and she wore a wreath of scented flowers. Her hands were lovely. They were so small, so exquisitely formed, they gave your heart-strings a wrench. And in those days she laughed easily. Her smile was so delightful that it made your knees shake. Her skin was like a field of ripe corn on a summer day. Good Heavens, how can I describe her? She was too beautiful to be real.

"And these two young things, she was sixteen and he was twenty, fell in love with one another at first sight. That is the real love, not the love that comes from sympathy, common interests, or intellectual community, but love pure and simple. That is the love that Adam felt for Eve when he awoke and found her in the garden gazing at him with dewy eyes. That is the love that draws the beasts to one another, and the Gods. That is the love that makes the world a miracle. That is the love which gives life its pregnant meaning. You have never heard of the wise, cynical French duke who said that with two lovers there is always one who loves and one who lets himself be loved; it is a bitter truth to which most of us have to resign ourselves; but now and then there are two who love and two who let themselves be loved. Then one might fancy that the sun stands still as it stood when Joshua prayed to the God of Israel.

"And even now after all these years, when I think of these two, so young, so fair, so simple, and of their love, I feel a pang. It tears my heart just as my heart is torn when on certain nights I watch the full moon shining on the lagoon from an unclouded sky. There is always pain in the contemplation of perfect beauty.

"They were children. She was good and sweet and kind. I know nothing of him, and I like to think that then at all events he was ingenuous and frank. I like to think that his soul was as comely as his body. But I daresay he had no more soul than the creatures of the woods and forests who made pipes from reeds and bathed in the mountain streams when the world was young, and you might catch sight of little fawns galloping through the glade on the back of a bearded centaur. A soul is a troublesome possession and when man developed it he lost the Garden of Eden.

"Well, when Red came to the island it had recently been visited by one of those epidemics which the white man has brought to the South Seas, and one third of the inhabitants had died. It seems that the girl had lost all her near kin and she lived now in the house of distant cousins. The household consisted of two ancient crones, bowed and wrinkled, two younger women, and a man and a boy. For a few days he stayed there. But perhaps he felt himself too near the shore, with the possibility that he might fall in with white men who would reveal his hiding-place; perhaps the lovers could not bear that the company of others should rob them for an instant of the delight of being together. One morning they set out, the pair of them, with the few things that belonged to the girl, and walked along a grassy path under the coconuts, till they came to the creek you see. They had to cross the bridge you crossed, and the girl laughed gleefully because he was afraid. She held his hand till they came to the end of the first tree, and then his courage failed him and he had to go back. He was obliged to take off all his clothes before he could risk it, and she carried

them over for him on her head. They settled down in the
empty hut that stood here. Whether she had any rights
over it (land tenure is a complicated business in the islands), or whether the owner had died during the epi-
demic, I do not know, but anyhow no one questioned
them, and they took possession. Their furniture consisted
of a couple of grass-mats on which they slept, a fragment
of looking-glass, and a bowl or two. In this pleasant land
that is enough to start housekeeping on.

"They say that happy people have no history, and certainly a happy love has none. They did nothing all day
long and yet the days seemed all too short. The girl had
a native name, but Red called her Sally. He picked up
the easy language very quickly, and he used to lie on the
mat for hours while she chattered gaily to him. He was
a silent fellow, and perhaps his mind was lethargic. He
smoked incessantly the cigarettes which she made him
out of the native tobacco and pandanus leaf, and he
watched her while with deft fingers she made grass mats.
Often natives would come in and tell long stories of the
old days when the island was disturbed by tribal wars.
Sometimes he would go fishing on the reef, and bring
home a basket full of coloured fish. Sometimes at night
he would go out with a lantern to catch lobster. There
were plantains round the hut and Sally would roast them
for their frugal meal. She knew how to make delicious
messes from coconuts, and the breadfruit tree by the side
of the creek gave them its fruit. On feast-days they
killed a little pig and cooked it on hot stones. They
bathed together in the creek; and in the evening they
went down to the lagoon and paddled about in a dugout,
with its great outrigger. The sea was deep blue, wine-
coloured at sundown, like the sea of Homeric Greece;
but in the lagoon the colour had an infinite variety, aq-
uamarine and amethyst and emerald; and the setting sun
turned it for a short moment to liquid gold. Then there
was the colour of the coral, brown, white, pink, red, purple; and the shapes it took were marvellous. It was like

a magic garden, and the hurrying fish were like butterflies. It strangely lacked reality. Among the coral were pools with a floor of white sand and here, where the water was dazzling clear, it was very good to bathe. Then, cool and happy, they wandered back in the gloaming over the soft grass road to the creek, walking hand in hand, and now the mynah birds filled the coconut trees with their clamour. And then the night, with that great sky shining with gold, that seemed to stretch more widely than the skies of Europe, and the soft airs that blew gently through the open hut, the long night again was all too short. She was sixteen and he was barely twenty. The dawn crept in among the wooden pillars of the hut and looked at those lovely children sleeping in one another's arms. The sun hid behind the great tattered leaves of the plantains so that it might not disturb them, and then, with playful malice, shot a golden ray, like the outstretched paw of a Persian cat, on their faces. They opened their sleepy eyes and they smiled to welcome another day. The weeks lengthened into months, and a year passed. They seemed to love one another as—I hesitate to say passionately, for passion has in it always a shade of sadness, a touch of bitterness or anguish, but as whole heartedly, as simply and naturally as on that first day on which, meeting, they had recognised that a god was in them.

"If you had asked them I have no doubt that they would have thought it impossible to suppose their love could ever cease. Do we not know that the essential element of love is a belief in its own eternity? And yet perhaps in Red there was already a very little seed, unknown to himself and unsuspected by the girl, which would in time have grown to weariness. For one day one of the natives from the cove told them that some way down the coast at the anchorage was a British whaling-ship.

" 'Gee,' he said, 'I wonder if I could make a trade of some nuts and plantains for a pound or two of tobacco.'

"The pandanus cigarettes that Sally made him with untiring hands were strong and pleasant enough to smoke, but they left him unsatisfied; and he yearned on a sudden for real tobacco, hard, rank, and pungent. He had not smoked a pipe for many months. His mouth watered at the thought of it. One would have thought some premonition of harm would have made Sally seek to dissuade him, but love possessed her so completely that it never occurred to her any power on earth could take him from her. They went up into the hills together and gathered a great basket of wild oranges, green, but sweet and juicy; and they picked plantains from around the hut, and coconuts from their trees, and breadfruit and mangoes; and they carried them down to the cove. They loaded the unstable canoe with them, and Red and the native boy who had brought them the news of the ship paddled along outside the reef.

"It was the last time she ever saw him.

"Next day the boy came back alone. He was all in tears. This is the story he told. When after their long paddle they reached the ship and Red hailed it, a white man looked over the side and told them to come on board. They took the fruit they had brought with them and Red piled it up on the deck. The white man and he began to talk, and they seemed to come to some agreement. One of them went below and brought up tobacco. Red took some at once and lit a pipe. The boy imitated the zest with which he blew a great cloud of smoke from his mouth. Then they said something to him and he went into the cabin. Through the open door the boy, watching curiously, saw a bottle brought out and glasses. Red drank and smoked. They seemed to ask him something, for he shook his head and laughed. The man, the first man who had spoken to them, laughed too, and he filled Red's glass once more. They went on talking and drinking, and presently, growing tired of watching a sight that meant nothing to him, the boy curled himself up on the deck and slept. He was awakened by a kick; and, jumping to his feet, he saw that the ship was slowly sailing out of the lagoon. He caught sight of Red seated at the table, with his head resting heavily on his arms, fast asleep. He made a movement towards him, intending to wake him, but a rough hand seized his arm, and a man, with a scowl and words which he did not understand, pointed to the side. He shouted to Red, but in a moment he was seized and flung overboard. Helpless, he swam round to his canoe which was drifting a little way off, and pushed it on to the reef. He climbed in and, sobbing all the way, paddled back to shore.

"What had happened was obvious enough. The whaler, by desertion or sickness, was short of hands, and the captain when Red came aboard had asked him to sign on; on his refusal he had made him drunk and kidnapped him.

"Sally was beside herself with grief. For three days she screamed and cried. The natives did what they could to comfort her, but she would not be comforted. She would not eat. And then, exhausted, she sank into a sullen apathy. She spent long days at the cove, watching the lagoon, in the vain hope that Red somehow or other would manage to escape. She sat on the white sand, hour after hour, with the tears running down her cheeks, and at night dragged herself wearily back across the creek to the little hut where she had been happy. The people with whom she had lived before Red came to the island wished her to return to them, but she would not; she was convinced that Red would come back, and she wanted him to find her where he had left her. Four months later she was delivered of a still-born child, and the old woman who had come to help her through her confinement remained with her in the hut. All joy was taken from her life. If her anguish with time became less intolerable it was replaced by a settled melancholy. You would not have thought that among these people, whose emotions, though so violent, are very transient, a woman could be found capable of so enduring a passion. She never lost the profound conviction that sooner or later Red would come back. She watched for him, and every time someone crossed this slender little bridge of coconut trees she looked. It might at last be he."

Neilson stopped talking and gave a faint sigh.

"And what happened to her in the end?" asked the skipper.

Neilson smiled bitterly.

"Oh, three years afterwards she took up with another white man."

The skipper gave a fat, cynical chuckle.

"That's generally what happens to them," he said.

The Swede shot him a look of hatred. He did not know why that gross, obese man excited in him so violent a repulsion. But his thoughts wandered and he found his mind filled with memories of the past. He went back five and twenty years. It was when he first came to the island, weary of Apia, with its heavy drinking, its gambling and coarse sensuality, a sick man, trying to resign himself to the loss of the career which had fired his imagination with ambitious thoughts. He set behind him resolutely all his hopes of making a great name for himself and strove to content himself with the few poor months of careful life which was all that he could count on. He was boarding with a half-caste trader who had a store a couple of miles along the coast at the edge of a native village; and one day, wandering aimlessly along the grassy paths of the coconut groves, he had come upon the hut in which Sally lived. The beauty of the spot had filled him with a rapture so great that it was almost painful, and then he had seen Sally. She was the loveliest creature he had ever seen, and the sadness in those dark, magnificent eyes of hers affected him strangely. The Kanakas were a handsome race, and beauty was not rare among them, but it was the beauty of shapely animals. It was empty. But those tragic eyes were dark with mystery, and you felt in them the bitter complexity of the groping, human soul. The trader told him the story and it moved him.

"Do you think he'll ever come back?" asked Neilson.

"No fear. Why, it'll be a couple of years before the ship is paid off, and by then he'll have forgotten all about her. I bet he was pretty mad when he woke up and found he'd been shanghaied, and I shouldn't wonder but he wanted to fight somebody. But he'd got to grin and bear it, and I guess in a month he was thinking it the best thing that had ever happened to him that he got away from the island."

But Neilson could not get the story out of his head. Perhaps because he was sick and weakly, the radiant health of Red appealed to his imagination. Himself an ugly man, insignificant of appearance, he prized very highly comeliness in others. He had never been passionately in love, and certainly he had never been passionately loved. The mutual attraction of those two young things gave him a singular delight. It had the ineffable beauty of the Absolute. He went again to the little hut by the creek. He had a gift for languages and an energetic mind, accustomed to work, and he had already given much time to the study of the local tongue. Old habit was strong in him and he was gathering together material for a paper on the Samoan speech. The old crone who shared the hut with Sally invited him to come in and sit down. She gave him *kava* to drink and cigarettes to smoke. She was glad to have someone to chat with and while she talked he looked at Sally. She reminded him of the Psyche in the museum at Naples. Her features had the same clear purity of line, and though she had borne a child she had still a virginal aspect.

It was not till he had seen her two or three times that he induced her to speak. Then it was only to ask him if he had seen in Apia a man called Red. Two years had passed since his disappearance, but it was plain that she still thought of him incessantly.

It did not take Neilson long to discover that he was in love with her. It was only by an effort of will now that he prevented himself from going every day to the creek, and when he was not with Sally his thoughts were. At first, looking upon himself as a dying man, he asked only to look at her, and occasionally hear her speak, and his love gave him a wonderful happiness. He exulted in its purity. He wanted nothing from her but the opportunity to weave around her graceful person a web of beautiful fancies. But the open air, the equable temperature, the rest, the simple fare, began to have an unexpected effect on his health. His temperature did not soar at night to such alarming heights, he coughed less and began to put on weight; six months passed without his having a hæmorrhage; and on a sudden he saw the possibility that he might live. He had studied his disease carefully, and the hope dawned upon him that with great care he might arrest its course. It exhilarated him to look forward once more to the future. He made plans. It was evident that any active life was out of the question, but he could live on the islands, and the small income he had, insufficient elsewhere, would be ample to keep him. He could grow coconuts; that would give him an occupation; and he would send for his books and a piano; but his quick mind saw that in all this he was merely trying to conceal from himself the desire which obsessed him.

He wanted Sally. He loved not only her beauty, but that dim soul which he divined behind her suffering eyes. He would intoxicate her with his passion. In the end he would make her forget. And in an ecstasy of surrender he fancied himself giving her too the happiness which he had thought never to know again, but had now so miraculously achieved.

He asked her to live with him. She refused. He had expected that and did not let it depress him, for he was sure that sooner or later she would yield. His love was irresistible. He told the old woman of his wishes, and found somewhat to his surprise that she and the neigh-

bours, long aware of them, were strongly urging Sally to
accept his offer. After all, every native was glad to keep
house for a white man, and Neilson according to the
standards of the island was a rich one. The trader with
whom he boarded went to her and told her not to be a
fool; such an opportunity would not come again, and
after so long she could not still believe that Red would
ever return. The girl's resistance only increased Neilson's
desire, and what had been a very pure love now became
an agonising passion. He was determined that nothing
should stand in his way. He gave Sally no peace. At last,
worn out by his persistence and the persuasions, by turns
pleading and angry, of everyone around her, she con-
sented. But the day after when, exultant, he went to see
her he found that in the night she had burnt down the
hut in which she and Red had lived together. The old
crone ran towards him full of angry abuse of Sally, but
he waved her aside; it did not matter; they would build
a bungalow on the place where the hut had stood. A Eu-
ropean house would really be more convenient if he
wanted to bring out a piano and a vast number of books.

And so the little wooden house was built in which he
had now lived for many years, and Sally became his
wife. But after the first few weeks of rapture, during
which he was satisfied with what she gave him he had
known little happiness. She had yielded to him, through
weariness, but she had only yielded what she set no store
on. The soul which he had dimly glimpsed escaped him.
He knew that she cared nothing for him. She still loved
Red, and all the time she was waiting for his return. At a
sign from him, Neilson knew that, notwithstanding his
love, his tenderness, his sympathy, his generosity, she
would leave him without a moment's hesitation. She
would never give a thought to his distress. Anguish seized
him and he battered at that impenetrable self of hers
which sullenly resisted him. His love became bitter. He
tried to melt her heart with kindness, but it remained as
hard as before; he feigned indifference, but she did not

notice it. Sometimes he lost his temper and abused her, and then she wept silently. Sometimes he thought she was nothing but a fraud, and that soul simply an invention of his own, and that he could not get into the sanctuary of her heart because there was no sanctuary there. His love became a prison from which he longed to escape, but he had not the strength merely to open the door—that was all it needed—and walk out into the open air. It was torture and at last he became numb and hopeless. In the end the fire burnt itself out and, when he saw her eyes rest for an instant on the slender bridge, it was no longer rage that filled his heart but impatience. For many years now they had lived together bound by the ties of habit and convenience, and it was with a smile that he looked back on his old passion. She was an old woman, for the women on the islands age quickly, and if he had no love for her any more he had tolerance. She left him alone. He was contented with his piano and his books.

His thoughts led him to a desire for words.

"When I look back now and reflect on that brief passionate love of Red and Sally, I think that perhaps they should thank the ruthless fate that separated them when their love seemed still to be at its height. They suffered, but they suffered in beauty. They were spared the real tragedy of love."

"I don't know exactly as I get you," said the skipper.

"The tragedy of love is not death or separation. How long do you think it would have been before one or other of them ceased to care? Oh, it is dreadfully bitter to look at a woman whom you have loved with all your heart and soul, so that you felt you could not bear to let her out of your sight, and realise that you would not mind if you never saw her again. The tragedy of love is indifference."

But while he was speaking a very extraordinary thing happened. Though he had been addressing the skipper he had not been talking to him, he had been putting his

thoughts into words for himself, and with his eyes fixed
on the man in front of him he had not seen him. But now
an image presented itself to them, an image not of the
man he saw, but of another man. It was as though he
were looking into one of those distorting mirrors that
make you extraordinarily squat or outrageously elongate,
but here exactly the opposite took place, and in the
obese, ugly old man he caught the shadowy glimpse of a
stripling. He gave him now a quick, searching scrutiny.
Why had a haphazard stroll brought him just to this
place? A sudden tremor of his heart made him slightly
breathless. An absurd suspicion seized him. What had
occurred to him was impossible, and yet it might be a
fact.

"What is your name?" he asked abruptly.

The skipper's face puckered and he gave a cunning
chuckle. He looked then malicious and horribly vulgar.

"It's such a damned long time since I heard it that I
almost forget it myself. But for thirty years now in the
islands they've always called me Red."

His huge form shook as he gave a low, almost silent
laugh. It was obscene. Neilson shuddered. Red was
hugely amused, and from his bloodshot eyes tears ran
down his cheeks.

Neilson gave a gasp, for at that moment a woman
came in. She was a native, a woman of somewhat commanding presence, stout without being corpulent, dark,
for the natives grow darker with age, with very grey
hair. She wore a black Mother Hubbard, and its thinness
showed her heavy breasts. The moment had come.

She made an observation to Neilson about some household matter and he answered. He wondered if his voice
sounded as unnatural to her as it did to himself. She
gave the man who was sitting in the chair by the window
an indifferent glance, and went out of the room. The moment had come and gone.

Neilson for a moment could not speak. He was
strangely shaken. Then he said:

"I'd be very glad if you'd stay and have a bit of dinner with me. Pot luck."

"I don't think I will," said Red. "I must go after this fellow Gray. I'll give him his stuff and then I'll get away. I want to be back in Apia tomorrow."

"I'll send a boy along with you to show you the way."

"That'll be fine."

Red heaved himself out of his chair, while the Swede called one of the boys who worked on the plantation. He told him where the skipper wanted to go, and the boy stepped along the bridge. Red prepared to follow him.

"Don't fall in," said Neilson.

"Not on your life."

Neilson watched him make his way across and when he had disappeared among the coconuts he looked still. Then he sank heavily in his chair. Was that the man who had prevented him from being happy? Was that the man whom Sally had loved all these years and for whom she had waited so desperately? It was grotesque. A sudden fury seized him so that he had an instinct to spring up and smash everything around him. He had been cheated. They had seen each other at last and had not known it. He began to laugh, mirthlessly, and his laughter grew till it became hysterical. The Gods had played him a cruel trick. And he was old now.

At last Sally came in to tell him dinner was ready. He sat down in front of her and tried to eat. He wondered what she would say if he told her now that the fat old man sitting in the chair was the lover whom she remembered still with the passionate abandonment of her youth. Years ago, when he hated her because she made him so unhappy, he would have been glad to tell her. He wanted to hurt her then as she hurt him, because his hatred was only love. But now he did not care. He shrugged his shoulders listlessly.

"What did that man want?" she asked presently.

He did not answer at once. She was old too, a fat old native woman. He wondered why he had ever loved her so madly. He had laid at her feet all the treasures of his soul, and she had cared nothing for them. Waste, what waste! And now, when he looked at her, he felt only contempt. His patience was at last exhausted. He answered her question.

"He's the captain of a schooner. He's come from Apia."

"Yes."

"He brought me news from home. My eldest brother is very ill and I must go back."

"Will you be gone long?"

He shrugged his shoulders.

Gun Crazy

By MACKINLAY KANTOR

I FIRST met Nelson Tare when he was around five or six years old, and I was around the same. I had watched his family moving into the creek house on a cold, snowless morning in early winter.

Two lumber wagons went by, with iron beds and old kitchen chairs and mattresses tied all over them. They rumbled down the hill past Mr. Boston's barn and stopped in front of the creek house. I could see men and girls working, carrying the stuff inside.

In midafternoon I was outdoors again, and I coasted to the corner in my little wagon to see whether the moving-in activities were still going on.

Then Nelson Tare appeared. He had climbed the hill by himself; probably he was looking for guns, although I couldn't know that at the time. He was a gaunt little child with bright blue beads for eyes, and a sharp-pointed nose.

He said, "Hello, kid. Want to pway?"

Nelson was only about a month younger than I, it turned out, but he still talked a lot of baby talk. I think kids are apt to do that more when their parents don't talk to them much.

I told him that I did want to play, and asked him what he wanted to do.

He asked, "Have you got any guns?" What he actually said was, "Dot any duns?" and for a while I didn't know what he was talking about. Then, when I understood, I coasted back to the house in my wagon, with Nelson walking beside me. We went into the living room.

I had three guns: a popgun with the pop gone, and a glass pistol that used to have candy inside—but now the candy was all eaten up—and a cap gun and holster.

The cap gun was the best. It was nickel-plated, and the holster was made of black patent leather. It was the shape and possibly half the size of an ordinary .32-caliber revolver.

Nelson Tare's eyes pushed out a little when he saw it. He made a grab, and belted it on before I had time to protest and tell him that I wanted to play with the cap gun and he could play with the glass pistol or the broken pop rifle. He went swaggering around with the gun on, and it kind of scared me the way he did it—all of a sudden he'd snatch the revolver out of its holster and aim it at me.

I took the glass pistol and tried to imitate him. But the glass pistol couldn't click, and at least the hammer of the cap gun would come down with a resounding click. Nelson, or Nelly, as I came to know him, fairly shot the daylights out of me. I began to protest, and he kept on advancing and kind of wrangling and threatening me, until he had me backed up in a corner.

He hadn't taken off his little red coat with its yellow horn buttons, and he was perspiring inside it. I still recollect how he smelled when he got close enough to wool me around; I had never smelled a smell like that before. I remember his face, too, when he came close—the tiny, expressionless turquois eyes, the receding chin and baby mouth still marked with the tag ends of his dinner; and in between them, that inhuman nose whittled out to a point.

I tried to push him away as he kept battling me and shooting me, and I guess I began to cry.

Nelson said that it wasn't a real gun.

"It might go off!"

He said that it couldn't go off; that it wasn't "weal."

"'Course it isn't real!" I cried. "I guess there isn't any boy in the world got a real gun!"

Well, he said that he had one, and when I was still disbelieving he said that he would go home and fetch it. His coat had come unbuttoned in our scufflings, and I remember how he looked as I watched through the window and saw him flapping down the last length of concrete sidewalk past the big maple tree.

My mother came from upstairs while I waited at the window. She said that she had heard voices. "Did you have company?" she asked.

"It was a new boy."

"What new boy?"

"He moved into the creek house down there."

My mother said doubtfully, "Oh, yes. I heard there was a ditcher's family moving in down there."

Well, I wanted to know what a ditcher was, and while mother was explaining to me about drainage ditches out on the prairie and how the tile was laid in them, here came Nelly hustling up the road as fast as he could leg it. He had something big and heavy that he had to carry in both hands. When he got into the yard we could see that he did have a revolver, and it looked like a real one.

Mother exclaimed, and went to open the door for him. He ducked inside, bareheaded and cold, with his dirty, thin, straw-colored hair sticking every which way, and the old red coat still dangling loose.

"I dot my dun," he said.

At the air-rifle stage of our development, Nelly could shoot rings around any of us. He and I used to go up in our barn and lie on the moldy, abandoned hay of the old mow. There were rats that sometimes came into the chicken run next door, to eat the chickens' food. I never did shoot a rat with my BB gun, and for some reason Nelly never did either. That was funny, because he was such a good shot. We used to amuse ourselves, while waiting for rats, by trying to peck away at the chickens' water pan. It was a good healthy distance, and I'd usually miss. But the side of the pan which faced our way had the enamel all spotted off by Nelly's accurate fire.

He owned an air-pump gun of his own, but not for long. He traded it to somebody for an old .22, and after that there was little peace in the neighborhood. He was always shooting at tin cans or bottles on the roadside dump. He was always hitting too.

In the winter of 1914, Nelly and I went hunting with Clyde Boston. Clyde was a huge, ruddy-faced young man at least ten years older than Nelly and I. He lived with his parents across from our corner.

One day there was deep snow, and Nelly and I were out exploring. He had his .22, and every now and then he'd bang away at a knot on a fence post. At last we wandered into Bostons' barnyard, and found Clyde in the barn, filling his pockets with shotgun shells.

He had a shotgun too—a fine repeater, gleaming blue steel—and Nelly wanted to know what Clyde was doing. "Going hunting?"

"Come on, Clyde," I said, "let us go! Nelly's got his gun."

Clyde took the little rifle and examined it critically. "This won't do for hunting around here," he said. "I'm going out after rabbits, and you got to have a shotgun for that. Rifle bullets are apt to carry too far and hit somebody, or maybe hit a pig or something. Anyway, you couldn't hit a cottontail on the run with that."

"Hell I couldn't," said Nelly.

I said, "Clyde, you let us go with you and we'll beat up the game. We'll scare the rabbits out of the weeds, because you haven't got any dog. Then you can shoot them when they run out. Maybe you'll let us have one shot each, huh, Clyde—maybe?"

Clyde said that he would see, and he made Nelly leave his rifle at the barn. We went quartering off through the truck garden on the hillside.

The snow had fallen freshly, but already there was a mass of rabbit tracks everywhere. You could see where the cottontails had run into the thickest, weediest coverts to feed upon dry seeds.

Clyde walked in the middle, with his face apple-colored with the cold and his breath blowing out. Nelly and I spread wide, to scare up the game. We used sticks and snowballs to alarm the thickets, and we worked hard at it. The big twelve-gauge gun began to bang every once in a while. Clyde had three cottontails hanging furry from his belt before we got to the bend in the creek opposite the Catholic cemetery. Then finally he passed the gun over to me and told me I could have the next chance.

It came pretty soon. We saw a cottontail in his set—a gray little mound among the vervain stalks. I lifted the muzzle, but Clyde said that it wasn't fair to shoot rabbits in the set, and made Nelly throw a snowball. The cottontail romped out of there in a hurry, and I whaled away with the shotgun and managed to wound the rabbit and slow him down. I fired again and missed, and Clyde caught up with the rabbit after a few strides. He put the poor peeping thing out of its misery by rapping it on the head.

I tied the rabbit to the belt of my mackinaw, and Clyde passed the shotgun over to Nelly.

Nelly's face was pale.

"Watch your step," said Clyde. "Remember to keep the safety on until you see something to shoot."

"Sure," said Nelly Tare.

We crossed the creek without starting any more rabbits, and came down the opposite side of the stream. Then a long-legged jack jumped up out of a deep furrow where there had been some fall plowing, and ran like a mule ahead of us.

"Look at those black ears!" Clyde sang out. "It's a jack! Get him, Nelly—get him!"

Well, Nelson had the gun at his shoulder; at first I thought he had neglected to touch the safety—I thought he couldn't pull the trigger because the safety was on. He kept swinging the muzzle of the gun, following the jack rabbit in its erratic course, until the rabbit slowed up a little.

The jack bobbed around behind a tree stump, and then came out on the other side. It squatted down on top of the snow and sat looking at us. It hopped a few feet farther and then sat up again to watch.

"For gosh sakes," said Clyde Boston, "what's the matter with you, kid? There he is, looking at you."

Nelson Tare just stood like a snow man, or rather like a snow boy. He kept the rabbit covered; his dirty blue finger didn't move. The trigger waited, the shell in the barrel waited, and so did we.

Nelly's face was deathly white under the dirt that streaked it. The eyes were blank little marbles, as always; even his nose seemed pointed like the sights of a gun. And yet he did not shoot.

Clyde said, half under his breath, "I guess that's what they call buck fever. You got the buck, Nelly." He hurried over to take the shotgun.

Blood from the last-killed rabbit made little dots on the snow around my feet, though the animal was freezing fast.

"Can't you see him, Nelly?"

Nelson said, "Yes. I——"

Clyde lost all patience. "Oh, for gosh sake!" he exclaimed, and grabbed the gun. But our combined motions startled the jack rabbit, and he vanished into the creek gorge beyond.

Something had happened there in the snow; none of us knew exactly what had happened. But whatever it was, it took the edge off our sport. We tramped along a cattle path next to the stream, with Clyde carrying the shotgun. We boys didn't scare up any more game. Nelly kept looking at the rabbits which bounced and rubbed their frozen red against Clyde Boston's overalls.

Clyde teased him, all the way back to the Boston barnyard. He'd say, "Nelly, I thought you were supposed to be the Daniel Boone of the neighborhood. Gosh, Nelly, I thought you could shoot. I thought you were just gun crazy!"

We walked through the fresh warm mire behind the Boston barn. Clyde said that he didn't need three rabbits; that his mother could use only two, and would Nelly want the other one?

"No," said Nelson. We went into the barn, and Nelly picked up his .22 rifle.

"Look out while you're on the way home," said Clyde, red-faced and jovial as ever. "Look out you don't meet a bear. Maybe he wouldn't set around and wait like that jack rabbit did."

Nelson Tare sucked in his breath. "You said I couldn't shoot, didn't you, Mister Clyde?"

"You had your chance. Look at Dave there. He's got a rabbit to take home that he shot himself, even though he didn't kill it first crack."

"I can shoot," said Nelly. He worked a cartridge into the breech of his rifle. "Dave," he said to me, "you throw up a snowball."

"Can't anybody hit a snowball with a twenty-two," said big Clyde Boston.

Nelly said, "Throw a snowball, Dave."

I stepped down from the sill of the barn door and made a ball about the size of a Duchess apple. I threw it high toward the telephone wires across the road. Nelly Tare pinked it apart with his .22 before the ball ever got to the wires. Then he went down the road to the

creek house, with Clyde Boston and me looking after
him. Clyde was scratching his head, but I just looked.

Nelly began to get into trouble when he was around
fourteen. His first trouble that anyone knew about happened in the cloakroom of the eighth grade at school.
Miss Cora Petersen was a great believer in corporal punishment, and when Nelly was guilty of some infraction of
rules, Miss Petersen prepared to thrash him with a little
piece of white rubber hose. Teachers used to be allowed
to do that.

But if the pupil did not permit it to be done to him,
but instead drew a loaded revolver from inside his shirt
and threatened to kill his teacher, that was a different
story. It was a story in which the superintendent of
schools and the local chief of police and hard-faced old
Mr. Tare were all mixed together in the climax.

There was some talk about the reform school, too, but
the reform school did not materialize until a year later.

That was after Meisner's Hardware and Harness
Store had been robbed. The thief or thieves had a peculiar taste in robbery; the cash drawer was untouched,
but five revolvers and a lot of ammunition were taken
away. A mile and a quarter away, to be exact. They were
hidden beneath planks and straw in Mr. Barton Tare's
wagon shed, and Chief of Police Kelcy found them after
the simplest kind of detective work.

This time the story had to be put in the paper, no matter how much my father regretted it. This time it was
the reform school for sure.

We boys in the south end of town sat solemnly on our
new concrete curbstone and talked of Nelly Tare in
hushed voices. The judge had believed, sternly and simply, that Nelly was better off at Eldora than at home. He
gave him two years. Nelly didn't serve all of that time.
He got several months off for good behavior, which must
have come as a surprise to many people in Elm City.

He emerged from the Eldora reformatory in the spring

of 1918. His parents were out of the picture by this time. His mother was dead; his father had moved to South Dakota with the two youngest girls, and the other girls had married or drifted away.

Nelly may have been under age, but when he expressed a preference for the cavalry, and when he flourished a good report sheet from the reformatory superintendent, no one cared to say him nay. Once he came home on furlough from a camp in New Mexico. I remember how he looked, standing in front of Frank Wanda's Recreation Pool Hall, with the flashing badge of a pistol expert pinned upon his left breast, and all the little kids grouped around to admire the polish on his half-leather putts.

He never got a chance to use any guns against the Germans. He wasn't sent to France, and came back to Elm City in the spring of 1919. It was reasonable for him to come there. Elm City was the only real home town he had, and one of his sisters was married to Ira Flagler, a garage mechanic who lived out on West Water Street. Nelly went to live with the Flaglers.

He began working at Frank Wanda's pool hall. I have spoken about his skill with his hands; he employed that skill to good advantage in the pool hall. He had developed into a remarkable player during his year in the Army. He also ran the cigar counter and soft drinks for Frank Wanda, who was getting old and couldn't stand on his feet very long at a time.

It used to be that in every pool hall there was somebody who played for the house, if people came along and really wanted to bet anything. Nelly would play on his own, too, taking money away from farm boys or from some out-of-towner who thought he was good. He was soon making real money, but he didn't spend it in the usual channels. He spent it on guns.

All sorts. Sometimes he'd have an especially good revolver down there in the billiard parlor with him, and he'd show it to me when I dropped in for cigarettes. He had a kind of private place out along the Burlington tracks where he used to practice shooting on Sundays. And in 1923 a carnival came to town.

Miss Antoinette McReady, the Outstanding Six-Gun Artiste of Two Nations, was supposed to come from Canada. Maybe she did. They built up a phony Royal Canadian Mounted Police atmosphere for her act. A fellow in a shabby red coat and yellow-striped breeches sold tickets out in front. An extra girl in the same kind of comic uniform assisted the artiste with her fancy shooting. They had a steel backstop at the rear of the enclosure to stop the bullets. I went to the carnival on the first night, and dropped in to see the shooting act.

The girl was pretty good. Her lady assistant put on a kind of crown with white chalks sticking up in it, and Miss McReady shot the chalks out of the crown quite accurately, missing only one or two shots and not killing the lady assistant at all. She did mirror shooting and upside-down-leaning-backward shooting; she balanced on a chair and shot. She was a very pretty redhead, though necessarily painted.

Then the Royal Canadian Mounted manager made a speech. He said that frequently during her extensive travels, Miss McReady had been challenged by local pistol artists, but that she was so confident of her ability that she had a standing offer of one hundred dollars to anybody who could outshoot her.

The only condition was that the challenging local artist should agree to award Miss McReady an honorarium of twenty dollars, provided she outshot him.

Nelly Tare climbed up on the platform; he showed the color of his money and the bet was on.

Miss Antoinette McReady shot first, shooting at the tiny target gong with great deliberation; she rang the gong five out of six times. Nelly took her gun, aimed and snapped it a few times before ejecting the empty shells, to acquaint himself with the trigger pull. Then he loaded up, with the whole audience standing to watch him. He fired his six rounds, rapid fire, and everyone yipped when he rang the gong with every shot.

Miss Antoinette McReady smiled and bowed as if she had done the shooting instead of Nelly; she went over to congratulate him. They got ready for the next competition. The girl assistant started to put on the crown thing with its chalks sticking out of the sockets. Nelly talked to her a minute in a low voice; he took the crown and put it on his own head.

He stood against the backstop. His face was very red, but he stood there stiff at Army attention, with his hands against his sides.

"Go ahead, sister," he told Miss McReady.

Well, they made him sign a waiver first, in case of accident. You could have heard an ant sneeze in that place when Miss McReady stood up to do her shooting. She fired six times and broke four of the chalks. The people in the audience proceeded to wake up babies two blocks away, and Miss Antoinette McReady went over to Nelly with those little dancing, running steps that circus and vaudeville folks use. She made him come down to the front and take applause with her. Then she said she'd wear the crown for Nelly, and this time there was no waiver signed.

Nelly broke all six chalks in six steady shots, and Miss Antoinette McReady kissed him, and Frank Wanda had to get a new fellow for the pool hall when Nelly left town with the show after the last performance on Saturday night.

It was six months later when I heard my father exclaim, while he was taking press dispatches over the out-of-town wire. He often did that when some news came through which particularly interested or excited him. I left my desk and went to look over his shoulder, while his fat old fingers pushed out the story on the typewriter.

HAMPTON, COLORADO, April 2.—Two desperate trick-shot artists gave Hampton residents an unscheduled

exhibition today. When the smoke had cleared away the
Hampton County Savings Bank discovered it had paid
more than $7000 to watch the show.

Shortly after the bank opened this morning, a young
man and a young woman, identified by witnesses as
"Cowboy" Nelson Tare and Miss Antoinette McReady,
walked into the bank and commanded tellers and customers to lie down on the floor. They scooped up $7150
in small bills, and were backing toward an exit, when
Vice-President O. E. Simms tried to reach for a telephone.

The trick-shot bandits promptly shot the telephone off
the desk. They pulverized chandeliers, interior glass and
window lights in a rapid fusillade which covered their
retreat to their car.

Within a few minutes a posse was in hot pursuit, but
lost the trail near Elwin, ten miles south of this place. A
stolen car, identified as the one used by the bandits, was
found abandoned this noon near Hastings City. State
and county officers immediately spread a dragnet on sur-
rounding highways.

Nelson Tare and his female companion were easily
recognized as stunt shooters with a traveling carnival
which became stranded in Elwin a week ago. A full de-
scription of the hard-shooting pair has been broadcast to
officials of five near-by states.

All the time I was reading it, I kept thinking of Nelly
Tare, half-pint size in a dirty red coat, asking me, "Dot
any duns?"

They were captured in Oklahoma that summer, after
another robbery. Antoinette McReady, whose real name
turned out to be Ruth Riley, was sent to a women's penal institution; Nelly Tare went to McAlester Prison. He
managed his escape during the winter two years later,
and started off on a long series of holdups which carried
him south into Texas, over to Arkansas, and north into
Missouri.

Those were the days of frequent and daring bank robberies throughout that region. There were a lot of other bad boys around, and Nelly was only one of the herd. Still, he began to appear in the news dispatches with increasing regularity, and when some enterprising reporter called him Nice Nelly, the name stuck and spread. It was a good news name, like Baby-face or Pretty Boy.

They recaptured him in Sedalia; the story of his escape from the Jefferson City Penitentiary in 1933 was front-page stuff all over the nation. It was always the same—he was always just as hard to catch up with. He was always just as able to puncture the tires of pursuing cars, to blast the headlights that tried to pick him out through the midnight dust.

Federal men didn't enter the picture until the next January, when Nelly kidnaped a bank cashier in Hiawatha, Kansas, and carried him nearly to Lincoln, Nebraska. That little state line made all the difference in the world. The so-called Lindbergh Law had come into existence, and Nice Nelly Tare became a public enemy on an elaborate scale.

It is not astonishing that some people of Elm City basked in this reflected notoriety.

Reporters from big city papers, photographers from national magazines, came poking around all the time. They interviewed Nelly's sister, poor Mrs. Ira Flagler, until she was black in the face—until she was afraid to let her children play in the yard.

They took pictures of Frank Wanda's pool hall, and they would have taken pictures of Frank if he hadn't been dead. They managed to shake Miss Cora Petersen, late of Elm City's eighth grade, from asthmatic retirement. Her homely double-chinned face appeared in a fine-screen cut, in ugly halftones—a million different impressions of it. READ TEACHER'S STORY OF HOW NICE NELLY, BABY BANDIT, DREW HIS FIRST BEAD ON HER. OTHER PICTURES ON PAGE SEVEN.

Clyde Boston and I used to talk about it, over in Clyde's office in the courthouse. Clyde Boston had been sheriff for two terms; he was just as apple-cheeked and good-natured as ever, though most of his hair was gone. He would shake his head when we talked about Nelly Tare, which we did often.

"You know," he'd say, "a lot of people probably doubt those stories about Nelly's fancy shooting—people who haven't seen him shoot. But I still remember that time he had you throw a snowball for him to break with a rifle. He certainly is gun crazy."

It was during the late summer of 1934—the bad drought year—when Nelly held up a bank at Northfield, Minnesota, and was promptly dubbed The Modern Jesse James.

Officers picked up Nelly's trail in Sioux Falls, and that was a relief to us in Elm City, because people had always feared that Nelly might be struck with a desire to revisit his boyhood haunts and stage a little shooting right there in the lobby of the Farmers' National Bank. Nelly's trail was lost again, and for two weeks he slid out of the news.

Then came the big story. Federal men very nearly re-captured him in Council Bluffs, though he got away from them even there. Then silence again.

About two o'clock of the following Thursday after-noon, I went up to the courthouse on printing business. I had stopped in at Sheriff Clyde Boston's office and was chewing the rag with Clyde, when his telephone rang.

Clyde picked up the phone. He said, "Yes. . . . Yes, Barney. . . . He did? . . . Yes. . . . Glad you called me." He hung up the receiver and sat drumming his fin-gers against a desk blotter.

"Funny thing," he said. "That was young Barney Meisner, down at the hardware store."

"What did he have to say?"

"He said that one of the Flagler kids was in there a while ago and bought two boxes of forty-five shells. Funny, isn't it?"

We looked at each other. "Maybe Ira Flagler's decided to emulate his wife's folks," I said, "and take up trick shooting on the side."

Clyde Boston squeezed out a smile. "Guess I'll ride up to their house and ask about it."

So I went along with him, and when we got to the green-and-white Flagler house on West Water Street, we saw a coupé parked in the drive. Clyde breathed rapidly for a moment; I saw his hands tighten on the steering wheel, until he could read the license number of the car. Clyde relaxed. It was a Vera Cruz County number; it was one of our own local cars; I remembered that I had seen Ira Flagler driving that car sometimes.

Clyde parked across the street, although down a little way. He got out on the driver's side and I got out on the other side. When I walked around the rear of the car and looked up at the Flagler house, Nelly Tare was standing on the porch with a revolver in his hand.

I guess neither Clyde nor I could have said anything if we had been paid. Clyde didn't have his own gun on; sheriffs didn't habitually carry guns in our county any more. There was Nelly on the porch, covering us and looking just about the same as ever, except that his shoulders had sagged and his chin seemed to have receded a good deal more.

He said, "Lay down on the ground. That's right—both of you. Lay down. That's right—keep your hands up."

When we were on the ground, or rather on the asphalt pavement which formed the last block of Water Street, Nelly fired four shots. He put them all into the hood and engine of the car, and then we heard his feet running on the ground. I didn't look for a minute, but Clyde had more nerve than I, and got up on his haunches immediately.

By that time Nelly was in the Flagler coupé. He drove

it right across their vegetable garden, across Lou Miller's yard, and out onto the pavement of Prospect Street. Prospect Street connected with a wide gravel road that went south toward the Rivermouth country and the town of Liberty beyond. Nelly put his foot on the gas; dust went high.

Those four bullets had made hash out of the motor. The starter was dead when Clyde got his foot on it; gas and water were leaking out underneath. Mrs. Ira Flagler stumbled out upon the porch with one of her children; they were both crying hysterically.

She said, "Oh, thank God he didn't shoot you, Mr. Boston!"

Later she told her story. Nelly had showed up there via boxcar early that morning, but Ira was working on a hurry-up job at the garage and didn't know about it. Nelly had made his sister and the children stay in the house all day. Finally he persuaded the youngest boy that it would be great fun and a joke on everybody if he would go downtown and buy him two boxes of .45 shells.

But all this revelation came later, for Clyde Boston was well occupied at the telephone. He called the courthouse and sent a carload of vigilantes after Nelly on Primary No. 37. He called the telephone office and had them notify authorities in Liberty, Prairie Flower, Mannville and Fort Hood. Then he called the state capital and talked to Federal authorities himself. Government men started arriving by auto and airplane within two hours.

About suppertime Nelly showed up at a farmhouse owned by Larry Larsen, fourteen miles southwest of Elm City. He had been circling around all afternoon, trying to break through the cordon. They had heavy trucks across all the roads; late-summer cornfields don't make for good auto travel, even when there has been a drought.

He took Larsen's sedan and made the farmer fill it with gas out of his tractor tank. Nelly had cut the telephone wires; he forced the farmer's family to tie one another up, and then he tied the last one himself. Nelly saw to it that the tying was well done; it was after eight o'clock before one of the kids got loose and they shouted forth their story over a neighbor's telephone.

Things were wild enough down at the Chronicle office that evening. But I had a reliable staff, and at eight-thirty I thought it was safe to take a run up to the courthouse.

"I kind of expected you'd be up, Dave," said Clyde Boston.

I told him that I thought he'd be out on the road somewhere.

"Been out for the last four hours." He took his feet down off the desk, and then put them up again. "If I can get loose from all these state and national efficiency experts, how'd you like to take a little drive with me in your car? Mine's kind of out of order."

Well, I told him that I'd be glad to drive him anywhere he said, but I didn't want to come back with bullet holes in the cowling. So he got loose from the efficiency experts, and he made me strike out south of town and then east, on Primary No. 6.

Clyde didn't talk. Usually it was his way to talk a lot, in a blissful, middle-aged, bald-headed fashion. We passed two gangs of guards and identified ourselves each time, and finally Clyde had me stop at a farm where some cousins of his lived. He borrowed a log chain—a good big one with heavy links. This rusty mass Clyde dumped down into my clean back seat, and then he directed me to drive south again.

The katydids exclaimed in every grove.

"You know," said Clyde, "I used to do a lot of rabbit hunting and prairie-chicken hunting down this way, when I was younger. And you used to do a lot of hiking around down here with the boys. Fact is, only boys who were raised in these parts would know this country completely. Isn't that a fact? Outside officers wouldn't know it."

Well, I agreed that they wouldn't, and then Clyde

began to talk about Nelly Tare. He said that Nelly's one chance to get out of those several hundred square miles that he was surrounded in was to ride out on a railroad train. He wouldn't be likely to try it on foot, not unless he was crazy, and Clyde Boston didn't think he was crazy. Except gun crazy, as always.

"Now, the railroads all cross up here in this end of the county, up north of the river. Don't they?"

"That's right."

"So to get from where Nelly was at suppertime to where he'd like to be, he'd have to go diagonally from southwest to northeast. Now, the river timber runs diagonally from southwest to northeast——"

I began to see a little light. "You're talking about the old Rivermouth road." And Clyde said that he was.

He said that he had picnicked there with his family in recent years. The ancient timber road was still passable by car, if a driver proceeded slowly and cautiously enough. It meant fording several creeks; it couldn't be managed when the creeks were up.

"It comes out on the prairie just below the old Bemis farm," said Clyde. "You go down between pastures on a branch-off lane, and then you're right in the woods. That's where I think maybe he'll come out."

When he got to the Bemis place we turned off on the side lane and drove to the edge of the timber. The forest road emerged—a wandering sluice with yellow leaves carpeting it. We left my car parked at the roadside, and Clyde dragged the log chain down the timber road until he found a good place.

Cottonwoods and thin saplings made a wall along either side, where the road twisted out of the gully. A driver couldn't tell that the road was blocked until he had climbed the last curve in low gear.

Clyde wrapped the log chain around two cottonwoods. It sagged, stiff and heavy, across the path.

I said, "He'll kill you, Clyde. Don't expect me to help you try to grab him and get killed at the same time."

"There won't be any killing." Clyde settled himself in the darkness. "I'm going to take Nelly Tare back to Elm City. Alive."

Old logs and gullies are thick in the Rivermouth country; hazel brush fairly blocks the forgotten road in a hundred places. It was long before Nelly's headlights came sneaking through the trees. The katydids spoke a welcome; the dull parking lights went in and out, twisting, exploring, poking through the brush; they came on, with the motor growling in low.

Nelly made quite a spurt and went into second for a moment as the car swung up out of the gorge; sleek leaves flew from under his rear wheels; little rocks pattered back into the shrubbery.

Then Nelly saw the log chain. He jammed his brakes and the car slewed around until it was broadside. Nelly turned off the motor and lights in half a second; the car door swung; he was out on the log-chain side, and he had a gun in his hand.

"Don't shoot, Nelly," said Clyde Boston, stepping in front of the trees and turning on his flashlight.

I didn't want to be killed, so I stood behind a tree and watched them. The flashlight thrust out a long, strong beam; Clyde stood fifteen feet away from the car's radiator, but the shaft of his lamp was like whitewash on Nelly Tare.

"It's Clyde," the sheriff said. "Clyde Boston. You remember me? I was up at your sister's place today."

Nelly cried, "Turn off that light!"

"No," Clyde said. "And I'm warning you not to shoot the light out, because I'm holding it right in front of my stomach. My stomach's a big target. You wouldn't want to shoot my stomach, would you, Nelly?"

Nelson Tare's hair was too long, and he needed a shave. He looked like some wild thing that had been dug out of the woods. "Clyde! I'm telling you for the last time! Turn it off!"

Clyde's voice was a smooth rumble, "Remember one time when we went hunting rabbits?" He edged forward a little. "You and Dave and me. Remember? A big jack sat down, waiting for you to kill him. And you couldn't pull the trigger. You couldn't kill him."

Nelly had his face screwed into a wad, and his teeth showed between his lips.

"Never shot anything or anybody, did you, Nelly?" There was a snapping sound, and I jumped. It was only a stick breaking under Clyde's foot as he moved nearer to the car. "You never shot a soul. Not a jack rabbit or anything. You couldn't."

He was only ten feet away from Nelly and Nelly's gun.

"You just pretended you could. But the guards in Oklahoma and Missouri didn't know you the way I do. They hadn't ever gone hunting with you, had they?"

He took another step forward. Another. Nelly was something out of a waxworks in a side show, watching him come. Then a vague suffusion of light began to show around them; a carload of deputies had spotted my car at the head of the lane; their head lamps came hurtling toward us.

"You shot telephones off of desks," Clyde purred to Nelly, "and tires off of cars. You've been around and you've done a lot of shooting. But you never shot things that the blood ran out of. . . . Now, you drop your gun, Nelly. Drop it on the ground. Gosh, I was crazy this afternoon. I shouldn't have laid down when you told me to. I should have just stood there."

Maybe he was right and maybe he was wrong; I don't know. The car stopped and I heard men yell, "Look out, sheriff!" They were ready with their machine guns, trying to hustle themselves into some position where they could spatter the daylights out of Nelly Tare without shooting Clyde Boston too. Clyde didn't give them a chance to do it. He dove forward; he flung his arms around Nelly and crushed him to the ground.

Nelly cried, and I don't like to think about it; sometimes I wake up in the night and think I hear him crying. My memory goes back to our haymow days and to the rats in the chicken pen—the rats that Nelly couldn't shoot—and I remember the bloody cottontails dangling from Clyde's belt.

Nelly cried, but not solely because he was captured and would never be free again. He wept because the world realized something he had tried to keep hidden, even from himself. When he was taken back into prison, he wore an expression of tragic perplexity. It must have been hideous for him to know that he, who had loved guns his whole life long, should at last be betrayed by them.

Escape from the Mine

By WALTER D. EDMONDS

THERE were about sixty men on the sand. Some sat with their backs propped against the stone. Some of them lay sprawled out. Few talked. It wasn't a good place to talk in, nor did they look like men who were given to talking. They didn't look very much like men, somehow, at all.

They had the shape of men, though. They wore men's clothes, but, for the most part, these were in rags, and all had a sodden, rotten look in the dim light from the charcoal fires.

The fires burned in old sap kettles, cooking pots, whatever could contain charcoal. It was necessary to keep them burning; two or three of the men were appointed every night to watch them. If the fires were permitted to go out, a few of the old hands said, the whole sixty prisoners would die inside of an hour.

They kept the fires burning close to the waterside to get the benefit of the reflected light, but light of any kind made small impression there. The shaft of the old mine was fifty feet across and seventy feet high, with only a four-foot opening at the top. This opening was secured by iron bars grouted into the stone—as if a prisoner could possibly have climbed the inside of a cone of smooth rock with forty pounds of iron on him.

When they looked up at those bars, during the few minutes that daylight slanted through them, some of the men felt that they would like to kill the man who had put in those bars.

They were all ironed by four chains that joined wrists and ankles. When a man entered the prison, the warden offered him his choice of a new set for two pounds English, or a rusty set for nothing. Though rusty sets made scars quicker than new ones, most of the prisoners could not afford to spend two pounds. Most of them didn't have that much.

Whenever the guard up above happened to think of it —sometimes it was every day, or every other day, or once a week—they were allowed up to exercise in the open air, to bring up their filth buckets and enjoy the world inside the walls that surrounded the prison buildings. They went up one at a time, up a fifty-foot iron ladder grouted into the rocky wall, heaving and jerking themselves to lift their fettered hands and feet from rung to rung. They went through a trap door into the guardhouse cellar, and when four had been allowed through, the trap was closed on the men on the ladder, and the first four passed up another ladder into the guardroom proper. Then four more were allowed in the cellar, and so on, so that the four armed guards in the cellar were never outnumbered. It was a foolproof system. There was no way out.

Of course, they had explored the drifts of the old mine. There were seven or eight of them, in which they slept;

but they all ended in blind ends. And no one could dig through stone without tools.

The richer prisoners bought boards from the guards at two shilling a foot, for the purpose of raising their straw pallets off the damp, and those that could not afford boards were envious. Anything that contributed to keeping the damp from a man's bones in that place was a treasure. The whole place was damp. The walls were always sweating and dropping water. Then there was the pool beyond the sand, under the main shaft. No one knew how deep it was, though two once had tried wading out into it. They had gone over their heads within a dozen feet. It had taken them two weeks to dry out. With irons on, a man could not take his clothes off, and the fires gave scarcely enough heat to counteract the dampness of the air itself.

The water filled half the area at the bottom of the shaft. On the side on which the ladder descended from the trap door of the guardroom cellar was the sandy beach. On the other, the water licked up against the wall of living rock. It backed off into two drifts, so no one knew how much water there really was inside the hill. But there was enough to make the temperature invariable. In the hottest summer weather it stayed at fifty-two degrees; and the same in winter, no matter how far below zero it was outside the guardhouse. But a man could never feel warm, even in winter.

The reason most of the men did not talk was that a human voice seemed to get lost as soon as it left the lips. It was the bigness of the place, the darkness, and, perhaps, the consciousness of all the mass of the hill overhead. The rebels, in 1776, called it Newgate Prison; but the prisoners still called it by its old name of Simsbury Mines.

The few who did talk during the summer of 1777 discussed torpidly the progress of Burgoyne's army, which was supposed to be coming down Lake Champlain from Canada. It was their great hope; though a good many wondered whether, if Burgoyne actually captured Albany and the Hudson Valley, he would explore as far east as Simsbury, Connecticut. It did not seem likely. To send out a letter, a man had to bribe the guard with ten shilling, the regular price.

Most of them were poor men anyway. Men who had been arrested rather through their neighbors' fear than through any overt act on their own part. One was a minister who had preached for the maintenance of established government and deplored the action of such hotheaded people as General Washington. He tried to preach in the prison, but in there no one wanted to listen to him.

Another man was a New York farmer who had tried to protect his wife and daughter from being molested by New England militia at a place called Bemis Heights. He had knocked down a sergeant. He never denied having been a Tory, but he had never done anything but knock down the sergeant. He said that everybody in the upper Hudson had been having trouble with the New England troops quartered in that district.

There were some Albany gentry who were known Tories. These men kept by themselves and talked politics, and these were the men who had information that Burgoyne was coming against Ticonderoga. They were quite cheerful at times, but, as often as not, they seemed to drop into the queer animal-pack instinct that belonged to the place, as if most of the men's minds had been touched when they came down the ladder into the darkness.

There was also the man John Wolff, who had been transferred to the prison in the early fall of 1776. He was listed on the prison ledger as "No. 17, store-keeper, Cosby's Manor, Tryon County; arrested by the Tryon County Committee of Safety; convicted of being a Loyalist."

But, while truthful in that meager outline, the ledger did not add that John Wolff had been proved of nothing more treasonable than giving food to hungry refugee Loyalists. Cosby's Manor was far up the Mohawk River, beyond the German Flats settlements in which he was tried, and people there were conscious of the Indians and the fact that the Iroquois were generally loyal to the crown, the Johnsons and the Butlers, who had already fled to Canada. The ledger, further, did not state that John Wolff was married and that he had left his wife with two pounds cash money to find her way to safety out of a hostile neighborhood. It did not say that John Wolff had never much considered his wife until the time of his trial, and that only when he was carried off from Fort Dayton under escort, to be sent to the mines, did he realize what a loyal person she was. The fact that he had never appreciated her preyed on John Wolff's mind. She was a colorless sort of woman, a woman without a great deal of spunk at any time.

He had passed her what money he had had on him, and he had told her to try to get to Canada, where John Butler might be willing to help her out. He had saved eight shilling with which to pay for sending a letter, but down here he found it cost ten shilling just to bribe the guard.

He still could not understand why he had been imprisoned. The sentence of the militia court had been execution, but somehow that had been changed to imprisonment at the last minute. He did not understand that either.

John Wolff, No. 17, had been in Newgate Prison for more than a year, but he was no longer sure, himself, how long it was. He seemed to have lost the sense of time. There were days when he couldn't have said offhand whether they were today, or yesterday. Generally it turned out that they were days beyond track.

Sometimes he would catch himself saying the days of the week, "Monday, Tuesday, Wednesday——" Or the months of the year. There were many things he used to say. "Lucy Locket, lost her pocket——" Sometimes he would wake up the near-by prisoners and they would throw pieces of rock at his bed and yell. It was awful when the men yelled. It started echoes whirling in the air shaft; one could hear them traveling up and down between the water and the grating. They would seem to carry John Wolff's thoughts up to that grating until he was nearly mad with the thought of it. What with the charcoal smoke, a man could hardly tell when the sun was in the sky above that grating, except at noon. A little before and a little after the equinox, a man could see the sun, itself, if he waded out into the water far enough. He could even feel it on his head, very faintly warm. John Wolff had so felt it, and the man next to him had felt it also, but he started a convulsion, and they had to haul him out of the water to save him from drowning.

But when the men started yelling and got the echoes going, it used to make John Wolff feel sick. The voices would start picking one another up, catching and passing one another, and coming up and down, until the echoes managed to acquire individual personalities of their own, and the echoes then had echoes, and it went on and on, a bedlam that wouldn't die even when the trap door opened at the top of the iron ladder and the guard looked down and yelled back furiously. Then the men would work on the echoes, and a queer singsong rise and fall would be worked out of the echoes that, even after everyone was tired, kept the echoes working endlessly.

It was like the eternal drip of water magnified. The drip of water had the same effect when all the men were silent. At first John Wolff would notice it on the wall right beside him. Drip, and a pause; drip, and a pause. Gradually, this soft impingement of a single drop would lead him to listen for drops farther away, and soon his ears would become attuned to drops much farther off. Then he would begin to be aware of the graduation in loudness that distance made, and all at once the drop he had first noticed would have the regular clang of a ringing bell. He couldn't, then, put it back into its proper equivalent in the sound of sense.

Sometimes he, or another man, would get up from his wet straw and work at the bare rock for hours to change the direction of an individual drip, so that its sound would be altered and thus restored to a sane proportion.

But one night when the men were making their singsong, and the guard happened to be drunk, maybe the guard went a little crazy himself. Anyway, he opened the trap and fired his musket down into the shaft. They could all see him, high above their heads, his furious red face, and the musket barrel pointing down like the finger of wrathful retribution. The bullet striking made no sound through the yelling voices, and they kept yelling, increasing the tumult. Even John Wolff yelled that night. The guard lost his head entirely. He fired again and again, and finally a ball ricocheted and killed one of his prisoners. He was the man who had knocked down a sergeant for molesting his wife. But they did not notice his death till it was time for them to go up the next day.

They had to hoist his body with a rope and carry him to the smithy, so that his irons could be taken off. Then he was buried, and the warden, Captain Viets, had half a dozen men flogged; choosing the ones the indignant guard who had committed the murder pointed out; and one man who owed that particular guard three shilling was hung by his heels for an hour and a half. No prisoner was served food for two days, but the guard did well instead, for it was necessary for the prison to consume its full ration of beef, if the warden were to receive his regular allowance.

It was odd, after that, to think of the dead man. He was buried in the prison yard. And yet he was sixty feet above any of the live prisoners. He was decomposing somewhere underground, but they were still more underground than he. Waiting for him to come down, one man said—to come down in drops of water. He embarked on an intricate calculation of how long it would take the first drop to come down to their level. John Wolff started watching the drops on the stone beside his bed.

Now and then, long, fiery discussions began to start up over the progress of the British Army under General Burgoyne. The discussions ended in futility, for the guard refused to give them any news. The guard struck a man if he asked. They gathered, from that, that the army was making progress. But one night the warden, himself, opened the trap, and they saw his bare, nourished legs squatting under his nightshirt as he bawled down: Did they want to hear about Gen. Johnny Burgoyne? They let the drops answer. But Captain Viets wasn't to be deprived of his fun. "He's surrendered!" he shouted. "His entire army! Six thousand men!" They could see him haul in his breath and swell himself. "The Hessians have got licked at Bennington, Vermont, and St. Leger has been drove off from Fort Stanwix by Benedict Arnold. How do you like that? Hey?"

Purely from habit, they started their singsong, and he had to slam the trap down. But they kept the singsong up all night. They knew now that all hope of their being rescued from the cavern must be deferred. In fact, it was a question now if they ever would get out. People didn't know where they were, a lot of them. They didn't really know themselves. They were conscious only of the vast formation of rock that was above them. They thought a person wouldn't think of looking for a man so deep down in solid rock.

For a week afterward they beguiled themselves by saying what they thought of General Burgoyne for getting whipped. They imagined General Burgoyne's being put down among them. They wondered whether there were a chance of that. But people like General Burgoyne, who made war and brought Indians and wore epaulets and carried his private whisky with him, weren't ever put in places like the mines. Only a person who preached in the pulpit for the King and constitutional government and the rights of property, or a person who said he was a Loyalist and refused to take the new oath, or who owed some upstart Yankee judge some money, or who hit a Continental soldier who was molesting his wife —then that person was an atrocious villain.

II

A good many of the other prisoners thought that John Wolff was going crazy. He was not aware of it himself. Only, he liked to repeat things he knew. And he also dictated himself letters to his wife every week. At first he tried writing these in the sand, but, as time went on, he just sat hunched over his knees and repeated what was in his mind, speaking the words being the next best thing to setting them down in writing.

He would ask her to write what she was doing, and then he would say what had happened in the prison. The letters sounded pretty much alike, even to himself. He got tired of them. The day after Captain Viets delivered the news of Burgoyne's surrender, John Wolff wrote his wife, Ally, about that, but then he could think of nothing to add. A Mr. Francis, who had been in the caverns when he first arrived, asked what the trouble was. "I'm writing my wife Alice," explained John Wolff, "but I can't think of anything new to tell her."

"Have you described this lovely home of ours?" asked Mr. Francis.

"No, I haven't."

"Why don't you? Take a look around and see what there is to see."

Several of the men laughed, but John Wolff did not mind. It was an idea. He began looking round and made up his letter, about the air shaft and the beds and the beach of sand and the water. "The water is queer," he dictated; "the water keeps dropping down off the walls all the while, and the water don't ever get higher nor lower." He realized that he was saying something nobody had noticed.

Suddenly John Wolff came out of his daze, and he had a long fit of the shakes. But they weren't the damp shakes that everybody had. He was shaking with excitement. He went and looked at the water .

He asked, "Has anybody ever tried to wade out there?"

"It's too deep," one of the men said.

"Has anybody tried to swim?" asked John Wolff.

A roar of laughter went up. One of the men reached out and rattled the chains connecting Wolff's anklets and wrist fetters. "Try and swim with forty pounds," he suggested. John Wolff stood in their midst, looking at their faces, gaunt, and filthy with rock dust and charcoal smoke and unwashed beards. It came to him that he must look like that himself. His hand went to his beard. He had never had a beard before. He had always shaved.

Then his eyes grew cunning. He felt them growing so, and closed the lids lest the other men see it, and he went and lay down. They were still making jokes about him when the guard opened the trap door and shouted down at them to heave up for their exercise.

From his bed, John Wolff watched them clambering toilsomely up the ladder, their chains clashing against the iron rungs as they fought upward with one hand and lugged the filth buckets with the other. The smoke from the braziers drew into the guardroom, and the guard stepped away from the door and closed it after the fourth man. It was a slow business. John Wolff lay there till they had all gone up.

"Hey, you!" shouted the guard.

John Wolff did not answer.

"Come up."

John Wolff remembered all the filth he had ever heard and sent it up to the guard. The guard laughed at him. "All right," he said, "stay down. Stay down for a week." Wolff was a harmless man, not worth going down for and lugging up and flogging. He slammed the trap shut.

John Wolff got up. He clanked slowly down to the beach and looked at the water. Then he started rummaging in the straw beds for pieces of plank. He hadn't been able to afford any himself. Moving with the slow, half-hopping motion the irons forced him to use, he took down planks and put them in the water. They floated soggily. He got more. He laid them on top of each other, side by side. Then he waded out and straddled them and tentatively pulled up his feet. The planks sank under him and he rummaged for more. He finally collected enough to float his weight, and he tied them together with strips torn from blankets.

He straddled the clumsy raft and pushed it out with his feet. He paddled with his hands. The weight of the irons made his hands splash, no matter how careful he was. But he had only a little way to go to get out of the light from the braziers.

John Wolff had been thinking about which shaft to choose. But as he could not make up his mind, he chose the farthest. When he entered it, the noise of his splashing diminished. The light behind him was circumscribed by the low ceiling of the shaft and the flat level of the water. Looking back, it seemed to him that he had come a great distance. He could not see far ahead, because the shaft made a turn. He paddled slowly round that, and then, in the darkness that instantly became complete, he felt the front of his raft strike the rock. The impact was very slight, but it almost knocked him off balance. He barely saved himself by lifting his hands and bracing them against the rock wall. He realized that the drift was filled to the ceiling, and that there was no way out. He felt all round the water level to make sure, and then tried to turn his raft.

There was not room to turn it, and he had to back out. It was a laborious and painful process. His arms dragged and his legs had gone numb with cold, except for the ache the cold made in his ankle scars.

When he came into view of the sand beach and the smoldering charcoal fires and the mussed straw beds he had violated of their planks, he was sobbing with exhaustion. He lay forward along the planks, eyes shut. From a vague sense of habit, he started dictating a letter to Ally:

"The right drift is full of water, so I can't get out that

way. I have got to try the other way. It is so hard to paddle."

Then it occurred to him that he could not wait another day to try. It would take almost as long to get fifty feet back to shore as to paddle into the other drift. In either case, he would have no time to put the planks back under the straw. They ducked men who monkeyed with the beds of others. It took two weeks to get dry.

John Wolff decided to paddle into the other drift.

Again the splashing he made seemed to crash against the upward walls of the shaft. But again the noise was shut off when he finally entered the second drift. He had been working an hour to cover his hundred feet or so of progress, and the men would be coming down soon. He forced himself to keep at his work until the last reflected light on the water was left behind. Then he came to a slight curve and continued round that, and then he stopped.

He had a sudden new sensation. The sweat was pouring out of his skin. It was the first time he had sweated for months. It made him feel weak, as if the whole energy of his body had been put to work at the process of creating sweat in him; but at the same time he felt an access of courage because he was still able to sweat.

It gave his hands power to paddle on. Behind, and far away, shut off by the rock wall, he heard the muffled clanking as the men started down the ladder. He kept on.

It was pitch dark now. The raft was scraping the side of the drift. But he kept on paddling, and the echoes that entered the drift were mere whispers of his name—John Wolff, John Wolff—like voices for a person departing the world.

His arms lifted and fell and lifted. He had gone a long way. He was not completely conscious any more of what he was doing. He was quite unprepared when the raft struck a projection of the wall, dumping him sideways off the plank into the water. His last flurry broke the wrappings of the raft and the planks came apart. He thought he was going to drown. Then he struck bottom. He stood up and his head came out of water. Against his wet face, in the dark, he felt an icy draft of air.

He started wading. The bottom was quite smooth, but the water deepened. It reached his chin. He knew that he was going in the right direction, because the air drew against his forehead.

The boards had drifted out of his reach and it was too dark to see anything anyway. John Wolff stood still in the water, thinking aloud, as he had got the habit of dictating to himself: "Dear Ally, the water is up to my mouth. It is getting deeper. But there is surely air coming along this drift. And I can't get back and I figure to go ahead. It is better to drown than to stand still in the water. It is not very cold water, but it makes me shake some. Otherwise I am well, and hoping you are the same——" He drew a deep breath and took a full stride forward.

The water fell away from his chin, from his throat. He felt the cold air against his wishbone. He drew another breath and took still another step, and the water dropped halfway to his waist. He shouted.

It was thin sound he made, and it was drowned by his threshing in the water. All at once he was reaching down, holding tight the chains to his ankles and floundering knee-deep along a narrow stream. The air was cold all over him. He went on for a dozen yards and shouted again. There was light on the right-hand wall. Faint but actual light. Daylight. He turned the corner to the left and saw the shine of the light on the water, which now ran downhill quite swiftly through a small tunnel, lined with stone, that seemed to narrow to the dimension of a large culvert. He had to bend and get on his knees. He took another turn as he dragged himself in the water, and he saw ahead of him the gray of woods in October.

But between him and the woods was a wooden grille.

It shocked and amazed him to find that grille, after so long and baffling a distance. It seemed to him of a piece with all the malicious godlessness of the mines. In its way it seemed to him infinitely more wicked than the trial which had sent him to the prison in the first place.

He dragged himself up to it and put his hands against the lower bar and rested his head on his hands. The shakes were taking hold of him again. He closed his eyes and let go of his body.

He felt the grille shaking as he shook, and opened his eyes. It came to him that the wood was old and the joints the crossbars made with the frame were very rotten. He braced his feet against a crease in the stone and threw his weight against the grille.

The whole business gave way, tumbling out under him down the steep hillside. He fell with it, with a last clank of his irons, rolled over down the slope, and came to rest with his face upward, seeing the breast of the hill against the sky. He lay still, weeping.

A cold rain was falling steadily.

III

In two hours he had covered a mile and a half through the woods. He had gone beyond caring about the noise he made. Just after sunset, he struck a path that led him into a pasture.

The pasture sloped toward a valley through which a road ran. On the road were a small house, with a barn attached to it by a woodshed, and an outbuilding that had a chimney and looked like a forge. The wet bricks shone faintly in the light from the house window. He stopped, while the rain beat down on him, and stared at the lighted fire visible through the kitchen window. Where he was the whole world smelled wet and cold.

Presently a man came out of the house and went to the barn. John Wolff could hardly credit his good luck as he saw the man lead out a horse and take it to the front door. The man waited there until a woman came out, shawling herself against the rain. The man helped her onto the pillion. He then mounted in front of her, and while the horse shifted sidewise under them, he shouted to someone in the house to bar the door till they came back.

John Wolff could hear the answer through the rain—a Negro voice. It sounded like a woman's. The man said they would return in two or three hours. He kicked the horse to a trot down the road.

As soon as the horse had gone, John Wolff started down the hill. He went first to the building he thought might be a smithy and opened the door. There was enough light in the banked fire to show him, dimly, the anvil and the hammers and files on the bench beside it.

He was like a man obsessed. He made no effort to be quiet, but picked up one of the hammers and started striking on the seams of his wristbands. It was hard to get a good swing. His aim was clumsy from the cold and the weight of the chain, and the hammer head kept rolling off the iron onto his arm. But the seam cracked finally and he pulled the iron loose. For a minute he stood looking at the rusty imprint on his wrist, as if he saw the iron in his flesh. Then he slowly flexed the arm and raised it over his head. He felt as if his fist could strike high heaven.

He broke the other fetter more handily and began work on the anklets. These were harder to break, for it was almost impossible to keep his leg on the anvil within striking distance of his arm and yet get a free swing with the hammer. Finally he thought of tipping the anvil over.

It took all his strength to accomplish that, and the anvil teetered a long time before he could overbalance it. It fell with a terrific thud, but John Wolff did not seem to notice the noise until the screaming of the Negro woman in the house broke in on his hearing. He lifted his chin and instinctively started to join her voice with his—as if it were the singsong starting back in the mine.

Then he remembered what he was doing and held his ankle against the anvil and swung the hammer with both hands. The fetter smashed all to pieces. He broke the other at the first blow.

The Negress was still shrieking over in the house, and John Wolff listened to her, cocking his head a little, while a strained look of cunning came into his eyes. The hand which held the hammer began to swing with little jerks. Suddenly he became aware of the motion of his hand and stopped it. He stood quite still, with a growing excitement in his eyes and his breath coming and going sharply.

At his first step, he nearly toppled over on his face. He recovered himself, went out through the door and closed it behind him with great care. He stopped for a moment more, turning his head toward the house as if he tasted the fear in the black woman's shrieks. The hand holding the hammer started again its premonitory twitching. He started for the house.

Habit forced his legs into the hobbling gait the shackles had trained them to, but the release from weight deprived them of all sense of balance. He kept lurching forward, and on the second hop he measured his length in the muddy yard. He scrambled up and forced himself to move more slowly until he had got to the porch. He knocked on the door. At the first blow, the woman stopped her screeching.

He compelled his free hand to knock gently again; this started the woman off on her shrieks, and he listened with his ear to the panel. When she stopped, the house was quiet as death, with only the sound of the rain dripping from the eaves.

The drip distracted him until he heard the woman moan inside the house, and then the sound of her feet sneaking toward the back.

It infuriated him. He raised the hammer with both hands and battered it against the door. It was an eight-pound hammer and he broke in a panel in half a dozen blows. He became intoxicated with the destruction he was making of the door and forgot all about the woman.

He knocked in the panels one by one and hammered at the bar behind them until it fell away, brackets and all. Then he opened the door and walked into the lighted room.

A fire was burning on the hearth and a kettle was steaming. He had not seen a kettle with a spout for more than a year. The hammer dropped out of his hand, clanked on the hearthstones, but he let it lie.

He thought he was standing steady, but he was weaving on his feet. He had forgotten all about the woman; even when she stole down the stairs to see what had become of him, he did not hear her.

She stood there watching him with her round eyes rolling the whites in her black face and her lips hanging flabbily open.

She saw a man so thin he hardly seemed a man at all, with a mess of light-brown hair showing white streaks and hanging down on his shoulders and a matted beard and a torn shirt and rotten wet trousers and bare feet. The feet were bleeding. She saw the blood on the hearthstones. And then she saw the fetter scars on his ankles and wrists.

"Lan' sakes," she breathed. "You ain' no booger, is you?"

His chin lifted, but his glazed eyes did not shift from the kettle.

"If I could have a cup of tea——" He sat down weakly.

The Negress was a young wench. Her curiosity and sympathy were powerfully aroused. "You one of de prison people," she announced. She nodded, as he did not contradict her. "Soon as I lay my eyes on you, I say, 'Leeza, dat am one of de prison people. He got put in jes' like ol' massa. Dat's what he did.'" She came forward. "Co'se you can have some tea. Dey ain' so many places where you can get it, neither," she added proudly. "An' I'll jes' bring along some eatables wid it." She flurried about her job, chattering: "Dey take away de hones' people. Dey take me 'way fum dem. Mistah Phelps, he jine de Committee of Safety and he get to be powerful big man, and he get me when dey lock up my ol' fambly. He gone to de committee to-night. He used to go by his-se'f, but since he tuk to fallen off di horseback, missis she jes' naturally 'bliged to go wid um. Lot of de wimmen folks does dat. Dey have their party, and de men dey have theirs."

John Wolff shivered with the tea. It scalded him, but the taste was so penetrating that he could not stop drinking. Warmth flooded him. The Negress stood at his side, offering a collop of cold pork and a slice of heavy white bread. She watched him with a kind of pride.

"Whar you gwine?" she asked softly. "You cain' stay here."

"No," said John Wolff. "No, I'm going to Canada."

The Negress eyed him more critically. "You cain' go lookin' de way you is," she said. "I'll fix you fo' de trip. I use' to shave ol' massa."

John Wolff was content just to sit still. He let the black wench work on him. She shaved him with her master's razor and she hacked his hair short. Then she went up-stairs and rummaged an old pair of shoes and a coat and a pair of trousers.

"Dey're kind of monst'us lookin'," she said, "but we're 'bliged to cover up dem iron marks."

Her face was proud over her handiwork. She was a clean-looking wench, quite young.

"Thanks," said John Wolff. "Maybe I better be going."

"You take me wid you?" she suggested, making eyes at him.

He said, "I've got to find Ally. My wife, Ally."

"I he'p you, massa."

"No," he said. "It's too far. I'm going out to Niagara."

He felt his strength coming back to him. He hadn't thought, till now, of going to Niagara. But now he remembered that that was where most of the refugees from the western part of the Mohawk Valley had headed for.

It occurred to him that at that place he might find someone who had heard of Ally, if she hadn't got there herself.

The Negress sighed.

"I guess you wouldn't take me along wid you nohow.
I guess I jes' naturally got to stay here."

She watched him sidelong.

"I'll jes' have to chase myself out into de rain," she went
on, as he made no sign of having heard her. "Less'n you
bash de top of my head wid de hammer a couple of times."

He shivered.

"No."

"Den I got to say you bus' in here and took dese things.
Oh, Mr. Phelps, he'll lay into me. But he ain't so smart.
Ain' none of dese new folks is so smart."

John Wolff took his eyes from the hammer. He turned
and went out into the rain. The Negress called after him
shrilly: "You take de lef' branch, massa. Dat bring you
into Canaan, bimeby."

IV

He followed strange roads furtively by night, or by day
only if it rained, but he encountered few militia bands.
The smell of fall was in the air, and the militia were going
home. His greatest danger was the spying system of the
local committees, men jealous of their new and unexpected
power, constantly on the watch for easy money by
picking up a deserter or a wandering man, like John
Wolff himself, who might have escaped from jail, or
against whom evidence might be manufactured for the
sake of the reward. They might be found in any tavern or
in any crossroads house. John Wolff spent two weeks
getting to the Hudson Valley.

He crossed the river at the mouth of the Hoosic and
made his way to Ballston village, and there, by a fortunate
chance, he picked up two men named Kennedy and Miller
who had come down from St. John's to visit their families. They had used their British leave to paddle the length

of Champlain Lake and tramp sixty miles of wilderness and enemy country, and the night John Wolff found them they were planning to return. They took him with them. At St. John's he learned that Major John Butler was in garrison at Fort Niagara. There was talk that since the breakdown of the regular army in the west, before Fort Stanwix, John Butler was recruiting a regiment of rangers of his own. Nobody knew very much about it, but John Butler would be a good man to serve under. If you liked frontier service.

From St. John's, John Wolff worked his way to Montreal, where he found that the last westward sloop was making ready to sail for Niagara. The master was a man named Grange. He agreed to take John Wolff aboard.

Now, six weeks after his escape from Simsbury, John Wolff was coming in sight of the British fort. It was at the very tail end of November.

A light snow had begun early in the afternoon. It drifted down without noticeable wind. But a heavy gathering of cloud in the northwest promised the storm to come.

The walls of the fort looked brown and close to the earth. Even the stone mess house and its two flanking towers seemed to huddle between the parallel expanses of lake and sky. The river and the flat of the land were gray with cold. The smokes from the barracks and the officers mess rose thinly against the falling flakes and mingled with the smokes from the Indian camp and huts of trappers, traders and independent rangers that made a straggling kind of village behind the gates. The people moving desultorily down to the shore seemed pinched. A squad of soldiers in their scarlet coats marched down among them and took their station at the head of the makeshift dock. John Wolff, on the foredeck, watched them and the low land they waited on creep toward the boat. He was gaunt and footsore. He looked like an unhealthy man in spite of the waning of his prison pallor. Or it may have been his expectancy that brought the slight flush to his cheeks.

He thought that now, at last, he would get news of his wife. He thought he couldn't help getting news, having come so far. It had been in his mind for weeks now.

The master of the sloop moved up behind John Wolff, smoking his short pipe, the tail of his red knitted cap hanging down beside his cheek. He said, "Well, here's where you get off," as if it were a joke he expected Wolff to laugh at.

John Wolff said, "Maybe I can see Mr. Butler and he'll lend me the passage money."

The master spat over the side.

"No hurry. I'll collect it next spring. He can't get away from me here. You neither." He sucked the pipestem open and stared west across the river. "That's where you'll live, I reckon."

"Over there? I thought that was the fort."

" 'Tis. But that's where Butler's building the barracks for his rangers. They ain't got any nails. I just as soon not see Butler till I got nails to bring him. Maybe I'll have them next spring."

Well back from the river shore, a low line of log buildings looked even more huddled under the snow than the fort.

The master said, "I don't see how people can stand to live here. They must be crazy. Ain't more than fifty women in the whole place, barring Indians." He glanced companionably at Wolff. "You said you lost your wife, didn't you?"

"Yes."

"That's how it is with women. You lose them, or something." He gestured with his pipe. "But out here you can't even find them. I don't see why you come out here."

He cocked his head.

"Listen to them falls. When they sound that way, I begin to expect ice. Well, you might as well get off."

The sloop was now half unloaded, and the dock sagged under boxes, bales and barrels of shoes, flour, rum, powder kegs, lead, pork, salt beef, blankets and Indian goods.

"I wish there was some nails, though," said the master. He shook hands with John Wolff. "There's a couple of them new rangers coming down. Maybe it's Butler. Guess I'll get below."

Wolff saw three men in green coats coming down to the opposite shore. They got into a skiff and rowed over the river. In the stern sat a short gray-haired man with a red face and dark eyes and a long Irish lip to his mouth.

"Mr. Grange!" he shouted. "Mr. Grange! Did you bring any nails?"

"No, I didn't!" bawled the master of the sloop.

"Why didn't you?"

"I couldn't get them, that's why!"

"Did you hand in my requisition?"

"Yes, I did."

"Didn't they say anything?" Butler asked angrily.

"They said nails was scarce!"

"That's a lie!"

"I ain't saying it ain't, am I?"

"What did they say?"

"They said, 'You'd think the old dumbhead was going to win the war with a kag of nails!'"

Major Butler drew in his breath. Then he seemed to collapse back into himself and his eyes became helpless. But he started to grin.

"Why didn't you tell me that in the first place, Grange?"

The master grinned back.

"I didn't want to crucify you all to once, major. Here's a man I've brought who wants to talk to you. Come all the way from Simsbury prison in Connecticut. I thought he might kind of take the place of a kag of nails. He's built kind of like a nail, ain't he?"

John Wolff flinched at the major's direct stare.

"What's your name?" Butler asked him.

"John Wolff."

"Wolff? Wolff? I seem to remember the name."

"I kept the store at Cosby's Manor."

"Oh, I remember you now. Do you want to join Butler's Rangers?"

His voice was proud, naming them, as if the organization were something tangible that he had achieved, like handwork.

"I don't know," said John Wolff. He didn't. He was a mild man by nature; he always had been. He looked like one now, with his pale, thin, tired face.

Butler said kindly, "You've been in jail?"

"Yes, sir. I was arrested a year ago last August."

"That's a long time." The major's face showed sympathy. He was used to these stories though. "But you get into the boat and come back with us. Old neighbors?" The words were sad in his mouth. "This is Sergeant McLonis. He came from your part of the valley. You may know him?"

Getting into the boat, John Wolff shook hands with the young man. He felt shy, aware of his own misshapen clothes as he studied the man's new uniform. A green coat with crossed buff breast straps. The lining of the coat was scarlet woolen. The hat was a skullcap of black leather, with a leather cockade over the left ear and a brass plate over the forehead. The waistcoat was of heavy green woolen, and the full-length leggings of Indian-tanned buckskin. It was a good uniform, Wolff thought, fixed for service in the woods.

"Sit down, Wolff," said Major Butler. . . . "We'll row back, lads. I don't want to see Commandant Bolton to-day. I don't feel like it." He turned to Wolff. "How did you happen to find your way here?"

John Wolff swallowed.

"I thought somebody here would know about Cosby's." He couldn't bring himself to mention Ally right off.

Butler said grimly:

"Well, I can tell you. They burned Thompson's house, the rebels did, and your store too. It's too bad, Wolff. It's going to be a long time before you can get back, or any of us can, to live. St. Leger made a mess of our best chance. So did Burgoyne. Up here we can't get government support for another real campaign. We can't even get nails from the government!"

John Wolff was silent as the skiff smacked over the light ripple. The drip from the oars had an icy sound. The air was raw and piercing.

"We'll have to do the best we can for ourselves. How old are you, Wolff?"

"Fifty-three."

"Hard at your time of life."

"I ain't so strong right now," said John Wolff. "But I'll be all right. I used to have good health."

The other men kept watching him. Then he saw that Major Butler was looking too. He saw that his sleeves had drawn back to show the fetter scars.

"You've had a hard time," Butler said grimly. "Maybe you can't forget it. But it's better to try, I guess." He raised himself stiffly as the boat touched shore. "They've kept my wife and children down there. Prisoners. Hostages they call them. They won't exchange them," he finished with abrupt harshness.

"Yes, sir." Wolff's face started to work. He blurted out, "Do any women get here from the valley, sir?"

"Some got through." Butler was brief. "Why?"

"You haven't seen my wife? Alice Wolff. Ally, she's called, generally. Kind of a pale woman? A little younger than me?"

Butler shook his head and glanced away. The men shook their heads too. McLonis said, "It would be known if she was here. It would be bound to be known."

Butler said almost angrily, "It's two hundred miles through the woods. We know that some started, that got driven out. We know they started, that's all."

"Can a man send a letter down there?" John Wolff asked.

Butler said, "I can send one under a flag, if you like, next spring. But a letter's not likely to reach her unless you know where she is."

John Wolff, shivering a little, walked behind Butler toward the low log barracks. "Yes, I'd forgot. My store got burned, didn't it?"

"Yes, Wolff."

"Squire," Wolff said suddenly.

"Yes?"

"Could a man my age join your Rangers?"

"Yes," Butler said, shortly.

The snow began to drive a little before the first lifting of the wind.

The Most Dangerous Game

By RICHARD CONNELL

THERE was no sound in the night as Rainsford sat there but the muffled throb of the engine that drove the yacht swiftly through the darkness, and the swish and ripple of the wash of the propeller. Rainsford, reclining in a steamer chair, indolently puffed on his favorite brier. "It's so dark," he thought, "that I could sleep without closing my eyes; the night would be my eyelids—"

An abrupt sound startled him. Off to the right he heard it, and his ears, expert in such matters, could not be mistaken. Again he heard the sound, and again. Somewhere, off in the blackness, someone had fired a gun three times. Rainsford sprang up and moved quickly to the rail, mystified. He strained his eyes in the direction from which the reports had come, but it was like trying to see through a blanket. He leaped upon the rail and balanced himself there, to get greater elevation; his pipe, striking a rope, was knocked from his mouth. He lunged for it; a short, hoarse cry came from his lips as he realized he had reached too far and had lost his balance. The cry was pinched off short as the blood-warm waters of the Caribbean Sea closed over his head.

He struggled up to the surface and tried to cry out, but the wash from the speeding yacht slapped him in the face and the salt water in his open mouth made him gag and strangle. Desperately he struck out with strong strokes after the receding lights of the yacht, but he stopped before he had swum fifty feet. A certain coolheadedness had come to him; it was not the first time he had been in a tight place. There was a chance that his cries could be heard by someone aboard the yacht, but that chance was slender, and grew more slender as the yacht raced on. He wrestled himself out of his clothes, and shouted with all his power. The lights of the yacht became faint and ever-vanishing fireflies; then they were blotted out entirely by the night.

Rainsford remembered the shots. They had come from the right, and doggedly he swam in that direction, swimming with slow, deliberate strokes, conserving his strength. For a seemingly endless time he fought the sea. He began to count his strokes; he could do possibly a hundred more, he thought, and then—

Rainsford heard a sound. It came out of the darkness, a high, screaming sound, the sound of an animal in an extremity of anguish and terror. He did not recognize the animal that made the sound; he did not try to; with fresh vitality he swam toward the sound. He heard it again; then it was cut short by another noise, crisp, staccato.

"Pistol shot," muttered Rainsford, swimming on.

Ten minutes of determined effort brought another sound to his ears—the most welcome he had ever heard—the muttering and growling of the sea breaking on a rocky shore. He was almost on the rocks before he saw them; on a night less calm he would have been shattered against them. With his remaining strength he dragged himself from the swirling waters. Gasping, his hands raw, he reached a flat place at the top. Dense jungle came down to the very edge of the cliffs. What perils that tangle of trees and underbrush might hold for him did not concern Rainsford just then. All he knew was that he was safe from his enemy, the sea, and that utter weariness was on him. He flung himself down at the jungle edge and tumbled headlong into the deepest sleep of his life.

When he opened his eyes he knew from the position of the sun that it was late in the afternoon. Sleep had given him new vigor; a sharp hunger was picking at him. He looked about him, almost cheerfully.

"Where there are pistol shots, there are men. Where there are men, there is food," he thought. But what kind of men, he wondered, in so forbidding a place? An unbroken front of snarled and ragged jungle fringed the shore.

He saw no sign of a trail through the closely knit web of weeds and trees; it was easier to go along the shore, and Rainsford floundered along by the water. Not far from where he had landed, he stopped. Some wounded thing, by the evidence a large animal, had thrashed about in the underbrush; the jungle weeds were crushed down and the moss was lacerated; one patch of weeds was stained crimson. A small, glittering object not far away caught Rainsford's eye and he picked it up. It was an empty cartridge.

"A twenty-two," he remarked. "That's odd. It must have been a fairly large animal, too. The hunter had his nerve with him to tackle it with a light gun. It's clear that the brute put up a fight."

He examined the ground closely and found what he had hoped to find—the print of hunting boots. They pointed along the cliff in the direction he had been going. Eagerly he hurried along, now slipping on a rotten log or a loose stone, but making headway; night was beginning to settle down on the island.

Bleak darkness was blacking out the sea and jungle when Rainsford sighted the lights. He came upon them as he turned a crook in the coast line, and his first thought was that he had come upon a village, for there were many lights. But as he forged his way along he saw to his astonishment that all the lights were in one enormous building—a lofty structure with pointed towers plunging upward into the gloom. His eyes made out the shadowy outlines of a palatial château; it was set on a high bluff, and on three sides of it cliffs dived down to where the sea licked greedy lips in the shadows.

"Mirage," thought Rainsford. But it was no mirage, he found, when he opened the tall spiked iron gate. The stone steps were real enough; the massive door with a leering gargoyle for a knocker was real enough; yet about it all hung an air of unreality. He lifted the knocker, and it creaked up stiffly as if it had never before been used. He let it fall, and it startled him with its booming loudness. He thought he heard steps within; the door remained closed. Again Rainsford lifted the heavy knocker, and let it fall. The door opened then, opened as suddenly as if it were on a spring, and Rainsford stood blinking in the river of glaring gold light that poured out. The first thing his eyes discerned was the largest man Rainsford had ever seen—a gigantic creature, solidly made and black-bearded to the waist. In his hand the man held a long-barreled revolver, and he was pointing it straight at Rainsford's heart. Out of the snarl of beard two small eyes regarded Rainsford.

"Don't be alarmed," said Rainsford, with a smile which he hoped was disarming. "I'm no robber. I fell off a yacht. My name is Sanger Rainsford of New York City."

The menacing look in the eyes did not change. The revolver pointed as rigidly as if the giant were a statue. He gave no sign that he understood Rainsford's words, or that he had even heard them. He was dressed in uniform, a black uniform trimmed with gray astrakhan.

"I'm Sanger Rainsford of New York," Rainsford began again. "I fell off a yacht. I am hungry."

The man's only answer was to raise with his thumb the hammer of his revolver. Then Rainsford saw the man's free hand go to his forehead in a military salute, and he saw him click his heels together and stand at attention. Another man was coming down the broad marble steps, an erect, slender man in evening clothes. He advanced to Rainsford and held out his hand. In a cultivated voice marked by a slight accent that gave it added precision and deliberateness, he said: "It is a very great pleasure and honor to welcome Mr. Sanger Rainsford, the celebrated hunter, to my home. I've read your book about hunting snow leopards in Tibet, you see," explained the man. "I am General Zaroff."

Rainsford's first impression was that the man was singularly handsome; his second was that there was an original, almost bizarre quality about the general's face. He was a tall man past middle age, for his hair was a vivid white; but his thick eyebrows and pointed military mustache were as black as the night from which Rainsford had come. His eyes, too, were black and very bright. He had high cheek bones, a sharp-cut nose, a spare, dark face, the face of a man used to giving orders, the face of an aristocrat. Turning to the giant in uniform, the general made a sign. The giant put away his pistol, saluted, withdrew.

"Ivan is an incredibly strong fellow," remarked the general, "but he has the misfortune to be deaf and dumb. A simple fellow, but, I'm afraid, like all his race, a bit of a savage."

"Is he Russian?"

"He is a Cossack," said the general, and his smile showed red lips and pointed teeth. "So am I."

"Come," he said, "we shouldn't be chatting here. We can talk later. Now you want clothes, food, rest. You shall have them. This is a most restful spot. Follow Ivan, if you please, Mr. Rainsford. I was about to have my dinner when you came. I'll wait for you. You'll find that my clothes will fit you, I think."

It was to a huge beam-ceiling bedroom with a canopied bed big enough for six men that Rainsford followed the silent giant. Ivan laid out an evening suit, and Rainsford, as he put it on, noticed that it came from a London tailor who ordinarily cut and sewed for none below the rank of duke.

The dining room to which Ivan conducted him was in many ways remarkable. It suggested a baronial hall of feudal times with its oaken panels, its high ceiling, its vast refectory table where two score men could sit down to eat. About the hall were the mounted heads of many animals—lions, tigers, elephants, moose, bears; larger or more perfect specimens Rainsford had never seen. The table appointments were of the finest—the linen, the crystal, the silver, the china.

Half apologetically General Zaroff said: "We do our best to preserve the amenities of civilization here. Please forgive any lapses. We are well off the beaten track, you know."

The general seemed a most thoughtful and affable host, a true cosmopolite. But whenever he looked up from his plate Rainsford found the general studying him, appraising him narrowly.

"Perhaps," said General Zaroff, "you were surprised that I recognized your name. You see, I read all books on hunting published in English, French, and Russian. I have but one passion in my life, Mr. Rainsford, and it is the hunt."

"You have some wonderful heads here," said Rainsford. "That Cape buffalo is the largest I ever saw. I've always thought that the Cape buffalo is the most dangerous of all big game."

For a moment the general did not reply; he was smiling his curious red-lipped smile. Then he said slowly: "No. You are wrong, sir. The Cape buffalo is not the most dangerous big game." He sipped his wine. "Here in my preserve on this island," he said, in the same slow tone, "I hunt more dangerous game."

Rainsford expressed his surprise. "Is there big game on this island?"

"Oh, it isn't here naturally, of course, I have to stock the island."

"What have you imported, General?" Rainsford asked. "Tigers?"

The general smiled. "No," he said. "Hunting tigers ceased to interest me some years ago. No thrill left in tigers, no real danger. I live for danger, Mr. Rainsford. We will have some capital hunting, you and I. I shall be most glad to have your society."

"But what game——" began Rainsford.

"I'll tell you," said the general. "You will be amused, I know. I think I may say, in all modesty, that I have done a rare thing. I have invented a new sensation."

The general continued: "God makes some men poets. Some He makes kings, some beggars. Me He made a hunter. My hand was made for the trigger, my father said. When I was only five years old he gave me a little gun, specially made in Moscow for me, to shoot sparrows with. I killed my first bear when I was ten. My whole life has been one prolonged hunt. I went into the army and for a time commanded a division of Cossack cavalry, but my real interest was always the hunt. I have hunted every kind of game in every land. It would be impossible for me to tell you how many animals I have killed.

"After the debacle in Russia I left the country, for it was imprudent for an officer of the Tsar to stay there. Luckily, I had invested heavily in American securities, so I shall never have to open a tea room in Monte Carlo or drive a taxi in Paris. Naturally, I continued to hunt—grizzlies in your Rockies, crocodiles in the Ganges, rhinoceroses in East Africa. I went to the Amazon to hunt jaguars, for I had heard that they were unusually cunning. They weren't." The Cossack sighed. "They were no match at all for a hunter with his wits about him, and a high-powered rifle. I was bitterly disappointed. I was lying in my tent with a splitting headache one night when a terrible thought pushed its way into my mind. Hunting was beginning to bore me! And hunting, remember, had been my life. I asked myself why the hunt no longer fascinated me. You are much younger than I am, Mr. Rainsford, and have not hunted as much, but you perhaps can guess the answer."

"What was it?"

"Simply this: hunting had ceased to be what you call 'a sporting proposition.' It had become too easy. I always got my quarry. Always. There is no greater bore than perfection."

The general lit a fresh cigarette. "No animal had a chance with me any more. That is no boast; it is a mathematical certainty. The animal had nothing but his legs and his instinct. Instinct is no match for reason. When I thought of this it was a tragic moment for me, I tell you."

Rainsford leaned across the table, absorbed in what his host was saying.

"It came to me as an inspiration what I must do," the general went on.

"And that was?"

The general smiled the quiet smile of one who has faced an obstacle and surmounted it with success. "I had to invent a new animal to hunt," he said.

"A new animal? You're joking."

"Not at all," said the general. "I never joke about hunting. I bought this island, built this house, and here I do my hunting. The island is perfect for my purposes— there are jungles with a maze of trails in them, hills, swamps—"

"But the animal, General Zaroff?"

"Oh," said the general, "it supplies me with the most exciting hunting in the world. Every day I hunt, and I never grow bored now, for I have a quarry with which I can match my wits."

Rainsford's bewilderment showed in his face.

"I wanted the ideal animal to hunt," explained the general. "So I said: 'What are the attributes of an ideal quarry?' And the answer was, of course: 'It must have courage, cunning, and, above all, it must be able to reason.' "

"But no animal can reason," objected Rainsford.

"My dear fellow," said the general, "there is one that can."

"But you can't mean—" gasped Rainsford.

"And why not?"

"I can't believe you are serious, General Zaroff. This is a grisly joke."

"Why should I not be serious? I am speaking of hunting."

"Hunting? Good God, General Zaroff, what you speak of is murder."

The general laughed. He regarded Rainsford quizzically. "I refuse to believe that so modern a man harbors romantic ideas about the value of human life. Surely your experiences in the war—"

"Did not make me condone cold-blooded murder," finished Rainsford, stiffly.

Laughter shook the general. "How extraordinarily droll you are!" he said. "One does not expect nowadays to find a young man of the educated class, even in America, with such a naive, and, if I may say so, mid-Victorian point of view. It's like finding a snuffbox in a limousine. I'll wager you'll forget your notions when you go hunting with me. You've a genuine new thrill in store for you, Mr. Rainsford."

"Thank you, I'm a hunter, not a murderer."

"Dear me," said the general, quite unruffled, "again that unpleasant word. But I think I can show you that your scruples are quite ill-founded."

"Yes?"

"Life is for the strong, to be lived by the strong, and if needs be, taken by the strong. The weak of the world were put here to give the strong pleasure. I am strong. Why should I not use my gift? If I wish to hunt, why should I not? I hunt the scum of the earth—sailors from tramp ships—lascars, blacks, Chinese, whites, mongrels

—a thoroughbred horse or hound is worth more than a score of them."

"But where do you get them?"

"This island is called Ship Trap," he answered. "Sometimes an angry god of the high seas sends them to me. Sometimes, when Providence is not so kind, I help Providence a bit. Come to the window with me.

"Watch! Out there!" exclaimed the general, pointing into the night. As the general pressed a button, far out to sea Rainsford saw the flash of lights.

The general chuckled. "They indicate a channel," he said, "where there's none: giant rocks with razor edges crouch like a sea monster with wide-open jaws. They can crush a ship as easily as I crush this nut." He dropped a walnut on the hardwood floor and brought his heel grinding down on it. "Oh, yes," he said, casually, as if in answer to a question, "I have electricity. We try to be civilized here."

"Civilized? And you shoot down men?"

A trace of anger was in the general's black eyes, but it was there for but a second, and he said, in his most pleasant manner: "Dear me, what a righteous young man you are! That would be barbarous. I treat these visitors with every consideration. They get plenty of good food and exercise. They get into splendid physical condition. You shall see for yourself tomorrow."

"What do you mean?"

"We'll visit my training school," smiled the general. "It's in the cellar. I have about a dozen pupils down there now. They're from the Spanish bark *Sanlucar* that had the bad luck to go on the rocks out there. A very inferior lot, I regret to say. Poor specimens and more accustomed to the deck than to the jungle."

He raised his hand, and Ivan brought thick Turkish coffee. Rainsford, with an effort, held his tongue in check.

"It's a game, you see," pursued the general, blandly. "I suggest to one of them that we go hunting. I give him a supply of food and an excellent hunting knife. I give him three hours' start. I am to follow, armed only with a pistol of the smallest caliber and range. If my quarry eludes me for three whole days, he wins the game. If I find him"—the general smiled—"he loses."

"Suppose he refuses to be hunted?"

"Oh," said the general, "I give him his option, of course. If he does not wish to hunt, I turn him over to Ivan. Ivan once had the honor of serving as official knouter to the Great White Tsar, and he has his own ideas of sport. Invariably, Mr. Rainsford, invariably they choose the hunt."

"And if they win?"

The smile on the general's face widened. "To date I have not lost," he said. Then he added, hastily, "I don't wish you to think me a braggart, Mr. Rainsford. Many of them afford only the most elementary sort of problem. Occasionally I strike a tartar. One almost did win. I eventually had to use the dogs."

The general steered Rainsford to a window. The lights from the windows sent a flickering illumination that made grotesque patterns on the courtyard below, and Rainsford could see moving about there a dozen or so huge black shapes; as they turned toward him, their eyes glittered greenly.

"A rather good lot, I think," observed the general. "They are let out at seven every night. If anyone should try to get into my house—or out of it—something extremely regrettable would occur to him." He hummed a snatch of song.

"And now," said the general, "I want to show you my new collection of heads. Will you come with me to the library?"

"I hope," said Rainsford, "that you will excuse me tonight, General. I'm really not feeling at all well."

"Ah, indeed?" the general inquired, solicitously. "Well, I suppose that's only natural, after your long swim. Tomorrow, you'll feel like a new man, I'll wager.

Then we'll hunt, eh? I've one rather promising prospect—"

Rainsford was hurrying from the room.

"Sorry you can't go with me tonight," called the general. "I expect rather fair sport—a big, strong black. He looks resourceful— Well, good night, Mr. Rainsford; I hope you have a good night's rest."

The bed was good, and the pajamas of the softest silk, and he was tired in every fiber of his being, but nevertheless Rainsford could not quiet his brain with the opiate of sleep. He lay, eyes wide open. Once he thought he heard stealthy steps in the corridor outside his room. He sought to throw open the door; it would not open. He went to the window and looked out. His room was high up in one of the towers. The lights of the château were out now and it was dark and silent, but there was a fragment of sallow moon, and by its light he could see, dimly, the courtyard; there, weaving in and out in the pattern of shadow, were black, noiseless forms; the hounds heard him at the window and looked up expectantly, with their green eyes. Rainsford went back to the bed and lay down. He had achieved a doze when just as morning began to come, he heard, far off in the jungle, the faint report of a pistol.

General Zaroff did not appear until luncheon. He was dressed faultlessly in the tweeds of a country squire. He was solicitous about the state of Rainsford's health.

"As for me," sighed the general, "I do not feel so well. I am worried, Mr. Rainsford. Last night I detected traces of my old complaint. The hunting was not good last night. The fellow lost his head. He made a straight trail that offered no problems at all. That's the trouble with these sailors; they have dull brains to begin with, and they do not know how to get about in the woods. It's most annoying."

"General," said Rainsford, firmly, "I wish to leave this island at once."

The general raised his thickets of eyebrows; he

seemed hurt. "But, my dear fellow," the general protested, "you've only just come. You've had no hunting—"

"I wish to go today," said Rainsford. He saw the dead black eyes of the general on him, studying him. General Zaroff's face suddenly brightened.

"Tonight," said the general, "we will hunt—you and I."

Rainsford shook his head. "No, General," he said. "I will not hunt."

The general shrugged his shoulders. "As you wish, my friend," he said. "The choice rests entirely with you. But may I not venture to suggest that you will find my idea of sport more diverting than Ivan's?"

"You don't mean—" cried Rainsford.

"My dear fellow," said the general, "have I not told you I always mean what I say about hunting? This is really an inspiration. I drink to a foeman worthy of my steel—at last."

The general raised his glass, but Rainsford sat staring at him.

"You'll find this game worth playing," the general said, enthusiastically. "Your brain against mine. Your woodcraft against mine. Your strength and stamina against mine. And the stake is not without value, eh?"

"And if I win—" began Rainsford huskily.

"I'll cheerfully acknowledge myself defeated if I do not find you by midnight of the third day," said General Zaroff. "My sloop will place you on the mainland near a town. I will give you my word as a gentleman and a sportsman. Of course, you, in turn, must agree to say nothing of your visit here."

"I'll agree to nothing of the kind," said Rainsford.

"Oh," said the general, "in that case— But why discuss that now?" Then a business-like air animated him. "Ivan," he said to Rainsford, "will supply you with hunting clothes, food, a knife. I suggest you wear moccasins; they leave a poorer trail. I suggest, too, that you avoid the big swamp in the southeast corner of the island. We call it Death Swamp. There's quicksand there. One foolish fellow tried it. The deplorable part of it was that Lazarus followed him. I loved Lazarus; he was the finest hound in my pack. Well, I must beg you to excuse me now. I always take a siesta after lunch. You'll hardly have time for a nap, I fear. You'll want to start, no doubt. I shall not follow till dusk. Hunting at night is so much more exciting than by day, don't you think? Au revoir, Mr. Rainsford, au revoir."

General Zaroff, with a deep, courtly bow, strolled from the room. From another door came Ivan. Under one arm he carried khaki hunting clothes, a haversack of food, a leather sheath containing a long-bladed hunting knife; his right hand rested on a cocked revolver thrust in the crimson sash about his waist.

Rainsford had fought his way through the bush for two hours. "I must keep my nerve. I must keep my nerve," he said, through tight teeth.

He had not been entirely clear-headed when the château gates snapped shut behind him. His whole idea at first was to put distance between himself and General Zaroff, and to this end, he had plunged along, spurred on by panic. Now he had got a grip on himself, had stopped, and was taking stock of himself and the situation.

He saw that straight flight was futile; inevitably it would bring him face to face with the sea. "I'll give him a trail to follow," muttered Rainsford, and he struck off from the rude path he had been following into the trackless wilderness.

He executed a series of intricate loops; he doubled on his trail again and again, recalling all the lore of the fox hunt, and all the dodges of the fox. Night found him leg-weary with hands and face lashed by the branches, on a thickly wooded ridge. A big tree with a thick trunk and outspread branches was near by, and taking care to leave not the slightest mark, he climbed up into the crotch, and stretching out on one of the broad limbs, after a fashion, rested. Rest brought him new confidence and almost a feeling of security. Even so zealous a hunter as General Zaroff could not trace him there, he told himself; only the devil himself could follow that complicated trail through the jungle after dark.

Toward morning, when a dingy gray was varnishing the sky the cry of some startled bird focused Rainsford's attention. Something was coming by the same winding way Rainsford had come. He flattened himself down on the limb, and through a screen of leaves almost as thick as tapestry, he watched. The thing that was approaching was a man.

It was General Zaroff. He made his way along with his eyes fixed in utmost concentration on the ground before him. He paused almost beneath the tree, dropped to his knees, and studied the ground. Rainsford's impulse was to hurl himself down like a panther, but he saw that the general's right hand held something metallic—a small automatic pistol.

The hunter shook his head several times, as if he were puzzled. Then he straightened up and took from his case one of his black cigarettes; its pungent smoke floated up to Rainsford's nostrils.

Rainsford held his breath. The general's eyes had left the ground and were traveling inch by inch up the tree. Rainsford froze there, every muscle tensed for a spring. But the sharp eyes of the hunter stopped before they reached the limb where Rainsford lay; a smile spread over his face. Very deliberately he blew a smoke ring into the air; then he turned his back on the tree and walked carelessly away, back along the trail he had come. Swish of the underbrush against his hunting boots grew fainter and fainter.

The pent-up air burst hotly from Rainsford's lungs. His first thought made him feel sick and numb. The general could follow a trail through the woods at night; he could follow an extremely difficult trail; only by the merest chance had the Cossack failed to see his quarry.

Rainsford's second thought was even more terrible. Why had the general smiled? Why had he turned back? Rainsford did not want to believe what his reason told him was true. The general was playing with him! The general was saving him for another day's sport! The Cossack was the cat; he was the mouse. Then it was that Rainsford knew the full meaning of terror.

"I will not lose my nerve. I will not."

He slid down from the tree, and struck off again into the woods. His face was set and he forced the machinery of his mind to function. Three hundred yards from his hiding place he stopped where a huge dead tree leaned precariously on a smaller, living one. Throwing off his sack of food Rainsford took his knife from its sheath and began to work with all his energy.

The job was finished at last, and he threw himself down behind a fallen log a hundred feet away. He did not have to wait long. The cat was coming again to play with the mouse.

Following the trail with the sureness of a bloodhound came General Zaroff. Nothing escaped those searching black eyes, no crushed blade of grass, no bent twig, no mark, no matter how faint, in the moss. So intent was the Cossack on his stalking that he was upon the thing Rainsford had made before he saw it. His foot touched the protruding bough that was the trigger. Even as he touched it, the general sensed his danger and leaped back with the agility of an ape. But he was not quite quick enough; the dead tree struck the general a glancing blow on the shoulder as it fell; he staggered, but he did not fall; nor did he drop his revolver. He stood there, rubbing his injured shoulder, and Rainsford, with fear again gripping his heart, heard the general's mocking laugh ring through the jungle.

"Rainsford," called the general, "if you are within sound of my voice, as I suppose you are, let me congratulate you. Not many men know how to make a Malay man-catcher. Luckily for me, I too have hunted in Malacca. You are proving of interest, Mr. Rainsford. I am going now to have my wound dressed; it's only a slight one. But I shall be back. I shall be back."

When the general, nursing his bruised shoulder, had gone, Rainsford took up his flight again. It was flight now, a desperate, hopeless flight. Dusk came, then darkness, and still he pressed on. The ground grew softer under his moccasins; the vegetation grew ranker, denser; insects bit him savagely. Then, as he stepped forward, his foot sank into the ooze. He tried to wrench it back, but the muck sucked viciously at his foot. With a violent effort he tore his foot loose. He knew where he was now. Death Swamp and its quicksand. The softness of the earth gave him an idea. He stepped back from the quicksand a dozen feet or so and began to dig. The pit grew deeper; when it was above his shoulders, he climbed out and from some hard saplings cut stakes and sharpened them to a fine point. These stakes he planted in the bottom of the pit with the points sticking up. With flying fingers he wove a rough carpet of weeds and branches and with it he covered the mouth of the pit. Then, wet with sweat and aching with tiredness, he crouched behind the stump of a lightning-charred tree.

He knew his pursuer was coming; he heard the padding sound of feet on the soft earth, and the night breeze brought him the perfume of the general's cigarette. Rainsford, crouching there, lived a year in a minute. Then he felt an impulse to cry aloud with joy, for he heard the sharp crackle of the breaking branches as the cover of the pit gave way; he heard the sharp scream of pain as the pointed stakes found their mark. He leaped up from his place of concealment. Then he cowered back. Three feet from the pit a man was standing, with an electric torch in his hand.

"You've done well, Rainsford," the voice of the general called. "Your Burmese tiger pit has claimed one of my best dogs. Again you score. I think, Mr. Rainsford,

I'll see what you can do against my whole pack. I'm going home for a rest now. Thank you for a most amusing evening."

At daybreak Rainsford, lying near the swamp, was awakened by a sound that made him know that he had new things to learn about fear. It was the baying of a pack of hounds. For a moment he stood there, thinking. An idea that held a wild chance came to him, and tightening his belt, he headed away from the swamp.

The baying of the hounds drew nearer, then still nearer, nearer, ever nearer. On a ridge Rainsford climbed a tree. Down a watercourse, not a quarter of a mile away, he could see the bush moving. Straining his eyes, he saw the lean figure of General Zaroff; just ahead of him, Rainsford made out another figure whose wide shoulders surged through the tall jungle weeds; it was the giant Ivan, holding the pack in leash.

They would be on him any minute now. His mind worked frantically. He thought of a native trick he had learned in Uganda. He slid down the tree. He caught hold of a springy young sapling and to it he fastened his hunting knife, with the blade pointing down the trail; with a bit of wild grapevine he tied back the sapling. Then he ran for his life. The hounds raised their voices as they hit the fresh scent.

He had to stop to get his breath. The baying of the hounds stopped abruptly, and Rainsford's heart stopped, too. They must have reached the knife.

He shinned excitedly up a tree and looked back, but the hope in his brain died, for he saw in the shallow valley that General Zaroff was still on his feet. Ivan was not. The knife, driven by the recoil of the springing tree, had not wholly failed.

Rainsford had hardly tumbled to the ground when the pack took up the cry again.

"Nerve, nerve, nerve!" he panted, as he dashed along. A blue gap showed between the trees dead ahead. Rainsford forced himself on toward that gap. It was the shore of the sea. Across a cove he could see the gloomy gray stone of the château. Twenty feet below him the sea rumbled and hissed. Rainsford hesitated. He heard the hounds. Then he leaped far out into the sea. . . .

When the general and his pack reached the place by the sea, the Cossack stopped. For some minutes he stood regarding the blue-green expanse of water. He shrugged his shoulders. Then he sat down, took a drink of brandy from a silver flask, and hummed a bit from "Madame Butterfly."

General Zaroff had an exceedingly good dinner in his great paneled dining hall that evening. Two slight annoyances kept him from perfect enjoyment. One was the thought that it would be difficult to replace Ivan; the other was that his quarry had escaped him. In his library he read, to soothe himself, from the works of Marcus Aurelius. At ten he went up to his bedroom. He was deliciously tired, he said to himself, as he locked himself in. There was a little moonlight, so before turning on his light he went to the window and looked down at the courtyard. He could see the great hounds, and he called: "Better luck another time," to them. Then he switched on the light.

A man who had been hiding in the curtains of the bed was standing there.

"Rainsford!" cried the general. "How in God's name did you get here?"

"Swam," said Rainsford. "I found it quicker than walking through the jungle."

The general sucked in his breath and smiled. "I congratulate you," he said. "You have won the game."

Rainsford did not smile. "I am still a beast at bay," he said, in a low, hoarse voice. "Get ready, General Zaroff."

The general made one of his deepest bows. "I see," he said. "Splendid! One of us is to furnish a repast for the hounds. The other will sleep in this very excellent bed. On guard, Rainsford. . . ."

He had never slept in a better bed, Rainsford decided.

The Fourth Man

By JOHN RUSSELL

THE RAFT might have been taken for a swath of cut
sedge or a drifting tangle of roots as it slid out of the
shadowy river mouth at dawn and dipped into the first
ground swell. But while the sky brightened and the
breeze came fresh offshore it picked a way among shoals
and swampy islets with purpose and direction, and when
at last the sun leaped up and cleared his bright eye of the
morning mists it had passed the wide entrance to the bay
and stood to open sea.

It was a curious craft for such a venture, of a type
that survives here and there in the obscure corners of the
world. The coracle maker would have scorned it. The
first navigating pithecanthrope built nearly as well with
his log and bush. A mat of pandanus leaves served for its
sail and a paddle of niaouli wood for its helm. But it had
a single point of real seaworthiness. Its twin floats,
paired as a catamaran, were woven of reed bundles and
bamboo sticks upon triple rows of bladders. It was light
as a bladder itself, elastic, fit to ride any weather. One
other quality this raft possessed which recommended it
beyond all comfort and safety to its present crew. It was
very nearly invisible. They had only to unstep its mast
and lie flat in the cup of its soggy platform and they
could not be spied half a mile away.

Four men occupied the raft. Three of them were
white. Their bodies had been scored with brambles and
blackened with dried blood, and on wrist and ankle they
bore the black and wrinkled stain of the gyves. The hair
upon them was long and matted. They wore only the

rags of blue canvas uniforms. But they were whites, members of the superior race—members of a highly superior race according to those philosophers who rate criminal aberration as a form of genius.

The fourth was the man who had built the raft and was now sailing it. There was nothing superior about him. His skin was a layer of soot. His prognathous jaw carried out the angle of a low forehead. No line of beauty redeemed his lean limbs and knobby joints. Nature had set upon him her plainest stamp of inferiority, and his only attempts to relieve it were the twist of bark about his middle and the prong of pig ivory through the cartilage of his nose. Altogether a very ordinary specimen of one of the lowest branches of the human family—the Canaques of New Caledonia.

The three whites sat together well forward, and so they had sat in silence for hours. But at sunrise, as if some spell had been raised by the clang of that great copper gong in the east, they stirred and breathed deep of the salt air and looked at one another with hope in their haggard faces, and then back toward the land which was now no more than a gray-green smudge behind them.

"Friends," said the eldest, whose temples were bound with a scrap of crimson scarf, "Friends—the thing is done."

With a gesture like conjuring he produced from the breast of his tattered blouse three cigarettes, fresh and round, and offered them.

"Nippers!" cried the one at his right. "True nippers—name of a little good man! And here? Doctor, I always said you were a marvel. See if they be not new from the box!"

Dr. Dubosc smiled. Those who had known him in very different circumstances about the boulevards, the lobbies, the clubs, would have known him again and in spite of all disfigurement by that smile. And here, at the bottom of the earth, it had set him still apart in the prisons, the cobalt mines, the chain gangs of a community not much given to mirth. Many a crowded lecture hall in Montpellier had seen him touch some intellectual firework with just such a twinkle behind his bristly gray brows, with just such a thin curl of the lip.

"By way of celebration," he explained. "Consider. There are seventy-five evasions from Noumea every six months, of which not more than one succeeds. I had the figures myself from Dr. Pierre at the infirmary. He is not much of a physician, but a very honest fellow. Could anybody win on that percentage without dissipating? I ask you."

"Therefore you prepared for this?"

"It is now three weeks since I bribed the night guard to get these same nippers."

The other regarded him with admiration. Sentiment came readily upon this beardless face, tender and languid, but overdrawn, with eyes too large and soft and oval too long. It was one of those faces familiar enough to the police which might serve as model for an angel were it not associated with some revolting piece of deviltry. Fenayrou himself had been condemned "to perpetuity" as an incorrigible.

"Is not our doctor a wonder?" he inquired as he handed a cigarette along to the third white man. "He thinks of everything. You should be ashamed to grumble. See—we are free, after all. Free!"

The third was a gross, pock-marked man with hairless lids, known sometimes as Niniche, Trois Huit, Le Tordeur, but chiefly among copains as Perroquet—a name derived perhaps from his beaked nose, or from some perception of his jailbird character. He was a garroter by profession, accustomed to rely upon his fists only for the exchange of amenities. Dubosc might indulge a fancy and Fenayrou seek to carry it as a pose, but The Parrot remained a gentleman of strictly serious turn. There is perhaps a tribute to the practical spirit of penal administration in the fact that while Dubosc was the most dangerous of these three and Fenayrou the most depraved, Perroquet was the one with the official reputation, whose escape would be signaled first among the "Wanted." He accepted the cigarette because he was glad to get it, but he said nothing until Dubosc passed a tin box of matches and the first gulp of picadura filled his lungs. . . .

"Wait till you've got your two feet on a pavé, my boy. That will be the time to talk of freedom. What? Suppose there came a storm."

"It is not the season of storms," observed Dubosc.

But The Parrot's word had given them a check. Such spirits as these, to whom the land had been a horror, would be slow to feel the terror of the sea. Back there they had left the festering limbo of a convict colony, oblivion. Out here they had reached the rosy threshold of the big round world again. They were men raised from the dead, charged with all the furious appetites of lost years, with the savor of life strong and sweet on their lips. And yet they paused and looked about in quickened perception, with the clutch at the throat that takes landsmen on big waters. The spaces were so wide and empty. The voices in their ears were so wide and murmurous. There was a threat in each wave that came from the depths, a sinister vibration. None of them knew the sea. None knew its ways, what tricks it might play, what traps it might spread—more deadly than those of the jungle.

The raft was running now before a brisk chop with alternate spring and wallow, while the froth bubbled in over the prow and ran down among them as they sat.

"Where is that cursed ship that was to meet us here?" demanded Fenayrou.

"It will meet us right enough." Dubosc spoke carelessly, though behind the blown wisp of his cigarette he had been searching the outer horizon with keen glance. "This is the day, as agreed. We will be picked up off the mouth of the river."

"You say," growled Perroquet. "But where is any river now? Or any mouth? Sacred name! this wind will blow us to China if we keep on."

"We dare not lie in any closer. There is a government launch at Torrien. Also the traders go armed hereabouts, ready for chaps like us. And don't imagine that the native trackers have given us up. They are likely to be following still in their proas."

"So far!"

Fenayrou laughed, for The Parrot's dread of their savage enemies had a morbid tinge.

"Take care, Perroquet. They will eat you yet."

"Is it true?" demanded the other, appealing to Dubosc. "I have heard it is even permitted these devils to keep all runaways they can capture—Name of God!—to fatten on."

"An idle tale," smiled Dubosc. "They prefer the reward. But one hears of convicts being badly mauled. There was a forester who made a break from Baie du Sud and came back lacking an arm. Certainly these people have not lost the habit of cannibalism."

"Piecemeal," chuckled Fenayrou. "They will only sample you, Perroquet. Let them make a stew of your brains. You would miss nothing."

But The Parrot swore.

"Name of a name—what brutes!" he said, and by a gesture recalled the presence of that fourth man who was of their party and yet so completely separated from them that they had almost forgotten him.

The Canaque was steering the raft. He sat crouched at the stern, his body glistening like varnished ebony with spray. He held the steering paddle, immobile as an image, his eyes fixed upon the course ahead.

There was no trace whatever of expression on his face, no hint of what he thought or felt or whether he thought or felt anything. He seemed not even aware of their regard, and each one of them experienced somehow that twinge of uneasiness with which the white always confronts his brother of color—this enigma brown or yellow or black he is fated never wholly to understand or to fathom. . . .

"It occurs to me," said Fenayrou in a pause, "that our friend here who looks like a shiny boot is able to steer us God knows where. Perhaps to claim the reward."

"Reassure yourself," answered Dubosc. "He steers by my order. Besides, it is a simple creature—an infant, truly, incapable of any but the most primitive reasoning."

"Is he incapable of treachery?"

"Of any that would deceive us. Also, he is bound by his duty. I made my bargain with his chief, up the river, and this one is sent to deliver us on board our ship. It is the only interest he has in us."

"And he will do it. Such is the nature of the native."

"I am glad you feel so," returned Fenayrou, adjusting himself indolently among the drier reeds and nursing the last of his cigarette. "For my part I wouldn't trust a figurehead like that for two sous. Mazette! What a monkey face!"

"Brute!" repeated Perroquet, and this man, sprung from some vile river-front slum of Argenteuil, whose home had been the dock pilings, the grog shop, and the jail, even this man viewed the black Canaque from an immeasurable distance with the look of hatred and contempt. . . .

Under the heat of the day the two younger convicts lapsed presently into dozing. But Dubosc did not doze. His tormented soul peered out behind its mask as he stood to sweep the sky line again under shaded hand. His theory had been so precise, the fact was so different. He had counted absolutely on meeting the ship—some small schooner, one of those flitting, half-piratical traders of the copra islands that can be hired like cabs in a dark street for any questionable enterprise. Now there was no ship, and here was no crossroads where one might sit and

wait. Such a craft as the catamaran could not be made
to lie to.

The doctor foresaw ugly complications for which he
had prepared and whereof he must bear the whole burden. The escape had been his own conception, directed
by him from the start. He had picked his companions deliberately from the whole forced labor squad, Perroquet
for his great strength, Fenayrou as a ready echo. He had
made it plain since their first dash from the mine, during
their skirmish with the military guards, their subsequent
wanderings in the brush with bloodhounds and trackers
on the trail—through every crisis—that he alone should
be the leader.

For the others, they had understood well enough
which of their number was the chief beneficiary. Those
mysterious friends on the outside that were reaching half
round the world to further their release had never heard
of such individuals as Fenayrou and The Parrot. Dubosc
was the man who had pulled the wires: that brilliant
physician whose conviction for murder had followed so
sensationally, so scandalously, upon his sweep of aca-
demic and social honors. There would be clacking
tongues in many a Parisian salon, and white faces in
some, when news should come of his escape. Ah, yes, for
example, they knew the highflyer of the band, and they
submitted—so long as he led them to victory. They submitted, while reserving a depth of jealousy, the inevitable
remnant of caste still persisting in this democracy of
stripes and shame.

By the middle of the afternoon the doctor had taken
certain necessary measures.

"Ho," said Fenayrou sleepily. "Behold our colors at
the masthead. What is that for, comrade?"

"To help them sight us when the ship comes."

"What wisdom!" cried Fenayrou. "Always he thinks
of everything, our doctor; everything——"

He stopped with the phrase on his lips and his hand
outstretched toward the center of the platform. Here, in

a damp depression among the reeds, had lain the wicker-covered bottle of green glass in which they carried their water. It was gone.

"Where is that flask?" he demanded. "The sun has grilled me like a bone."

"You will have to grill some more," said Dubosc grimly. "This crew is put on rations."

Fenayrou stared at him wide-eyed, and from the shadow of a folded mat The Parrot thrust his purpled face. "What do you sing me there? Where is that water?"

"I have it," said Dubosc.

They saw, in fact, that he held the flask between his knees, along with their single packet of food in its wrapping of cocoanut husk.

"I want a drink," challenged Perroquet.

"Reflect a little. We must guard our supplies like reasonable men. One does not know how long we may be floating here. . . ."

Fell a silence among them, heavy and strained, in which they heard only the squeaking of the frail basket-work as their raft labored in the wash. Slow as was their progress, they were being pushed steadily outward and onward, and the last cliffs of New Caledonia were no longer even a smudge in the west, but only a hazy line. And still they had seen no moving thing upon the great round breast of the sea that gleamed in its corselet of brass plates under a brazen sun.

"So that is the way you talk now?" began The Parrot, half choking. "You do not know how long? But you were sure enough when we started."

"I am still sure," returned Dubosc. "The ship will come. Only she cannot stay for us in one spot. She will be cruising to and fro until she intercepts us. We must wait."

"Ah, good! We must wait. And in the meantime, what? Fry here in the sacred heat with our tongue hanging out while you deal us drop by drop—*hein?*"

"Perhaps."

"But no!" The garroter clenched his hands. "Blood of God, there is no man big enough to feed me with a spoon!"

Fenayrou's chuckle came pat, as it had more than once, and Dubosc shrugged.

"You laugh!" cried Perroquet, turning in fury. "But how about this Lascar of a captain that lets us put to sea unprovided? What? He thinks of everything, does he? He thinks of everything! . . . Sacred farceur—let me hear you laugh again!"

Somehow Fenayrou was not so minded.

"And now he bids us be reasonable," concluded The Parrot. "Tell that to the devils in hell. You and your cigarettes, too. Bah—comedian!"

"It is true," muttered Fenayrou, frowning. "A bad piece of work for a captain of runaways."

But the doctor faced mutiny with his thin smile.

"All this alters nothing. Unless we would die very speedily, we must guard our water."

"By whose fault?"

"Mine," acknowledged the doctor. "I admit it. What then? We can't turn back. Here we are. Here we must stay. We can only do our best with what we have."

"I want a drink," repeated The Parrot, whose throat was afire since he had been denied.

"You can claim your share, of course. But take warning of one thing. After it is gone, do not think to sponge on us—on Fenayrou and me."

"He would be capable of it, the pig!" exclaimed Fenayrou, to whom this thrust had been directed. "I know him. See here, my old, the doctor is right. Fair for one, fair for all."

"I want a drink."

Dubosc removed the wooden plug from the flask.

"Very well," he said quietly.

With the delicacy that lent something of legerdemain to all his gestures, he took out a small canvas wallet, the crude equivalent of the professional black bag, from which he drew a thimble. Meticulously he poured a brimming measure, and Fenayrou gave a shout at the grumbler's fallen jaw as he accepted that tiny cup between his big fingers. Dubosc served Fenayrou and himself with the same amount before he recorked the bottle.

"In this way we should have enough to last us three days—maybe more—with equal shares among the three of us."

Such was his summing of the demonstration, and it passed without comment, as a matter of course in the premises, that he should count as he did—ignoring that other who sat alone at the stern of the raft, the black Canaque, the fourth man.

Perroquet had been outmaneuvered, but he listened sullenly while for the hundredth time Dubosc recited his easy and definite plan for their rescue, as arranged with his secret correspondents.

"That sounds very well," observed The Parrot at last. "But what if these jokers only mock themselves of you. What if they have counted it good riddance to let you rot here? And us? Sacred name, that would be a famous jest! To let us wait for a ship and they have no ship!"

"Perhaps the doctor knows better than we how sure a source he counts upon," suggested Fenayrou slyly.

"That is so," said Dubosc with great good humor. "My faith, it would not be well for them to fail me. Figure to yourselves that there is a safety vault in Paris full of papers to be opened at my death. Certain friends of mine could hardly afford to have some little confessions published that would be found there. . . . Such a tale as this, for instance——"

And to amuse them he told an indecent anecdote of high life, true or fictitious, it mattered nothing, so he could make Fenayrou's eyes glitter and The Parrot growl in wonder. Therein lay his means of ascendancy over such men, the knack of eloquence and vision. Harried, worn, oppressed by fears that he could sense so much more sharply than they, he must expend himself now in vulgar marvels to distract these ruder minds. He succeeded so far that when the wind fell at sunset they were almost cheerful, ready to believe that the morning would bring relief. They dined on dry biscuit and another thimbleful of water apiece and took watch by amiable agreement. And through that long clear night of stars, whenever the one of the three who lay awake between his comrades chanced to look aft, he could see the vague blot of another figure—the naked Canaque, who slumbered there apart.

It was an evil dawning. Fenayrou, on the morning trick, was aroused by a foot as hard as a hoof, and started up at Perroquet's wrathful face, with the doctor's graver glance behind.

"Idler! Good-for-nothing! Will you wake at least before I smash your ribs? Name of God, here is a way to stand watch!"

"Keep off!" cried Fenayrou wildly. "Keep off! Don't touch me!"

"Eh, and why not, fool? Do you know that the ship could have missed us? A ship could have passed us a dozen times while you slept!"

"*Bourrique!*"

"*Vache!*"

They spat the insults of the prison while Perroquet knotted his great fist over the other, who crouched away catlike, his mobile mouth twisted to a snarl. Dubosc stood aside in watchful calculation until against the angry red sunrise in which they floated there flashed the naked red gleam of steel. Then he stepped between.

"Enough. Fenayrou, put up that knife."

"The dog kicked me."

"You were at fault," said Dubosc sternly. "Perroquet!"

"Are we all to die that he may sleep?" stormed The Parrot.

"The harm is done. Listen now, both of you. Things

are bad enough already. We may need all our energies. Look about."

They looked and saw the far, round horizon and the empty desert of the sea and their own long shadows that slipped slowly before them over its smooth, slow heaving, and nothing else. The land had sunk away from them in the night—some one of the chance currents that sweep among the islands had drawn them none could say where or how far. The trap had been sprung.

"Good God, how lonely it is!" breathed Fenayrou in a hush.

No more was said. They dropped their quarrel. Silently they shared their rations as before, made shift to eat something with their few drops of water, and sat down to pit themselves one against another in the vital struggle that each could feel was coming—a sort of tacit test of endurance.

A calm had fallen as it does between trades in this flawed belt, an absolute calm. The air hung weighted. The sea showed no faintest crinkle, only the maddening, unresting heave and fall in polished undulations on which the lances of the sun broke and drove in under their eyelids as white, hot splinters; a savage sun that kindled upon them with the power of a burning glass, that sucked the moisture from poor human bits of jelly and sent them crawling .to the shelter of their mats and brought them out again, gasping, to shrivel anew. The water, the world of water, seemed sleek and thick as oil. They came to loathe it and the rotting smell of it, and when the doctor made them dip themselves overside they found little comfort. It was warm and sluggish, slimed. But a curious thing resulted. . . .

While they clung along the edge of the raft they all faced inboard, and there sat the black Canaque. He did not join them. He did not glance at them. He sat hunkered on his heels in the way of the native, with arms hugging his knees. He stayed in his place at the stern, motionless under that shattering sun, gazing out into vacancy. Whenever they raised their eyes, they saw him. He was the only thing to see.

"Here is one who appears to enjoy himself quite well," remarked Dubosc.

"I was thinking so myself," said Fenayrou.

"The animal!" rumbled Perroquet.

They observed him, and for the first time with direct interest, with thought of him as a fellow being—with the beginning of envy.

"He does not seem to suffer."

"What is going on in his brain? What does he dream of there? One would say he despises us."

"The beast!"

"Perhaps he is waiting for us to die," suggested Fenayrou with a harsh chuckle. "Perhaps he is waiting for the reward. He would not starve on the way home at least. And he could deliver us—piecemeal."

They studied him.

"How does he do it, doctor? Has he no feeling?"

"I have been wondering," said Dubosc. "It may be that his fibres are tougher—his nerves."

"Yet we have had water and he none."

"But look at his skin, fresh and moist."

"And his belly, fat as a football!"

The Parrot hauled himself aboard.

"Don't tell me this black beast knows thirst!" he cried with a strange excitement. "Is there any way he could steal our supplies?"

"Certainly not."

"Then, name of a dog, what if he has supplies of his own hidden about?"

The same monstrous notion struck them all, and the others swarmed to help. They knocked the black aside. They searched the platform where he sat, burrowing among the rushes, seeking some hidden cache, another bottle or a gourd. They found nothing.

"We were mistaken," said Dubosc.

But Perroquet had a different expression for disappointment. He turned on the Canaque and caught him by the kinky mop of hair and proceeded to give him what is known as gruel in the cobalt mines. This was a little specialty of The Parrot's. He paused only when he himself was breathless and exhausted and threw the limp, unresisting body from him.

"There, lump of dirt! That will teach you. Maybe you're not so chipper now, my boy—*hein?* Not quite so satisfied with your luck. Pig! That will make you feel. . . ."

It was a ludicrous, a wanton, a witless thing. But the others said nothing. The learned Dubosc made no protest. Fenayrou had none of his usual jests at the garroter's stupidity. They looked on as at the satisfaction of a common grudge. The white trampled the black with or without cause, and that was natural. And the black crept away into his place with his hurts and his wrongs and made no sign and struck no blow. And that was natural too.

The sun declined into a blazing furnace whereof the gates stood wide, and they prayed to hasten it and cursed because it hung so long enchanted. But when it was gone their blistered bodies still held the heat like things incandescent. The night closed down over them like a purple bowl, glazed and impermeable. They would have divided the watches again, though none of them thought of sleep, but Fenayrou made a discovery.

"Idiots!" he rasped. "Why should we look and look? A whole navy of ships cannot help us now. If we are becalmed, why so are they!"

The Parrot was singularly put out.

"Is this true?" he asked Dubosc.

"Yes, we must hope for a breeze first."

"Then, name of God, why didn't you tell us so? Why did you keep on playing out the farce?"

He pondered it for a time. "See here," he said. "You are wise, eh? You are very wise. You know things we do

not and you keep them to yourself." He leaned forward
to peer into the doctor's face. "Very good. But if you
think you are going to use that cursed smartness to get
the best of us in any way—see here, my zig, I pull your
gullet out like the string of an orange. . . . Like that.
What?"

Fenayrou gave a nervous giggle and Dubosc shrugged,
but it was perhaps about this time that he began to regret his intervention in the knife play.

For there was no breeze and there was no ship.

By the third morning each had sunk within himself,
away from the rest. The doctor was lost in a profound
depression, Perroquet in dark suspicion, and Fenayrou in
bodily suffering, which he supported ill. Only two effective ties still bound their confederacy. One was the flask
which Dubosc had slung at his side by a strip of wicker-
work. Every move he made with it, every drop he
poured, was followed with burning eyes. And he knew
and he had no advantage of them in knowing that the
will to live was working its relentless formula aboard
that raft. Under his careful saving there still remained
nearly half of their original store.

The other bond, as it had come to be by strange muta-
tion, was the presence of the black Canaque.

There was no forgetting the fourth man now, no over-
looking him. He loomed upon their consciousness, more
formidable, more mysterious, more exasperating with
every hour. Their own powers were ebbing. The naked
savage had yet to give the slightest sign of complaint or
weakness.

During the night he had stretched himself out on the
platform as before, and after a time he had slept.
Through the hours of darkness and silence while each of
the whites wrestled with despair, this black man had
slept as placidly as a child, with easy, regular breathing.
Since then he had resumed his place aft. And so he remained, unchanged, a fixed fact and a growing wonder.

The brutal rage of Perroquet, in which he had vented his distorted hate of the native, had been followed by superstitious doubts.

"Doctor," he said at last, in awed huskiness, "is this a man or a fiend?"

"It is a man."

"A miracle," put in Fenayrou.

But the doctor lifted a finger in a way his pupils would have remembered.

"It is a man," he repeated, "and a very poor and wretched example of a man. You will find no lower type anywhere. Observe his cranial angle, the high ears, the heavy bones of his skull. He is scarcely above the ape. There are educated apes more intelligent."

"Ah? Then what?"

"He has a secret," said the doctor.

That was a word to transfix them.

"A secret! But we see him—every move he makes, every instant. What chance for a secret?"

The doctor rather forgot his audience, betrayed by chagrin and bitterness.

"How pitiful!" he mused. "Here are we three—children of the century, products of civilization—I fancy none would deny that, at least. And here is this man who belongs before the Stone Age. In a set trial of fitness, of wits, of resource, is he to win? Pitiful!"

"What kind of a secret?" demanded Perroquet, fuming.

"I cannot say," admitted Dubosc with a baffled gesture. "Possibly some method of breathing, some peculiar posture that operates to cheat the sensations of the body. Such things are known among primitive peoples—known and carefully guarded—like the properties of certain drugs, the uses of hypnotism and complex natural laws. Then, again, it may be psychologic—a mental attitude persistently held. Who knows? . . .

"To ask him? Useless. He will not tell. Why should he? We scorn him. We give him no share with us. We abuse him. He simply remains inscrutable—as he has always been and will always be. He never tells those innermost secrets. They are the means by which he has survived from the depth of time, by which he may yet survive when all our wisdom is dust."

"I know several very excellent ways of learning secrets," said Fenayrou as he passed his dry tongue over his lips. "Shall I begin?"

Dubosc came back with a start and looked at him.

"It would be useless. He could stand any torture you could invent. No, that is not the way."

"Listen to me," said Perroquet with sudden violence. "Me, I am wearied of the gab. You say he is a man. Very well. If he is a man, he must have blood in his veins. That would be, anyway, good to drink."

"No," returned Dubosc. "It would be hot. Also it would be salt. For food—perhaps. But we do not need food."

"Kill the animal then, and throw him over."

"We gain nothing."

"Well, sacred name, what do you want?"

"To beat him!" cried the doctor, curiously agitated. "To beat him at the game—that's what I want! For our own sakes, for our racial pride, we must, we must. To outlast him, to prove ourselves his masters. By better brain, by better organization and control. Watch him, watch him, friends—that we may ensnare him, that we may detect and defeat him in the end!"

But the doctor was miles beyond them.

"Watch?" growled The Parrot. "I believe you, old windbag. It is all one watch. I sleep no more and leave any man alone with that bottle."

To this the issue finally sharpened. Such craving among such men could not be stayed much longer by driblets. They watched. They watched the Canaque. They watched each other. And they watched the falling level in their flask—until the tension gave.

Another dawn upon the same dead calm, rising like a conflagration through the puddled air, cloudless, hopeless! Another day of blinding, slow-drawn agony to meet. And Dubosc announced that their allowance must be cut to half the thimbleful.

There remained perhaps a quarter of a liter—a miserable reprieve of bare life among the three of them, but one good swallow for a yearning throat.

At sight of the bottle, at the tinkle of its limpid content, so cool and silvery green inside the glass, Fenayrou's nerve snapped.

"More!" he begged, with pleading hands. "I die. More!"

When the doctor refused him, he groveled among the reeds, then rose suddenly to his knees and tossed his arms abroad with a hoarse cry.

"A ship! A ship!"

The others span about. They saw the thin, unbroken ring of this greater and more terrible prison to which they had exchanged; and that was all they saw, though they stared and stared. They turned back to Fenayrou and found him in the act of tilting the bottle. A cunning slash of his knife had loosed it from its sling at the doctor's side. . . . Even now he was sucking at the mouth, spilling the precious liquid——

With one sweep Perroquet caught up their paddle and flattened him, crushed him.

Springing across the prostrate man, Dubosc snatched the flask upright and put the width of the raft between himself and the big garroter who stood wide-legged, his bloodshot eyes alight, rumbling in his chest.

"There is no ship," said The Parrot. "There will be no ship. We are done. Because of you and your rotten promises that have brought us here—doctor, liar, ass!"

Dubosc stood firm.

"Come a step nearer and I break bottle and all over your head."

They stood regarding each other, and Perroquet's brows gathered in a slow effort of thought.

"Consider," urged Dubosc with his quaint touch of pedantry. "Why should you and I fight? We are rational men. We can see this trouble through and win yet. Such weather cannot last forever. Besides, here are only two of us to divide the water now."

"That is true," nodded The Parrot. "That is true, isn't it? Fenayrou kindly leaves us his share. An inheritance—what? A famous idea. I'll take mine now."

Dubosc probed him keenly.

"My share at once, if you please," insisted Perroquet, with heavy docility. "Afterwards we shall see. Afterwards."

The doctor smiled his grim and wan little smile.

"So be it."

Without relinquishing the flask, he brought out his canvas wallet once more—that wallet which replaced the professional black bag—and rolled out the thimble by some swift sleight of his flexible fingers while he held Perroquet's glance with his own.

"I will measure it for you."

He poured the thimbleful and handed it over quickly, and when Perroquet had tossed it off he filled again and again.

"Four—five," he counted. "That is enough."

But The Parrot's big grip closed quietly around his wrist at the last offering and pinioned him and held him helpless.

"No, it is not enough. Now I will take the rest. Ha, wise man! Have I fooled you at last?"

There was no chance to struggle and Dubosc did not try, only stayed smiling up at him, waiting.

Perroquet took the bottle.

"The best man wins," he remarked. "Eh, my zig? A bright notion of yours. The—best——"

His lips moved, but no sound issued. A look of the most intense surprise spread upon his round face. He stood swaying a moment, and collapsed like a huge hinged toy when the string is cut.

Dubosc stooped and caught the bottle again, looking down at his big adversary, who sprawled in a brief con-

vulsion and lay still, a bluish scum oozing between his
teeth. . . .

"Yes, the best man wins," repeated the doctor, and
laughed as he in turn raised the flask for a draft.

"The best man wins!" echoed a voice in his ear.

Fenayrou, writhing up and striking like a wounded
snake, drove the knife home between his shoulders.

The bottle fell and rolled to the middle of the platform, and there, while each strove vainly to reach it, it
poured out its treasure in a tiny stream that trickled away
and was lost.

It may have been minutes or hours later—for time has
no count in emptiness—when next a sound proceeded
from that frail slip of a raft, hung like a mote between sea
and sky. It was a phrase of song, a wandering strain in
half tones and fluted accidentals, not unmelodious. The
black Canaque was singing. He sang without emotion
or effort, quite casually and softly to himself. So he
might sing by his forest hut to ease some hour of idle-
ness. Clasping his knees and gazing out into space,
untroubled, unmoved, enigmatic to the end, he sang—
he sang.

And, after all, the ship came.

She came in a manner befitting the sauciest little tops'l
schooner between Nukahiva and the Pelews—as her
owner often averred and none but the envious denied—
in a manner worthy too of that able Captain Jean Guil-
bert, the merriest little scamp that ever cleaned a pearl
bank or snapped a cargo of labor from a scowling coast.
Before the first whiff out of the west came the *Petite
Suzanne*, curtsying and skipping along with a flash of
white frill by her forefoot, and brought up startled and
stood shaking her skirts and keeping herself quite daintily
to windward.

"And 'ere they are sure enough, by dam!" said the
polyglot Captain Jean in the language of commerce and
profanity. "Zose passengers for us, hey? They been here

all the time, not ten mile off—I bet you, Marteau. Ain't it 'ell? What you zink, by gar?"

His second, a tall and excessively bony individual of gloomy outlook, handed back the glasses.

"More bad luck. I never approved this job. And now—see—we have had our voyage for nothing. What misfortune!"

"Marteau, if that good Saint Pierre gives you some day a gold 'arp, still you would holler bad luck—bad job!" retorted Captain Jean. "Do I 'ire you to stand zere and cry about ze luck? Get a boat over, and quicker zan zat!"

M. Marteau aroused himself sufficiently to take command of the boat's crew that presently dropped away to investigate. . . .

"It is even as I thought," he called up from the quarter when he returned with his report. "I told you how it would be, Captain Jean."

"Hey?" Captain Jean cried, bouncing at the rail. "Have you got those passengers yet, *enfant de salaud?*"

"I have not," said Marteau in the tone of lugubrious triumph. There was nothing in the world that could have pleased him quite so much as this chance to prove Captain Jean the loser on a venture. "We are too late. Bad luck, bad luck—that calm. What misfortune! They are all dead!"

"Will you mind your business?" shouted the skipper.

"But still the gentlemen are dead——"

"What is zat to me? All ze better, they will cost nozing to feed."

"But how——"

"Hogsheads, my gar," said Captain Jean paternally. "Zose hogsheads in the afterhold. Fill them nicely with brine, and zere we are!" And after having drawn all possible satisfaction from the other's amazement, he sprang the nub of his joke with a grin. "Ze gentlemen's passage is all paid, Marteau. Before we left Sydney, Marteau. I contrac' to bring back three escape' convicts and so by 'ell I do—in pickle! And now if you'll kindly get zose passengers aboard like I said and bozzer less about ze goddam luck, I be much oblige'. Also, zere is no green on my eye, Marteau, and you can dam well smoke it!"

Marteau recovered himself with difficulty in time to recall another trifling detail. "There is a fourth man on board that raft, Captain Jean. He is a Canaque—still alive. What shall we do with him?"

"A Canaque?" snapped Captain Jean. "A Canaque! I had no word in my contrac' about any Canaque. . . . Leave him zere. . . . He is only a dam nigger. He'll do well enough where he is."

And Captain Jean was right, perfectly right, for while the *Petite Suzanne* was taking aboard her grisly cargo the wind freshened from the west, and just about the time she was shaping away for Australia the "dam nigger" spread his own sail of pandanus leaves and twirled his own helm of niaouli wood and headed the catamaran eastward, back toward New Caledonia.

Feeling somewhat dry after his exertions, he plucked at random from the platform a hollow reed with a sharp end and, stretching himself at full length in his accustomed place at the stern, he thrust the reed down into one of the bladders underneath and drank his fill of the sweet water. . . .

He had a dozen such storage bladders remaining, built into floats at intervals above the water line—quite enough to last him safely home again.

The Man Who Saw through Heaven

By WILBUR DANIEL STEELE

PEOPLE have wondered (there being obviously no question of romance involved) how I could ever have allowed myself to be let in for the East African adventure of Mrs. Diana in search of her husband. There were several reasons. To begin with, the time and effort and money weren't mine; they were the property of the wheel of which I was but a cog, the Society through which Diana's life had been insured, along with the rest of that job lot of missionaries. The "letting in" was the firm's. In the second place, the wonderers have not counted on Mrs. Diana's capacity for getting things done for her. Meek and helpless. Yes, but God was on her side. Too meek, too helpless to move mountains herself, if those who happened to be handy didn't move them for her then her God would know the reason why. Having dedicated her all to making straight the Way, why should her neighbor cavil at giving a little? The writer for one, a colonial governor-general for another, railway magnates, insurance managers, *safari* leaders, the ostrich farmer of Ndua, all these and a dozen others in their turns have felt the hundred-ton weight of her thin-lipped meekness—have seen her in metaphor sitting grimly on the doorsteps of their souls.

A third reason lay in my own troubled conscience. Though I did it in innocence, I can never forget that it was I who personally conducted Diana's party to the Observatory on that fatal night in Boston before it sailed. Had it not been for that kindly intentioned "hunch" of mine, the astonished eye of the Reverend Hubert Diana would never have gazed through the floor of Heaven, and he would never have undertaken to measure the Infinite with the foot rule of his mind.

It all started so simply. My boss at the shipping-and-insurance office gave me the word in the morning. "Bunch of missionaries for the *Platonic* tomorrow. They're on our hands in a way. Show 'em the town." It wasn't so easy when you think of it: one male and seven females on their way to the heathen; though it was easier in Boston than it might have been in some other towns. The evening looked the simplest. My friend Krum was at the Observatory that semester; there at least I was sure their sensibilities would come to no harm.

On the way out in the street car, seated opposite to Diana and having to make conversation, I talked of Krum and of what I knew of his work with the spiral nebulæ. Having to appear to listen, Diana did so (as all day long) with a vaguely indulgent smile. He really hadn't time for me. That night his life was exalted as it had never been, and would perhaps never be again. Tomorrow's sailing, the actual fact of leaving all to follow Him, held his imagination in thrall. Moreover, he was a bridegroom of three days with his bride beside him, his nerves at once assuaged and thrilled. No, but more. As if a bride were not enough, arrived in Boston, he had found himself surrounded by a very galaxy of womanhood gathered from the four corners; already within hours one felt the chaste tentacles of their feminine dependence curling about the party's unique man; already their contacts with the world of their new lives began to be made through him; already they saw in part through his eyes. I wonder what he would have said if I had told him he was a little drunk.

In the course of the day I think I had got him fairly well. As concerned his Church he was at once an asset and a liability. He believed its dogma as few still did, with a simplicity, "the old-time religion." He was born that kind. Of the stuff of the fanatic, the reason he was not a fanatic was that, curiously impervious to little questionings, he had never been aware that his faith was anywhere attacked. A self-educated man, he had accepted the necessary smattering facts of science with a serene indulgence, as simply so much further proof of what the Creator could do when He put His Hand to it. Nor was he conscious of any conflict between these facts and the fact that there existed a substantial Heaven, geographically up, and a substantial Hot Place, geographically down.

So, for his Church, he was an asset in these days. And so, and for the same reason, he was a liability. The Church must after all keep abreast of the times. For home consumption, with modern congregations, especially urban ones, a certain streak of "healthy" scepticism is no longer amiss in the pulpit; it makes people who read at all more comfortable in their pews. A man like Hubert Diana is more for the cause than a hundred. But what to do with him? Well, such things arrange themselves. There's the Foreign Field. The blacker the heathen the whiter the light they'll want, and the solider the conception of a God the Father enthroned in a Heaven of which the sky above them is the visible floor.

And that, at bottom, was what Hubert Diana believed. Accept as he would with the top of his brain the fact of a spherical earth zooming through space, deep in his heart he knew that the world lay flat from modern Illinois to ancient Palestine, and that the sky above it, blue by day and by night festooned with guiding stars for wise men, was the nether side of a floor on which the resurrected trod.

I shall never forget the expression of his face when he realized he was looking straight through it that night. In the quiet dark of the dome I saw him remove his eye from the eyepiece of the telescope up there on the staging and turn it, in the ray of a hooded bulb, on the demon's keeper, Krum.

"What's that, Mr. Krum? I didn't get you!"

"I say, that particular cluster you're looking at——"

"This star, you mean?"

"You'd have to count awhile to count the stars describing their orbits in that 'star,' Mr. Diana. But what I was saying—have you ever had the wish I used to have as a boy—that you could actually look back into the past? With your own two eyes?"

Diana spoke slowly. He didn't know it, but it had already begun to happen; he was already caught. "I have often wished, Mr. Krum, that I might actually look back into the time of our Lord. Actually. Yes."

Krum grunted. He was young. "We'd have to pick a nearer neighbor than *Messier* 79 then. The event you see when you put your eye to that lens is happening much too far in the past. The lightwaves thrown off by that particular cluster on the day, say, of the Crucifixion—*you* won't live to see them. They've hardly started yet—a mere twenty centuries on their way—leaving them something like eight hundred and thirty centuries yet to come before they reach the earth."

Diana laughed the queerest catch of a laugh. "And—and there—there won't be any earth here, then, to welcome them."

"*What?*" It was Krum's turn to look startled. So for a moment the two faces remained in confrontation, the one, as I say, startled, the other exuding visibly little sea-green globules of sweat. It was Diana that caved in first, his voice hardly louder than a whisper.

"W-w-will there?"

None of us suspected the enormousness of the thing that had happened in Diana's brain. Krum shrugged his shoulders and snapped his fingers. Deliberately. *Snap!* "What's a thousand centuries or so in the cosmic reckoning?" He chuckled. "We're just beginning to get out among 'em with *Messier*, you know. In the print room, Mr. Diana, I can show you photographs of clusters to which, if you cared to go, traveling at the speed of light——"

The voice ran on; but Diana's eye had gone back to

the eyepiece, and his affrighted soul had re-entered the big black tube sticking its snout out of the slit in the iron hemisphere. . . . "At the speed of light!" . . . That unsuspected, that wildly chance-found chink in the armor of his philosophy! The body is resurrected and it ascends to Heaven instantaneously. At what speed must it be borne to reach instantaneously that city beyond the ceiling of the sky? At a speed inconceivable, mystical. At, say (as he had often said to himself), *the speed of light.* . . . And now, hunched there in the trap that had caught him, black rods, infernal levers and wheels, he was aware of his own eye passing vividly through unpartitioned emptiness, *eight hundred and fifty centuries at the speed of light!*

"And still beyond these," Krum was heard, "we begin to come into the regions of the spiral nebulæ. We've some interesting photographs in the print room, if you've the time."

The ladies below were tired of waiting. One had "lots of packing to do." The bride said, "Yes, I do think we should be getting along, Hubert, dear; if you're ready——"

The fellow actually jumped. It's lucky he didn't break anything. His face looked greener and dewier than ever amid the contraptions above. "If you—you and the ladies, Cora—wouldn't mind—if Mr.—Mr.—(he'd mislaid my name) would see you back to the hotel——" Meeting silence, he began to expostulate. "I feel that this is a rich experience. I'll follow shortly; I know the way."

In the car going back into the city Mrs. Diana set at rest the flutterings of six hearts. Being unmarried they couldn't understand men as she did. When I think of that face of hers, to which I was destined to grow only too accustomed in the weary, itchy days of the trek into Kavirondoland, with its slightly tilted nose, its irregular pigmentation, its easily inflamed lids, and long moist cheeks, like those of a hunting dog, glorying in weariness, it seems incredible that a light of coyness could have found lodgment there. But that night it did. She sat serene among her virgins.

"You don't know Bert. You wait; he'll get a perfectly wonderful sermon out of all that tonight, Bert will."

Krum was having a grand time with his neophyte. He would have stayed up all night. Immured in the little print room crowded with files and redolent of acids, he conducted his disciple "glassy-eyed" through the dim frontiers of space, holding before him one after another the likenesses of universes sister to our own, islanded in immeasurable vacancy, curled like glimmering crullers on their private Milky Ways, and hiding in their wombs their myriad "coal-pockets," star-dust fœtuses of which—their quadrillion years accomplished—their litters of new suns would be born, to bear their planets, to bear their moons in turn.

"And beyond these?"

Always, after each new feat of distance, it was the same. "And beyond?" Given an ell, Diana surrendered to a pop-eyed lust for nothing less than light-years. "And still beyond?"

"Who knows?"

"The mind quits. For if there's no end to these nebulæ——"

"But supposing there is?"

"An end? But, Mr. Krum, in the very idea of an ending——"

"An end to what we might call this particular category of magnitudes. Eh?"

"I don't get that."

"Well, take this—take the opal in your ring there. The numbers and distances inside that stone may conceivably be to themselves as staggering as ours to us in our own system. Come! that's not so far-fetched. What are we learning about the structure of the atom? A nucleus (call it a sun) revolved about in eternal orbits by electrons (call them planets, worlds). Infinitesimal; but after all what are bigness and littleness but matters of comparison?

To eyes on one of those electrons (don't be too sure there aren't any) its tutelary sun may flame its way across a heaven a comparative ninety million miles away. Impossible for them to conceive of a boundary to their billions of atomic systems, molecular universes. In that category of magnitudes its diameter is infinity; once it has made the leap into our category and become an opal it is merely a quarter of an inch. That's right, Mr. Diana, you may well stare at it: between *now* and *now* ten thousand histories may have come and gone down there. . . . And just so the diameter of our own cluster of universes, going over into another category, may be——"

"May be a—a ring—a little stone—in a—a—a—ring."

Krum was tickled by the way the man's imagination jumped and engulfed it.

"Why not? That's as good a guess as the next. A ring, let's say, worn carelessly on the—well, say the tentacle—of some vast organism—some inchoate creature hobnobbing with its cloudy kind in another system of universes—which in turn——"

It is curious that none of them realized next day that they were dealing with a stranger, a changed man. Why he carried on, why he capped that night of cosmic debauch by shaving, eating an unremarkable breakfast, packing his terrestrial toothbrush and collars, and going up the gangplank in tow of his excited convoy to sail away, is beyond explanation—unless it was simply that he was in a daze.

It wasn't until four years later that I was allowed to know what had happened on that ship, and even then the tale was so disjointed, warped, and opinionated, so darkly seen in the mirror of Mrs. Diana's orthodoxy, that I had almost to guess what it was *really* all about.

"When Hubert turned irreligious . . ." That phrase, recurrent on her tongue in the meanderings of the East African quest to which we were by then committed, will serve to measure her understanding. Irreligious! Good Lord! But from that sort of thing I had to reconstruct the drama. Evening after evening beside her camp fire (appended to the Mineral Survey Expedition Toward Uganda through the kindness—actually the worn-down surrender—of the Protectorate government) I lingered a while before joining the merrier engineers, watched with fascination the bumps growing under the mosquitoes on her forehead, and listened to the jargon of her mortified meekness and her scandalized faith.

There had been a fatal circumstance, it seems, at the very outset. If Diana could but have been seasick, as the rest of them were (horribly), all might still have been well. In the misery of desired death, along with the other contents of a heaving midriff, he might have brought up the assorted universes of which he had been led too rashly to partake. But he wasn't. As if his wife's theory was right, as if Satan was looking out for him, he was spared to prowl the swooping decks immune. Four days and nights alone. Time enough to digest and assimilate into his being beyond remedy that lump of whirling magnitudes and to feel himself surrendering with a strange new ectasy to the drunkenness of liberty.

Such liberty! Given Diana's type, it is hard to imagine it adequately. The abrupt, complete removal of the toils of reward and punishment; the withdrawal of the surveillance of an all-seeing, all-knowing Eye; the windy assurance of being responsible for nothing, important to no one, no longer (as the police say) "wanted"! It must have been beautiful in those few days of its first purity, before it began to be discolored by his contemptuous pity for others, the mask of his inevitable loneliness and his growing fright.

The first any of them knew of it—even his wife—was in mid-voyage, the day the sea went down and the seven who had been sick came up. There seemed an especial Providence in the calming of the waters; it was Sunday morning and Diana had been asked to conduct the services.

He preached on the text: "For of such is the kingdom of Heaven."

"If our concept of God means anything it means a God *all*-mighty, Creator of *all* that exists, Director of the *infinite*, cherishing in His Heaven the saved souls of *all space and all time*."

Of course; amen. And wasn't it nice to feel like humans again, and real sunshine pouring up through the lounge ports from an ocean suddenly grown kind? . . . But—then—*what* was Diana *saying*?

Mrs. Diana couldn't tell about it coherently even after a lapse of fifty months. Even in a setting as remote from that steamer's lounge as the equatorial bush, the ember-reddened canopy of thorn trees, the meandering camp fires, the chant and tramp somewhere away of Kikuyu porters dancing in honor of an especial largesse of fat zebra meat—even here her memory of that impious outburst was too vivid, too aghast.

"It was Hubert's look! The way he stared at us! As if you'd said he was licking his chops! . . . That '*Heaven*' of his!"

It seems they hadn't waked up to what he was about until he had the dimensions of his sardonic Paradise irreparably drawn in. The final haven of all right souls. Not alone the souls released from this our own tiny earth. In the millions of solar systems we see as stars how many millions of satellites must there be upon which at some time in their histories conditions suited to organic life subsist? Uncounted hordes of wheeling populations! Of men? God's creatures at all events, a portion of them reasoning. Weirdly shaped perhaps, but what of that? And that's only to speak of our own inconsiderable cluster of universes. That's to say nothing of other systems of magnitudes, where God's creatures are to our world what we are to the worlds in the atoms in our finger rings. (He had shaken *his*, here, in their astounded faces.) And all these, all the generations of these enormous and microscopic beings harvested through a time beside which the life span of our earth is as a second in a million centuries: all these brought to rest for an eternity to which time itself is a watch tick—all crowded to rest pellmell, thronged, serried, packed, packed to suffocation in layers unnumbered light-years deep. This must needs be our concept of Heaven if God is the God of the Whole. If, on the other hand——

The other hand was the hand of the second officer, the captain's delegate at divine worship that Sabbath day. He at last had "come to."

I don't know whether it was the same day or the next; Mrs. Diana was too vague. But here's the picture. Seven women huddled in the large stateroom on B-deck, conferring in whispers, aghast, searching one another's eye obliquely even as they bowed their heads in prayer for some light—and of a sudden the putting back of the door and the in-marching of the Reverend Hubert. . . .

As Mrs. Diana tried to tell me, "You understand, don't you, he had just taken a bath? And he hadn't—he had forgotten to——"

Adam-innocent there he stood. Not a stitch. But I don't believe for a minute it was a matter of forgetting. In the high intoxication of his soul release, already crossed (by the second officer) and beginning to show his zealot claws, he needed some gesture stunning enough to witness to his separation, his unique rightness, his contempt of match-flare civilizations and infinitesimal taboos.

But I can imagine that stateroom scene: the gasps, the heads colliding in aversion, and Diana's six weedy feet of birthday suit towering in the shadows, and ready to sink through the deck I'll warrant, now the act was irrevocable, but still grimly carrying it off.

"And if, on the other hand, you ask me to bow down before a God peculiar to this one earth, this one grain of dust lost among the giants of space, watching its sparrows fall, profoundly interested in a speck called Palestine no

ing the tongue. I was a bit nonplussed, to put it mildly, when I discovered what he was up to."

What things Diana had been up to the Major showed us in one of the huts in the native kraal—a round dozen of them, modeled in mud and baked. Blackened blobs of mud, that's all. Likenesses of nothing under the sun, fortuitous masses sprouting haphazard tentacles, only two among them showing postules that might have been experimental heads. . . . The ostrich farmer saw our faces.

"Rum, eh? O course I realized the chap was anything but fit. A walking skeleton. Nevertheless, whatever it is about these beasties, there's not a nigger in the village has dared set foot inside this hut since Diana left. You can see for yourselves it's about to crash. There's another like it he left at Suki, above here. Taboo, no end!"

So Diana's "hunch" had been right. He had found his virgin field, indeed, fit soil for his cosmic fright. A religion in the making, here before our eyes.

"This was at the very last before he left," Wyeside explained. "He took to making these mud pies quite of a sudden; the whole lot within a fortnight's time. Before that he had simply talked, harangued. He would sit here in the doorway of an evening with the niggers squatted around and harangue 'em by the hour. I knew something of it through my house-boys. The most amazing rot. All about the stars to begin with, as if these black baboons could half grasp *astronomy!* But that seemed all proper. Then there was talk about a something a hundred times as big and powerful as the world, sun, moon, and stars put together—some perfectly enormous stupendous awful being—but knowing how mixed the boys can get, it still seemed all regular—simply the parson's way of getting at the notion of an Almighty God. But no, they insisted, there wasn't any God. That's the point, they said; there *is no* God. . . . Well, that impressed me as a go. That's when I decided to come down and get the rights of this star-swallowing monstrosity the beggar was feeding my labor on. And here he sat in the doorway with one of these beasties—here it is, this one—waving it furiously in the niggers' benighted faces. And do you know what he'd done?—you can see the mark here still on this wabble-leg, this tentacle-business—he had taken off a ring he had and screwed it on just here. His finger ring, my word of honor! And still, if you'll believe it, I didn't realize he was just daft. Not until he spoke to me. 'I find,' he was good enough to enlighten me, 'I find I have to make it somehow concrete.' . . . 'Make what?' . . . 'Our wearer.' 'Our *what, where?*' . . . 'In the following category.' . . . His actual words, honor bright. I was going to have him sent down-country where he could be looked after. He got ahead of me though. He cleared out. When I heard he'd turned up at Suki I ought, I suppose, to have attended to it. But I was having trouble with leopards. And you know how things go."

From there we went to Suki, the Major accompanying. It was as like Ndua as one flea to its brother, a stockade inclosing round houses of mud, wattles, and thatch, and full of naked heathen. The Kavirondo are the nakedest of all African peoples and, it is said, the most moral. It put a great strain on Mrs. Diana; all that whole difficult anxious time, as it were detachedly, I could see her itching to get them into Mother Hubbard and cast-off Iowa pants.

Here too, as the Major had promised, we found a holy of holies, rather a dreadful of dreadfuls, "taboo no end," its shadows cluttered with the hurlothrumbos of Diana's artistry. What puzzled me was their number. Why this appetite for experimentation? There was an uncertainty; one would think its effect on potential converts would be bad. Here, as in Ndua, Diana had contented himself at first with words and skyward gesticulations. Not for so long however. Feeling the need of giving his concept of the cosmic "wearer" a substance much earlier, he had shut himself in with the work, literally—a fever of creation. We counted seventeen of the nameless "blobs," all done, we were told, in the seven days and nights before their maker had again cleared out. The villagers would hardly speak of him; only after spitting to protect themselves, their eyes averted, and in an undertone, would they mention him: "He of the Ring." Thereafter we were to hear of him only as "He of the Ring."

Leaving Suki, Major Wyeside turned us over (thankfully, I warrant) to a native who told us his name was Charlie Kamba. He had spent some years in Nairobi, running for an Indian outfitter, and spoke English remarkably well. It was from him we learned, quite casually, when our modest eight-load *safari* was some miles on its way, that the primary object of our coming was nonexistent. Hubert Diana was dead.

Dead nearly five weeks—a moon and a little—and buried in the mission church at Tara Hill.

Mission church! There was a poser for us. *Mission church?*

Well then, Charlie Kamba gave us to know that he was paraphrasing in a large way suitable to our habits of thought. We wouldn't have understood *his* informant's "wizard house" or "house of the effigy."

I will say for Mrs. Diana that in the course of our halt of lugubrious amazement she shed tears. That some of them were not tears of unrealized relief it would be hardly natural to believe. She had desired loyally to find her husband, but when she should have found him—what? This problem, sturdily ignored so long, was now removed.

Turn back? Never! Now it would seem the necessity for pressing forward was doubled. In the scrub-fringed ravine of our halt the porters resumed their loads, the dust stood up again, the same caravan moved on. But how far it was now from being the same.

From that moment it took on, for me at least, a new character. It wasn't the news especially; the fact that Diana was dead had little to do with it. Perhaps it was simply that the new sense of something aimfully and cumulatively dramatic in our progress had to have a beginning, and that moment would do as well as the next.

Six villages: M'nann, Leika, Leikapo, Shamba, Little

Tara, and Tara, culminating in the apotheosis of Tara Hill. Six stops for the night on the road it had cost Diana as many months to cover in his singular pilgrimage to his inevitable goal. Or in his flight to it. Yes, his stampede. Now the pipers at that four-day orgy of liberty on the *Platonic's* decks were at his heels for their pay. Now that his strength was failing, the hosts of loneliness were after him, creeping out of their dreadful magnitudes, the hounds of space. Over all that ground it seemed to me we were following him not by the word of hearsay but, as one follows a wounded animal making for its earth, by the droppings of his blood.

Our progress had taken on a pattern; it built itself with a dramatic artistry; it gathered suspense. As though it were a story at its most breathless places "continued in our next," and I a reader forgetting the road's weariness, the dust, the torment of insects never escaped, the inadequate food, I found myself hardly able to keep from running on ahead to reach the evening's village, to search out the inevitable repository of images left by the white stranger who had come and tarried there awhile and gone again.

More concrete and ever more concrete. The immemorial compromise with the human hunger for a symbol to see with the eyes, touch with the hands. Hierarchy after hierarchy of little mud effigies—one could see the necessity pushing the man. Out of the protoplasmic blobs of Ndua, Suki, even M'nann, at Leikapo Diana's concept of infinity (so pure in that halcyon epoch at sea), of categories nested within categories like Japanese boxes, of an over-creature wearing our cosmos like a trinket, unawares, had become a mass with legs to stand on and a real head. The shards scattered about in the filth of the hut there (as if in violence of despair) were still monstrosities, but with a sudden stride of concession their monstrousness was the monstrousness of lizard and turtle and crocodile. At Shamba there were dozens of huge-footed birds.

It is hard to be sure in retrospect, but I do believe that

by the time we reached Little Tara I began to see the
thing as a whole—the fœtus, working out slowly, blindly,
but surely, its evolution in the womb of fright. At Little
Tara there was a change in the character of the exhibits;
their numbers had diminished, their size had grown. There
was a boar with tusks and a bull the size of a dog with
horns, and on a tusk and on a horn an indentation left by
a ring.

I don't believe Mrs. Diana got the thing at all. Toward
the last she wasn't interested in the huts of relics; at Little
Tara she wouldn't go near the place; she was "too tired."
It must have been pretty awful, when you think of it,
even if all she saw in them was the mud-pie play of a
man reverted to a child.

There was another thing at Little Tara quite as mo-
mentous as the jump to boar and bull. Here at last a mask
had been thrown aside. Here there had been no pretense
of proselyting, no astronomical lectures, no doorway
harangues. Straightway he had arrived (a fabulous figure
already, long heralded), he had commandeered a house
and shut himself up in it and there, mysterious, assiduous,
he had remained three days and nights, eating nothing,
but drinking gallons of the foul water they left in gourds
outside his curtain of reeds. No one in the village had
ever seen what he had done and left there. Now, candidly,
those labors were for himself alone.

Here at last in Tara the moment of that confession had
overtaken the fugitive. It was he, ill with fever and dying
of nostalgia—not these naked black baboon men seen now
as little more than blurs—who had to give the Beast of
the Infinite a name and a shape. And more and more, not
only a shape, but a *shapeliness*. From the instant when, no
longer able to live alone with nothingness, he had given it
a likeness in Ndua mud, and perceived that it was intolerable and fled its face, the turtles and distorted crocodiles
of Leikapo and the birds of Shamba had become inevitable, and no less inevitable the Little Tara boar and
bull. Another thing grows plain in retrospect: the reason

why, done to death (as all the way they reported him) he couldn't die. He didn't dare to. Didn't dare to close his eyes.

It was at Little Tara we first heard of him as "Father Witch," a name come back, we were told, from Tara, where he had gone. I had heard it pronounced several times before it suddenly obtruded from the native context as actually two English words. That was what made it queer. It was something they must have picked up by rote, uncomprehending; something then they could have had from no lips but his own. When I repeated it after them with a better accent they pointed up toward the north, saying "Tara! Tara!"—their eagerness mingled with awe.

I shall never forget Tara as we saw it, after our last blistering scramble up a gorge, situated in the clear air on a slope belted with cedars. A mid-African stockade left by some blunder in an honest Colorado landscape, or a newer and bigger Vermont. Here at the top of our journey, black savages, their untidy *shambas*, the very Equator, all these seemed as incongruous as a Gothic cathedral in a Congo marsh. I wonder if Hubert Diana knew whither his Instinct was guiding him on the long road of his journey here to die. . . .

He had died and he was buried, not in the village, but about half a mile distant, on the ridge; this we were given to know almost before we had arrived. There was no need to announce ourselves, the word of our coming had outrun us; the populace was at the gates.

"Our Father Witch! Our Father Witch!" They knew what we were after; the funny parrot-wise English stood out from the clack and clatter of their excited speech. "Our Father Witch! Ay! Ay!" With a common eagerness they gesticulated at the hilltop beyond the cedars.

Certainly here was a change. No longer the propitiatory spitting, the averted eyes, the uneasy whispering allusion to him who had passed that way: here in Tara they would shout him from the housetops, with a kind of civic pride.

We learned the reason for this on our way up the hill. It was because they were his chosen, the initiate.

We made the ascent immediately, against the village's advice. It was near evening; the return would be in the dark; it was a bad country for goblins; wouldn't tomorrow morning do? . . . No, it wouldn't do the widow. Her face was set. . . . And so, since we were resolved to go, the village went with us, armed with rattles and drums. Charlie Kamba walked beside us, sifting the information a hundred were eager to give.

These people were proud, he said, because their wizard was more powerful than all the wizards of all the other villages "in the everywhere together." If he cared to he could easily knock down all the other villages in the "everywhere," destroying all the people and all the cattle. If he cared to he could open his mouth and swallow the sky and the stars. But Tara he had chosen. Tara he would protect. He made their mealies to grow and their cattle to multiply.

I protested, "But he is *dead* now!"

Charlie Kamba made signs of deprecation. I discerned that he was far from being clear about the thing himself.

Yes, he temporized, this Father Witch was dead, quite dead. On the other hand he was up there. On the other hand he would never die. He was longer than forever. Yes, quite true, he was dead and buried under the pot.

I gave it up. "How did he die?"

Well, he came to this village of Tara very suffering, very sick. The dead man who walked. His face was very sad. Very eaten. Very frightened. He came to this hill. So he lived here for two full moons, very hot, very eaten, very dead. These men made him a house as he commanded them, also a stockade. In the house he was very quiet, very dead, making magic two full moons. Then he came out and they that were waiting saw him. He had made the magic, and the magic had made him well. His face was kind. He was happy. He was full fed. He was full fed, these men said, without any eating. Yes, they carried up to him very fine food, because they were full of wonder and some fear, but he did not eat any of it. Some water he drank. So, for two days and the night between them, he continued sitting in the gate of the stockade, very happy, very full fed. He told these people very much about their wizard, who is bigger than everywhere and longer than forever and can, if he cares to, swallow the sky and stars. From time to time however, ceasing to talk to these people, he got to his knees and talked in his own strange tongue to Our Father Witch, his eyes held shut. When he had done this just at sunset of the second day he fell forward on his face. So he remained that night. The next day these men took him into the house and buried him under the pot. On the other hand Our Father Witch is longer than forever. He remains there still. . . .

The first thing I saw in the hut's interior was the earthen pot at the northern end, wrong-side-up on the ground. I was glad I had preceded Mrs. Diana. I walked across and sat down on it carelessly, hoping so that her afflicted curiosity might be led astray. It gave me the oddest feeling, though, to think of what was there beneath my nonchalant sitting-portion—aware as I was of the Kavirondo burial of a great man—up to the neck in mother earth, and the rest of him left out in the dark of the pot for the undertakings of the ants. I hoped his widow wouldn't wonder about that inverted vessel of clay.

I needn't have worried. Her attention was arrested otherwheres. I shall not forget the look of her face, caught above me in the red shaft of sundown entering the western door, as she gazed at the last and the largest of the Reverend Hubert Diana's gods. That long, long cheek of hers, buffeted by sorrow, startled now and mortified. Not till that moment, I believe, had she comprehended the steps of mud-images she had been following for what they were, the steps of idolatry.

For my part, I wasn't startled. Even before we started up the hill, knowing that her husband had dared to die here, I could have told her pretty much what she would find.

This overlord of the cosmic categories that he had fashioned (at last) in his own image sat at the other end of the red-streaked house upon a bench—a throne?—of mud. Diana had been no artist .An ovoid two-eyed head, a cylindrical trunk, two arms, two legs, that's all. But indubitably man, man-sized. Only one finger of one of the hands had been done with much care. It wore an opal, a two-dollar stone from Mexico, set in a silver ring. This was the hand that was lifted, and over it the head was bent.

I've said Diana was no artist. I'll take back the words. The figure was crudeness itself, but in the relation between that bent head and that lifted hand there was something which was something else. A sense of scrutiny one would have said no genius of mud could ever have conveyed. An attitude of interest centered in that bauble, intense and static, breathless and eternal all in one—penetrating to its bottom atom, to the last electron, to a hill upon it, and to a two-legged mite about to die. Marking (yes, I'll swear to the incredible) the sparrow's fall.

The magic was made. The road that had commenced with the blobs of Ndua—the same that commenced with our hairy ancestors listening to the night-wind in their caves—was run.

And from here Diana, of a sudden happy, of a sudden looked after, "full fed," had walked out——

But no; I couldn't stand that mortified sorrow on the widow's face any longer. She had to be made to see what she wanted to see. I said it aloud:

"From here, Mrs. Diana, your husband walked out——"

"He had sunk to idolatry. *Idolatry!*"

"To the bottom, yes. And come up its whole history again. And from here he walked out into the sunshine to kneel and talk with 'Our Father Which——' "

She got it. She caught it. I wish you could have seen the light going up those long, long cheeks as she got it:

"Our Father which art in Heaven, Hallowed be Thy Name!"

We went down hill in the darkness, protected against goblins by a vast rattling of gourds and beating of goat-hide drums.

The Open Boat

By STEPHEN CRANE

NONE OF them knew the color of the sky. Their eyes glanced level, and were fastened upon the waves that swept toward them. These waves were of the hue of slate, save for the tops, which were of foaming white, and all of the men knew the colors of the sea. The horizon narrowed and widened, and dipped and rose, and at all times its edge was jagged with waves that seemed thrust up in points like rocks. Many a man ought to have a bath-tub larger than the boat which here rode upon the sea. These waves were most wrongfully and barbarously abrupt and tall, and each froth top was a problem in small boat navigation.

The cook squatted in the bottom and looked with both eyes at the six inches of gunwhale which separated him from the ocean. His sleeves were rolled over his fat fore-arms, and two flaps of his unbuttoned vest dangled as he bent to bail out the boat. Often he said: "Gawd! That was a narrow clip." As he remarked it he invariably gazed eastward over the broken sea.

The oiler, steering with one of the two oars in the boat, sometimes raised himself suddenly to keep clear of water that swirled in over the stern. It was a thin little oar and it seemed often ready to snap.

The correspondent, pulling at the other oar, watched the waves and wondered why he was there.

The injured captain, lying in the bow, was at this time buried in that profound dejection and indifference which comes, temporarily at least, to even the bravest and most enduring when, willy-nilly, the firm fails, the army loses, the ship goes down. The mind of the master of a vessel is rooted deep in the timbers of her, though he commanded for a day or a decade, and this captain had on him the stern impression of a scene in the grays of dawn of seven turned faces, and later a stump of a top mast with a white ball on it that slashed to and fro at the waves, went low and lower, and down. Thereafter there was something strange in his voice. Although steady, it was deep with mourning, and of a quality beyond oration or tears.

"Keep 'er a little more south, Billie," said he.

" 'A little more south,' sir," said the oiler in the stern.

A seat in this boat was not unlike a seat upon a bucking broncho, and by the same token, a broncho is not much smaller. The craft pranced and reared, and plunged like an animal. As each wave came, and she rose for it, she seemed like a horse making at a fence outrageously high. The manner of her scramble over these walls of water is a mystic thing, and, moreover, at the top of them were ordinarily these problems in white water, the foam racing down from the summit of each wave, requiring a new leap, and a leap from the air. Then, after scornfully bumping a crest, she would slide, and race, and splash down a long incline, and arrive bobbing and nodding in front of the next menace.

A singular disadvantage of the sea lies in the fact that after successfully surmounting one wave you discover that there is another behind it just as important and just as nervously anxious to do something effective in the way of swamping boats. In a ten-foot dingey one can get an idea of the resources of the sea in the line of waves that is not probable to the average experience which is never at sea in a dingey. As each slatey wall of water approached, it shut all else from the view of the men in the boat, and it was not difficult to imagine that this particular wave was the final outburst of the ocean, the last effort of the grim water. There was a terrible grace in the move of the waves, and they came in silence, save for the snarling of the crests.

In the wan light, the faces of the men must have been gray. Their eyes must have glinted in strange ways as they gazed steadily astern. Viewed from a balcony, the whole thing would doubtless have been weirdly picturesque. But the men in the boat had no time to see it, and if they had had leisure there were other things to occupy their minds. The sun swung steadily up the sky, and they knew it was broad day because the color of the sea changed from slate to emerald green, streaked with amber lights, and the foam was like tumbling snow. The process of the breaking day was unknown to them. They were aware only of this effect upon the color of the waves that rolled toward them.

In disjointed sentences the cook and the correspondent argued as to the difference between a life-saving station and a house of refuge. The cook had said: "There's a house of refuge just north of the Mosquito Inlet Light, and as soon as they see us, they'll come off in their boat and pick us up."

"As soon as who see us?" said the correspondent.

"The crew," said the cook.

"Houses of refuge don't have crews," said the correspondent. "As I understand them, they are only places where clothes and grub are stored for the benefit of shipwrecked people. They don't carry crews."

"Oh, yes, they do," said the cook.

"No, they don't," said the correspondent.

"Well, we're not there yet, anyhow," said the oiler, in the stern.

"Well," said the cook, "perhaps it's not a house of

refuge that I'm thinking of as being near Mosquito Inlet Light. Perhaps it's a life-saving station."

"We're not there yet," said the oiler, in the stern.

II

As the boat bounced from the top of each wave, the wind tore through the hair of the hatless men, and as the craft plopped her stern down again the spray splashed past them. The crest of each of these waves was a hill, from the top of which the men surveyed, for a moment, a broad tumultuous expanse, shining and wind-riven. It was probably splendid. It was probably glorious, this play of the free sea, wild with lights of emerald and white and amber.

"Bully good thing it's an on-shore wind," said the cook. "If not, where would we be? Wouldn't have a show."

"That's right," said the correspondent.

The busy oiler nodded his assent.

Then the captain, in the bow, chuckled in a way that expressed humor, contempt, tragedy, all in one. "Do you think we've got much of a show now, boys?" said he.

Whereupon the three were silent, save for a trifle of hemming and hawing. To express any particular optimism at this time they felt to be childish and stupid, but they all doubtless possessed this sense of the situation in their mind. A young man thinks doggedly at such times. On the other hand, the ethics of their condition was decidedly against any open suggestion of hopelessness. So they were silent.

"Oh, well," said the captain, soothing his children, "we'll get ashore all right."

But there was that in his tone which made them think, so the oiler quoth: "Yes! If this wind holds!"

The cook was bailing: "Yes! If we don't catch hell in the surf."

Canton flannel gulls flew near and far. Sometimes they sat down on the sea, near patches of brown seaweed that rolled on the waves with a movement like carpets on a line in a gale. The birds sat comfortably in groups, and they were envied by some in the dingey, for the wrath of the sea was no more to them than it was to a covey of prairie chickens a thousand miles inland. Often they came very close and stared at the men with black bead-like eyes. At these times they were uncanny and sinister in their unblinking scrutiny, and the men hooted angrily at them, telling them to be gone. One came, and evidently decided to alight on the top of the captain's head. The bird flew parallel to the boat and did not circle, but made short sidelong jumps in the air in chicken fashion. His black eyes were wistfully fixed upon the captain's head. "Ugly brute," said the oiler to the bird. "You look as if you were made with a jack-knife." The cook and the correspondent swore darkly at the creature. The captain naturally wished to knock it away with the end of the heavy painter; but he did not dare do it, because anything resembling an emphatic gesture would have capsized this freighted boat, and so with his open hand, the captain gently and carefully waved the gull away. After it had been discouraged from the pursuit the captain breathed easier on account of his hair, and others breathed easier because the bird struck their minds at this time as being somehow gruesome and ominous.

In the meantime the oiler and the correspondent rowed. And also they rowed.

They sat together in the same seat, and each rowed an oar. Then the oiler took both oars; then the correspondent took both oars; then the oiler; then the correspondent. They rowed and they rowed. The very ticklish part of the business was when the time came for the reclining one in the stern to take his turn at the oars. By the very last star of truth, it is easier to steal eggs from under a hen than it was to change seats in the dingey. First the man in the stern slid his hand along the thwart and moved with care, as if he were of Sèvres. Then the man in the rowing seat slid his hand along the other thwart. It was all done with the most extraordinary care. As the two sidled past each other, the whole party kept watchful eyes on the coming wave, and the captain cried: "Look out now! Steady there!"

The brown mats of seaweed that appeared from time to time were like islands, bits of earth. They were traveling, apparently, neither one way nor the other. They were, to all intents, stationary. They informed the men in the boat that it was making progress slowly toward the land.

The captain, rearing cautiously in the bow, after the dingey soared on a great swell, said that he had seen the lighthouse at Mosquito Inlet. Presently the cook remarked that he had seen it. The correspondent was at the oars then, and for some reason he too wished to look at the lighthouse, but his back was toward the far shore and the waves were important, and for some time he could not seize an opportunity to turn his head. But at last there came a wave more gentle than the others, and when at the crest of it he swiftly scoured the western horizon.

"See it?" said the captain.

"No," said the correspondent slowly, "I didn't see anything."

"Look again," said the captain. He pointed. "It's exactly in that direction."

At the top of another wave, the correspondent did as he was bid, and this time his eyes chanced on a small still thing on the edge of the swaying horizon. It was precisely like the point of a pin. It took an anxious eye to find a lighthouse so tiny.

"Think we'll make it, captain?"

"If this wind holds and the boat don't swamp, we can't do much else," said the captain.

The little boat, lifted by each towering sea, and splashed viciously by the crests, made progress that in the absence of seaweed was not apparent to those in her. She seemed just a wee thing wallowing, miraculously top up, at the mercy of five oceans. Occasionally, a great spread of water, like white flames, swarmed into her.

"Bail her, cook," said the captain serenely.

"All right, captain," said the cheerful cook.

III

It would be difficult to describe the subtle brotherhood of men that was here established on the seas. No one said that it was so. No one mentioned it. But it dwelt in the boat, and each man felt it warm him. They were a captain, an oiler, a cook and a correspondent, and they were friends, friends in a more curiously iron-bound degree than may be common. The hurt captain, lying against the water jar in the bow, spoke always in a low voice and calmly, but he could never command a more ready and swiftly obedient crew than the motley three of the dingey. It was more than a mere recognition of what was best for the common safety. There was surely in it a quality that was personal and heartfelt. And after this devotion to the commander of the boat there was this comradeship that the correspondent, for instance, who had been taught to be cynical of men, knew even at the time was the best experience of his life. But no one said that it was so. No one mentioned it.

"I wish we had a sail," remarked the captain. "We might try my overcoat on the end of an oar and give you two boys a chance to rest." So the cook and the correspondent held the mast and spread wide the overcoat. The oiler steered, and the little boat made good way with her new rig. Sometimes the oiler had to scull sharply to keep a sea from breaking into the boat, but otherwise sailing was a success.

Meanwhile the lighthouse had been growing slowly larger. It had now almost assumed color, and appeared like a little gray shadow on the sky. The man at the oars could not be prevented from turning his head rather often to try for a glimpse of this little gray shadow.

At last, from the top of each wave the men in the tossing boat could see land. Even as the lighthouse was an upright shadow on the sky, this land seemed but a long black shadow on the sea. It certainly was thinner than paper. "We must be about opposite New Smyrna," said the cook, who had coasted this shore often in schooners. "Captain, by the way, I believe they abandoned that life-saving station there about a year ago."

"Did they?" said the captain.

The wind slowly died away. The cook and the corre-spondent were not now obliged to slave in order to hold high the oar. But the waves continued their old impetuous swooping at the dingey, and the little craft, no longer under way, struggled woundily over them. The oiler or the correspondent took the oars again.

Shipwrecks are *à propos* of nothing. If men could only train for them and have them occur when the men had reached pink condition, there would be less drowning at sea. Of the four in the dingey none had slept any time worth mentioning for two days and two nights previous to embarking in the dingey, and in the excitement of clambering about the deck of a foundering ship they had also forgotten to eat heartily.

For these reasons, and for others, neither the oiler nor the correspondent was fond of rowing at this time. The correspondent wondered ingenuously how in the name of all that was sane could there be people who thought it amusing to row a boat. It was not an amusement; it was a diabolical punishment, and even a genius of mental aber-rations could never conclude that it was anything but a horror to the muscles and a crime against the back. He mentioned to the boat in general how the amusement of rowing struck him, and the weary-faced oiler smiled in full sympathy. Previously to the foundering, by the way, the oiler had worked double-watch in the engine-room of the ship.

"Take her easy, now, boys," said the captain. "Don't spend yourselves. If we have to run a surf you'll need all your strength, because we'll sure have to swim for it. Take your time."

Slowly the land arose from the sea. From a black line

it became a line of black and a line of white, trees and sand. Finally, the captain said that he could make out a house on the shore. "That's the house of refuge, sure," said the cook. "They'll see us before long, and come out after us."

The distant lighthouse reared high. "The keeper ought to be able to make us out now, if he's looking through a glass," said the captain. "He'll notify the life-saving people."

"None of those other boats could have got ashore to give word of the wreck," said the oiler, in a low voice. "Else the lifeboat would be out hunting us."

Slowly and beautifully the land loomed out of the sea. The wind came again. It had veered from the northeast to the southeast. Finally, a new sound struck the ears of the men in the boat. It was the low thunder of the surf on the shore. "We'll never be able to make the lighthouse now," said the captain. "Swing her head a little more north, Billie," said he.

" 'A little more north,' sir," said the oiler.

Whereupon the little boat turned her nose once more down the wind, and all but the oarsman watched the shore grow. Under the influence of this expansion doubt and direful apprehension were leaving the minds of the men. The management of the boat was still most absorbing, but it could not prevent a quiet cheerfulness. In an hour, perhaps, they would be ashore.

Their backbones had become thoroughly used to balancing in the boat, and they now rode this wild colt of a dingey like circus men. The correspondent thought that he had been drenched to the skin, but happening to feel in the top pocket of his coat, he found therein eight cigars. Four of them were soaked with sea water; four were perfectly scatheless. After a search, somebody produced three dry matches, and thereupon the four waifs rode impudently in their little boat, and with an assurance of an impending rescue shining in their eyes, puffed at the big cigars and judged well and ill of all men. Everybody took a drink of water.

IV

"Cook," remarked the captain, "there don't seem to be any signs of life about your house of refuge."

"No," replied the cook. "Funny they don't see us!"

A broad stretch of lowly coast lay before the eyes of the men. It was of dunes topped with dark vegetation. The roar of the surf was plain, and sometimes they could see the white lip of a wave as it spun up the beach. A tiny house was blocked out black upon the sky. Southward, the slim lighthouse lifted its little gray length.

Tide, wind, and waves were swinging the dingey northward. "Funny they don't see us," said the men.

The surf's roar was here dulled, but its tone was, nevertheless, thunderous and mighty. As the boat swam over the great rollers, the men sat listening to this roar. "We'll swamp sure," said everybody.

It is fair to say here that there was not a life-saving station within twenty miles in either direction, but the men did not know this fact, and in consequence they made dark and opprobrious remarks concerning the eyesight of the nation's life-savers. Four scowling men sat in the dingey and surpassed records in the invention of epithets.

"Funny they don't see us."

The lightheartedness of a former time had completely faded. To their sharpened minds it was easy to conjure pictures of all kinds of incompetency and blindness and, indeed, cowardice. There was the shore of the populous land, and it was bitter and bitter to them that from it came no sign.

"Well," said the captain, ultimately, "I suppose we'll have to make a try for ourselves. If we stay out here too long, we'll none of us have strength left to swim after the boat swamps."

And so the oiler, who was at the oars, turned the boat

straight for the shore. There was a sudden tightening of muscle. There was some thinking.

"If we don't all get ashore——" said the captain. "If we don't all get ashore, I suppose you fellows know where to send news of my finish?"

They then briefly exchanged some addresses and admonitions. As for the reflections of the men, there was a great deal of rage in them. Perchance they might be formulated thus: "If I am going to be drowned—if I am going to be drowned—if I am to be drowned, why, in the name of the seven mad gods who rule the sea, was I allowed to come thus far and contemplate sand and trees? Was I brought here merely to have my nose dragged away as I was about to nibble the sacred cheese of life? It is preposterous. If this old ninny woman, Fate, cannot do better than this, she should be deprived of the management of men's fortunes. She is an old hen who knows not her intention. If she has decided to drown me, why did she not do it in the beginning and save me all this trouble? The whole affair is absurd. . . . But no, she cannot mean to drown me. She dare not drown me. She cannot drown me. Not after all this work." Afterward the man might have had an impulse to shake his fist at the clouds: "Just you drown me, now, and then hear what I call you!"

The billows that came at this time were more formidable. They seemed always just about to break and roll over the little boat in a turmoil of foam. There was a preparatory and long growl in the speech of them. No mind unused to the sea would have concluded that the dingey could ascend these sheer heights in time. The shore was still afar. The oiler was a wily surfman. "Boys," he said swiftly, "she won't live three minutes more, and we're too far out to swim. Shall I take her to sea again, captain?"

"Yes! Go ahead!" said the captain.

This oiler, by a series of quick miracles, and fast and steady oarsmanship, turned the boat in the middle of the surf and took her safely to sea again.

There was a considerable silence as the boat bumped over the furrowed sea to deeper water. Then somebody in gloom spoke. "Well, anyhow, they must have seen us from the shore by now."

The gulls went in slanting flight up the wind toward the gray desolate east. A squall, marked by dingy clouds, and clouds brick red, like smoke from a burning building, appeared from the southeast.

"What do you think of those life-saving people? Ain't they peaches?"

"Funny they haven't seen us."

"Maybe they think we're out here for sport! Maybe they think we're fishin'. Maybe they think we're damned fools."

It was a long afternoon. A changed tide tried to force them southward, but the wind and wave said northward. Far ahead, where coastline, sea, and sky formed their mighty angle, there were little dots which seemed to indicate a city on the shore.

"St. Augustine?"

The captain shook his head. "Too near Mosquito Inlet."

And the oiler rowed, and then the correspondent rowed. Then the oiler rowed. It was a weary business. The human back can become the seat of more aches and pains than are registered in books for the composite anatomy of a regiment. It is a limited area, but it can become the theater of innumerable muscular conflicts, tangles, wrenches, knots, and other comforts.

"Did you ever like to row, Billie?" asked the correspondent.

"No," said the oiler. "Hang it!"

When one exchanged the rowing seat for a place in the bottom of the boat, he suffered a bodily depression that caused him to be careless of everything save an obligation to wiggle one finger. There was cold sea water swashing to and fro in the boat, and he lay in it. His head, pillowed on a thwart, was within an inch of the swirl of a wave crest, and sometimes a particularly obstreperous sea came in-board and drenched him once more. But these matters did not annoy him. It is almost certain that if the boat had capsized he would have tumbled comfortably out upon the ocean as if he felt sure that it was a great soft mattress.

"Look! There's a man on the shore!"

"Where?"

"There! See 'im? See 'im?"

"Yes, sure! He's walking along."

"Now he's stopped. Look! He's facing us!"

"He's waving at us!"

"So he is! By thunder!"

"Ah, now we're all right! Now we're all right! There'll be a boat out here for us in half an hour."

"He's going on. He's running. He's going up to that house there."

The remote beach seemed lower than the sea, and it required a searching glance to discern the little black figure. The captain saw a floating stick and they rowed to it. A bath towel was by some weird chance in the boat, and, tying this on the stick, the captain waved it. The oarsman did not dare turn his head, so he was obliged to ask questions.

"What's he doing now?"

"He's standing still again. He's looking, I think. . . . There he goes again. Toward the house. . . . Now he's stopped again."

"Is he waving at us?"

"No, not now! he was, though."

"Look! There comes another man!"

"He's running."

"Look at him go, would you."

"Why, he's on a bicycle. Now he's met the other man. They're both waving at us. Look!"

"There comes something up the beach."

"What the devil is that thing?"

"Why it looks like a boat."

"Why, certainly it's a boat."

"No, it's on wheels."

"Yes, so it is. Well, that must be the life-boat. They drag them along shore on a wagon."

"That's the life-boat, sure."

"No, by——, it's—it's an omnibus."

"I tell you it's a life-boat."

"It is not! It's an omnibus. I can see it plain. See? One of these big hotel omnibuses."

"By thunder, you're right. It's an omnibus, sure as fate. What do you suppose they are doing with an omnibus? Maybe they are going around collecting the life-crew, hey?"

"That's it, likely. Look! There's a fellow waving a little black flag. He's standing on the steps of the omnibus. There come those other two fellows. Now they're all talking together. Look at the fellow with the flag. Maybe he ain't waving it."

"That ain't a flag, is it? That's his coat. Why, certainly, that's his coat."

"So it is. It's his coat. He's taken it off and is waving it around his head. But would you look at him swing it."

"Oh, say, there isn't any life-saving station there. That's just a winter resort hotel omnibus that has brought over some of the boarders to see us drown."

"What's that idiot with the coat mean? What's he signaling, anyhow?"

"It looks as if he were trying to tell us to go north. There must be a life-saving station up there."

"No! He thinks we're fishing. Just giving us a merry hand. See? Ah, there, Willie!"

"Well, I wish I could make something out of those signals. What do you suppose he means?"

"He don't mean anything. He's just playing."

"Well, if he'd just signal us to try the surf again, or to go to sea and wait, or go north, or go south, or go to hell—there would be some reason in it. But look at him. He just stands there and keeps his coat revolving like a wheel. The ass!"

"There come more people."

"Now there's quite a mob. Look! Isn't that a boat?"

"Where? Oh, I see where you mean. No, that's no boat."

"That fellow is still waving his coat."

"He must think we like to see him do that. Why don't he quit it? It don't mean anything."

"I don't know. I think he is trying to make us go north. It must be that there's a life-saving station there somewhere."

"Say, he ain't tired yet. Look at 'im wave."

"Wonder how long he can keep that up. He's been revolving his coat ever since he caught sight of us. He's an idiot. Why aren't they getting men to bring a boat out? A fishing boat—one of those big yawls—could come out here all right. Why don't he do something?"

"Oh, it's all right, now."

"They'll have a boat out here for us in less than no time, now that they've seen us."

A faint yellow tone came into the sky over the low land. The shadows on the sea slowly deepened. The wind bore coldness with it, and the men began to shiver.

"Holy smoke!" said one, allowing his voice to express his impious mood, "if we keep on monkeying out here! If we've got to flounder out here all night!"

"Oh, we'll never have to stay here all night! Don't you worry. They've seen us now, and it won't be long before they'll come chasing out after us."

The shore grew dusky. The man waving a coat blended gradually into this gloom, and it swallowed in the same manner the omnibus and the group of people. The spray, when it dashed uproariously over the side, made the voyagers shrink and swear like men who were being branded.

"I'd like to catch the chump who waved the coat. I feel like soaking him one, just for luck."

"Why? What did he do?"

"Oh, nothing, but then he seemed so damned cheerful."

In the meantime the oiler rowed, and then the correspondent rowed, and then the oiler rowed. Gray-faced and bowed forward, they mechanically, turn by turn, plied the leaden oars. The form of the lighthouse had vanished from the southern horizon, but finally a pale star appeared, just lifting from the sea. The streaked saffron in the west passed before the all-merging darkness, and the sea to the east was black. The land had vanished, and was expressed only by the low and drear thunder of the surf.

"If I am going to be drowned—if I am going to be drowned—if I am going to be drowned, why, in the name of the seven mad gods who rule the sea, was I allowed to come thus far and contemplate sand and trees? Was I brought here merely to have my nose dragged away as I was about to nibble the sacred cheese of life?"

The patient captain, drooped over the water jar, was sometimes obliged to speak to the oarsman.

"Keep her head up! Keep her head up!"

" 'Keep her head up,' sir." The voices were weary and low.

This was surely a quiet evening. All save the oarsman lay heavily and listlessly in the boat's bottom. As for him, his eyes were just capable of noting the tall black waves that swept forward in a most sinister silence, save for an occasional subdued growl of a crest.

The cook's head was on a thwart, and he looked without interest at the water under his nose. He was deep in other scenes. Finally he spoke. "Billie," he murmured, dreamily, "what kind of pie do you like best?"

V

"Pie," said the oiler and the correspondent, agitatedly. "Don't talk about those things, blast you!"

"Well," said the cook, "I was just thinking about ham sandwiches, and——"

A night on the sea in an open boat is a long night. As darkness settled finally, the shine of the light, lifting from the sea in the south, changed to full gold. On the northern horizon a new light appeared, a small bluish gleam on the edge of the waters. These two lights were the furniture of the world. Otherwise there was nothing but waves.

Two men huddled in the stern, and distances were so magnificent in the dingey that the rower was enabled to keep his feet partly warmed by thrusting them under his companions. Their legs indeed extended far under the rowing seat until they touched the feet of the captain forward. Sometimes, despite the efforts of the tired oarsman, a wave came piling into the boat, an icy wave of the night, and the chilling water soaked them anew. They would twist their bodies for a moment and groan, and sleep the dead sleep once more, while the water in the boat gurgled about them as the craft rocked.

The plan of the oiler and the correspondent was for one to row until he lost the ability, and then arouse the other from his sea water couch in the bottom of the boat.

The oiler plied the oars until his head drooped forward, and the overpowering sleep blinded him. And he rowed yet afterward. Then he touched a man in the bottom of the boat and called his name. "Will you spell me for a little while?" he said, meekly.

"Sure, Billie," said the correspondent, awakening and dragging himself to a sitting position. They exchanged places carefully, and the oiler, cuddling down in the sea water at the cook's side, seemed to go to sleep instantly.

The particular violence of the sea had ceased. The waves came without snarling. The obligation of the man at the oars was to keep the boat headed so that the tilt of the rollers would not capsize her, and to preserve her from filling when the crests rushed past. The black waves were silent and hard to be seen in the darkness. Often one was almost upon the boat before the oarsman was aware.

In a low voice the correspondent addressed the captain. He was not sure that the captain was awake, although this iron man seemed to be always awake. "Captain, shall I keep her making for that light north, sir?"

The same steady voice answered him. "Yes. Keep it about two points off the port bow."

The cook had tied a life belt around himself in order to get even the warmth which this clumsy cork contrivance could donate, and he seemed almost stove-like when a rower, whose teeth invariably chattered wildly as soon as he ceased his labor, dropped down to sleep.

The correspondent, as he rowed, looked down at the two men sleeping under foot. The cook's arm was around the oiler's shoulders, and, with their fragmentary clothing and haggard faces, they were the babes of the sea, a grotesque rendering of the old babes in the wood.

Later he must have grown stupid at his work, for suddenly there was a growling of water, and a crest came with a roar and a swash into the boat, and it was a wonder that it did not set the cook afloat in his life belt. The cook continued to sleep, but the oiler sat up, blinking his eyes and shaking with the new cold.

"Oh, I'm awfully sorry, Billie," said the correspondent contritely.

"That's all right, old boy," said the oiler, and lay down again and was asleep.

Presently it seemed that even the captain dozed, and the correspondent thought that he was the one man afloat on all the oceans. The wind had a voice as it came over the waves, and it was sadder than the end.

There was a long, loud swishing astern of the boat, and a gleaming trail of phosphorescence, like blue flame, was furrowed on the black waters. It might have been made by a monstrous knife.

Then there came a stillness, while the correspondent breathed with the open mouth and looked at the sea.

Suddenly there was another swish and another long flash of bluish light, and this time it was alongside the boat, and might almost have been reached with an oar. The correspondent saw an enormous fin speed like a shadow through the water, hurling the crystalline spray and leaving the long glowing trail.

The correspondent looked over his shoulder at the captain. His face was hidden, and he seemed to be asleep. He looked at the babes of the sea. They certainly were asleep. So, being bereft of sympathy, he leaned a little way to one side and swore softly into the sea.

But the thing did not then leave the vicinity of the boat. Ahead or astern, on one side or the other, at intervals long or short, fled the long sparkling streak, and there was to be heard the whirroo of the dark fin. The speed and power of the thing was greatly to be admired. It cut the water like a gigantic and keen projectile.

The presence of this biding thing did not affect the man with the same horror that it would if he had been a picnicker. He simply looked at the sea dully and swore in an undertone.

Nevertheless, it is true that he did not wish to be alone. He wished one of his companions to awaken by chance and keep him company with it. But the captain hung motionless over the water jar, and the oiler and the cook in the bottom of the boat were plunged in slumber.

VI

"If I am going to be drowned—if I am going to be drowned—if I am going to be drowned, why, in the name of the seven mad gods who rule the sea, was I allowed to come thus far and contemplate sand and trees?" During this dismal night, it may be remarked that a man would conclude that it was really the intention of the seven mad gods to drown him, despite the abominable injustice of it. For it was certainly an abominable injustice to drown a man who had worked so hard, so hard. The man felt it would be a crime most unnatural. Other people had drowned at sea since galleys swarmed with painted sails, but still——

When it occurs to a man that nature does not regard him as important, and that she feels she would not maim the universe by disposing of him, he at first wishes to

throw bricks at the temple, and he hates deeply the fact
that there are no bricks and no temples. Any visible
expression of nature would surely be pelleted with his
jeers.

Then, if there be no tangible thing to hoot he feels,
perhaps, the desire to confront a personification and
indulge in pleas, bowed to one knee, and with hands
supplicant, saying: "Yes, but I love myself."

A high cold star on a winter's night is the word he feels
that she says to him. Thereafter he knows the pathos of
his situation.

The men in the dingey had not discussed these matters,
but each had, no doubt, reflected upon them in silence
and according to his mind. There was seldom any expression upon their faces save the general one of complete
weariness. Speech was devoted to the business of the boat.

To chime the notes of his emotion, a verse mysteriously entered the correspondent's head. He had even forgotten that he had forgotten this verse, but it suddenly
was in his mind.

A soldier of the Legion lay dying in Algiers,
There was a lack of woman's nursing, there was dearth
of woman's tears;
But a comrade stood beside him, and he took that
comrade's hand,
And he said: "I shall never see my own, my native land."

In his childhood, the correspondent had been made
acquainted with the fact that a soldier of the Legion lay
dying in Algiers, but he had never regarded the fact as
important. Myriads of his school fellows had informed
him of the soldier's plight, but the dinning had naturally
ended by making him perfectly indifferent. He had never
considered it his affair that a soldier of the Legion lay
dying in Algiers, nor had it appeared to him as a matter
for sorrow. It was less to him than the breaking of a
pencil's point.

Now, however, it quaintly came to him as a human, living thing. It was no longer merely a picture of a few throes in the breast of a poet, meanwhile drinking tea and warming his feet at the grate; it was an actuality—stern, mournful, and fine.

The correspondent plainly saw the soldier. He lay on the sand with his feet out straight and still. While his pale left hand was upon his chest in an attempt to thwart the going of his life, the blood came between his fingers. In the far Algerian distance, a city of low square forms was set against a sky that was faint with the last sunset hues. The correspondent, plying the oars and dreaming of the slow and slower movements of the lips of the soldier, was moved by a profound and perfectly impersonal comprehension. He was sorry for the soldier of the Legion who lay dying in Algiers.

The thing which had followed the boat and waited, had evidently grown bored at the delay. There was no longer to be heard the slash of the cut water, and there was no longer the flame of the long trail. The light in the north still glimmered, but it was apparently no nearer to the boat. Sometimes the boom of the surf rang in the correspondent's ears, and he turned the craft seaward then and rowed harder. Southward, someone had evidently built a watch fire on the beach. It was too low and too far to be seen, but it made a shimmering, roseate reflection upon the bluff back of it, and this could be discerned from the boat. The wind came stronger, and sometimes a wave suddenly raged out like a mountain cat, and there was to be seen the sheen and sparkle of a broken crest.

The captain, in the bow, moved on his water jar and sat erect. "Pretty long night," he observed to the correspondent. He looked at the shore. "Those life-saving people take their time."

"Did you see that shark playing around?"

"Yes, I saw him. He was a big fellow, all right."

"Wish I had known you were awake."

Later the correspondent spoke into the bottom of the boat.

"Billie!" There was a slow and gradual disentanglement. "Billie, will you spell me?"

"Sure," said the oiler.

As soon as the correspondent touched the cold comfortable sea water in the bottom of the boat, and had huddled close to the cook's life belt he was deep in sleep, despite the fact that his teeth played all the popular airs. This sleep was so good to him that it was but a moment before he heard a voice call his name in a tone that demonstrated the last stages of exhaustion. "Will you spell me?"

"Sure, Billie."

The light in the north had mysteriously vanished, but the correspondent took his course from the wide-awake captain.

Later in the night they took the boat farther out to sea, and the captain directed the cook to take one oar at the stern and keep the boat facing the seas. He was to call out if he should hear the thunder of the surf. This plan enabled the oiler and the correspondent to get respite together. "We'll give those boys a chance to get into shape again," said the captain. They curled down and, after a few preliminary chatterings and trembles, slept once more the dead sleep. Neither knew they had bequeathed to the cook the company of another shark, or perhaps the same shark.

As the boat caroused on the waves, spray occasionally bumped over the side and gave them a fresh soaking, but this had no power to break their repose. The ominous slash of the wind and the water affected them as it would have affected mummies.

"Boys," said the cook, with the notes of every reluctance in his voice, "she's drifted in pretty close. I guess one of you had better take her to sea again." The correspondent, aroused, heard the crash of the toppled crests.

As he was rowing, the captain gave him some whisky

and water, and this steadied the chills out of him. "If I ever get ashore and anybody shows me even a photograph of an oar——"

At last there was a short conversation.

"Billie. . . . Billie, will you spell me?"

"Sure," said the oiler.

VII

When the correspondent again opened his eyes, the sea and the sky were each of the gray hue of the dawning. Later, carmine and gold was painted upon the waters. The morning appeared finally, in its splendor, with a sky of pure blue, and the sunlight flamed on the tips of the waves.

On the distant dunes were set many little black cottages, and a tall white windmill reared above them. No man, nor dog, nor bicycle appeared on the beach. The cottages might have formed a deserted village.

The voyagers scanned the shore. A conference was held in the boat. "Well," said the captain, "if no help is coming we might better try a run through the surf right away. If we stay out here much longer we will be too weak to do anything for ourselves at all." The others silently acquiesced in this reasoning. The boat was headed for the beach. The correspondent wondered if none ever ascended the tall wind tower, and if then they never looked seaward. This tower was a giant, standing with its back to the plight of the ants. It represented in a degree, to the correspondent, the serenity of nature amid the struggles of the individual—nature in the wind, and nature in the vision of men. She did not seem cruel to him then, nor beneficent, nor treacherous, nor wise. But she was indifferent, flatly indifferent. It is, perhaps, plausible that a man in this situation, impressed with the unconcern of the universe, should see the innumerable flaws of his life, and have them taste wickedly in his mind and wish for another chance. A distinction between right and wrong seems absurdly clear to him, then, in this new ignorance of the grave edge, and he understands that if he were given another opportunity he would mend his conduct and his words, and be better and brighter during an introduction or at a tea.

"Now, boys," said the captain, "she is going to swamp, sure. All we can do is to work her in as far as possible, and then when she swamps, pile out and scramble for the beach. Keep cool now, and don't jump until she swamps sure."

The oiler took the oars. Over his shoulders he scanned the surf. "Captain," he said, "I think I'd better bring her about, and keep her head-on to the seas and back her in."

"All right, Billie," said the captain. "Back her in." The oiler swung the boat then and, seated in the stern, the cook and the correspondent were obliged to look over their shoulders to contemplate the lonely and indifferent shore.

The monstrous in-shore rollers heaved the boat high until the men were again enabled to see the white sheets of water scudding up the slanted beach. "We won't get in very close," said the captain. Each time a man could wrest his attention from the rollers, he turned his glance toward the shore, and in the expression of the eyes during this contemplation there was a singular quality. The correspondent, observing the others, knew that they were not afraid, but the full meaning of their glances was shrouded.

As for himself, he was too tired to grapple fundamentally with the fact. He tried to coerce his mind into thinking of it, but the mind was dominated at this time by the muscles, and the muscles said they did not care. It merely occurred to him that if he should drown it would be a shame.

There were no hurried words, no pallor, no plain agitation. The men simply looked at the shore. "Now, remember to get well clear of the boat when you jump," said the captain.

Seaward the crest of a roller suddenly fell with a thunderous crash, and the long white comber came roaring down upon the boat.

"Steady now," said the captain. The men were silent. They turned their eyes from the shore to the comber and waited. The boat slid up the incline, leaped at the furious top, bounced over it, and swung down the long back of the wave. Some water had been shipped and the cook bailed it out.

But the next crashed also. The tumbling, boiling flood of white water caught the boat and whirled it almost perpendicular. Water swarmed in from all sides. The correspondent had his hands on the gunwale at this time, and when the water entered at that place he swiftly withdrew his fingers, as if he objected to wetting them.

The little boat, drunken with this weight of water, reeled and snuggled deeper into the sea.

"Bail her out, cook! Bail her out," said the captain.

"All right, captain," said the cook.

"Now, boys, the next one will do for us, sure," said the oiler. "Mind to jump clear of the boat."

The third wave moved forward, huge, furious, implacable. It fairly swallowed the dingey, and almost simultaneously the men tumbled into the sea. A piece of life belt had lain in the bottom of the boat, and as the correspondent went overboard he held this to his chest with his left hand.

The January water was icy, and he reflected immediately that it was colder than he had expected to find it on the coast of Florida. This appeared to his dazed mind as a fact important enough to be noted at the time. The coldness of the water was sad; it was tragic. This fact was somehow so mixed and confused with his opinion of his own situation that it seemed almost a proper reason for tears. The water was cold.

When he came to the surface he was conscious of little but the noisy water. Afterward he saw his companions in the sea. The oiler was ahead in the race. He was swimming strongly and rapidly. Off to the correspondent's left, the cook's great white and corked back bulged out of the water, and in the rear the captain was hanging with his one good hand to the keel of the overturned dingey.

There is a certain immovable quality to a shore, and the correspondent wondered at it amid the confusion of the sea.

It seemed also very attractive, but the correspondent knew that it was a long journey, and he paddled leisurely. The piece of life preserver lay under him, and sometimes he whirled down the incline of a wave as if he were on a hand-sled.

But finally he arrived at a place in the sea where travel was beset with difficulty. He did not pause swimming to inquire what manner of current had caught him, but there his progress ceased. The shore was set before him like a bit of scenery on a stage, and he looked at it and understood with his eyes each detail of it.

As the cook passed, much farther to the left, the captain was calling to him, "Turn over on your back, cook! Turn over on your back and use the oar."

"All right, sir." The cook turned on his back, and, paddling with an oar, went ahead as if he were a canoe.

Presently the boat also passed to the left of the correspondent with the captain clinging with one hand to the keel. He would have appeared like a man raising himself to look over a board fence, if it were not for the extraordinary gymnastics of the boat. The correspondent marveled that the captain could still hold to it.

They passed on, nearer to shore—the oiler, the cook, the captain—and following them went the water jar, bouncing gayly over the seas.

The correspondent remained in the grip of this strange new enemy—a current. The shore, with its white slope of sand and its green bluff, topped with little silent cottages, was spread like a picture before him. It was very near to him then, but he was impressed as one who in a gallery looks at a scene from Brittany or Holland.

He thought: "I am going to drown? Can it be possible? Can it be possible? Can it be possible?" Perhaps an individual must consider his own death to be the final phenomenon of nature.

But later a wave perhaps whirled him out of this small, deadly current, for he found suddenly that he could again make progress toward the shore. Later still, he was aware that the captain, clinging with one hand to the keel of the dingey, had his face turned away from the shore and toward him, and was calling his name. "Come to the boat! Come to the boat!"

In his struggle to reach the captain and the boat, he reflected that when one gets properly wearied, drowning must really be a comfortable arrangement, a cessation of hostilities accompanied by a large degree of relief, and he was glad of it, for the main thing in his mind for some months had been horror of the temporary agony. He did not wish to be hurt.

Presently he saw a man running along the shore. He was undressing with most remarkable speed. Coat, trousers, shirt, everything flew magically off him.

"Come to the boat," called the captain.

"All right, captain." As the correspondent paddled, he saw the captain let himself down to bottom and leave the boat. Then the correspondent performed his one little marvel of the voyage. A large wave caught him and flung him with ease and supreme speed completely over the boat and far beyond it. It struck him even then as an event in gymnastics, and a true miracle of the sea. An overturned boat in the surf is not a plaything to a swimming man.

The correspondent arrived in water that reached only to his waist, but his condition did not enable him to stand for more than a moment. Each wave knocked him into a heap, and the undertow pulled at him.

Then he saw the man who had been running and undressing, and undressing and running, come bounding
into the water. He dragged ashore the cook, and then
waded towards the captain, but the captain waved him
away, and sent him to the correspondent. He was naked,
naked as a tree in winter, but a halo was about his head,
and he shone like a saint. He gave a strong pull, and a
long drag, and a bully heave at the correspondent's hand.
The correspondent, schooled in the minor formulæ,
said: "Thanks, old man." But suddenly the man cried:
"What's that?" He pointed a swift finger. The correspondent said: "Go."

In the shallows, face downward, lay the oiler. His
forehead touched sand that was periodically, between
each wave, clear of the sea.

The correspondent did not know all that transpired
afterward. When he achieved safe ground he fell, striking the sand with each particular part of his body. It was
as if he had dropped from a roof, but the thud was grateful to him.

It seems that instantly the beach was populated with
men with blankets, clothes, and flasks, and women with
coffee pots and all the remedies sacred to their minds.
The welcome of the land to the men from the sea was
warm and generous, but a still and dripping shape was
carried slowly up the beach, and the land's welcome for
it could only be the different and sinister hospitality of
the grave.

When it came night, the white waves paced to and fro
in the moonlight, and the wind brought the sound of the
sea's great voice to the men on shore, and they felt that
they could then be interpreters.

The Man Who Would Be King

By RUDYARD KIPLING

"Brother to a Prince and fellow to a beggar if he be found worthy."

THE LAW, as quoted, lays down a fair conduct of life, and one not easy to follow. I have been fellow to a beggar again and again under circumstances which prevented either of us finding out whether the other was worthy. I have still to be brother to a Prince, though I once came near to kinship with what might have been a veritable King and was promised the reversion of a Kingdom—army, law-courts, revenue and policy all complete. But, to-day, I greatly fear that my King is dead, and if I want a crown I must go and hunt it for myself.

The beginning of everything was in a railway train upon the road to Mhow from Ajmir. There had been a Deficit in the Budget, which necessitated traveling, not Second-class, which is only half as dear as First-class, but by Intermediate, which is very awful indeed. There are no cushions in the Intermediate class, and the population are either Intermediate, which is Eurasian, or native, which for a long night journey is nasty, or Loafer, which is amusing though intoxicated. Intermediates do not patronize refreshment-rooms. They carry their food in bundles and pots, and buy sweets from the native sweet-meat-sellers, and drink the roadside water. That is why in the hot weather Intermediates are taken out of the carriages dead, and in all weathers are most properly looked down upon.

My particular Intermediate happened to be empty till I reached Nasirabad, when a huge gentleman in shirt-sleeves entered, and, following the custom of Intermediates, passed the time of day. He was a wanderer and a vagabond like myself, but with an educated taste for whiskey. He told tales of things he had seen and done, of out-of-the-way corners of the Empire into which he had penetrated, and of adventures in which he risked his life for a few days' food. "If India was filled with men like you and me, not knowing more than the crows where they'd get their next day's rations, it isn't seventy millions of revenue the land would be paying—it's seven hundred millions," said he; and as I looked at his mouth and chin I was disposed to agree with him. We talked politics—the politics of Loaferdom that sees things from the underside where the lath and plaster is not smoothed off—and we talked postal arrangements because my friend wanted to send a telegram back from the next station to Ajmir, which is the turning-off place from the Bombay to the Mhow line as you travel westward. My friend had no money beyond eight annas which he wanted for dinner, and I had no money at all, owing to the hitch in the Budget before mentioned. Further, I was going into a wilderness where, though I should resume touch with the Treasury, there were no telegraph offices. I was, therefore, unable to help him in any way.

"We might threaten a Station-master, and make him send a wire on tick," said my friend, "but that'd mean inquiries for you and for me, and I've got my hands full these days. Did you say you are traveling back along this line within any days?"

"Within ten," I said.

"Can't you make it eight?" said he. "Mine is rather urgent business."

"I can send your telegram within ten days if that will serve you," I said.

"I couldn't trust the wire to fetch him now I think of it. It's this way. He leaves Delhi on the 23d for Bombay. That means he'll be running through Ajmir about the night of the 23d."

"But I am going into the Indian Desert," I explained.

"Well and good," said he. "You'll be changing at Marwar Junction to get into Jodhpore territory—you must do that—and he'll be coming through Marwar Junction in the early morning of the 24th by the Bombay Mail. Can you be at Marwar Junction on that time? 'Twon't be inconveniencing you because I know that there's precious few pickings to be got out of these Central India States—even though you pretend to be correspondent of the *Backwoodsman*."

"Have you ever tried that trick?" I asked.

"Again and again, but the Residents find you out, and then you get escorted to the Border before you've time to get your knife into them. But about my friend here. I *must* give him a word o'mouth to tell him what's come to me or else he won't know where to go. I would take it more than kind of you if you was to come out of Central India in time to catch him at Marwar Junction, and say to him:—'He has gone South for the week.' He'll know what that means. He's a big man with a red beard, and a great swell he is. You'll find him sleeping like a gentleman with all his luggage round him in a Second-class compartment. But don't you be afraid. Slip down the window, and say:—'He has gone South for the week,' and he'll tumble. It's only cutting your time of stay in those parts by two days. I ask you as a stranger—going to the West," he said, with emphasis.

"Where have *you* come from?" said I.

"From the East," said he, "and I am hoping that you will give him the message on the Square—for the sake of my Mother as well as your own."

Englishmen are not usually softened by appeals to the memory of their mothers, but for certain reasons, which will be fully apparent, I saw fit to agree.

"It's more than a little matter," said he, "and that's why I ask you to do it—and now I know that I can depend on you doing it. A Second-class carriage at Marwar Junction, and a red-haired man asleep in it. You'll be sure to remember. I get out at the next station, and I must hold on there till he comes or sends me what I want."

"I'll give the message if I catch him," I said, "and for the sake of your Mother as well as mine I'll give you a word of advice. Don't try to run the Central India States just now as the correspondent of the *Backwoodsman*. There's a real one knocking about here, and it might lead to trouble."

"Thank you," said he, simply, "and when will the swine be gone? I can't starve because he's ruining my work. I wanted to get hold of the Degumber Rajah down here about his father's widow, and give him a jump."

"What did he do to his father's widow, then?"

"Filled her up with red pepper and slippered her to death as she hung from a beam. I found that out myself and I'm the only man that would dare going into the State to get hush-money for it. They'll try to poison me, same as they did in Chortumna when I went on the loot there. But you'll give the man at Marwar Junction my message?"

He got out at a little roadside station, and I reflected. I had heard, more than once, of men personating correspondents of newspapers and bleeding small Native States with threats of exposure, but I had never met any of the caste before. They lead a hard life, and generally die with great suddenness. The Native States have a wholesome horror of English newspapers, which may throw light on their peculiar methods of government, and do their best to choke correspondence with champagne, or drive them out of their mind with four-in-hand barouches. They do not understand that nobody cares a straw for the internal administration of Native States so long as oppression and crime are kept within decent limits, and the ruler is not drugged, drunk, or diseased from one end of the year to the other. Native States were created by Providence in order to supply picturesque scenery, tigers, and tall-writing. They are the dark places of the earth, full of unimaginable cruelty, touching the Railway and the Telegraph on one side, and, on the other, the days of Harun-al-Raschid. When I left the train I did business with divers Kings, and in eight days passed through many changes of life. Sometimes I wore dress-clothes and consorted with Princes and Politicals, drinking from crystal and eating from silver. Sometimes I lay out upon the ground and devoured what I could get, from a plate made of a flapjack, and drank the running water, and slept under the same rug as my servant. It was all in the day's work.

Then I headed for the Great Indian Desert upon the proper date, as I had promised, and the Night Mail set me down at Marwar Junction, where a funny little, happy-go-lucky, native-managed railway runs to Jodhpore. The Bombay Mail from Delhi makes a short halt at Marwar. She arrived as I got in, and I had just time to hurry to her platform and go down the carriages. There was only one Second-class on the train. I slipped the window and looked down upon a flaming red beard, half covered by a railway rug. That was my man, fast asleep, and I dug him gently in the ribs. He woke with a grunt and I saw his face in the light of the lamps. It was a great and shining face.

"Tickets again?" said he.

"No," said I. "I am to tell you that he is gone South for the week. He is gone South for the week!"

The train had begun to move out. The red man rubbed his eyes. "He has gone South for the week," he repeated. "Now that's just like his impidence. Did he say that I was to give you anything?—'Cause I won't."

"He didn't," I said, and dropped away, and watched the red lights die out in the dark. It was horribly cold because the wind was blowing off the sands. I climbed into my own train—not an Intermediate Carriage this time—and went to sleep.

If the man with the beard had given me a rupee I should have kept it as a memento of a rather curious affair. But the consciousness of having done my duty was my only reward.

Later on I reflected that two gentlemen like my friends could not do any good if they foregathered and personated correspondents of newspapers, and might, if they "stuck up" one of the little rat-trap states of Central India or Southern Rajputana, get themselves into serious difficulties. I therefore took some trouble to describe them as accurately as I could remember to people who would be interested in deporting them: and succeeded, so I was later informed, in having them headed back from the Degumber border.

Then I became respectable, and returned to an Office where there were no Kings and no incidents except the daily manufacture of a newspaper. A newspaper office seems to attract every conceivable sort of person, to the prejudice of discipline. Zenana-mission ladies arrive, and beg that the Editor will instantly abandon all his duties to describe a Christian prize-giving in a back-slum of a perfectly inaccessible village; Colonels who have been over-passed for commands sit down and sketch the outline of a series of ten, twelve, or twenty-four leading articles on Seniority *versus* Selection; missionaries wish to know why they have not been permitted to escape from their regular vehicles of abuse and swear at a brother-missionary under special patronage of the editorial We; stranded theatrical companies troop up to explain that they cannot pay for their advertisements, but on their return from New Zealand or Tahiti will do so with interest; inventors of patent punkah-pulling machines, carriage couplings and unbreakable swords and axle-trees call with specifications in their pockets and hours at their disposal; tea-companies enter and elaborate their prospectuses with the office pens; secretaries of ball-committees clamor to have the glories of their last dance more fully expounded; strange ladies rustle in and say: —"I want a hundred lady's cards printed *at once*, please," which is manifestly part of an Editor's duty;

and every dissolute ruffian that ever tramped the Grand Trunk Road makes it his business to ask for employment as a proof-reader. And, all the time, the telephone-bell is ringing madly, and Kings are being killed on the Continent, and Empires are saying—"You're another," and Mister Gladstone is calling down brimstone upon the British Dominions, and the little black copy-boys are whining, *"kaa-pi chay-ha-yeh"* (copy wanted) like tired bees, and most of the paper is as blank as Modred's shield.

But that is the amusing part of the year. There are other six months wherein none ever come to call, and the thermometer walks inch by inch up to the top of the glass, and the office is darkened to just above reading-light, and the press machines are red-hot of touch, and nobody writes anything but accounts of amusements in the Hill-stations or obituary notices. Then the telephone becomes a tinkling terror, because it tells you of the sudden deaths of men and women that you knew intimately, and the prickly-heat covers you as with a garment, and you sit down and write:—"A slight increase of sickness is reported from the Khuda Janta Khan District. The outbreak is purely sporadic in its nature, and, thanks to the energetic efforts of the District authorities, is now almost at an end. It is, however, with deep regret we record the death, etc."

Then the sickness really breaks out, and the less recording and reporting the better for the peace of the subscribers. But the Empires and the Kings continue to divert themselves as selfishly as before, and the Foreman thinks that a daily paper really ought to come out once in twenty-four hours, and all the people at the Hill-stations in the middle of their amusements say:—"Good gracious! Why can't the paper be sparkling? I'm sure there's plenty going on up here."

That is the dark half of the moon, and, as the advertisements say, "must be experienced to be appreciated."

It was in that season, and a remarkably evil season,

that the paper began running the last issue of the week on Saturday night, which is to say Sunday morning, after the custom of a London paper. This was a great convenience, for immediately after the paper was put to bed, the dawn would lower the thermometer from 96° to almost 84° for half an hour, and in that chill—you have no idea how cold is 84° on the grass until you begin to pray for it—a very tired man could set off to sleep ere the heat roused him.

One Saturday night it was my pleasant duty to put the paper to bed alone. A King or courtier or a courtesan or a community was going to die or get a new Constitution, or do something that was important on the other side of the world, and the paper was to be held open till the latest possible minute in order to catch the telegram. It was a pitchy black night, as stifling as a June night can be, and the *loo,* the red-hot wind from the westward, was booming among the tinder-dry trees and pretending that the rain was on its heels. Now and again a spot of almost boiling water would fall on the dust with the flop of a frog, but all our weary world knew that was only pretence. It was a shade cooler in the press-room than the office, so I sat there, while the type ticked and clicked, and the night-jars hooted at the windows, and the all but naked compositors wiped the sweat from their foreheads and called for water. The thing that was keeping us back, whatever it was, would not come off, though the *loo* dropped and the last type was set, and the whole round earth stood still in the choking heat, with its finger on its lip, to wait the event. I drowsed, and wondered whether the telegraph was a blessing, and whether this dying man, or struggling people, was aware of the inconvenience the delay was causing. There was no special reason beyond the heat and worry to make tension, but, as the clock hands crept up to three o'clock and the machines spun their fly-wheels two and three times to see that all was in order, before I said the word that would set them off, I could have shrieked aloud.

Then the roar and rattle of the wheels shivered the quiet into little bits. I rose to go away, but two men in white clothes stood in front of me. The first one said:— "It's him!" The second said:—"So it is!" And they both laughed almost as loudly as the machinery roared, and mopped their foreheads. "We see there was a light burning across the road and we were sleeping in that ditch there for coolness, and I said to my friend here, The office is open. Let's come along and speak to him as turned us back from the Degumber State," said the smaller of the two. He was the man I had met in the Mhow train, and his fellow was the red-bearded man of Marwar Junction. There was no mistaking the eyebrows of the one or the beard of the other.

I was not pleased, because I wished to go to sleep, not to squabble with loafers. "What do you want?" I asked.

"Half an hour's talk with you cool and comfortable, in the office," said the red-bearded man. "We'd *like* some drink—the Contrack doesn't begin yet, Peachey, so you needn't look—but what we really want is advice. We don't want money. We ask you as a favor, because you did us a bad turn about Degumber."

I led from the press-room to the stifling office with the maps on the walls, and the red-haired man rubbed his hands. "That's something like," said he. "This was the proper shop to come to. Now, Sir, let me introduce to you Brother Peachey Carnehan, that's him, and Brother Daniel Dravot, that is *me*, and the less said about our professions the better, for we have been most things in our time. Soldier, sailor, compositor, photographer, proof-reader, street-preacher, and correspondents of the *Back-woodsman* when we thought the paper wanted one. Carnehan is sober, and so am I. Look at us first and see that's sure. It will save you cutting into my talk. We'll take one of your cigars apiece, and you shall see us light."

I watched the test. The men were absolutely sober, so I gave them each a tepid peg.

"Well *and* good," said Carnehan of the eyebrows, wiping the froth from his moustache. "Let me talk now, Dan. We have been all over India, mostly on foot. We have been boiler-fitters, engine-drivers, petty contractors, and all that, and we have decided that India isn't big enough for such as us."

They certainly were too big for the office. Dravot's beard seemed to fill half the room and Carnehan's shoulders the other half, as they sat on the big table. Carnehan continued:—"The country isn't half worked out because they that governs it won't let you touch it. They spend all their blessed time in governing it, and you can't lift a spade, nor chip a rock, nor look for oil, nor anything like that without all the Government saying— 'Leave it alone and let us govern.' Therefore, such as it is, we will let it alone, and go away to some other place where a man isn't crowded and can come to his own. We are not little men, and there is nothing that we are afraid of except Drink, and we have signed a Contrack on that. *Therefore*, we are going away to be Kings."

"Kings in our own right," muttered Dravot.

"Yes, of course," I said. "You've been tramping in the sun, and it's a very warm night, and hadn't you better sleep over the notion? Come to-morrow."

"Neither drunk nor sunstruck," said Dravot. "We have slept over the notion half a year, and require to see Books and Atlases, and we have decided that there is only one place now in the world that two strong men can Sar-a-*whack*. They call it Kafiristan. By my reckoning it's the top right-hand corner of Afghanistan, not more than three hundred miles from Peshawur. They have two and thirty heathen idols there, and we'll be the thirty-third. It's a mountainous country, and the women of those parts are very beautiful."

"But that is provided against in the Contrack," said Carnehan. "Neither Women nor Liqu-or, Daniel."

"And that's all we know, except that no one has gone there, and they fight, and in any place where they fight a man who knows how to drill men can always be a King. We shall go to those parts and say to any King we find— 'D' you want to vanquish your foes?' and we will show him how to drill men; for that we know better than anything else. Then we will subvert that King and seize his Throne and establish a Dynasty."

"You'll be cut to pieces before you're fifty miles across the Border," I said. "You have to travel through Afghanistan to get to that country. It's one mass of mountains and peaks and glaciers, and no Englishman has been through it. The people are utter brutes, and even if you reached them you couldn't do anything."

"That's more like," said Carnehan. "If you could think us a little more mad we would be more pleased. We have come to you to know about this country, to read a book about it, and to be shown maps. We want you to tell us that we are fools and to show us your books." He turned to the bookcases.

"Are you at all in earnest?" I said.

"A little," said Dravot, sweetly. "As big a map as you have got, even if it's all blank where Kafiristan is, and any books you've got. We can read, though we aren't very educated."

I uncased the big thirty-two-miles-to-the-inch-map of India, and two smaller Frontier maps, hauled down volume INFKAN of the *Encyclopædia Britannica*, and the men consulted them.

"See here!" said Dravot, his thumb on the map. "Up to Jagdallak, Peachey and me know the road. We was there with Roberts's Army. We'll have to turn off to the right at Jagdallak through Laghmann territory. Then we get among the hills—fourteen thousand feet—fifteen thousand—it will be cold work there, but it don't look very far on the map."

I handed him Wood on the *Sources of the Oxus*. Carnehan was deep in the *Encyclopædia*.

"They're a mixed lot," said Dravot, reflectively; "and

it won't help us to know the names of their tribes. The more tribes the more they'll fight, and the better for us. From Jagdallak to Ashang. H'mm!"

"But all the information about the country is as sketchy and inaccurate as can be," I protested. "No one knows anything about it really. Here's the file of the *United Services' Institute*. Read what Bellew says."

"Blow Bellew!" said Carnehan. "Dan, they're an all-fired lot of heathens, but this book here says they think they're related to us English."

I smoked while the men pored over *Raverty*, *Wood*, the maps and the *Encyclopædia*.

"There is no use your waiting," said Dravot, politely. "It's about four o'clock now. We'll go before six o'clock if you want to sleep, and we won't steal any of the papers. Don't you sit up. We're two harmless lunatics, and if you come, to-morrow evening, down to the Serai we'll say good-bye to you."

"You *are* two fools," I answered. "You'll be turned back at the Frontier or cut up the minute you set foot in Afghanistan. Do you want any money or a recommendation down-country? I can help you to the chance of work next week."

"Next week we shall be hard at work ourselves, thank you," said Dravot. "It isn't so easy being a King as it looks. When we've got our Kingdom in going order we'll let you know, and you can come up and help us to govern it."

"Would two lunatics make a Contrack like that?" said Carnehan, with subdued pride, showing me a greasy half-sheet of note-paper on which was written the following. I copied it, then and there, as a curiosity:

This Contrack between me and you persuing witnesseth in the name of God—Amen and so forth.

(*One*) *That me and you will settle this matter together: i.e., to be Kings of Kafiristan.*

(*Two*) *That you and me will not, while this matter*

> *is being settled, look at any Liquor, nor any*
> *Woman, black, white or brown, so as to get*
> *mixed up with one or the other harmful.*
>
> (*Three*) *That we conduct ourselves with dignity and*
> *discretion, and if one of us gets into trouble*
> *the other will stay by him.*
>
> *Signed by you and me this day.*
> > *Peachey Taliaferro Carnehan.*
> > *Daniel Dravot.*
> > *Both Gentlemen at Large.*

"There was no need for the last article," said Carne-han, blushing modestly; "but it looks regular. Now you know the sort of men that loafers are—we *are* loafers, Dan, until we get out of India—and *do* you think that we would sign a Contrack like that unless we was in earnest? We have kept away from the two things that make life worth having."

"You won't enjoy your lives much longer if you are going to try this idiotic adventure. Don't set the office on fire," I said, "and go away before nine o'clock."

I left them still poring over the maps and making notes on the back of the "Contrack." "Be sure to come down to the Serai to-morrow," were their parting words.

The Kumharsen Serai is the great four-square sink of humanity where the strings of camels and horses from the North load and unload. All the nationalities of Central Asia may be found there, and most of the folk of India proper. Balkh and Bokhara there meet Bengal and Bombay, and try to draw eye-teeth. You can buy ponies, turquoises, Persian pussy-cats, saddle-bags, fat-tailed sheep and musk in the Kumharsen Serai, and get many strange things for nothing. In the afternoon I went down there to see whether my friends intended to keep their word or were lying about drunk.

A priest attired in fragments of ribbons and rags stalked up to me, gravely twisting a child's paper whirli-gig. Behind him was his servant bending under the load of a crate of mud toys. The two were loading up two camels, and the inhabitants of the Serai watched them with shrieks of laughter.

"The priest is mad," said a horse-dealer to me. "He is going up to Kabul to sell toys to the Amir. He will either be raised to honor or have his head cut off. He came in here this morning and has been behaving madly ever since."

"The witless are under the protection of God," stammered a flat-cheeked Usbeg in broken Hindi. "They foretell future events."

"Would they could have foretold that my caravan would have been cut up by the Shinwaris almost within shadow of the Pass!" grunted the Eusufzai agent of a Rajputana trading-house whose goods had been feloniously diverted into the hands of other robbers just across the Border, and whose misfortunes were the laughing-stock of the bazar. "Ohé, priest, whence come you and whither do you go?"

"From Roum have I come," shouted the priest, waving his whirligig; "from Roum, blown by the breath of a hundred devils across the sea! O thieves, robbers, liars, the blessing of Pir Khan on pigs, dogs, and perjurers! Who will take the Protected of God to the North to sell charms that are never still to the Amir? The camels shall not gall, the sons shall not fall sick, and the wives shall remain faithful while they are away, of the men who give me place in their caravan. Who will assist me to slipper the King of the Roos with a golden slipper with a silver heel? The protection of Pir Khan be upon his labors!" He spread out the skirts of his gaberdine and pirouetted between the lines of tethered horses.

"There starts a caravan from Peshawur to Kabul in twenty days, *Huzrut*," said the Eusufzai trader. "My camels go therewith. Do thou also go and bring us good-luck."

"I will go even now!" shouted the priest. "I will depart upon my winged camels, and be at Peshawur in a day! Ho! Hazar Mir Khan," he yelled to his servant, "drive out the camels, but let me first mount my own."

He leaped on the back of his beast as it knelt, and, turning round to me, cried:—"Come thou also, Sahib, a little along the road and I will sell thee a charm—an amulet that shall make thee King of Kafiristan."

Then the light broke upon me and I followed the two camels out of the Serai till we reached open road and the priest halted.

"What d' you think o' that?" said he in English. "Carnehan can't talk their patter, so I've made him my servant. He makes a handsome servant. 'Tisn't for nothing that I've been knocking about the country for fourteen years. Didn't I do that talk neat? We'll hitch on to a caravan at Peshawur till we get to Jagdallak, and then we'll see if we can get donkeys for our camels, and strike into Kafiristan. Whirligigs for the Amir, O Lor! Put your hand under the camel-bags and tell me what you feel."

I felt the butt of a Martini, and another and another.

"Twenty of 'em," said Dravot, placidly. "Twenty of 'em, and ammunition to correspond, under the whirligigs and the mud dolls."

"Heaven help you if you are caught with those things!" I said. "A Martini is worth her weight in silver among the Pathans."

"Fifteen hundred rupees of capital—every rupee we could beg, borrow, or steal—are invested on these two camels," said Dravot. "We won't get caught. We're going through the Khaiber with a regular caravan. Who'd touch a poor mad priest?"

"Have you got everything you want?" I asked, overcome with astonishment.

"Not yet, but we shall soon. Give us a memento of your kindness, Brother. You did me a service yesterday, and that time in Marwar. Half my Kingdom shall you have, as the saying is." I slipped a small charm compass from my watch-chain and handed it up to the priest.

"Good-bye," said Dravot, giving me a hand cautiously. "It's the last time we'll shake hands with an

Englishman these many days. Shake hands with him, Carnehan," he cried, as the second camel passed me.

Carnehan leaned down and shook hands. Then the camels passed away along the dusty road, and I was left alone to wonder. My eye could detect no failure in the disguises. The scene in Serai attested that they were complete to the native mind. There was just the chance, therefore, that Carnehan and Dravot would be able to wander through Afghanistan without detection. But, beyond, they would find death, certain and awful death.

Ten days later a native friend of mine, giving me the news of the day from Peshawur, wound up his letter with:—"There has been much laughter here on account of a certain mad priest who is going in his estimation to sell petty gauds and insignificant trinkets which he ascribes as great charms to H. H. the Amir of Bokhara. He passed through Peshawur and associated himself to the Second Summer caravan that goes to Kabul. The merchants are pleased because through superstition they imagine that such mad fellows bring good-fortune."

The two, then, were beyond the Border. I would have prayed for them, but, that night, a real King died in Europe and demanded an obituary notice.

The wheel of the world swings through the same phases again and again. Summer passed and winter thereafter, and came and passed again. The daily paper continued and I with it, and upon the third summer there fell a hot night, a night-issue, and a strained waiting for something to be telegraphed from the other side of the world, exactly as had happened before. A few great men had died in the past two years, the machines worked with more clatter, and some of the trees in the Office garden were a few feet taller. But that was all the difference.

I passed over to the press-room, and went through just such a scene as I have already described. The nervous tension was stronger than it had been two years before, and I felt the heat more acutely. At three o'clock I cried, "Print off," and turned to go, when there crept to my chair what was left of a man. He was bent into a circle, his head was sunk between his shoulders, and he moved his feet one over the other like a bear. I could hardly see whether he walked or crawled—this rag-wrapped, whining cripple who addressed me by name, crying that he was come back, "Can you give me a drink?" he whimpered. "For the Lord's sake, give me a drink!"

I went back to the office, the man following with groans of pain, and I turned up the lamp.

"Don't you know me?" he gasped, dropping into a chair, and he turned his drawn face, surmounted by a shock of grey hair, to the light.

I looked at him intently. Once before had I seen eyebrows that met over the nose in an inch-broad black band, but for the life of me I could not tell where.

"I don't know you," I said, handing him the whiskey. "What can I do for you?"

He took a gulp of the spirit raw, and shivered in spite of the suffocating heat.

"I've come back," he repeated; "and I was the King of Kafiristan—me and Dravot—crowned Kings we was! In this office we settled it—you setting there and giving us the books. I am Peachey—Peachey Taliaferro Carnehan, and you've been setting here ever since—O Lord!"

I was more than a little astonished, and expressed my feelings accordingly.

"It's true," said Carnehan, with a dry cackle, nursing his feet, which were wrapped in rags. "True as gospel. Kings we were, with crowns upon our heads—me and Dravot—poor Dan—oh, poor, poor Dan, that would never take advice, not though I begged of him!"

"Take the whiskey," I said, "and take your own time. Tell me all you can recollect of everything from beginning to end. You got across the border on your camels, Dravot dressed as a mad priest and you his servant. Do you remember that?"

"I ain't mad—yet, but I shall be that way soon. Of course I remember. Keep looking at me, or maybe my words will go all to pieces. Keep looking at me in my eyes and don't say anything."

I leaned forward and looked into his face as steadily as I could. He dropped one hand upon the table and I grasped it by the wrist. It was twisted like a bird's claw, and upon the back was a ragged, red, diamond-shaped scar.

"No, don't look there. Look at *me*," said Carnehan.

"That comes afterward, but for the Lord's sake don't distrack me. We left with that caravan, me and Dravot playing all sorts of antics to amuse the people we were with. Dravot used to make us laugh in the evenings when all the people were cooking their dinners—cooking their dinners, and . . . what did they do then? They lit little fires with sparks that went into Dravot's beard, and we all laughed—fit to die. Little red fires they was, going into Dravot's big red beard—so funny." His eyes left mine and he smiled foolishly.

"You went as far as Jagdallak with that caravan," I said, at a venture, "after you had lit those fires. To Jagdallak, where you turned off to try to get into Kafiristan."

"No, we didn't neither. What are you talking about? We turned off before Jagdallak, because we heard the roads was good. But they wasn't good enough for our two camels—mine and Dravot's. When we left the caravan, Dravot took off all his clothes and mine too, and said we would be heathen, because the Kafirs didn't allow Mohammedans to talk to them. So we dressed betwixt and between, and such a sight as Daniel Dravot I never saw yet nor expect to see again. He burned half his beard, and slung a sheep-skin over his shoulder, and shaved his head into patterns. He shaved mine, too, and made me wear outrageous things to look like a heathen. That was in a most mountainous country, and our camels couldn't go along any more because of the mountains. They were tall and black, and coming home I saw them fight like wild goats—there are lots of goats in Kafiristan. And these mountains, they never keep still, no more than the goats. Always fighting they are, and don't let you sleep at night."

"Take some more whiskey," I said, very slowly. "What did you and Daniel Dravot do when the camels could go no further because of the rough roads that led into Kafiristan?"

"What did which do? There was a party called Peachey Taliaferro Carnehan that was with Dravot. Shall I tell you about him? He died out there in the cold. Slap from the bridge fell old Peachey, turning and twisting in the air like a penny whirligig that you can sell to the Amir.—No; they was two for three ha'pence, those whirligigs, or I am much mistaken and woful sore. And then these camels were no use, and Peachey said to Dravot—'For the Lord's sake, let's get out of this before our heads are chopped off,' and with that they killed the camels all among the mountains, not having anything in particular to eat, but first they took off the boxes with the guns and the ammunition, till two men came along driving four mules. Dravot up and dances in front of them, singing,—'Sell me four mules.' Says the first man, —'If you are rich enough to buy, you are rich enough to rob'; but before ever he could put his hand to his knife, Dravot breaks his neck over his knee, and the other party runs away. So Carnehan loaded the mules with the rifles that was taken off the camels, and together we starts forward into those bitter cold mountainous parts, and never a road broader than the back of your hand."

He paused for a moment, while I asked him if he could remember the nature of the country through which he had journeyed.

"I am telling you as straight as I can, but my head isn't as good as it might be. They drove nails through it to make me hear better how Dravot died. The country was mountainous and the mules were most contrary, and the inhabitants was dispersed and solitary. They went up and up, and down and down, and that other party, Carnehan, was imploring of Dravot not to sing and whistle so loud, for fear of bringing down the tremenjus avalanches. But Dravot says that if a King couldn't sing it wasn't worth being King, and whacked the mules over the rump, and never took no heed for ten cold days. We came to a big level valley all among the mountains, and the mules were near dead, so we killed them, not having anything in special for them or us to eat. We sat upon the boxes, and played odds and even with the cartridges that was jolted out.

"Then ten men with bows and arrows ran down that valley, chasing twenty men with bows and arrows, and the row was tremenjus. They was fair men—fairer than you or me—with yellow hair and remarkable well built. Says Dravot, unpacking the guns—'This is the beginning of the business. We'll fight for the ten men,' and with that he fires two rifles at the twenty men, and drops one of them at two hundred yards from the rock where we was sitting. The other men began to run but Carnehan and Dravot sits on the boxes picking them off at all ranges, up and down the valley. Then we goes up to the ten men that had run across the snow too, and they fires a footy little arrow at us. Dravot he shoots above their heads and they all falls down flat. Then he walks over them and kicks them, and then he lifts them up and shakes hands all round to make them friendly like. He calls them and gives them the boxes to carry, and waves his hand for all the world as though he was King already. They takes the boxes and him across the valley and up the hill into a pine wood on the top, where there was half a dozen big stone idols. Dravot he goes to the biggest—a fellow they call Imbra—and lays a rifle and cartridge at his feet, rubbing his nose respectful with his own nose, patting him on the head, and saluting in front of it. He turns round to the men and nods his head, and says,— 'That's all right. I'm in the know too, and all these old jim-jams are my friends.' Then he opens his mouth and points down it, and when the first man brings him food, he says—'No'; and when the second man brings him food, he says 'No'; but when one of the old priests and the boss of the village brings him food, he says—'Yes'; very haughty, and eats it slow. That was how we came to our first village, without any trouble, just as though we had tumbled from the skies. But we tumbled from one of those damned rope-bridges, you see, and you couldn't expect a man to laugh much after that."

"Take some more whiskey and go on," I said. "That was the first village you came into. How did you get to be King?"

"I wasn't King," said Carnehan. "Dravot he was the King, and a handsome man he looked with the gold crown on his head and all. Him and the other party stayed in that village, and every morning Dravot sat by the side of old Imbra, and the people came and worshipped. That was Dravot's order. Then a lot of men came into the valley, and Carnehan and Dravot picks them off with the rifles before they knew where they was, and runs down into the valley and up again the other side, and finds another village, same as the first one, and the people all falls down flat on their faces, and Dravot says,—'Now what is the trouble between you two villages?' and the people points to a woman, as fair as you or me, that was carried off, and Dravot takes her back to the first village and counts up the dead—eight there was. For each dead man Dravot pours a little milk on the ground and waves his arms like a whirligig and 'That's all right,' says he. Then he and Carnehan takes the big boss of each village by the arm and walks them down into the valley, and shows them how to scratch a line with a spear right down the valley, and gives each a sod of turf from both sides o' the line. Then all the people comes down and shouts like the devil and all, and Dravot says,—'Go and dig the land, and be fruitful and multiply,' which they did, though they didn't understand.

Then we asks the names of things in their lingo—bread and water and fire and idols and such, and Dravot leads the priest of each village up to the idol, and says he must sit there and judge the people, and if anything goes wrong he is to be shot.

"Next week they was all turning up the land in the valley as quiet as bees and much prettier, and the priests heard all the complaints and told Dravot in dumb show what it was about. 'That's just the beginning,' said Dravot. 'They think we're Gods.' He and Carnehan picks out twenty good men and shows them how to click off a rifle, and form fours, and advance in line, and they was very pleased to do so, and clever to see the hang of it. Then he takes out his pipe and his baccy-pouch and leaves one at one village and one at the other, and off we two goes to see what was to be done in the next valley. That was all rock, and there was a little village there, and Carnehan says,—'Send 'em to the old valley to plant,' and takes 'em there and gives 'em some land that wasn't took before. They were a poor lot, and we blooded 'em with a kid before letting 'em into the new Kingdom. That was to impress the people, and then they settled down quiet, and Carnehan went back to Dravot who had got into another valley, all snow and ice and most mountainous. There was no people there and the Army got afraid, so Dravot shoots one of them, and goes on till he finds some people in a village, and the Army explains that unless the people wants to be killed they had better not shoot their little matchlocks; for they had matchlocks. We make friends with the priest and I stays there alone with two of the Army, teaching the men how to drill, and a thundering big Chief comes across the snow with kettle-drums and horns twanging, because he heard there was a new God kicking about. Carnehan sights for the brown of the men half a mile across the snow and wings one of them. Then he sends a message to the Chief that, unless he wished to be killed, he must come and shake hands with me and leave his arms behind. The chief comes alone first, and Carnehan shakes hands with him and whirls his arms about, same as Dravot used, and very much surprised that Chief was, and strokes my eyebrows. Then Carnehan goes alone to the Chief, and asks him in dumb show if he had an enemy he hated. 'I have,' says the Chief. So Carnehan weeds out the pick of his men, and sets the two of the Army to show them drill and at the end of two weeks the men can manœuvre about as well as Volunteers. So he marches with the Chief to a great big plain on the top of a mountain, and the Chief's men rushes into a village and takes it; we three Martinis firing into the brown of the enemy. So we took that village too, and I gives the Chief a rag from my coat and says, 'Occupy till I come': which was scriptural. By way of a reminder, when me and the Army was eighteen hundred yards away, I drops a bullet near him standing on the snow, and all the•people falls flat on their faces. Then I sends a letter to Dravot, wherever he be by land or by sea."

At the risk of throwing the creature out of train I interrupted, "How could you write a letter up yonder?"

"The letter? Oh!—The letter! Keep looking at me between the eyes, please. It was a string-talk letter, that we'd learned the way of it from a blind beggar in the Punjab."

I remember that there had once come to the office a blind man with a knotted twig and a piece of string which he wound round the twig according to some cypher of his own. He could, after the lapse of days or hours, repeat the sentence which he had reeled up. He had reduced the alphabet to eleven primitive sounds; and tried to teach me his method, but failed.

"I sent that letter to Dravot," said Carnehan; "and told him to come back because this Kingdom was growing too big for me to handle, and then I struck for the first valley, to see how the priests were working. They called the village we took along with the Chief, Bashkai, and the first village we took, Er-Heb. The priests at Er-

Heb were doing all right, but they had a lot of pending cases about land to show me, and some men from another village had been firing arrows at night. I went out and looked for that village and fired four rounds at it from a thousand yards. That used all the cartridges I cared to spend, and I waited for Dravot, who had been away two or three months, and I kept my people quiet.

"One morning I heard the devil's own noise of drums and horns, and Dan Dravot marches down the hill with his Army and a tail of hundreds of men, and, which was the most amazing—a great gold crown on his head. 'My Gord, Carnehan,' says Daniel, 'this is a tremendjus business, and we've got the whole country as far as it's worth having. I am the son of Alexander by Queen Semiramis, and you're my younger brother and a God too! It's the biggest thing we've ever seen. I've been marching and fighting for six weeks with the Army, and every footy little village for fifty miles has come in rejoiceful; and more than that, I've got the key of the whole show, as you'll see, and I've got a crown for you! I told 'em to make two of 'em at a place called Shu, where the gold lies in the rock like suet in mutton. Gold I've seen, and turquoise I've kicked out of the cliffs, and there's garnets in the sands of the river, and here's a chunk of amber that a man brought me. Call up all the priests and, here, take your crown.'

"One of the men opens a black hair bag and I slips the crown on. It was too small and too heavy, but I wore it for the glory. Hammered gold it was—five pound weight, like a hoop of a barrel.

" 'Peachey,' says Dravot, 'we don't want to fight no more. The Craft's the trick so help me!' and he brings forward that same Chief that I left at Bashkai—Billy Fish we called him afterward, because he was so like Billy Fish that drove the big tank-engine at Mach on the Bolan in the old days. 'Shake hands with him,' says Dravot, and I shook hands and nearly dropped, for Billy Fish gave me the Grip. I said nothing, but tried him with the Fellow Craft Grip. He answers, all right, and I tried the Master's Grip, but that was a slip. 'A Fellow Craft he is!' I says to Dan. 'Does he know the word?' 'He does,' says Dan, 'and all the priests know. It's a miracle! The Chiefs and the priests can work a Fellow Craft Lodge in a way that's very like ours, and they've cut the marks on the rocks, but they don't know the Third Degree, and they've come to find out. It's Gord's Truth. I've known these long years that the Afghans knew up to the Fellow Craft Degree, but this is a miracle. A God and a Grand-Master of the Craft am I, and a Lodge in the Third Degree I will open, and we'll raise the head priests and the Chiefs of the villages.'

" 'It's against all the law,' I says, 'holding a Lodge without warrant from any one; and we never held office in any Lodge.'

" 'It's a master-stroke of policy,' says Dravot. 'It means running the country as easy as a four-wheeled bogy on a down grade. We can't stop to inquire now, or they'll turn against us. I've forty Chiefs at my heel, and passed and raised according to their merit they shall be. Billet these men on the villages and see that we run up a Lodge of some kind. The temple of Imbra will do for the Lodge-room. The women must make aprons as you show them. I'll hold a levee of Chiefs to-night and Lodge to-morrow.'

"I was fair run off my legs, but I wasn't such a fool as not to see what a pull this Craft business gave us. I showed the priests' families how to make aprons of the degrees, but for Dravot's apron the blue border and marks was made of turquoise lumps on white hide, not cloth. We took a great square stone in the temple for the Master's chair, and little stones for the officers' chairs, and painted the black pavement with white squares, and did what we could to make things regular.

"At the levee which was held that night on the hillside with big bonfires, Dravot gives out that him and me were Gods and sons of Alexander, and Past Grand-Masters in

the Craft, and was come to make Kafiristan a country
where every man should eat in peace and drink in quiet,
and specially obey us. Then the Chiefs come round to
shake hands, and they was so hairy and white and fair it
was just shaking hands with old friends. We gave them
names according as they was like men we had known in
India—Billy Fish, Holly Dilworth, Pikky Kergan that
was Bazar-master when I was at Mhow, and so on and
so on.

"The *most* amazing miracle was at Lodge next night.
One of the old priests was watching us continuous, and I
felt uneasy, for I knew we'd have to fudge the Ritual,
and I didn't know what the men knew. The old priest
was a stranger come in from beyond the village of Bashkai. The minute Dravot puts on the Master's apron that
the girls had made for him, the priest fetches a whoop
and a howl, and tries to overturn the stone that Dravot
was sitting on. 'It's all up now,' I says. 'That comes of
meddling with the Craft without warrant!' Dravot never
winked an eye, not when ten priests took and tilted over
the Grand-Master's chair—which was to say the stone of
Imbra. The priest begins rubbing the bottom end of it to
clear away the black dirt, and presently he shows all the
other priests the Master's Mark, same as was on Dravot's
apron, cut into the stone. Not even the priests of the
temple of Imbra knew it was there. The old chap falls
flat on his face at Dravot's feet and kisses 'em. 'Luck
again,' says Dravot, across the Lodge to me, 'they say it's
the missing Mark that no one could understand the why
of. We're more than safe now.' Then he bangs the butt of
his gun for a gavel and says:—'By virtue of the author-
ity vested in me by my own right hand and the help of
Peachey, I declare myself Grand-Master of all Freema-
sonry in Kafiristan in this the Mother Lodge o' the country, and King of Kafiristan equally with Peachey!' At
that he puts on his crown and I puts on mine—I was doing Senior Warden—and we opens the Lodge in most
ample form. It was an amazing miracle! The priests

moved in Lodge through the first two degrees almost without telling, as if the memory was coming back to them. After that, Peachey and Dravot raised such as was worthy—high priests and Chiefs of far-off villages. Billy Fish was the first, and I can tell you we scared the soul out of him. It was not in any way according to Ritual, but it served our turn. We didn't raise more than ten of the biggest men because we didn't want to make the Degree common. And they was clamoring to be raised.

" 'In another six months,' says Dravot, 'we'll hold another Communication and see how you are working.' Then he asks them about their villages, and learns that they was fighting one against the other and were fair sick and tired of it. And when they wasn't doing that they was fighting with the Mohammedans. 'You can fight those when they come into our country,' says Dravot. 'Tell off every tenth man of your tribes for a Frontier guard, and send two hundred at a time to this valley to be drilled. Nobody is going to be shot or speared any more so long as he does well, and I know that you won't cheat me because you're white people—sons of Alexander—and not like common, black Mohammedans. You are *my* people and by God,' says he, running off into English at the end—'I'll make a damned fine Nation of you, or I'll die in the making!'

"I can't tell all we did for the next six months because Dravot did a lot I couldn't see the hang of, and he learned their lingo in a way I never could. My work was to help the people plough, and now and again go out with some of the Army and see what the other villages were doing, and make 'em throw rope-bridges across the ravines which cut up the country horrid. Dravot was very kind to me, but when he walked up and down in the pine wood pulling that bloody red beard of his with both fists I knew he was thinking plans I could not advise him about, and I just waited for orders.

"But Dravot never showed me disrespect before the people. They were afraid of me and the Army, but they loved Dan. He was the best of friends with the priests and the Chiefs; but any one could come across the hills with a complaint and Dravot would hear him out fair, and call four priests together and say what was to be done. He used to call in Billy Fish from Bashkai, and Pikky Kergan from Shu, and an old Chief we called Kafuzelum—it was like enough to his real name—and hold councils with 'em when there was any fighting to be done in small villages. That was his Council of War, and the four priests of Bashkai, Shu, Khawak, and Madora was his Privy Council. Between the lot of 'em they send me, with forty men and twenty rifles, and sixty men carrying turquoises, into the Ghorband country to buy those hand-made Martini rifles, that come out of the Amir's workshops at Kabul, from one of the Amir's Herati regiments that would have sold the very teeth out of their mouths for turquoises.

"I stayed in Ghorband a month, and gave the Governor there the pick of my baskets for hush-money, and bribed the Colonel of the regiment some more, and, between the two and the tribes-people, we got more than a hundred hand-made Martinis, a hundred good Kohat Jezails, that'll throw to six hundred yards, and forty man-loads of very bad ammunition for the rifles. I came back with what I had, and distributed 'em among the men that the Chiefs sent to me to drill. Dravot was too busy to attend to those things, but the old Army that we first made helped me, and we turned out five hundred men that could drill, and two hundred that knew how to hold arms pretty straight. Even those cork-screwed, hand-made guns was a miracle to them. Dravot talked big about powder-shops and factories, walking up and down in the pine wood when the winter was coming on.

"'I won't make a Nation,' says he, 'I'll make an Empire! These men aren't niggers; they're English! Look at their eyes—look at their mouths. Look at the way they stand up. They sit on chairs in their own houses. They're the Lost Tribes, or something like it, and they've grown to be English. I'll take a census in the spring if the priests don't get frightened. There must be a fair two million of 'em in these hills. The villages are full o' little children. Two million people—two hundred and fifty thousand fighting men—and all English! They only want the rifles and a little drilling. Two hundred and fifty thousand men, ready to cut in on Russia's right flank when she tries for India! Peachey, man,' he says, chewing his beard in great hunks, 'we shall be Emperors—Emperors of the Earth! Rajah Brooke will be a suckling to us. I'll treat with the Viceroy on equal terms. I'll ask him to send me twelve picked English—twelve that I know of—to help us govern a bit. There's Mackray, Sergeant-pensioner at Segowli—many's the good dinner he's given me, and his wife a pair of trousers. There's Donkin, the Warder of Tounghoo Jail; there's hundreds that I could lay my hand on if I was in India. The Viceroy shall do it for me. I'll send a man through in the spring for those men, and I'll write for a dispensation from the Grand Lodge for what I've done as Grand-Master. That —and all the Sniders that'll be thrown out when the native troops in India take up the Martini. They'll be worn smooth, but they'll do for fighting in these hills. Twelve English, a hundred thousand Sniders run through the Amir's country in driblets—I'd be content with twenty thousand in one year—and we'd be an Empire. When everything was shipshape, I'd hand over the crown—this crown I'm wearing now—to Queen Victoria on my knees, and she'd say: "Rise up, Sir Daniel Dravot." Oh, it's big! It's big, I tell you! But there's so much to be done in every place—Bashkai, Khawak, Shu, and everywhere else.'

" 'What is it?' I says. 'There are no more men coming in to be drilled this autumn. Look at those fat, black clouds. They're bringing the snow.'

" 'It isn't that,' says Daniel, putting his hand very hard on my shoulder; 'and I don't wish to say anything that's against you, for no other living man would have followed me and made me what I am as you have done. You're a first-class Commander-in-Chief, and the people know you; but—it's a big country, and somehow you can't help me, Peachey, in the way I want to be helped.'

"'Go to your blasted priests then!' I said, and I was sorry when I made that remark, but it did hurt me sore to find Daniel talking so superior when I'd drilled all the men, and done all he told me.

"'Don't let's quarrel, Peachey,' says Daniel, without cursing. 'You're a King too, and the half of this Kingdom is yours; but can't you see, Peachey, we want cleverer men than us now—three or four of 'em, that we can scatter about for our Deputies. It's a hugeous great State, and I can't always tell the right thing to do, and I haven't time for all I want to do, and here's the winter coming on and all.' He put half his beard into his mouth, and it was as red as the gold of his crown.

"'I'm sorry, Daniel,' says I. 'I've done all I could. I've drilled the men and shown the people how to stack their oats better; and I've brought in those tinware rifles from Ghorband—but I know what you're driving at. I take it Kings always feel oppressed that way.'

"'There's another thing too,' says Dravot, walking up and down. 'The winter's coming and these people won't be giving much trouble, and if they do we can't move about. I want a wife.'

"'For God's sake leave the women alone!' I says. 'We've both got all the work we can, though I *am* a fool. Remember the Contrack, and keep clear o' women.'

"'The Contrack only lasted till such time as we was Kings; and Kings we have been these months past,' says Dravot, weighing his crown in his hand. 'You go get a wife too, Peachey—a nice, strappin', plump girl that'll keep you warm in the winter. They're prettier than English girls, and we can take the pick of 'em. Boil 'em once or twice in hot water, and they'll come as fair as chicken and ham.'

"'Don't tempt me!' I says. 'I will not have any deal-

ings with a woman not till we are a dam' side more settled than we are now. I've been doing the work o' two
men, and you've been doing the work o' three. Let's lie
off a bit, and see if we can get some better tobacco from
Afghan country and run in some good liquor; but no
women.'

" 'Who's talking o' *women?*' says Dravot. 'I said *wife*
—a Queen to breed a King's son for the King. A Queen
out of the strongest tribe, that'll make them your blood-
brothers, and that'll lie by your side and tell you all the
people thinks about you and their own affairs. That's
what I want.'

" 'Do you remember that Bengali woman I kept at
Mogul Serai when I was a plate-layer?' says I. 'A fat lot
o' good she was to me. She taught me the lingo and one
or two other things; but what happened? She ran away
with the Station Master's servant and half my month's
pay. Then she turned up at Dadur Junction in tow of a
half-caste, and had the impidence to say I was her husband—all among the drivers in the running-shed!'

" 'We've done with that,' says Dravot. 'These women
are whiter than you or me, and a Queen I will have for
the winter months.'

" 'For the last time o' asking, Dan, do *not*,' I says.
'It'll only bring us harm. The Bible says that Kings ain't
to waste their strength on women, 'specially when
they've got a new raw Kingdom to work over.'

" 'For the last time of answering I will,' said Dravot,
and he went away through the pine-trees looking like a
big red devil. The low sun hit his crown and beard on
one side and the two blazed like hot coals.

"But getting a wife was not as easy as Dan thought.
He put it before the Council, and there was no answer
till Billy Fish said that he'd better ask the girls. Dravot
damned them all round. 'What's wrong with me?' he
shouts, standing by the idol Imbra. 'Am I a dog or am I
not enough of a man for your wenches? Haven't I put
the shadow of my hand over this country? Who stopped

the last Afghan raid?' It was me really, but Dravot was too angry to remember. 'Who brought your guns? Who repaired the bridges? Who's the Grand-Master of the sign cut in the stone?' and he thumped his hand on the block that he used to sit on in Lodge, and at Council, which opened like Lodge always. Billy Fish said nothing and no more did the others. 'Keep your hair on, Dan,' said I; 'and ask the girls. That's how it's done at Home, and these people are quite English.'

" 'The marriage of the King is a matter of State,' says Dan, in a white-hot rage, for he could feel, I hope, that he was going against his better mind. He walked out of the Council-room, and the others sat still, looking at the ground.

" 'Billy Fish,' says I to the Chief of Bashkai, 'what's the difficulty here? A straight answer to a true friend.' 'You know,' says Billy Fish. 'How should a man tell you who knows everything? How can daughters of men marry Gods or Devils? It's not proper.'

"I remember something like that in the Bible; but, if, after seeing us as long as they had they still believed we were Gods, it wasn't for me to undeceive them.

" 'A God can do anything,' says I. 'If the King is fond of a girl he'll not let her die.' 'She'll have to,' said Billy Fish. 'There are all sorts of Gods and Devils in these mountains, and now and again a girl marries one of them and isn't seen any more. Besides, you two know the Mark cut in the stone. Only the Gods know that. We thought you were men till you showed the sign of the Master.'

"I wished then that we had explained about the loss of the genuine secrets of a Master-Mason at the first go-off; but I said nothing. All that night there was a blowing of horns in a little dark temple halfway down the hill, and I heard a girl crying fit to die. One of the priests told us that she was being prepared to marry the King.

" 'I'll have no nonsense of that kind,' says Dan. 'I don't want to interfere with your customs, but I'll take my own wife.' 'The girl's a little bit afraid,' says the priest. 'She thinks she's going to die, and they are a-heartening of her up down in the temple.'

" 'Hearten her very tender, then,' says Dravot, 'or I'll hearten you with the butt of a gun so that you'll never want to be heartened again.' He licked his lips, did Dan, and stayed up walking about more than half the night, thinking of the wife that he was going to get in the morning. I wasn't any means comfortable, for I knew that dealings with a woman in foreign parts, though you was a crowned King twenty times over, could not but be risky. I got up very early in the morning while Dravot was asleep, and I saw the priests talking together in whispers, and the Chiefs talking together too, and they looked at me out of the corners of their eyes.

" 'What is up, Fish?' I says to the Bashkai man, who was wrapped up in his furs and looking splendid to behold.

" 'I can't rightly say,' says he; 'but if you can induce the King to drop all this nonsense about marriage, you'll be doing him and me and yourself a great service.'

" 'That I do believe,' says I. 'But sure, you know, Billy, as well as me, having fought against and for us, that the King and me are nothing more than two of the finest men that God Almighty ever made. Nothing more, I do assure you.'

" 'That may be,' says Billy Fish, 'and yet I should be sorry if it was.' He sinks his head upon his great fur cloak for a minute and thinks. 'King,' says he, 'be you man or God or Devil, I'll stick by you to-day. I have twenty of my men with me, and they will follow me. We'll go to Bashkai until the storm blows over.'

"A little snow had fallen in the night, and everything was white except the greasy fat clouds that blew down and down from the north. Dravot came out with his crown on his head, swinging his arms and stamping his feet, and looking more pleased than Punch.

" 'For the last time, drop it, Dan,' says I, in a whisper. 'Billy Fish here says that there will be a row.'

" 'A row among my people!' says Dravot. 'Not much. Peachey, you're a fool not to get a wife too. Where's the girl?' says he, with a voice as loud as the braying of a jackass. 'Call up all the Chiefs and priests, and let the Emperor see if his wife suits him.'

"There was no need to call any one. They were all there leaning on their guns and spears round the clearing in the centre of the pine wood. A deputation of priests went down to the little temple to bring up the girl, and the horns blew up fit to wake the dead. Billy Fish saunters round and gets as close to Daniel as he could, and behind him stood his twenty men with matchlocks. Not a man of them under six feet. I was next to Dravot, and behind me was twenty men of the regular Army. Up comes the girl, and a strapping wench she was, covered with silver and turquoises but white as death, and looking back every minute at the priests.

" 'She'll do,' said Dan, looking her over. 'What's to be afraid of, lass? Come and kiss me.' He puts his arm round her. She shuts her eyes, gives a bit of a squeak, and down goes her face in the side of Dan's flaming red beard.

" 'The slut's bitten me!' says he, clapping his hand to his neck, and, sure enough, his hand was red with blood. Billy Fish and two of his matchlock-men catches hold of Dan by the shoulders and drags him into the Bashkai lot, while the priests howls in their lingo,—'Neither God nor Devil but a man!' I was all taken aback, for a priest cut at me in front, and the Army behind began firing into the Bashkai men.

" 'God A-mighty!' says Dan. 'What is the meaning o' this?'

" 'Come back! Come away!' says Billy Fish. 'Ruin and Mutiny is the matter. We'll break for Bashkai if we can.'

"I tried to give some sort of orders to my men—the men o' the regular Army—but it was no use, so I fired into the brown of 'em with an English Martini and drilled three beggars in a line. The valley was full of shouting, howling creatures, and every soul was shrieking, 'Not a God nor a Devil but only a man!' The Bashkai troops stuck to Billy Fish all they were worth, but their matchlocks wasn't half as good as the Kabul breach-loaders, and four of them dropped. Dan was bellowing like a bull, for he was very wrathy; and Billy Fish had a hard job to prevent him running out at the crowd.

"'We can't stand,' says Billy Fish. 'Make a run for it down the valley! The whole place is against us.' The matchlock-men ran, and we went down the valley in spite of Dravot's protestations. He was swearing horribly and crying out that he was a King. The priests rolled great stones on us, and the regular Army fired hard, and there wasn't more than six men, not counting Dan, Billy Fish, and Me, that came down to the bottom of the valley alive.

"Then they stopped firing and the horns in the temple blew again. 'Come away—for Gord's sake come away!' says Billy Fish. 'They'll send runners out to all the villages before ever we get to Bashkai. I can protect you there, but I can't do anything now.'

"My own notion is that Dan began to go mad in his head from that hour. He stared up and down like a stuck pig. Then he was all for walking back alone and killing the priests with his bare hands; which he could have done. 'An Emperor am I,' says Daniel, 'and next year I shall be a Knight of the Queen.'

"'All right, Dan,' says I; 'but come along now while there's time.'

"'It's your fault,' says he, 'for not looking after your Army better. There was mutiny in the midst, and you didn't know—you damned engine-driving, plate-laying, missionary's-pass-hunting hound!' He sat upon a rock and called me every foul name he could lay tongue to. I was too heart-sick to care, though it was all his foolishness that brought the smash.

" 'I'm sorry, Dan,' says I, 'but there's no accounting for natives. This business is our Fifty-Seven. Maybe we'll make something out of it yet, when we've got to Bashkai.'

" 'Let's get to Bashkai, then,' says Dan, 'and, by God, when I come back here again I'll sweep the valley so there isn't a bug in a blanket left!'

"We walked all that day, and all that night Dan was stumping up and down on the snow, chewing his beard and muttering to himself.

" 'There's no hope o' getting clear,' said Billy Fish. 'The priests will have sent runners to the villages to say that you are only men. Why didn't you stick on as Gods till things was more settled? I'm a dead man,' says Billy Fish, and he throws himself down on the snow and begins to pray to his Gods.

"Next morning we was in a cruel bad country—all up and down, no level ground at all, and no food either. The six Bashkai men looked at Billy Fish hungry-wise as if they wanted to ask something, but they said never a word. At noon we came to the top of a flat mountain all covered with snow, and when we climbed up into it, behold, there was an Army in position waiting in the middle!

" 'The runners have been very quick,' says Billy Fish, with a little bit of a laugh. 'They are waiting for us.'

"Three or four men began to fire from the enemy's side, and a chance shot took Daniel in the calf of the leg. That brought him to his senses. He looks across the snow at the Army, and sees the rifles that we had brought into the country.

" 'We're done for,' says he. 'They are Englishmen, these people,—and it's my blasted nonsense that has brought you to this. Get back, Billy Fish, and take your men away; you've done what you could, and now cut for it. Carne-han,' says he, 'shake hands with me and go along with Billy. Maybe they won't kill you. I'll go and meet 'em alone. It's me that did it. Me, the King!'

"'Go!' says I. 'Go to Hell, Dan. I'm with you here. Billy Fish, you clear out, and we two will meet those folk.'

"'I'm a Chief,' says Billy Fish, quite quiet. 'I stay with you. My men can go.'

"The Bashkai fellows didn't wait for a second word but ran off, and Dan and Me and Billy Fish walked across to where the drums were drumming and the horns were horning. It was cold—awful cold. I've got that cold in the back of my head now. There's a lump of it there."

The punkah-coolies had gone to sleep. Two kerosene lamps were blazing in the office, and the perspiration poured down my face and splashed on the blotter as I leaned forward. Carnehan was shivering, and I feared that his mind might go. I wiped my face, took a fresh grip of the piteously mangled hands, and said:—"What happened after that?"

The momentary shift of my eyes had broken the clear current.

"What was you pleased to say?" whined Carnehan. "They took them without any sound. Not a little whisper all along the snow, not though the King knocked down the first man that set hand on him—not though old Peachey fired his last cartridge into the brown of 'em. Not a single solitary sound did those swines make. They just closed up tight, and I tell you their furs stunk. There was a man called Billy Fish, a good friend of us all, and they cut his throat, Sir, then and there, like a pig; and the King kicks up the bloody snow and says: 'We've had a dashed fine run for our money. What's coming next?' But Peachey, Peachey Taliaferro, I tell you, Sir, in confidence as betwixt two friends, he lost his head, Sir. No, he didn't neither. The King lost his head, so he did, all along o' one of those cunning rope-bridges. Kindly let me have the paper-cutter, Sir. It tilted this way. They marched him a mile across that snow to a rope-bridge over a ravine with a river at the bottom. You may have seen such. They prodded him behind like an ox. 'Damn your eyes!' says the King 'D'you suppose I can't die like a gentleman?' He turns to Peachey—Peachey that was crying like a child. 'I've brought you to this, Peachey,' says he. 'Brought you out of your happy life to be killed in Kafiristan, where you was late Commander-in-Chief of the Emperor's forces. Say you forgive me, Peachey.' 'I do,' says Peachey. 'Fully and freely do I forgive you, Dan.' 'Shake hands, Peachey,' says he. 'I'm going now.' Out he goes, looking neither right nor left, and when he was plump in the middle of those dizzy dancing ropes. 'Cut, you beggars,' he shouts; and they cut, and old Dan fell, turning round and round and round twenty thousand miles, for he took half an hour to fall till he struck the water, and I could see his body caught on a rock with the gold crown close beside.

"But do you know what they did to Peachey between two pine trees? They crucified him, Sir, as Peachey's hand will show. They used wooden pegs for his hands and his feet; and he didn't die. He hung there and screamed, and they took him down next day, and said it was a miracle that he wasn't dead. They took him down—poor old Peachey that hadn't done them any harm—that hadn't done them any. . . ."

He rocked to and fro and wept bitterly, wiping his eyes with the back of his scarred hands and moaning like a child for some ten minutes.

"They were cruel enough to feed him up in the temple, because they said he was more of a God than old Daniel that was a man. Then they turned him out on the snow, and told him to go home, and Peachey came home in about a year, begging along the roads quite safe; for Daniel Dravot he walked before and said:—'Come along, Peachey. It's a big thing we're doing.' The mountains they danced at night, and the mountains they tried to fall on Peachey's head, but Dan he held up his hand, and Peachey came along bent double. He never let go of Dan's hand, and he never let go of Dan's head. They gave it to him as a present in the temple, to remind him not to come again, and though the crown was pure gold, and Peachey was starving, never would Peachey sell the same. You knew Dravot, Sir! You knew Right Worshipful Brother Dravot! Look at him now!"

He fumbled in the mass of rags round his bent waist; brought out a black horsehair bag embroidered with silver thread; and shook therefrom on to my table—the dried, withered head of Daniel Dravot! The morning sun that had long been paling the lamps struck the red beard and blind sunken eyes; struck, too, a heavy circlet of gold studded with raw turquoises, that Carnehan placed tenderly on the battered temples.

"You behold now," said Carnehan, "the Emperor in his habit as he lived—the King of Kafiristan with his crown upon his head. Poor old Daniel that was a monarch once!"

I shuddered, for, in spite of defacements manifold, I recognized the head of the man of Marwar Junction. Carnehan rose to go. I attempted to stop him. He was not fit to walk abroad. "Let me take away the whiskey and give me a little money," he gasped. "I was a King once. I'll go to the Deputy Commissioner and ask to set in the Poorhouse till I get my health. No, thank you, I can't wait till you get a carriage for me. I've urgent private affairs—in the south—at Marwar."

He shambled out of the office and departed in the direction of the Deputy Commissioner's house. That day at noon I had occasion to go down the blinding hot Mall, and I saw a crooked man crawling along the white dust of the roadside, his hat in his hand, quavering dolorously after the fashion of street-singers at Home. There was not a soul in sight and he was out of all possible earshot of the houses. And he sang through his nose, turning his head from right to left:

> *The Son of Man goes forth to war,*
> *A golden crown to gain;*
> *His blood-red banner streams afar—*
> *Who follows in his train?*

I waited to hear no more, but put the poor wretch into my carriage and drove him off to the nearest missionary for eventual transfer to the Asylum. He repeated the hymn twice while he was with me whom he did not in the least recognize, and I left him singing it to the missionary.

Two days later I inquired after his welfare of the Superintendent of the Asylum.

"He was admitted suffering from sun-stroke. He died early yesterday morning," said the Superintendent. "Is it true that he was half an hour bareheaded in the sun at midday?"

"Yes," said I, "but do you happen to know if he had anything upon him by any chance when he died!"

"Not to my knowledge," said the Superintendent.

And there the matter rests.

The King's Messenger

By RAFAEL SABATINI

ON A BRILLIANT May morning of the year 1690 a gentleman stepped ashore at Santiago de Porto Rico, followed by a negro servant shouldering a valise. He had been brought to the mole in a cock-boat from the yellow galleon standing in the roadstead, with the flag of Spain floating from her maintruck. Having landed him, the cock-boat went smartly about, and was pulled back to the ship, from which circumstance the gaping idlers on the mole assumed that this gentleman had come to stay.

They stared at him with interest, as they would have stared at any stranger. This, however, was a man whose exterior repaid their attention, a man to take the eye. Even the wretched white slaves toiling half-naked on the fortifications, and the Spanish soldiery guarding them, stood at gaze.

Tall, straight, and vigorously spare, our gentleman was dressed with sombre Spanish elegance in black and silver. The curls of his black periwig fell to his shoulders, and his keen shaven face with its high-bridged nose and disdainful lips was shaded by a broad black hat about the crown of which swept a black ostrich plume. Jewels flashed at his breast, a foam of Mechlin almost concealed his hands, and there were ribbons to the long gold-mounted ebony cane he carried. A fop from the Alameda he must have seemed but for the manifest vigour of him and the air of assurance and consequence with which he bore himself. He carried his dark finery with an indifference to the broiling tropical heat which argued an iron constitution, and his glance was so imperious that the eyes of the inquisitive fell away abashed before it.

He asked the way to the Governor's residence, and the officer commanding the guard over the toiling white prisoners detached a soldier to conduct him.

Beyond the square, which architecturally, and saving for the palm trees throwing patches of black shadow on the dazzling white sun-drenched ground, might have belonged to some little town in Old Spain, past the church with its twin spires and marble steps, they came, by tall, wrought-iron gates, into a garden, and by an avenue of acacias to a big white house with deep external galleries all clad in jessamine. Negro servants in ridiculously rich red-and-yellow liveries admitted our gentleman, and went to announce to the Governor of Porto Rico the arrival of Don Pedro de Queiroz on a mission from King Philip.

Not every day did a messenger from the King of Spain arrive in this almost the least of his Catholic Majesty's overseas dominions. Indeed, the thing had never happened before, and Don Jayme de Villamarga, whilst thrilled to the marrow by the announcement, knew not whether to assign the thrill to pride or to alarm.

A man of middle height, big of head and paunch, and of less than mediocre intelligence, Don Jayme was one of those gentlemen who best served Spain by being absent from her, and this no doubt had been considered in appointing him Governor of Porto Rico. Not even his awe of majesty, represented by Don Pedro, could repress his naturally self-sufficient manner. He was pompous in his reception of him, and remained unintimidated by the cold haughty stare of Don Pedro's eyes—eyes of a singularly deep blue, contrasting oddly with his bronzed face. A Dominican monk, elderly, tall and gaunt, kept his excellency company.

"Sir, I give you welcome." Don Jayme spoke as if his mouth were full. "I trust you will announce to me that I have the honour to meet with his majesty's approbation."

Don Pedro made him a deep obeisance, with a sweep of his plumed hat, which, together with his cane, he thereafter handed to one of the negro lackeys. "It is to signify the royal approbation that I am here, happily, after some adventures. I have just landed from the 'San Tomas,' after a voyage of many vicissitudes. She has gone on to San Domingo, and it may be three or four days before she returns to take me off again. For that brief while I must make free with your excellency's hospitality." He seemed to claim it as a right rather than ask it as a favour.

"Ah!" was all that Don Jayme permitted himself to answer. And with head on one side, a fatuous smile on the thick lips under his grizzled moustache, he waited for the visitor to enter into details of the royal message.

The visitor, however, displayed no haste. He looked about him at the cool spacious room with its handsome furnishings of carved oak and walnut, its tapestries and pictures, all imported from the Old World, and inquired, in that casual manner of the man who is at home in every environment, if he might be seated. His excellency with some loss of dignity made haste to set a chair.

Composedly, with a thin smile which Don Jayme disliked, the messenger sat down and crossed his legs.

"We are," he announced, "in some sort related, Don Jayme."

Don Jayme stared. "I am not aware of the honour."

"That is why I am at the trouble of informing you. Your marriage, sir, established the bond. I am a distant cousin of Doña Hernanda."

"Oh! My wife!" His excellency's tone in some subtle way implied contempt for that same wife and her relations. "I had remarked your name: Queiroz." This also explained to him the rather hard and open accent of Don Pedro's otherwise impeccable Castilian. "You will, then, be Portuguese, like Doña Hernanda?" and again his tone implied contempt of Portuguese, and particularly perhaps of Portuguese who were in the service of the King of Spain, from whom Portugal had re-established her independence a half-century ago.

"Half Portuguese, of course. My family——"

"Yes, yes." Thus the testy Don Jayme interrupted him. "But your message from his majesty?"

"Ah yes. Your impatience, Don Jayme, is natural." Don Pedro was faintly ironical. "You will forgive me that I should have intruded family matters. My message, then. It will be no surprise to you, sir, that eulogistic reports should have reached his majesty, whom God preserve"— he bowed his head in reverence, compelling Don Jayme to do the same—"not only of the good government of this important island of Porto Rico, but also of the diligence employed by you to rid these seas of the pestilent rovers, particularly the English buccaneers who trouble our shipping and the peace of our Spanish settlements."

There was nothing in this to surprise Don Jayme. Not even upon reflection. Being a fool, he did not suspect that Porto Rico was the worst governed of any Spanish settlement in the West Indies. As for the rest, he had certainly encouraged the extirpation of the buccaneers from the Caribbean. Quite recently, and quite fortuitously be it added, he had actually contributed materially to this desirable end as he was not slow to mention.

With chin high and chest puffed out, he moved, strutting, before Don Pedro as he delivered himself. It was gratifying to be appreciated in the proper quarter. It encouraged endeavour. He desired to be modest. Yet in justice to himself he must assert that under his government the island was tranquil and prosperous. Frey Luis here could bear him out in this. The Faith was firmly planted, and there was no heresy in any form in Porto Rico. And as for the matter of the buccaneers, he had done all that a man in his position could do. Not perhaps as much as he could have desired to do. After all, his office kept him ashore. Had Don Pedro remarked the new fortifications he was building? The work was all but complete, and he did not think that even the infamous Captain Blood would have the hardihood to pay him a visit. He had already shown that redoubtable buccaneer that he was not a man with whom it was prudent to trifle. A party of this Captain Blood's men had dared to land on the southern side of the island a few days ago. But Don Jayme's followers were vigilant. He saw to that. A troop of horse was in the neighbourhood at the time. It had descended upon the pirates and had taught them a sharp lesson. He laughed as he spoke of it; laughed at the thought of it; and Don Pedro politely laughed with him, desiring with courteous and appreciative interest to know more of this.

"You killed them all, of course?" he suggested, his contempt of them implicit in his tone.

"Not yet." His excellency spoke with a relish almost fierce. "But I have them under my hand. Six of them, who were captured. We have not yet decided upon their end. Perhaps the rope. Perhaps an auto-da-fé and the fires of the Faith for them. They are heretics all, of course. It is a matter I am still considering with Frey Luis here."

"Well, well," said Don Pedro, as if the subject began to weary him. "Will your excellency hear the remainder of my message?"

The Governor was annoyed by this suggestion that his lengthy exposition had amounted to an interruption.

Stiffly he bowed to the representative of majesty. "My apologies," said he in a voice of ice.

But the lofty Don Pedro paid little heed to his manner. He drew from an inner pocket of his rich coat a folded parchment and a small flat leather case.

"I have to explain, your excellency, the condition in which this comes to you. I have said, although I do not think you heeded it, that I arrive here after a voyage of many vicissitudes. Indeed, it is little short of a miracle that I am here at all, considering what I have undergone. I, too, have been a victim of that infernal dog, Captain Blood. The ship on which I originally sailed from Cadiz was sunk by him a week ago. More fortunate than my cousin Don Rodrigo de Queiroz, who accompanied me and who remains a prisoner in that infamous pirate's hands, I made my escape. It is a long tale with which I will not weary you."

"It would not weary me," exclaimed his excellency, forgetting his dignity in his interest.

But Don Pedro waved aside the implied request for details. "Later! Later, perhaps, if you care to hear of it. It is not important. What is important on your excellency's account is that I escaped. I was picked up by the 'San Tomas,' which has brought me here, and so I am happily able to discharge my mission." He held up the folded parchment. "I but mention it to explain how this has come to suffer by sea-water, though not to the extent of being illegible. It is a letter from his majesty's Secretary of State informing you that our Sovereign, whom God preserve, has been graciously pleased to create you, in recognition of the services I have mentioned, a knight of the most noble order of St. James of Compostella."

Don Jayme went first white, then red, in his incredulous excitement. With trembling fingers he took the letter and unfolded it. It was certainly damaged by sea-water. Some words were scarcely legible. The ink in which his own surname had been written had run into a smear, as had that

of his government of Porto Rico, and some other words
here and there. But the amazing substance of the letter
was indeed as Don Pedro announced, and the royal signa-
ture was unimpaired.

As Don Jayme raised his eyes at last from the document,
Don Pedro, proffering the leather case, touched a spring
in it. It flew open, and the Governor gazed upon rubies
that glowed like live coals against their background of
black velvet.

"And here," said Don Pedro, "is the insignia; the cross
of the most noble order in which you are invested."

Don Jayme took the case gingerly, as if it had been
some holy thing, and gazed upon the smouldering cross.
The friar came to stand beside him, murmuring congratu-
latory words. Any knighthood would have been an
honourable, an unexpected, reward for Don Jayme's services to the crown of Spain. But that of all orders this most
exalted and coveted order of St. James of Compostella
should have been conferred upon him was something that
almost defied belief. The Governor of Porto Rico was
momentarily awed by the greatness of the thing that had
befallen him.

And yet when a few minutes later the room was entered
by a little lady, young and delicately lovely, Don Jayme
had already recovered his habitual poise of self-sufficiency.

The lady, beholding a stranger, an elegant, courtly
stranger, who rose instantly upon her advent, paused in
the doorway, hesitating, timid. She addressed Don
Jayme.

"Pardon. I did not know you occupied."

Don Jayme appealed, sneering, to the friar. "She did not
know me occupied! I am the King's representative in
Porto Rico, his majesty's Governor of this island, and my
wife does not know that I am occupied, conceives that I
have leisure. It is unbelievable. But come in, Hernanda.
Come in." He grew more playful. "Acquaint yourself
with the honours the King bestows upon his poor servant.

This may help you to realise what his majesty does me the justice to realise, although you may have failed to do so: that my occupations here are onerous."

Timidly she advanced, obedient to his invitation. "What is it, Jayme?"

"What is it?" He seemed to mimic her. "It is merely this." He displayed the order. "His majesty invests me with the cross of Saint James of Compostella. That is all."

She grew conscious that she was mocked. Her pale, delicate face flushed a little. But there was no accompanying sparkle of her great, dark, wistful eyes to proclaim it a flush of pleasure. Rather, thought Don Pedro, she flushed from shame and resentment at being so contemptuously used before a stranger and at the boorishness of a husband who could so use her.

"I am glad, Jayme," she said in a gentle, weary voice. "I felicitate you. I am glad."

"Ah! You are glad. Frey Alonso, you will observe that Doña Hernanda is glad." Thus he sneered at her without even the poor grace of being witty. "This gentleman, by whose hand the order came, is a kinsman of yours, Hernanda."

She turned aside, to look again at that elegant stranger. Her gaze was blank. Yet she hesitated to deny him. Kinship when claimed by gentlemen charged by kings with missions of investiture is not lightly to be denied in the presence of such a husband as Don Jayme. And, after all, hers was a considerable family, and must include many with whom she was not personally acquainted.

The stranger bowed until the curls of his periwig met across his face. "You will not remember me, Doña Hernanda. I am, nevertheless, your cousin, and you will have heard of me from our other cousin Rodrigo. I am Pedro de Queiroz."

"You are Pedro?" She stared the harder. "Why, then . . ." She laughed a little. "Oh, but I remember Pedro. We played together as children. Pedro and I."

Something in her tone seemed to deny him. But he confronted her unperturbed.

"That would be at Santarem," said he.

"At Santarem it was." His readiness appeared now to bewilder her. "But you were a fat, sturdy boy then, and your hair was golden."

He laughed. "I have become lean in growing, and I favour a black periwig."

"Which makes your eyes a startling blue. I do not remember that you had blue eyes."

"God help us, ninny!" croaked her husband. "You never could remember anything."

She turned to look at him, and for all that her lip quivered, her eyes steadily met his sneering glance. She seemed about to speak, checked herself, and then spoke at last, very quietly. "Oh yes. There are some things a woman never forgets."

"And on the subject of memory," said Don Pedro, addressing the Governor with cold dignity, "I do not remember that there are any ninnies in our family."

"Faith, then, you needed to come to Porto Rico to discover it," his excellency retorted with his loud, coarse laugh.

"Ah!" Don Pedro sighed. "That may not be the end of my discoveries."

There was something in his tone which Don Jayme did not like. He threw back his big head and frowned. "You mean?" he demanded.

Don Pedro was conscious of an appeal in the little lady's dark, liquid eyes. He yielded to it, laughed, and answered:

"I have yet to discover where your excellency proposes to lodge me during the days in which I must inflict myself upon you. If I might now withdraw . . ."

The Governor swung to Doña Hernanda. "You hear? Your kinsman needs to remind us of our duty to a guest. It will not have occurred to you to make provision for him."

"But I did not know. . . . I was not told of his presence until I found him here."

"Well, well. You know now. And we dine in half an hour."

At dinner Don Jayme was in high spirits, which is to say that he was alternately pompous and boisterous, and occasionally filled the room with his loud jarring laugh.

Don Pedro scarcely troubled to dissemble his dislike of him. His manner became more and more frigidly aloof, and he devoted his attention and addressed his conversation more and more exclusively to the despised wife.

"I have news for you," he told her, when they had come to the dessert, "of our Cousin Rodrigo."

"Ah!" sneered her husband. "She'll welcome news of him. She ever had a particular regard for her Cousin Rodrigo, and he for her."

She flushed, keeping her troubled eyes lowered. Don Pedro came to the rescue, swiftly, easily. "Regard for one another is common among the members of our family. Every Queiroz owes a duty to every other, and is at all times ready to perform it." He looked very straightly at Don Jayme as he spoke, as if inviting him to discover more in the words than they might seem to carry. "And that is at the root of what I am to tell you, cousin Hernanda. As I have already informed his excellency, the ship in which Don Rodrigo and I sailed from Spain together was set upon and sunk by that infamous pirate Captain Blood. We were both captured, but I was so fortunate as to make my escape."

"You have not told us how. You must tell us how," the Governor interrupted him.

Don Pedro waved a hand disdainfully. "It is no great matter, and I soon weary of talking of myself. But . . . if you insist . . . some other time. At present I am to tell you of Rodrigo. He remains a prisoner in the hands of Captain Blood. But do not be unduly alarmed."

There was need for his reassuring tone. Doña Hernanda, who had been hanging on his words, had turned deathly white.

"Do not be alarmed. Rodrigo is in good health, and his life is safe. Also, from my own experience, I know that this Blood, infamous pirate though he be, is not without chivalrous ideals, and, piracy apart, he is a man of honour."

"Piracy apart?" Laughter exploded from Don Jayme. "On my soul, that's humorous! You deal in paradox, Don Pedro. Eh, Frey Alonso?"

The lean friar smiled mechanically. Doña Hernanda, pale and piteous, suffered in silence the interruption. Don Pedro frowned:

"The paradox is not in me, but in Captain Blood. An indemoniated robber, yet he practises no wanton cruelty, and he keeps his word. Therefore I say you need have no apprehension on the score of Don Rodrigo's fate. His ransom has been agreed between himself and Captain Blood, and I have undertaken to procure it. Meanwhile he is well and courteously entreated, and, indeed, a sort of friendship has come to exist between himself and his pirate captor."

"Faith, that I can believe!" cried the Governor, whilst Doña Hernanda sank back in her chair with a sigh of relief. "Rodrigo was ever ready to consort with rogues. Was he not, Hernanda?"

"I . . ." She bridled indignantly; then curbed herself. "I never observed it."

"You never observed it! I ask myself have you ever observed anything? Well, well, and so Rodrigo's to be ransomed. At what is his ransom fixed?"

"You desire to contribute?" cried Don Pedro with a certain friendly eagerness.

The Governor started as if he had been stung. His countenance became gravely blank. "Not I, by the Virgin! Not I. That is entirely a matter for the family of Queiroz."

Don Pedro's smile perished. He sighed. "True! True! And yet . . . I've a notion you'll come to contribute something before all is ended."

"Dismiss it," laughed Don Jayme, "for that way lies disappointment."

They rose from table soon thereafter and withdrew to the noontide rest the heat made necessary.

They did not come together again until supper, which was served in that same room, in the comparative cool of eventide and by the light of a score of candles in heavy silver branches brought from Spain.

The Governor's satisfaction at the signal honour of which he was the recipient appeared to have grown with contemplation of it. He was increasingly jovial and facetious, but not on this account did he spare Doña Hernanda his sneers. Rather did he make her the butt of coarse humours, inviting the two men to laugh with him at the shortcomings he indicated in her. Don Pedro, however, did not laugh. He remained preternaturally grave, indeed almost compassionate, as he observed the tragic patience on that long-suffering wife's sweet face.

She looked so slight and frail in her stiff black satin gown, which rendered more dazzling by contrast the whiteness of her neck and shoulders, even as her lustrous, smoothly-dressed black hair stressed the warm pallor of her gentle countenance. A little statue in ebony and ivory she seemed to Don Pedro's fancy, and almost as lifeless until after supper he found himself alone with her in the deep jessamine-clad galleries that stood open to the cool night breezes blowing from the sea.

His excellency had gone off to indite a letter of grateful acknowledgment to the King, and had taken the friar to assist him. He had commended his guest to the attention of his wife, whilst commiserating with him upon the necessity. She had led Don Pedro out into the scented purple tropic night, and stepping now beside him came at last to life, and addressed him in a breathless anxiety.

"What you told us to-day of Don Rodrigo de Queiroz,

is it true? That he is a prisoner in the hands of Captain Blood, but unhurt and safe, awaiting ransom?"

"Most scrupulously true in all particulars."

"You . . . you pledge your word for that? Your honour as a gentleman? For I must assume you a gentleman, since you bear commissions from the King."

"And on no other ground?" quoth he, a little taken aback.

"Do you pledge me your word?" she insisted.

"Unhesitatingly. My word of honour. Why should you doubt me?"

"You give me cause. You are not truthful in all things. Why, for instance, do you say you are my cousin?"

"You do not, then, remember me?"

"I remember Pedro de Queiroz. The years might have given you height and slenderness; the sun might have tanned your face, and under your black periwig your hair may still be fair, though I take leave to doubt it. But what, I ask myself, could have changed the colour of your eyes? For your eyes are blue, and Pedro's were dark brown."

He was silent a moment, like a man considering, and she watched his stern, handsome face, made plain by the light beating upon it from the windows of the house. He did not meet her glance. Instead his eyes sought the sea, gleaming under the bright stars and reflecting the twinkling lights of ships in the roadstead, watched the fireflies flitting among the bushes in pursuit of moths, looked anywhere but at the little figure at his side.

At last he spoke, quietly, almost humorously, in admission of the imposture. "We hoped you would have forgotten such a detail."

"We?" she questioned him.

"Rodrigo and I. He is at least my friend. He was hastening to you when this thing befell him. That is how we came to be on the same ship."

"And he desired you to do this?"

"He shall tell you so himself when he arrives. He will

be here in a few days, depend on it. As soon as I can ransom him, which will be very soon after my departure. When I was escaping—for, unlike him, I had given no parole—he desired that if I came here I should claim to be your cousin, so as to stand at need in his place until he comes."

She was thoughtful, and her bosom rose and fell in agitation. In silence they moved a little way in step.

"You took a foolish risk," she said, thereby showing her acceptance of his explanation.

"A gentleman," said he sententiously, "will always take a risk to serve a lady."

"Were you serving me?"

"Does it seem to you that I could be serving myself?"

"No. You could not have been doing that."

"Why question further, then? Rodrigo wished it so. He will explain his motives fully when he comes. Meanwhile, as your cousin, I am in his place. If this boorish husband burdens you overmuch . . ."

"What are you saying?" Her voice rang with alarm.

"That I am Rodrigo's deputy. So that you remember it, that is all I ask."

"I thank you, cousin," she said, and left him.

Three days Don Pedro continued as the guest of the Governor of Porto Rico, and they were much as that first day, saving that daily Don Jayme continued to increase in consciousness of his new dignity as a knight of Saint James of Compostella, and became, consequently, daily more insufferable. Yet Don Pedro suffered him with exemplary fortitude, and at times seemed even disposed to feed the Governor's egregious vanity. Thus, on the third night at supper, Don Pedro cast out the suggestion that his excellency should signalise the honour with which the King had distinguished him by some gesture that should mark the occasion and render it memorable in the annals of the island.

Don Jayme swallowed the suggestion avidly. "Ah yes!

That is an admirable thought. What do you counsel that I do?"

Don Pedro smiled with flattering deprecation. "Not for me to counsel Don Jayme de Villamarga. But the gesture should be worthy of the occasion."

"Indeed, yes. That is true." The dullard's wits, however, were barren of ideas. "The question now is what might be considered worthy?"

Frey Alonso suggested a ball at Government House, and was applauded in this by Doña Hernanda. Don Pedro, apologetically to the lady, thought a ball would have significance only for those who were bidden to it. Something was required that should impress all social orders in Porto Rico.

"Why not an amnesty?" he inquired at last.

"An amnesty?" The three of them looked at him in questioning wonder.

"Why not? It is a royal gesture, true. But is not a governor in some sort royal, a viceroy, a representative of royalty, the one to whom men look for royal gestures? To mark your accession to this dignity, throw open your gaols, Don Jayme, as do kings upon their coronation."

Don Jayme conquered his stupefaction at the magnitude of the act suggested, and smote the table with his fist, protesting that here was a notion worth adopting. To-morrow he would announce it in a proclamation, and set all prisoners free, their sentences remitted.

"That is," he added, "all but six, whose pardon would hardly please the colony."

"I think," said Don Pedro, "that exceptions would stultify the act. There should be no exceptions."

"But these are exceptional prisoners. Can you have forgotten that I told you I had made captive six buccaneers out of a party that had the temerity to land on Porto Rico?"

Don Pedro frowned, reflecting. "Ah, true!" he cried at last. "I remember."

"And did I tell you, sir, that one of these men is that dog Wolverstone?" He pronounced it Volverstohn.

"Wolverstone?" said Don Pedro, who also pronounced it Volverstohn. "You have captured Wolverstone!" It was clear that he was profoundly impressed; as well he might be, for Wolverstone, who was nowadays the foremost of Blood's lieutenants, was almost as well known to Spaniards and as detested by them as Blood himself. "You have captured Wolverstone!" he repeated, and for the first time looked at Don Jayme with eyes of unmistakable respect. "You did not tell me that. Why, in that case, my friend, you have clipped one of Blood's wings. Without Wolverstone he is shorn of half his power. His own destruction may follow now at any moment, and Spain will owe that to you."

Don Jayme spread his hands in an affectation of modesty. "It is something towards deserving the honour his majesty has bestowed upon me."

"Something!" echoed Don Pedro. "If the King had known this, he might have accounted the order of Saint James of Compostella inadequate."

Doña Hernanda looked at him sharply, to see whether he dealt in irony. But he seemed quite sincere, so much so that for once he had shed the hauteur in which he usually arrayed himself. He resumed after a moment's pause.

"Of course, of course, you cannot include these men in the amnesty. They are not common malefactors. They are enemies of Spain." Abruptly, with a hint of purpose, he asked: "How will you deal with them?"

Don Jayme thrust out a nether lip considering. "I am still undecided whether to hang them out of hand or to let Frey Alonso hold his auto-da-fé upon them and consign them to the fire as heretics. I think I told you so."

"Yes, yes. But I did not then know that Wolverstone is one of them. That makes a difference."

"What difference?"

"Oh, but consider. Give this matter thought. With

thought you'll see for yourself what you should do. It's plain enough."

Don Jayme considered awhile as he was bidden. Then shrugged his shoulders.

"Faith, sir, it may be plain enough to you. But I confess that I see no choice beyond that of rope or fire."

"Ultimately, yes. One or the other. But not here in Porto Rico. That is to smother the effulgence of your achievement. Send them to Spain, Don Jayme. Send them to his majesty, as an earnest of the zeal for which he has been pleased to honour you. Show him thus how richly you deserve that honour and even greater honours. Let that be your acknowledgment."

Don Jayme was staring at him with dilating eyes. His face glowed. "I vow to Heaven I should never have thought of it," he said at last.

"Your modesty made you blind to the opportunity."

"It may be that," Don Jayme admitted.

"But you perceive it now that I indicate it?"

"Oh, I perceive it. Yes, the King of Spain shall be impressed."

Frey Alonso seemed downcast. He had been counting upon his auto-da-fé. Doña Hernanda was chiefly puzzled by the sudden geniality of her hitherto haughty and disdainful pretended cousin. Meanwhile Don Pedro piled Pelion upon Ossa.

"It should prove to his majesty that your excellency is wasted in so small a settlement as Porto Rico. I see you as governor of some more important colony. Perhaps as viceroy. . . . Who shall say? You have displayed a zeal such as has rarely been displayed by any Spanish governor overseas."

"But how and when to send them to Spain?" wondered Don Jayme, who no longer questioned the expediency of doing so.

"Why, that is a matter in which I can serve your excellency. I can convey them for you on the 'San Tomas,' which should call for me at any moment now. You will write another letter to his majesty, offering him these evidences of your zeal, and I will bear it together with these captives. Your general amnesty can wait until I've sailed with them. Thus there will be nothing to mar it. It will be complete and properly imposing."

So elated and so grateful to his guest for his suggestion was Don Jayme that he actually went the length of addressing him as cousin in the course of thanking him.

The matter, it seemed, had presented itself for discussion only just in time. For early on the following morning Santiago was startled by the boom of a gun, and turning out to ascertain the reason, beheld again the yellow Spanish ship which had brought Don Pedro coming to anchor in the bay.

Don Pedro himself sought the Governor with the information that this was the signal for his departure, expressing a polite regret that duty did not permit him longer to encroach upon Don Jayme's princely hospitality.

Whilst his negro valet was packing his effects he went to take his leave of Doña Hernanda, and again assured that wistful little lady that she need be under no apprehension on the score of her cousin Rodrigo, who would soon now be with her.

After this Don Jayme, with an officer in attendance, carried Dón Pedro off to the town gaol, where the pirates were lodged.

In a dark, unpaved stone chamber, lighted only by a small, heavily-barred, unglazed window set near the ceiling, they were herded with perhaps a score of other malefactors of all kinds and colours. The atmosphere of the place was so indescribably foul and noisome that Don Pedro recoiled as from a blow when it first assailed him. Don Jayme's loud, coarse laugh derided his fastidiousness. Nevertheless, the Governor flicked out a handkerchief that was sprayed with verbena, and thereafter at intervals held it to his nostrils.

Wolverstone and his five associates, heavily loaded with irons, were in a group a little apart from their fellow-prisoners. They squatted against the wall on the foul dank straw that was their bedding. Unshaven, dishevelled and filthy, for no means of grooming themselves had been allowed them, they huddled together there as if seeking strength in union against the common rogues with whom they were confined. Wolverstone, almost a giant in build, might from his dress have been a merchant. Dyke, that sometime petty officer in the King's Navy, had similarly been arrayed like a citizen of some consequence. The other four wore the cotton shirts and leather breeches which had been the dress of the boucan-hunters before they took to the sea, and their heads were swathed in coloured kerchiefs.

They did not stir when the door creaked on its ponderous hinges and a half-dozen corseletted Spaniards with pikes entered to form a guard of honour as well as a protection for the Governor. When that august personage made his appearance attended by his officer and accompanied by his distinguished-looking guest, the other prisoners sprang up and ranged themselves in awe and reverence. The pirates stolidly sat on. But they were not quite indifferent. As Don Pedro sauntered in, languidly leaning on his beribboned cane, dabbing his lips with a handkerchief, which he, too, had deemed it well to produce, Wolverstone stirred on his foul bed, and his single eye (he had lost the other one at Sedgmoor) rolled with almost portentous ferocity.

Don Jayme indicated the group by a wave of his hand. "There are your cursed pirates, Don Pedro, hanging together like a brood of carrion birds."

"These?" quoth Don Pedro haughtily, and pointed with his cane. "Faith, they look their trade, the villains."

Wolverstone glared more fiercely than ever, but was contemptuously silent. A stubborn rogue, it was plain.

Don Pedro advanced towards them, superb in his black and silver, seeming to symbolise the pride and majesty of

Spain. The thick-set Governor, in pale green taffetas, kept pace with him, and presently, when they had come to a halt before the buccaneers, he addressed them.

"You begin to know, you English dogs, what it means to defy the might of Spain. And you'll know it better before all is done. I deny myself the pleasure of hanging you as I intended, so that you may go to Madrid, to feed a bonfire."

Wolverstone leered at him. "You are noble," he said, in execrable, but comprehensible Spanish. "Noble with the nobility of Spain. You insult the helpless."

The Governor raged at him, calling him the unprintably foul names that come so readily to an angry Spaniard's lips. This until Don Pedro checked him with a hand upon his arm.

"Is this waste of breath worth while?" He spoke disdainfully. "It but serves to detain us in this noisome place."

The buccaneers stared at him in a sort of wonder. Abruptly he turned on his heel.

"Come, Don Jayme." His tone was peremptory. "Have them out of this. The 'San Tomas' is waiting, and the tide is on the turn."

The Governor hesitated, flung a last insult at them, then gave an order to the officer, and stalked after his guest, who was already moving away. The officer transferred the order to his men. With the butts of their pikes and many foul words the soldiers stirred the buccaneers. They rose with clank of gyves and manacles, and went stumbling out into the clean air and the sunshine, herded by the pikemen. Hangdog, foul and weary, they dragged themselves across the square, where the palms waved in the sea breeze, and the islanders stood to watch them pass, and so they came to the mole, where a wherry of eight oars awaited them.

The Governor and his guest stood by whilst they were being packed into the sternsheets, whither the pikemen

followed them. Then Don Pedro and Don Jayme took
their places in the prow with Don Pedro's negro, who
carried his valise. The wherry pushed off and was rowed
across the blue water to the stately ship from whose masthead floated the flag of Spain.

They came bumping along her yellow side at the foot
of the entrance-ladder, to which a sailor hitched a boat-
hook.

Don Pedro, from the prow of the wherry, called per-
emptorily for a file of musketeers to stand to order in the
waist. A morioned head appeared over the bulwarks to
answer him that it was done already. Then, with the pikemen urging them, and moving awkwardly and painfully
in their irons, the buccaneer prisoners climbed the ladder
and dropped one by one over the ship's side.

Don Pedro waved his black servant after them with
the valise, and finally invited Don Jayme to precede him
aboard. Himself, Don Pedro followed close, and when at
the ladder's head Don Jayme came to a sudden halt, it was
Don Pedro's continuing ascent that thrust him forward,
and this so sharply that he almost tumbled headlong into
the vessel's waist. There were a dozen ready hands to
steady him, and a babble of voices to give him laughing
welcome. But the voices were English, and the hands
belonged to men whose garments and accoutrements pro-
claimed them buccaneers. They swarmed in the waist, and
already some of them were at work to strike the irons
from Wolverstone and his mates.

Gasping, livid, bewildered, Don Jayme de Villamarga
swung round to Don Pedro who followed. That very
Spanish gentleman had paused at the head of the ladder
and stood there steadying himself by a ratline, surveying
the scene below him. He was calmly smiling.

"You have nothing to apprehend, Don Jayme. I give
you my word for that. And my word is good. I am
Captain Blood."

He came down to the deck under the stare of the

bulging eyes of the Governor, who understood nothing. Before enlightenment finally came his dull, bewildered wits were to understand still less.

A tall, slight gentleman, very elegantly arrayed, stepped forward to meet the Captain. This, to the Governor's increasing amazement, was his wife's cousin, Don Rodrigo. Captain Blood greeted him in a friendly manner.

"I have brought your ransom, as you see, Don Rodrigo," and he waved a hand in the direction of the group of manacled prisoners. "You are free now to depart with Don Jayme. We'll cut short our farewells, for we take up the anchor at once. Hagthorpe, give the order."

Don Jayme thought that he began to understand. Furiously, he turned upon this cousin of his wife's.

"My God, are you in this? Have you plotted with these enemies of Spain to——?"

A hand gripped his shoulder, and a boatswain's whistle piped somewhere forward. "We are weighing the anchor," said Captain Blood. "You were best over the side, believe me. It has been an honour to know you. In future be more respectful to your wife. Go with God, Don Jayme."

The governor found himself, as in a nightmare, bustled over the side and down the ladder. Don Rodrigo followed him after taking courteous leave of Captain Blood.

Don Jayme collapsed limply in the sternsheets of the wherry as it put off. But soon he roused himself furiously to demand an explanation whilst at the same time overwhelming his companion with threats.

Don Rodrigo strove to preserve his calm. "You had better listen. I was on that ship, the 'San Tomas,' on my way to San Domingo, when Blood captured her. He put the crew ashore on one of the Virgin Islands. But me he retained for ransom because of my rank."

"And to save your skin and your purse you made this infamous bargain with him?"

"I have said that you had better listen. It was not so

at all. He treated me honourably, and we became in some sort friends. He is a man of engaging ways, as you may have discovered. In the course of our talks he gleaned from me a good deal of my private life and yours, which in a way, through my Cousin Hernanda, is linked with it. A week ago, after the capture of the men who had gone ashore with Wolverstone, he decided to use the knowledge he had gained; that and my papers, of which he had, of course, possessed himself. He told me what he intended to do, and promised me that if by the use of my name and the rest he succeeded in delivering those followers of his, he would require no further ransom from me."

"And you? You agreed?"

"Agreed? Sometimes, indeed often, you are fatuous. My agreement was not asked. I was merely informed. Your own foolishness and the order of Saint James of Compostella did the rest. I suppose he conferred it upon you, and so dazzled you with it that you were prepared to believe anything he told you?"

"You were bringing it to me? It was among your papers?" quoth Don Jayme, who thought he began to understand.

There was a grim smile on Don Rodrigo's long, sallow face. "I was taking it to the Governor of Hispaniola Don Jayme de Guzman, to whom the letter was addressed."

Don Jayme de Villamarga's mouth fell open. He turned pale. "Not even that, then? The order was not intended for me? It was part of his infernal comedy?"

"You should have examined the letter more attentively."

"It was damaged by sea-water!" roared the Governor furiously.

"You should have examined your conscience, then. It would have told you that you had done nothing to deserve the cross of Saint James."

Don Jayme was too stunned to resent the gibe. Not until he was home again and in the presence of his wife did he recover himself sufficiently to hector her with the tale of how he had been bubbled. Thus he brought upon himself his worst humiliation.

"How does it come, madam," he demanded, "that you recognized him for your cousin?"

"I did not," she answered him, and dared at last to laugh at him, taking payment in that moment for all the browbeating she had suffered at his hands.

"You did not! You mean that you knew he was not your cousin?"

"That is what I mean."

"And you did not tell me?" The world was rocking about him.

"You would not allow me. When I told him that I did not remember that my Cousin Pedro had blue eyes, you told me that I never remembered anything, and you called me ninny. Because I did not wish to be called ninny again before a stranger I said nothing further."

Don Jayme mopped the sweat from his brow, and appealed in livid fury to her cousin Rodrigo, who stood by. "And what do you say to that?" he demanded.

"For myself, nothing. But I might remind you of Captain Blood's advice to you at parting. I think it was that in future you be more respectful to your wife."

The Sire de Malétroit's Door

By ROBERT LOUIS STEVENSON

DENIS DE BEAULIEU was not yet two-and-twenty, but he counted himself a grown man, and a very accomplished cavalier into the bargain. Lads were early formed in that rough, warfaring epoch; and when one has been in a pitched battle and a dozen raids, has killed one's man in

an honourable fashion, and knows a thing or two of
strategy and mankind, a certain swagger in the gait is
surely to be pardoned. He had put up his horse with due
care, and supped with due deliberation; and then, in a very
agreeable frame of mind, went out to pay a visit in the
grey of the evening. It was not a very wise proceeding
on the young man's part. He would have done better to
remain beside the fire or go decently to bed. For the town
was full of the troops of Burgundy and England under a
mixed command; and though Denis was there on safe-
conduct, his safe-conduct was like to serve him little on
a chance encounter.

It was September, 1429; the weather had fallen sharp;
a flighty piping wind, laden with showers, beat about the
township; and the dead leaves ran riot along the streets.
Here and there a window was already lighted up; and the
noise of men-at-arms making merry over supper within,
came forth in fits and was swallowed up and carried away
by the wind. The night fell swiftly; the flag of England,
fluttering on the spire-top, grew ever fainter and fainter
against the flying clouds—a black speck like a swallow in
the tumultuous, leaden chaos of the sky. As the night fell
the wind rose, and began to hoot under archways and
roar amid the tree-tops in the valley below the town.

Denis de Beaulieu walked fast and was soon knocking
at his friend's door; but though he promised himself to
stay only a little while and make an early return, his welcome was so pleasant, and he found so much to delay
him, that it was already long past midnight before he said
good-bye upon the threshold. The wind had fallen again
in the meanwhile; the night was as black as the grave;
not a star, nor a glimmer of moonshine, slipped through
the canopy of cloud. Denis was ill-acquainted with the
intricate lanes of Chateau Landon; even by daylight he
had found some trouble in picking his way; and in this
absolute darkness he soon lost it altogether. He was certain of one thing only—to keep mounting the hill; for his
friend's house lay at the lower end, or tail, of Chateau

Landon, while the inn was up at the head, under the great church spire. With this clue to go upon he stumbled and groped forward, now breathing more freely in open places where there was a good slice of sky overhead, now feeling along the wall in stifling closes. It is an eerie and mysterious position to be thus submerged in opaque blackness in an almost unknown town. The silence is terrifying in its possibilities. The touch of cold window bars to the exploring hand startles the man like the touch of a toad; the inequalities of the pavement shake his heart into his mouth; a piece of denser darkness threatens an ambuscade or a chasm in the pathway; and where the air is brighter, the houses put on strange and bewildering appearances, as if to lead him farther from his way. For Denis, who had to regain his inn without attracting notice, there was real danger as well as mere discomfort in the walk; and he went warily and boldly at once, and at every corner paused to make an observation.

He had been for some time threading a lane so narrow that he could touch a wall with either hand, when it began to open out and go sharply downward. Plainly this lay no longer in the direction of his inn; but the hope of a little more light tempted him forward to reconnoitre. The lane ended in a terrace with a bartizan wall, which gave an outlook between high houses, as out of an embrasure, into the valley lying dark and formless several hundred feet below. Denis looked down, and could discern a few tree-tops waving and a single speck of brightness where the river ran across a weir. The weather was clearing up, and the sky had lightened, so as to show the outline of the heavier clouds and the dark margin of the hills. By the uncertain glimmer, the house on his left hand should be a place of some pretensions; it was surmounted by several pinnacles and turret-tops; the round stern of a chapel, with a fringe of flying buttresses, projected boldly from the main block; and the door was sheltered under a deep porch carved with figures and overhung by two long gargoyles. The windows of the chapel gleamed through their intricate tracery with a light as of many tapers, and threw out the buttresses and the peaked roof in a more intense blackness against the sky. It was plainly the hotel of some great family of the neighbourhood; and as it reminded Denis of a town house of his own at Bourges, he stood for some time gazing up at it and mentally gauging the skill of the architects and the consideration of the two families.

There seemed to be no issue to the terrace but the lane by which he had reached it; he could only retrace his steps, but he had gained some notion of his whereabouts, and hoped by this means to hit the main thoroughfare and speedily regain the inn. He was reckoning without that chapter of accidents which was to make this night memorable above all others in his career; for he had not gone back above a hundred yards before he saw a light coming to meet him, and heard loud voices speaking together in the echoing narrows of the lane. It was a party of men-at-arms going the night round with torches. Denis assured himself that they had all been making free with the wine-bowl, and were in no mood to be particular about safe-conducts or the niceties of chivalrous war. It was as like as not that they would kill him like a dog and leave him where he fell. The situation was inspiriting but nervous. Their own torches would conceal him from sight, he reflected; and he hoped that they would drown the noise of his footsteps with their own empty voices. If he were but fleet and silent, he might evade their notice altogether.

Unfortunately, as he turned to beat a retreat, his foot rolled upon a pebble; he fell against the wall with an ejaculation, and his sword rang loudly on the stones. Two or three voices demanded who went there—some in French, some in English; but Denis made no reply, and ran faster down the lane. Once upon the terrace, he paused to look back. They still kept calling after him, and just then began to double the pace in pursuit, with a considerable clank of armour, and great tossing of the torchlight to and fro in the narrow jaws of the passage.

Denis cast a look around and darted into the porch. There he might escape observation, or—if that were too much to expect—was in a capital posture whether for parley or defense. So thinking, he drew his sword and tried to set his back against the door. To his surprise, it yielded behind his weight; and though he turned in a moment, continued to swing back on oiled and noiseless hinges, until it stood wide open on a black interior. When things fall out opportunely for the person concerned, he is not apt to be critical about the how or why, his own immediate personal convenience seeming a sufficient reason for the strangest oddities and revolutions in our sublunary things; and so Denis, without a moment's hesitation, stepped within and partly closed the door behind him to conceal his place of refuge. Nothing was further from his thoughts than to close it altogether; but for some inexplicable reason—perhaps by a spring or a weight—the ponderous mass of oak whipped itself out of his fingers and clanked to, with a formidable rumble and a noise like the falling of an automatic bar.

The round, at that very moment, debouched upon the terrace and proceeded to summon him with shouts and curses. He heard them ferreting in the dark corners; the stock of a lance even rattled along the outer surface of the door behind which he stood; but these gentlemen were in too high a humour to be long delayed, and soon made on down a corkscrew pathway which had escaped Denis' observation, and passed out of sight and hearing along the battlements of the town.

Denis breathed again. He gave them a few minutes' grace for fear of accidents, and then groped about for some means of opening the door and slipping forth again. The inner surface was quite smooth, not a handle, not a moulding, not a projection of any sort. He got his finger-nails round the edges and pulled, but the mass was immovable. He shook it, it was as firm as a rock. Denis de Beaulieu frowned and gave vent to a little noiseless whistle. What ailed the door? he wondered. Why was it open? How came it to shut so easily and so effectually after him? There was something obscure and underhand about all this, that was little to the young man's fancy. It looked like a snare; and yet who could suppose a snare in such a quiet by-street and in a house of so prosperous and even noble an exterior? And yet—snare or no snare, intentionally or unintentionally—here he was, prettily trapped; and for the life of him he could see no way out of it again. The darkness began to weigh upon him. He gave ear; all was silent without, but within and close by he seemed to catch a faint sighing, a faint sobbing rustle, a little stealthy creak—as though many persons were at his side, holding themselves quite still, and governing even their respiration with the extreme of slyness. The idea went to his vitals with a shock, and he faced about suddenly as if to defend his life. Then, for the first time, he became aware of a light about the level of his eyes and at some distance in the interior of the house—a vertical thread of light, widening towards the bottom, such as might escape between two wings of arras over a doorway. To see anything was a relief to Denis; it was like a piece of solid ground to a man labouring in a morass; his mind seized upon it with avidity; and he stood staring at it and trying to piece together some logical conception of his surroundings. Plainly there was a flight of steps ascending from his own level to that of the illuminated doorway; and indeed he thought he could make out another thread of light, as fine as a needle and as faint as phosphorescence, which might very well be reflected along the polished wood of a handrail. Since he had begun to suspect that he was not alone, his heart had continued to beat with smothering violence, and an intolerable desire for action of any sort had possessed itself of his spirit. He was in deadly peril, he believed. What could be more natural than to mount the staircase, lift the curtain, and confront his difficulty at once? At least he would be dealing with something tangible; at least he would be no longer in the dark. He stepped slowly forward with outstretched hands, until his foot struck the bottom step; then he rapidly scaled the stairs, stood for a moment to compose his expression, lifted the arras and went in.

He found himself in a large apartment of polished stone. There were three doors; one on each of three sides; all similarly curtained with tapestry. The fourth side was occupied by two large windows and a great stone chimney-piece, carved with the arms of the Malétroits. Denis recognized the bearings, and was gratified to find himself in such good hands. The room was strongly illuminated; but it contained little furniture except a heavy table and a chair or two, the hearth was innocent of fire, and the pavement was but sparsely strewn with rushes clearly many days old.

On a high chair beside the chimney, and directly facing Denis as he entered, sat a little old gentleman in a fur tippet. He sat with his legs crossed and his hands folded, and a cup of spiced wine stood by his elbow on a bracket on the wall. His countenance had a strongly masculine cast; not properly human, but such as we see in the bull, the goat, or the domestic boar, something equivocal and wheedling, something greedy, brutal, and dangerous. The upper lip was inordinately full, as though swollen by a blow or a toothache; and the smile, the peaked eyebrows, and the small, strong eyes were quaintly and almost comically evil in expression. Beautiful white hair hung straight all round his head, like a saint's, and fell in a single curl upon the tippet. His beard and moustache were the pink of venerable sweetness. Age, probably in consequence of inordinate precautions, had left no mark upon his hands; and the Malétroit hand was famous. It would be difficult to imagine anything at once so fleshy and so delicate in design; the taper, sensual fingers were like those of one of Leonardo's

women; the fork of the thumb made a dimpled protuber-
ance when closed; the nails were perfectly shaped, and
of a dead, surprising whiteness. It rendered his aspect
tenfold more redoubtable, that a man with hands like
these should keep them devoutly folded in his lap like a
virgin martyr—that a man with so intense and startling
an expression of face should sit patiently on his seat and
contemplate people with an unwinking stare, like a god,
or a god's statue. His quiescence seemed ironical and
treacherous, it fitted so poorly with his looks.

Such was Alain, Sire de Malétroit.

Denis and he looked silently at each other for a second
or two.

"Pray step in," said the Sire de Malétroit. "I have
been expecting you all the evening."

He had not risen, but he accompanied his words with a
smile and a slight but courteous inclination of the head.
Partly from the smile, partly from the strange musical
murmur with which the Sire prefaced his observation,
Denis felt a strong shudder of disgust go through his
marrow. And what with disgust and honest confusion of
mind, he could scarcely get words together in reply.

"I fear," he said, "that this is a double accident. I am
not the person you suppose me. It seems you were looking for a visit; but for my part, nothing was further from
my thoughts—nothing could be more contrary·to my
wishes—than this intrusion."

"Well, well," replied the old gentleman indulgently,
"here you are, which is the main point. Seat yourself, my
friend, and put yourself entirely at your ease. We shall
arrange our little affairs presently."

Denis perceived that the matter was still complicated
with some misconception, and he hastened to continue
his explanation.

"Your door . . ." he began.

"About my door?" asked the other, raising his peaked
eyebrows. "A little piece of ingenuity." And he shrugged
his shoulders. "A hospitable fancy! By your own ac-

count, you were not desirous of making my acquaintance. We old people look for such reluctance now and then; and when it touches our honours, we cast about until we find some way of overcoming it. You arrive uninvited, but believe me, very welcome."

"You persist in error, sir," said Denis. "There can be no question between you and me. I am a stranger in this countryside. My name is Denis, damoiseau de Beaulieu. If you see me in your house, it is only——"

"My found friend," interrupted the other, "you will permit me to have my own ideas on that subject. They probably differ from yours at the present moment," he added with a leer, "but time will show which of us is in the right."

Denis was convinced he had to do with a lunatic. He seated himself with a shrug, content to wait the upshot; and a pause ensued, during which he thought he could distinguish a hurried gabbling as of prayer from behind the arras immediately opposite him. Sometimes there seemed to be but one person engaged, sometimes two; and the vehemence of the voice, low as it was, seemed to indicate either great haste or an agony of spirit. It occurred to him that this piece of tapestry covered the entrance to the chapel he had noticed from without.

The old gentleman meanwhile surveyed Denis from head to foot with a smile, and from time to time emitted little noises like a bird or a mouse, which seemed to indicate a high degree of satisfaction. This state of matters became rapidly insupportable; and Denis, to put an end to it, remarked politely that the wind had gone down.

The old gentleman fell into a fit of silent laughter, so prolonged and violent that he became quite red in the face. Denis got upon his feet at once, and put on his hat with a flourish.

"Sir," he said, "if you are in your wits, you have affronted me grossly. If you are out of them, I flatter myself I can find better employment for my brains than to talk with lunatics. My conscience is clear; you have

made a fool of me from the first moment; you have refused to hear my explanations; and now there is no
power under God will make me stay here any longer;
and if I cannot make my way out in a more decent fashion, I will hack your door in pieces with my sword."

The Sire de Malétroit raised his right hand and
wagged it at Denis with the fore and little fingers extended.

"My dear nephew," he said, "sit down."

"Nephew!" retorted Denis, "you lie in your throat";
and he snapped his fingers in his face.

"Sit down, you rogue!" cried the old gentleman, in a
sudden, harsh voice, like the barking of a dog. "Do you
fancy," he went on, "that when I had made my little
contrivance for the door I had stopped short with that?
If you prefer to be bound hand and foot till your bones
ache, rise and try to go away. If you choose to remain a
free young buck, agreeably conversing with an old gentleman—why, sit where you are in peace, and God be
with you."

"Do you mean I am a prisoner?" demanded Denis.

"I state the facts," replied the other. "I would rather
leave the conclusion to yourself."

Denis sat down again. Externally he managed to keep
pretty calm; but within, he was now boiling with anger,
now chilled with apprehension. He no longer felt convinced that he was dealing with a madman. And if the
old gentleman was sane, what, in God's name, had he to
look for? What absurd or tragical adventure had befallen
him? What countenance was he to assume?

While he was thus unpleasantly reflecting, the arras
that overhung the chapel door was raised, and a tall
priest in his robes came forth and, giving a long, keen
stare at Denis, said something in an undertone to Sire de
Malétroit.

"She is in a better frame of spirit?" asked the latter.

"She is more resigned, messire," replied the priest.

"Now the Lord help her, she is hard to please!"

sneered the old gentleman. "A likely stripling—not ill-born—and of her own choosing, too? Why, what more would the jade have?"

"The situation is not usual for a young damsel," said the other, "and somewhat trying to her blushes."

"She should have thought of that before she began the dance. It was none of my choosing, God knows that: but since she is in it, by our Lady, she shall carry it to the end." And then addressing Denis, "Monsieur de Beau-lieu," he asked, "may I present you to my niece? she has been waiting your arrival, I may say, with even greater impatience than myself."

Denis had resigned himself with a good grace—all he desired was to know the worst of it as speedily as possible; so he rose at once, and bowed in acquiescence. The Sire de Malétroit followed his example and limped, with the assistance of the chaplain's arm, towards the chapel door. The priest pulled aside the arras, and all three entered. The building had considerable architectural pretensions. A light groining sprang from six stout columns, and hung down in two rich pendants from the centre of the vault. The place terminated behind the altar in a round end, embossed and honeycombed with a superfluity of ornament in relief, and pierced by many little windows shaped like stars, trefoils, or wheels. These windows were imperfectly glazed, so that the night air circulated freely in the chapel. The tapers, of which there must have been half a hundred burning on the altar, were unmercifully blown about; and the light went through many different phases of brilliancy and semi-eclipse. On the steps in front of the altar knelt a young girl richly attired as a bride. A chill settled over Denis as he observed her costume; he fought with desperate energy against the conclusion that was being thrust upon his mind; it could not—it should not—be as he feared.

"Blanche," said the Sire, in his most flute-like tones, "I have brought a friend to see you, my little girl; turn round and give him your pretty hand. It is good to be devout; but it is necessary to be polite, my niece."

The girl rose to her feet and turned towards the newcomer. She moved all of a piece; and shame and exhaustion were expressed in every line of her fresh young body; and she held her head down and kept her eyes upon the pavement, as she came slowly forward. In the course of her advance, her eyes fell upon Denis de Beaulieu's feet—feet of which he was justly vain, be it remarked, and wore in the most elegant accoutrement even while traveling. She paused—stared, as if his yellow boots had conveyed some shocking meaning—and glanced suddenly up into the wearer's countenance. Their eyes met; shame gave place to horror and terror in her looks; the blood left her lips; with a piercing scream she covered her face with her hands and sank upon the chapel floor.

"That is not the man!" she cried. "My uncle, that is not the man!"

The Sire de Malétroit chirped agreeably. "Of course not," he said; "I expected as much. It was so unfortunate you could not remember his name."

"Indeed," she cried, "indeed, I have never seen this person till this moment—I have never so much as set eyes upon him—I never wish to see him again. Sir," she said, turning to Denis, "if you are a gentleman, you will bear me out. Have I ever seen you—have you ever seen me—before this accursed hour?"

"To speak for myself, I have never had that pleasure," answered the young man. "This is the first time, messire, that I have met with your engaging niece."

The old gentleman shrugged his shoulders.

"I am distressed to hear it," he said. "But it is never too late to begin. I had little more acquaintance with my own late lady ere I married her; which proves," he added with a grimace, "that these impromptu marriages may often produce an excellent understanding in the long-run. As the bridegroom is to have a voice in the matter, I will give him two hours to make up for lost time before we proceed with the ceremony." And he turned towards the door, followed by the clergyman.

The girl was on her feet in a moment. "My uncle, you cannot be in earnest," she said. "I declare before God I will stab myself rather than be forced on that young man. The heart rises at it; God forbids such marriages; you dishonour your white hair. Oh, my uncle, pity me! There is not a woman in all the world but would prefer death to such a nuptial. Is it possible," she added, faltering—"is it possible that you do not believe me—that you still think this"—and she pointed at Denis with a tremor of anger and contempt—"that you still think *this* to be the man?"

"Frankly," said the old gentleman, pausing on the threshold, "I do. But let me explain to you once for all, Blanche de Malétroit, my way of thinking about this affair. When you took it into your head to dishonour my family and the name that I have borne, in peace and war, for more than three-score years, you forfeited, not only the right to question my designs, but that of looking me in the face. If your father had been alive, he would have spat on you and turned you out of doors. His was the hand of iron. You may bless your God you have only to deal with the hand of velvet, mademoiselle. It was my duty to get you married without delay. Out of pure good-will, I have tried to find your own gallant for you. And I believe I have succeeded. But before God and all the holy angels, Blanche de Malétroit, if I have not, I care not one jack-straw. So let me recommend you to be polite to our young friend; for upon my word, your next groom may be less appetizing."

And with that he went out, with the chaplain at his heels; and the arras fell behind the pair.

The girl turned upon Denis with flashing eyes.

"And what, sir," she demanded, "may be the meaning of all this?"

"God knows," returned Denis gloomily. "I am a prisoner in this house, which seems full of mad people. More I know not; and nothing do I understand."

"And pray how came you here?" she asked.

He told her as briefly as he could. "For the rest," he added, "perhaps you will follow my example, and tell me the answer to all these riddles, and what, in God's name, is like to be the end of it."

She stood silent for a little, and he could see her lips tremble and her tearless eyes burn with a feverish lustre. Then she pressed her forehead in both hands.

"Alas, how my head aches!" she said wearily—"to say nothing of my poor heart! But it is due to you to know my story, unmaidenly as it must seem. I am called Blanche de Malétroit; I have been without father or mother for—oh! for as long as I can recollect, and indeed I have been most unhappy all my life. Three months ago a young captain began to stand near me every day in church. I could see that I pleased him; I am much to blame, but I was so glad that any one should love me; and when he passed me a letter, I took it home with me and read it with great pleasure. Since that time he has written many. He was so anxious to speak with me, poor fellow! and kept asking me to leave the door open some evening that we might have two words upon the stair. For he knew how much my uncle trusted me." She gave something like a sob at that, and it was a moment before she could go on. "My uncle is a hard man, but he is very shrewd," she said at last. "He has performed many feats in war, and was a great person at court, and much trusted by Queen Isabeau in old days. How he came to suspect me I cannot tell; but it is hard to keep anything from his knowledge; and this morning, as we came from mass, he took my hand in his, forced it open, and read my little billet, walking by my side all the while. When he had finished, he gave it back to me with great politeness. It contained another request to have the door left open; and this has been the ruin of us all. My uncle kept me strictly in my room until evening, and then ordered me to dress myself as you see me—a hard mockery for a young girl, do you not think so? I suppose, when he could not prevail with me to tell him the young captain's name, he must have laid a trap for him: into which, alas! you have fallen in the anger of God. I looked for much confusion; for how could I tell whether he was willing to take me for his wife on these sharp terms? He might have been trifling with me from the first; or I might have made myself too cheap in his eyes. But truly I had not looked for such a shameful punishment as this. I could not think that God would let a girl be so disgraced before a young man. And now I have told you all; and I can scarcely hope that you will not despise me."

Denis made her a respectful inclination.

"Madam," he said, "you have honoured me by your confidence. It remains for me to prove that I am not unworthy of the honour. Is Messire de Malétroit at hand?"

"I believe he is writing in the salle without," she answered.

"May I lead you thither, madam?" asked Denis, offering his hand with his most courtly bearing.

She accepted it; and the pair passed out of the chapel, Blanche in a very drooping and shamefaced condition, but Denis strutting and ruffling in the consciousness of a mission, and the boyish certainty of accomplishing it with honour.

The Sire de Malétroit rose to meet them with an ironical obeisance.

"Sir," said Denis, with the grandest possible air, "I believe I am to have some say in the matter of this marriage; and let me tell you at once, I will be no party to forcing the inclination of this young lady. Had it been freely offered to me, I should have been proud to accept her hand, for I perceive she is as good as she is beautiful; but as things are, I have now the honour, messire, of refusing."

Blanche looked at him with gratitude in her eyes; but the old gentleman only smiled and smiled, until his smile grew positively sickening to Denis.

"I am afraid," he said, "Monsieur de Beaulieu, that you do not perfectly understand the choice I have to offer you. Follow me, I beseech you, to this window." And he led the way to one of the large windows which stood open on the night. "You observe," he went on, "there is an iron ring in the upper masonry, and reeved through that, a very efficacious rope. Now, mark my words: if you should find your disinclination to my niece's person insurmountable, I shall have you hanged out of this window before sunrise. I shall only proceed to such an extremity with the greatest regret, you may believe me. For it is not at all your death that I desire, but my niece's establishment in life. At the same time, it must come to that if you prove obstinate. Your family, Monsieur de Beaulieu, is very well in its way; but if you sprang from Charlemagne, you should not refuse the hand of a Malétroit with impunity—not if she had been as common as the Paris road—not if she were as hideous as the gargoyle over my door. Neither my niece nor you, nor my own private feelings, move me at all in this matter. The honour of my house has been compromised; I believe you to be the guilty person; at least you are now in the secret; and you can hardly wonder if I request you to wipe out the stain. If you will not, your blood be on your own head! It will be no great satisfaction to me to have your interesting relics kicking their heels in the breeze below my windows; but half a loaf is better than no bread, and if I cannot cure the dishonour, I shall at least stop the scandal."

There was a pause.

"I believe there are other ways of settling such imbroglios among gentlemen," said Denis. "You wear a sword, and I hear you have used it with distinction."

The Sire de Malétroit made a signal to the chaplain, who crossed the room with long silent strides and raised the arras over the third of the three doors. It was only a moment before he let it fall again; but Denis had time to see a dusky passage full of armed men.

"When I was a little younger, I should have been delighted to honour you, Monsieur de Beaulieu," said Sire Alain; "but I am now too old. Faithful retainers are the sinews of age, and I must employ the strength I have. This is one of the hardest things to swallow as a man grows up in years; but with a little patience, even this becomes habitual. You and the lady seem to prefer the salle for what remains of your two hours; and as I have no desire to cross your preference, I shall resign it to your use with all the pleasure in the world. No haste!" he added, holding up his hand, as he saw a dangerous look come into Denis de Beaulieu's face. "If your mind revolts against hanging, it will be time enough two hours hence to throw yourself out of the window or upon the pikes of my retainers. Two hours of life are always two hours. A great many things may turn up in even as little a while as that. And besides, if I understand her appearance, my niece has still something to say to you. You will not disfigure your last hours by a want of politeness to a lady?"

Denis looked at Blanche, and she made him an imploring gesture.

It is likely that the old gentleman was hugely pleased at this symptom of an understanding; for he smiled on both, and added sweetly: "If you will give me your word of honour, Monsieur de Beaulieu, to await my return at the end of the two hours before attempting anything desperate, I shall withdraw my retainers, and let you speak in greater privacy with mademoiselle."

Denis again glanced at the girl, who seemed to beseech him to agree.

"I give you my word of honour," he said.

Messire de Malétroit bowed, and proceeded to limp about the apartment, clearing his throat the while with that odd musical chirp which had already grown so irritating in the ears of Denis de Beaulieu. He first possessed himself of some papers which lay upon the table; then he went to the mouth of the passage and appeared to give an order to the men behind the arras; and lastly he hobbled out through the door by which Denis had come in, turning upon the threshold to address a last smiling bow to the young couple, and followed by the chaplain with a hand-lamp.

No sooner were they alone than Blanche advanced towards Denis with her hands extended. Her face was flushed and excited, and her eyes shone with tears.

"You shall not die!" she cried, "you shall marry me after all."

"You seem to think, madam," replied Denis, "that I stand much in fear of death."

"Oh, no, no," she said, "I see you are no poltroon. It is for my own sake—I could not bear to have you slain for such a scruple."

"I am afraid," returned Denis, "that you underrate the difficulty, madam. What you may be too generous to refuse, I may be too proud to accept. In a moment of noble feeling towards me, you forget what you perhaps owe to others."

He had the decency to keep his eyes upon the floor as he said this, and after he had finished, so as not to spy upon her confusion. She stood silent for a moment, then walked suddenly away, and falling on her uncle's chair, fairly burst out sobbing. Denis was in the acme of embarrassment. He looked round, as if to seek for inspiration, and seeing a stool, plumped down upon it for something to do. There he sat, playing with the guard of his rapier, and wishing himself dead a thousand times over, and buried in the nastiest kitchen-heap in France. His eyes wandered round the apartment but found nothing to arrest them. There were such wide spaces between the furniture, the light fell so badly and cheerlessly over all, the dark outside air looked in so coldly through the windows, that he thought he had never seen a church so vast, nor a tomb so melancholy. The regular sobs of Blanche de Malétroit measured out the time like the ticking of a clock. He read the device upon the shield over and over again, until his eyes became obscured; he stared into shadowy corners until he imagined they were swarming with horrible animals; and every now and again he awoke with a start, to remember that his last two hours were running and death was on the march.

Oftener and oftener, as the time went on, did his glance settle on the girl herself. Her face was bowed forward and covered with her hands, and she was shaken at intervals by the convulsive hiccup of grief. Even thus she was not an unpleasant object to dwell upon, so plump and yet so fine, with a warm brown skin, and the most beautiful hair, Denis thought, in the whole world of womankind. Her hands were like her uncle's; but they were more in place at the end of her young arms, and looked infinitely soft and caressing. He remembered how her blue eyes had shone upon him, full of anger, pity, and innocence. And the more he dwelt on her perfections, the uglier death looked, and the more deeply was he smitten with penitence at her continued tears. Now he felt that no man could have the courage to leave a world which contained so beautiful a creature; and now he would have given forty minutes of his last hour to have unsaid his cruel speech.

Suddenly a hoarse and ragged peal of cockcrow rose to their ears from the dark valley below the windows. And this shattering noise in the silence all around was like a light in a dark place, and shook them both out of their reflections.

"Alas, can I do nothing to help you?" she said, looking up.

"Madam," replied Denis, with a fine irrelevancy, "if I have said anything to wound you, believe me, it was for your own sake and not for mine."

She thanked him with a tearful look.

"I feel your position cruelly," he went on. "The world

has been bitter hard on you. Your uncle is a disgrace to mankind. Believe me, madam, there is no young gentleman in all France but would be glad of my opportunity, to die in doing you a momentary service."

"I know already that you can be very brave and generous," she answered. "What I *want* to know is whether I can serve you—now or afterwards," she added, with a quaver.

"Most certainly," he answered with a smile. "Let me sit beside you as if I were a friend, instead of a foolish intruder; try to forget how awkwardly we are placed to one another; make my last moments go pleasantly; and you will do me the chief service possible."

"You are very gallant," she added, with a yet deeper sadness . . . "very gallant . . . and it somehow pains me. But draw nearer, if you please, and if you find anything to say to me, you will at least make certain of a very friendly listener. Ah! Monsieur de Beaulieu, how can I look you in the face?" And she fell to weeping again with a renewed effusion.

"Madam," said Denis, taking her hand in both of his, "reflect on the little time I have before me, and the great bitterness into which I am cast by the sight of your distress. Spare me, in my last moments, the spectacle of what I cannot cure even with the sacrifice of my life."

"I am very selfish," answered Blanche. "I will be braver, Monsieur de Beaulieu, for your sake. But think if I can do you no kindness in the future—if you have no friends to whom I could carry your adieux. Charge me as heavily as you can; every burden will lighten, by so little, the invaluable gratitude I owe you. Put it in my power to do something more for you than weep."

"My mother is married again, and has a young family to care for. My brother Guichard will inherit my fiefs; and if I am not in error, that will content him amply for my death. Life is a little vapour that passeth away, as we are told by those in holy orders. When a man is in a fair way and sees all life open in front of him, he seems to himself to make a very important figure in the world. His horse whinnies to him; the trumpets blow and the girls look out of windows as he rides into town before his company; he receives many assurances of trust and regard—sometimes by express in a letter—sometimes face to face, with persons of great consequence falling on his neck. It is not wonderful if his head is turned for a time. But once he is dead, were he as brave as Hercules or as wise as Solomon, he is soon forgotten. It is not ten years since my father fell, with many other knights around him, in a very fierce encounter, and I do not think that any one of them, nor so much as the name of the fight, is now remembered. No, no, madam, the nearer you come to it, you see that death is a dark and dusty corner, where a man gets into his tomb and has the door shut after him till the judgment day. I have few friends just now, and once I am dead I shall have none."

"Ah, Monsieur de Beaulieu!" she exclaimed, "you forget Blanche de Malétroit."

"You have a sweet nature, madam, and you are pleased to estimate a little service far beyond its worth."

"It is not that," she answered. "You mistake me if you think I am so easily touched by my own concerns. I say so, because you are the noblest man I have ever met; because I recognise in you a spirit that would have made even a common person famous in the land."

"And yet here I die in a mouse-trap—with no more noise about it than my own speaking," answered he.

A look of pain crossed her face, and she was silent for a little while. Then a light came into her eyes, and with a smile she spoke again.

"I cannot have my champion think meanly of himself. Any one who gives his life for another will be met in Paradise by all the heralds and angels of the Lord God. And you have no such cause to hang your head. For . . . Pray, do you think me beautiful?" she asked, with a deep flush.

"Indeed, madam, I do," he said.

"I am glad of that," she answered, heartily. "Do you think there are many men in France who have been asked in marriage by a beautiful maiden—with her own lips—and who have refused her to her face? I know you men would half despise such a triumph; but believe me, we women know more of what is precious in love. There is nothing that should set a person higher in his own esteem; and we women would prize nothing more dearly."

"You are very good," he said; "but you cannot make me forget that I was asked in pity and not for love."

"I am not so sure of that," she replied, holding down her head. "Hear me to an end, Monsieur de Beaulieu. I know how you must despise me; I feel you are right to do so; I am too poor a creature to occupy one thought of your mind, although, alas! you must die for me this morning. But when I asked you to marry me, indeed, and indeed, it was because I respected and admired you, and loved you with my whole soul, from the very moment that you took my part against my uncle. If you had seen yourself, and how noble you looked, you would pity rather than despise me. And now," she went on, hurriedly checking him with her hand, "although I have laid aside all reserve and told you so much, remember that I know your sentiments towards me already. I would not, believe me, being nobly born, weary you with importunities into consent. I too have a pride of my own: and I declare before the holy mother of God, if you should now go back from your word already given, I would no more marry you than I would marry my uncle's groom."

Denis smiled a little bitterly.

"It is a small love," he said, "that shies at a little pride."

She made no answer, although she probably had her own thought.

"Come hither to the window," he said, with a sigh. "Here is the dawn."

And indeed the dawn was already beginning. The hollow of the sky was full of essential daylight, colourless and clean; and the valley underneath was flooded with a grey reflection. A few thin vapors clung in the coves of the forest or lay along the winding course of the river. The scene disengaged a surprising effect of stillness, which was hardly interrupted when the cocks began once more to crow among the steadings. Perhaps the same fellow who had made so horrid a clangour in the darkness not half an hour before, now sent up the merriest cheer to greet the coming day. A little wind went bustling and eddying among the tree-tops underneath the windows. And still the daylight kept flooding insensibly out of the east, which was soon to grow incandescent and cast up that red-hot cannon-ball, the rising sun.

Denis looked out over all this with a bit of a shiver. He had taken her hand and retained it in his almost unconsciously.

"Has the day begun already?" she said; and then, illogically enough: "the night has been so long! Alas! what shall we say to my uncle when he returns?"

"What you will," said Denis, and he pressed her fingers in his.

She was silent.

"Blanche," he said, with a swift, uncertain, passionate utterance, "you have seen whether I fear death. You must know well enough that I would as gladly leap out of the window into the empty air as to lay a finger on you without your free and full consent. But if you care for me at all do not let me lose my life in a misapprehension; for I love you better than the whole world; and though I will die for you blithely, it would be like all the joys of Paradise to live on and spend my life in your service."

As he stopped speaking, a bell began to ring loudly in the interior of the house, and a clatter of armour in the corridor showed that the retainers were returning to their post, and the two hours were at an end.

"After all that you have heard?" she whispered, leaning towards him with her lips and eyes.

"I have heard nothing," he replied.

"The captain's name was Florimond de Champdivers," she said in his ear.

"I did not hear it," he answered taking her supple body in his arms and covering her wet face with kisses.

A melodious chirping was audible behind, followed by a beautiful chuckle, and the voice of Messire de Malétroit wished his new nephew a good morning.

POCKET BOOK BEST SELLERS